PENGUIN BOOKS

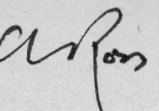

A Prodigal Child

David Storey was born in 1933 and is the third son of a mine-worker. He was educated at the Queen Elizabeth School at Wakefield and the Slade School of Fine Art. He has had various jobs ranging from professional footballer to school-teaching and showground tent-erecting. He is now both a novelist and a dramatist.

His novels include *This Sporting Life*, which won the Macmillan Fiction Award in 1960 and was also filmed; *Flight into Camden*, which won the John Llewelyn Rhys Memorial Prize and also the Somerset Maugham Award in 1963; *Radcliffe*; *Pasmore*, which won the Faber Memorial Prize in 1973; *A Temporary Life*; and *Saville*, which won the Booker Prize in 1976. He has received numerous drama awards including the New York Critics' Best Play of the Year Award in three years out of four. His plays include *The Restoration of Arnold Middleton*; *In Celebration*, which has been filmed; *The Contractor*; *Home*; *The Changing Room*; *The Farm*; *Life Class*; *Mother's Day*; *Sisters*; and *Early Days*. Several of David Storey's novels are published by Penguin as are three volumes of his plays.

David Storey lives in London. He was married in 1956 and has four children.

D1440103

DAVID STOREY

A
PRODIGAL
CHILD

PENGUIN BOOKS

Penguin Books Ltd, Harmondsworth, Middlesex, England
Penguin Books, 40 West 23rd Street, New York, New York 10010, U.S.A.
Penguin Books Australia Ltd, Ringwood, Victoria, Australia
Penguin Books Canada Ltd, 2801 John Street, Markham, Ontario, Canada L3R 1B4
Penguin Books (N.Z.) Ltd, 182–190 Wairau Road, Auckland 10, New Zealand

—

First published by Jonathan Cape 1982
Published in Penguin Books 1984

—

—

Made and printed in Great Britain by
Richard Clay (The Chaucer Press) Ltd, Bungay, Suffolk
Filmset in Monophoto Times by Northumberland Press Ltd, Gateshead

Stainforth estate succeeded to Spinney Moor.

At one time the Moor had been the haunt of deer, wild boar and pheasant; then the farmers came: they cut back the bracken, turned the clayey soil, and built stone walls coiling up to the flat-topped summit – the crest of a ridge which, sharply incised, fell southwards to the river. Later, the streams were blocked; mills were built, their grey stone shapes strewn out across the slope, one succeeding to another, the water stored in tiny dams, the river, finally, claiming it all where, polluted, the streams, coalescing, ran in from its northern bank: here, below a stone-faced weir, an ancient Chantry Bridge crossed over to the town – a hilly crest which overlooked, to the east, the less conspicuous summit of Spinney Top.

After the mills came the houses – rows of stone-built cottages scattered across the slope, the lanes linking them lined with mud, bounded by walls, stretching up towards the summit, at the very peak of which stood the ancient structure of Spinney House, a mansion, fallen into ruin, overgrown, its fabric picked at by the builders, the cottages on their outer walls bearing stones carved to a mullioned window or a grooved transom or shaped to the lintel above a door.

Then, after the mills, came the factories, scattered across the valley bottom, and, with the factories, came the brick-built houses, stretching in rows, the higher ground still left to the sheep, the slope thick with snow in winter, clogged by rain in spring and autumn, burned bare in summer: hawks hovered above the back gardens, and owls came down at night from the dark recesses of Spinney House.

After the mills and factories came the great manufactures;

5

longer streets were built until, in the middle '20s, the houses of Stainforth estate were planned, rising in pairs, semi-detached, reaching up across the untouched land, engulfing the last of the cottages, engulfing the older streets, engulfing even Spinney House, with its owls and its picked-at walls and long-since empty windows: a hospital was built, a school and, on a terrace above the river, before the last drop to the valley bottom, the stone structure of a church.

ONE

A cry, 'Alan!' came from the back door of the house and the short, stocky, fair-haired, blue-eyed figure of Mr Morley appeared. 'Alan!' he called again and made his way across the upturned clay and the builders' mounds to where the child was sitting. 'What're you playing at?' he said, lifting the boy above his head, shaking him to and fro so that the child, with his arms outstretched, his fingers flexed, laughed and kicked his booted legs: Mr Morley, finally, lowering his arms, pressed his head against the boy's chest.

The mother appeared at the back door of the house; small, dark-haired, dark-eyed, slim-featured, she stood in the porch, her eyes shaded against the morning light, gazing out to the field before her.

'Are you fetching this stuff in or not?' she called. 'Mr Patterson's doing it all himself.'

Mr Patterson appeared in the porch beside her: their neighbour, a thick-set man, balding, with a fringe of reddish hair, taller and more broadly built than Mr Morley, he waved his arm and shouted, 'Give him it, Alan. Don't let him off.'

'It's Arthur you should be shouting at,' Mrs Morley said. 'He's as much a baby as Alan is. Just look at him,' she added. 'Leaving you to all the work.'

'Nay, I'm fair easy,' Mr Patterson said, standing with his hands on his hips which, like his shoulders and his chest, were broad and heavy. 'Give him it,' he called. 'Don't let him off.'

'He's got me beat,' came Mr Morley's shout. 'He's got me licked. He's got me down.' He rolled on his back, the child suspended by its stomach, its legs kicking, its arms writhing.

'Are you doing this or aren't you?' came Mrs Morley's shout as she squeezed past Mr Patterson's shirt-sleeved figure and disappeared inside the kitchen, her voice continuing, inaudibly, from beyond the door.

'I'm coming,' came Mr Morley's shout. 'Come on. Get off!' holding the child above him, shaking it about. 'Let me up now, will you? Your mother's calling. Come on,' rolling on to his side, turning over, the child cradled beneath him until, getting to his knees, and then his feet, he set him on his shoulders. 'Theer, then. He's taken a ride. And I never said he could.'

Striding with his short, bow-shaped legs across the uncompleted garden and the builders' mounds, he approached the back door, calling, 'Are we ready, Harry, or has she done it all without us?'

'She's started.' Mr Patterson laughed.

'She's started,' Mr Morley agreed, jogging the child above him up and down. 'And it'll be a damn long time afore we're finished,' ducking his head, laughing, as, following Mr Patterson, he went inside the house.

The house on Spinney Moor Road was comprised of two rooms downstairs, one described as a living-room and the other as a scullery, and three rooms upstairs, together with a bathroom. The living-room ran through from the front of the house to the back: two windows looked out to the road, and a single window to the garden of upturned clay and the field at the back. Of the three rooms upstairs, the principal bedroom was sufficiently large to accommodate a double bed, a wardrobe and a chest of drawers, the secondary bedroom two single beds and a cupboard, and the tiny back bedroom a single bed only, leaving scarcely sufficient space to open the door. The bathroom, which was occupied by a bath, a toilet, a handbasin and two large cisterns, one for hot water, the other for cold, took up the remainder of the upper floor.

The Morleys' first morning in their new house – smelling of plaster, of paint, of cement and mortar, and of the freshly hammered-in and unvarnished wood – resolved itself into arranging precisely where the furniture should be put; there wasn't a great deal of it, which, rather than diminishing, increased the scope of each discussion: should the table be put in the kitchen or should it be placed opposite the black-enamelled range in the living-room, or should it be set to one side and the two easy chairs

8

given preference? Should the double bed in the main bedroom be facing the two windows which looked out to the road, or should it be placed sideways, in which case the light wouldn't shine each morning into Mr and Mrs Morley's eyes? Should the boy's cot be put in the second bedroom, or would it be better off in the back? Would the stair-carpet cover the stairs; and when the linoleum man came in one or two days' time, should any spare bits left over be used to cover the concrete floor of the scullery, or used to fill in the spaces in the double bedroom around or – should there be sufficient – underneath the bed?

Mr Patterson, who appeared to be as genial and as hard-working as he was chunky, bald and stout, listened to these arguments with a smile: his pale-blue eyes turned from the wife to the husband, back to the wife and then to the husband once again; he scratched his head, ran his hand over his remaining tufts of hair, smiled, nodded, nodded once again, extended his arm, made a suggestion, and finally sat down beside the figure of the child, glanced at it, tickled it, and even allowed it to bite his finger. 'Ow,' he said, laughing. 'Get off,' nevertheless allowing his finger, its knuckle bared, to remain inside the tiny mouth, while 'Upstairs,' came from Mrs Morley, and 'Downstairs,' from Mr Morley, until, finally, it was decided 'Upstairs,' after all. Chairs were lifted, set down, the table raised, lowered, turned, the bed hoisted, twisted, manoeuvred, levered, the wardrobe pushed, pulled, carried, the carpets tugged, rolled, unrolled, 'squared', and the few ornaments placed, unplaced, set, re-set, and, finally, with a sigh, Mrs Morley announced herself satisfied 'for the present' and Mr Morley invited Mr Patterson to have a ride on the cart.

It was on the cart – a four-wheeled, mud-encrusted, red-painted farm wagon pulled by a dark-brown horse – that the furniture had been brought that morning; a bag had been attached to the muzzle of the horse shortly after the cart's arrival and, while the furniture was being unloaded, the horse had delved and champed and blown out chaff, snorted, sneezed and chewed and snuffled, until, when the last of its load had been taken inside, Mr Morley had unhooked the bag and the horse had wandered off. When, finally, Mr Morley and Mr Patterson emerged from the house, followed by the boy, the cart, its wheels locked against the kerb, was standing some distance down the road, the horse, its head stooped, grazing at the rutted verge and blocking the movement of the builders' carts which, as a consequence, were obliged to go past it on the footpath.

'Whoa,' called Mr Morley from the wooden gate as the cart gave a lurch. 'Whoa,' he called down the road, while his wife, emerging from the door, called, 'You're surely not taking Alan with you? How're you going to get him back?'

'I'll fetch him on the bike,' Mr Morley said.

'He's not safe on your bike,' Mrs Morley said, standing in her apron and taking Alan's hand herself.

'I'll 'o'd him,' Mr Morley said, to whom simple things never seemed simpler than when they were questioned by his wife.

'For four miles?' Mrs Morley glanced at Mr Patterson who, content that his help was no longer required, had rolled down his sleeves. 'He's to pedal four miles with a child between his arms. Alan's only to drop off once and that's an accident,' she added.

Mr Patterson shook his head.

'I s'll leave him here, in that case,' Mr Morley said. 'He mu'n lift that settee while I'm gone, and help you with the chairs.'

'He's better here than with you,' Mrs Morley said, taking the child up the path to the door, and adding, 'How long are you going to be?'

'As long as it takes.'

'Is Mr Patterson going all the way?'

'Oh, just to the corner, missis,' Mr Patterson said, for the notion of having a 'lift' he had taken as an invitation to the Spinney Moor Hotel which stood, newly-erected, at the corner of Spinney Moor Avenue, where it joined the main road which led to the town.

'Don't be long,' Mrs Morley said, though whether to Mr Patterson or to Mr Morley, or to both, it was impossible to tell: with a certain spring in their step which had been absent before, and with a brushing down of their sleeves to confirm that that part of their work, at least, was finished, the two men set off down the road to where the horse, at the command of 'Whoa,' had raised its massive head, gazing out at the builders' carts from between it blackened blinkers.

The men climbed up on the cart; the cart set off.

At one point, where the descent was steepest, Mr Morley applied the brake, which involved Mr Patterson leaping off and tugging on a rope which in turn drew a metal-lined block against the wheel, sending up a shower of sparks. 'Steady, Major,' Mr Morley called and, once on the level, they turned out of the opening of Spinney Moor Avenue, past a row of newly-erected shops and, beyond a vacant building plot, entered the yard of the public house.

Taking the precaution of tethering the horse, Mr Morley and Mr Patterson went inside.

An hour passed; the two men reappeared.

Mr Patterson's shirt-sleeved shoulder was slapped; Mr Morley's hand was wrung: their heads were nodded, the slightly reddened eyes were blinked. With another slap at Mr Patterson's shoulder, and another, 'All right, Arthur, think nothing of it,' the two men parted, the smaller to climb, with some difficulty, on to the back of the cart, from where he was obliged to descend to untether the horse, the stouter to set off to the adjacent corner where, with a backward glance and a final wave, he disappeared.

The road Mr Morley took led out from the estate towards the countryside beyond; at the first junction he turned to the right and proceeded along a narrow lane which led across the valley.

Sitting with his legs beneath the shafts, he gazed with a bemused expression at the rhythmical movement of the horse's back: the road passed beneath a railway bridge, curved round a row of cottages, and ran on directly between hedged fields towards the valley's opposite flank. From a projecting spur in the valley side loomed the fortifications of Feltham Castle and, along the profile of the spur, behind the castle, a row of brick-built houses making up the suburb of Feltham itself.

Lulled by the horse's momentum, by his taking his drink on an empty stomach, by the delayed shock of moving house, Mr Morley closed his eyes, his reveries interrupted as a lorry rattled past and, shaking his head, flicking the reins, clicking his tongue, he called, 'Come up, Major,' as though it were the horse and not he who were falling asleep and then, having glanced round and ascertained that he was only halfway across the valley, that the canal had just been crossed and, before the canal, the river and, before the river, he had passed beneath the railway bridge, he returned his gaze to the view ahead, thinking, 'By God: he said have the cart back by one o'clock and it must have gone past two already.' He felt in his waistcoat pocket, remembered he'd left his watch on the mantelshelf in the living-room and, glancing up at the sun, timed, with the accuracy of an outdoor worker, that it must be ten minutes past two at least and it would be another twenty-five minutes before he got to Spencer's. 'Come up, Major,' he called again, and thought, 'It's a damn good house, I'm lucky to have it. It starts a whole new life for me. Not that I can afford it. Who can? Harry's a good man, a damn good man to have as a neighbour. We'll have one or two good times with him,' then – to his dismay – missing the opening to the lane, he turned the cart round and re-applied the horse's head to the narrow gap and, setting off along the curling and coiling strand of road beyond, he concluded. 'That drinking's cost a penny: if Patterson can sup as fast as that I'll be skint inside a week.'

Birds sang in the hedges; butterflies fluttered across the thick, grass verges; the hooves of the horse rasped against the road. To Mr Morley's right the fields stretched up to the valley side, and to his left, and slightly behind, rose the silhouetted summit of Spinney Top; beyond, and separated from it by a shallow dale, dense with houses, appeared the profile of the town – the dome of the County Hall, the porticoed entrance to the Courts of Law, the tower of the Town Hall, the tall, dog-toothed spire of All Saints Church.

As the lane approached the opposite valley side it was joined by a narrow road running laterally along the valley bottom: trees threw their shade across the cart. The road narrowed; it crossed a hump-backed bridge: to Mr Morley's right appeared the farm.

The lane was quiet; in a gravel yard, fronting a public house, opposite the entrance to the farm itself, a man sat at a table and, seeing Mr Morley, waved his arm.

'How go, Arthur?'

Mr Morley backed the cart beneath a shed, got down, unharnessed the horse and, opening a gate at the end of a yard, enclosed by the eroded walls of a barn on one side and a cowshed on the other, allowed the horse through to a field the other side: bowing its head, walking on two paces, it began to graze.

From the back of a shed he wheeled out his bike. The door of the farmhouse opened and a figure in jodhpurs and shirt-sleeves appeared: its head was balding, its skin florid, its arms, beneath its rolled shirt-sleeves, muscular and brown.

'How go, Arthur?' the man inquired. 'Has't flitted?'

'We're all fixed up, Mr Spencer,' Mr Morley said.

'I thought thy'd be back an hour ago.'

The barking of two dogs came from the open door behind.

'It took longer than I thought.'

'Major all right?'

'He's fine.'

'Shoved him i' the pasture?'

'Right.'

'Has't fastened the shed door?'

'I have.'

'I'll see you Monday.'

'I'll see you Monday, Mr Spencer.'

The farmer turned to the house: from one of its upstairs windows a curtain fluttered.

'He's thinking,' Morley thought, 'that I've been shifting some-one else's load and making one or two bob on the side and all because of his kindness in letting me use the cart for nought.'

'The cart all right?'

'I've put it i' the shed.'

'That brake wa're all right, wa're it?'

'Grand.'

Mr Morley stood with one foot on his pedal.

'See you, Arthur.'

'See you, Mr Spencer.'

Yet the delay in dismissing him had been sufficient of a re-primand to remind Mr Morley that, if he should ever ask to borrow the cart again, he'd be refused. 'I should never have gone into the pub with Patterson,' he thought. 'But then,' he concluded, 'he can't take the bloody cart back: he'll just wuk me harder next week and make up the difference, in one road or another.'

The figure at the table in the pub yard opposite called again.

'Wukking overtime, Arthur?'

'I've been flitting,' Mr Morley said.

'Wheer to?'

'Stainforth.'

'By go: won't be seeing you down here again.'

'Oh, I'll be here,' Mr Morley said, pausing where the pebbled forecourt of the pub came up to the road.

'Lent you his cart?' The man gestured to the farm.

'That's right.'

'Be cutting his bloody arm off next.'

'I s'll have to be off,' Mr Morley said.

'Have a pint.'

'I said I'd be back,' Mr Morley said. 'I'm late already.'

'Nay, if thy's flitted it's worth celebrating,' the man at the table said.

'I s'll have a quick 'un,' Mr Morley thought. 'What's five minutes for her after waiting an hour?'

Half an hour later he was still sitting by the wooden table and the doors of the public house were about to be closed.

'A last one,' he said, 'then I s'll have to be off.'

He skipped inside, jangling the last coins in his pocket, and came out with two glasses.

'Here's to it,' said the man for the fifth or sixth time since Mr Morley had joined him, and drank as quickly from his glass as he had from the first. 'Which road are you off?' he added.

'Straight back.' Mr Morley's speech was slurred.

'Wi' one or two wiggles.'

He got up from the table. 'Nay, I'm as steady now as I wa' when I started.' The glasses on the table jangled.

'I should walk home, Arthur, if I were you.'

'Nay,' Mr Morley said, conscious of the time if of nothing else. 'I have to get back.'

He got on his bike.

The front wheel wobbled.

'Want a shove?'

'No, thanks.'

He pedalled on.

'By God,' he thought, 'what a day to come a cropper.'

At the hump-backed bridge, where the stream from Spencer's Farm crossed under the road, he laid the bike down; he scrambled through the hedge and, where several ducks and geese were swimming up and down in the shadow of the bridge itself, he knelt on the bank, cupped his hands, drew up the water and splashed his face.

'Are you all right?' a man called from the pub across the stream.

Mr Morley waved his arm.

He cupped his hands again, drew up the water, missed his face, and drenched the front of his shirt and jacket.

He lay back in the grass; he was aware of the honking of the geese and the quacking of the ducks, of the dampness drying on the back of his hands. Lulled by the murmuring of the stream and the heat of the day, and thinking, 'She won't have the bed ready by the time I get back. I might as well rest here,' he fell asleep.

'Where on earth have you been to?' Sarah said.

Mr Morley could see that his wife had been crying and his resolve to describe in detail the farmer's conversation, a compendium of all Mr Spencer had told him over the previous week, melted at the sight of her tear-streaked face. 'Is anything up?'

'It's nearly seven o'clock.'

'Seven?'

'You've been gone six hours.'

'Six?'

He looked for his watch. The room had been tidied. It had, per-haps, been tidied several times: his watch had gone; the chairs were in place, the sideboard had been dusted; a fire was burning in the grate. Where on earth, he wondered, had she got the coal? Then he remembered Patterson had said he'd lend them some.

He sat down at the table; that, too, he noticed, had been re-arranged. The curtains had been put up on the windows.

'Where have you been?'

'I've been talking to Spencer.'

'All afternoon?'

'I met Jack Bannister. He wa're at the Three Bells.'

'Alan'll be in bed,' he thought. 'First night in a new home and I wasn't here to see it.'

'He wa' telling me about his job at Havercroft.'

'Jack Bannister was sacked at Spencer's. He was always drunk.'

'I near fell off the bike.'

He held up his hand: the back had been cut where he'd scrambled through the hedge.

'Mr Patterson was home five hours ago.'

'Aye.'

'This is our first day in our new home.'

He didn't look up. 'I lay down in Spencer's field and fell asleep. I meant to have a rest and come on again.'

She went out of the room; her feet came from the stairs: they sounded across the boards of the narrow landing; a door was closed above his head.

A moment later the sound of her sobbing came through the ceiling.

'Hell,' he thought, 'what a mess,' gazing out at the darkening road, with the sunset glowing on the houses opposite. 'All fresh and I go and bugger it up.' He gazed about him at the room: a feeling of sadness absorbed him entirely, not at his mistake, but at the evidence of his wife's preoccupation with the house, the innumerable touches with which she'd sought to eradicate the bareness of the room, the alignment of the chairs, the setting of a poker in the hearth, the sweeping away of the ashes.

'She'll cry long enough and loud enough to rub it in,' he thought, 'and I s'll have to sit down here and listen.'

Yet, having decided that, he got to his feet.

He climbed the stairs: he looked in the little back room, then he looked in the other bedroom at the front. The cot was empty.

He knocked on his bedroom door and stepped inside.

His wife lay curled up, her back to the door; the boy was sleeping on the bed beside her.

'Is he asleep?'

His wife didn't answer.

He knelt on the bed; the boy was wearing a patterned night-shirt, his feet bare, his arms outstretched.

He glanced at his wife across whose back he was leaning. 'Shall I put him in his cot?'

Her eyes were open, her figure stiff.

16

He got off the bed and went round the other side. Only when he was about to lift the boy did she say, 'Leave him,' and, as he paused, as if she suspected he hadn't heard, she added, 'Leave him,' once again. 'You're drunk.'

'I'm sober.'

'You're drunk,' she said, tonelessly. 'I can smell it.'

'Nay, I'll be damned. I've pedalled back miles.'

'Just think,' she said, 'if you'd taken him with you.'

'I'd have come straight home.'

'I'm glad I never let you. My God, just think of a drunken man with a child.'

'I'm not drunk,' he said. 'I'm telling you,' yet he stood back from the bed, gazing at the child, thinking, 'It might have more of me, but it's hers now, and always will be.'

'Look at your clothes,' she added.

'Nay, well, I s'll not give a damn next time,' he said. 'I s'll take my bloody time and be damned whether I come back here or not.'

'Lifting a child to its cot when you're not even safe to stand,' she said, not listening. 'All the furniture I've had to straighten. You've not given a hand since you lifted it in.'

'I'm here now, aren't I?' Morley said.

'My God, I wish you weren't,' she said. 'I wish I'd never met you.'

'That's soon arranged, is that. That soon is,' Morley said.

He closed the door.

He went back down. He looked in the scullery: there, too, the crockery and the cutlery had been put away and the pans set up on a wooden shelf, close to the ceiling, behind the scullery door. A gas-ring stood on a wooden-topped copper.

Unable to find the kettle he picked up a pan and filled it with water and set it on the ring.

He washed his hands, winced as he took the scab off his knuckles and, looking round for a towel and finding none, took out his handkerchief.

Steam rose from the pan. Finding the tea in the stone-slabbed pantry he mashed it in a pot.

He took the pot out to the porch.

The sun was setting: before him stretched the upturned garden

17

– clods of clay alternating with clumps of grass and builders' rubble – and, beyond the wooden rail designating the end of the garden, stretched the field, circumscribed on the opposite side by a row of uncompleted houses.

He was hungry; he'd had no lunch. He'd set off that morning before seven o'clock to fetch the cart; it was twelve hours since he'd eaten. 'She must think I live on fresh air,' he thought. 'She's never been fair to me, not ever.'

In the adjoining garden Mr Patterson was turning the soil: a neat patch of yellowish clay stretched out before him to the edge of the field.

'How go?' he said.

'All right,' Morley said, and considered that Patterson had heard, through the thin partitioning of the walls between the houses, something of the quarrel.

'Nought but clay.' Patterson gestured with his spade.

'I s'll have a go tomorrow.'

'Aye.'

The gasps of Mr Patterson as he stooped to the spade alternated with the cries of children playing in the field.

Morley watched their figures running to and fro: the sounds of their voices echoed between the houses.

'Have you had anything to eat?' His wife's voice sounded in the door behind.

'No.'

She was standing there as if nothing had happened: hearing his voice and Mr Patterson's replying, she had come down to indicate to the neighbour that nothing was amiss.

'I put your lunch in the oven,' she said. 'It'll be dried up by now.'

'You cooked something, did you?' Morley got up. 'Put it on the table,' he added, following her inside. 'If you've cooked it, love,' he continued, in a voice loud enough to be heard outside, 'it'll be good enough for me.'

TWO

Mrs Morley was the youngest of a family of eight: three sisters had alternated with four brothers and her own arrival had been greeted by her parents with despair. Despised by her brothers and abused by her sisters and disregarded entirely by her parents, she had lived amongst her family with scarcely more security than that of a household pet, condemned to be the last at table and the first to be called upon to do household tasks. A sullenness and capriciousness, like that of a beaten dog, characterized her early years, a tendency to go off, whenever she could, into corners and from there to gaze out at the world with a dark-eyed bitterness and fury. Not until she met Morley had she felt anything different: he had been in the army, a corporal, and home on leave when she met him at a dance hall. There, sheltering in the doorway during a shower of rain, he had offered her his greatcoat to put over her head. 'It won't bite,' he told her. 'There's nought inside.' They'd walked to her home together, their heads beneath the coat, his arm around her waist, and only as they neared the house and he realized they lived in adjoining streets had he suddenly released her and said, 'You're not one of the Wolmersley lasses, are you? I thought they were wed.'

'They're my sisters,' Sarah had said.

'I didn't know there wa're another,' he told her.

'Four of us,' she said.

'Four.' He gazed at her from beneath the shoulders of the coat. 'By go, they breed like rabbits in Hasleden Street.'

'And four brothers,' she added with a laugh.

'I know thy brothers. So you're the one that wa're alus roaring and had her knickers wet, and that.'

'Not me,' she said, withdrawing from the coat.

19

'Nay, it must have been,' he said. 'You were nobbut this high when I went away.' He raised his hand above his waist. 'Two foot o' nought, and a mucky nose.'

He'd laughed; she was used to abuse and gazed up at his genial, bright-eyed face and thought he must have recognized in her something of the beaten dog, for he placed his arm about her once again, and she felt the pressure of his hand through her waist, and felt the thrill, too, of that pressure go through her and thought, bitterly, 'This is the first man who has seen me away from my sisters and now he is anxious to put me back with them again.'

'I'd never have recognized you,' he said. 'You'll remember the Morleys, o' course, in Wentworth Street.'

'I've heard of them,' she said.

'I bet. There's not a policeman within ten miles that hasn't.' He laughed. 'I wa' sent i' the army. The old man said, "It's jankers in the Yorks and Lancs where your mother and I can't see you, or it's fending for yourself." They'd had enough of me.'

On two successive nights they'd walked beyond the town: his arm around her waist had been followed by their lying on the grass, and his kissing had been succeeded by his attempts to release her dress. Only then had Sarah protested.

'I shouldn't hurt you,' he said. 'What's up?'

'I can't go on until I'm married,' she said.

'That's not what I've heard of the Wolmersley lasses,' Morley said.

'It's what you'll have to hear from me,' she said, something of her sullenness returning.

Her father, like her sisters and most of her brothers, worked at the mill; living in the small, dark houses beside the river she compared their existence to that of the rats which lived in the dark holes and crevices along the bank: the soldier was a challenge, almost senseless.

In the Sarah Wolmersley girl Morley saw a confirmation of all he had achieved himself; in arousing her to smile, to cling to him, the world he'd moved out to was suddenly enhanced. He described to her his travels – a moonlit night off Madagascar, a storm-tossed crossing of the Bay of Biscay, a burning afternoon at Suez. He had thought of staying on in the army but, after a second, longer leave, he decided to come out. He was almost twenty-five; most of his brothers were married and all of his friends. He proposed to her at the end of the leave. She accepted: they had scarcely known each other a year and, during that time, they had never spent more than eight hours together.

Her parents didn't come to the wedding; neither did his. Her own parents didn't approve of someone who was a wastrel – though he had worked by that time nine months at Spencer's Farm – and his parents thought, patently, he might have married someone better.

Yet marriage brought all Sarah's virtues to the fore – her tenacity, her loyalty, her determination, in having set herself a task, to see it through, her capacity to take rebuffs and, while wilting, even hating her oppressors, to carry on. They lived, for a while, with her parents, since her other brothers and sisters, having married, had already moved out, and, when the rancour and the quarrelling, with which she was familiar and to which she was almost immune, depressed Morley himself and damped his spirits to a degree which began to frighten her, they moved to his parents' house and then, in succession, to the homes of his married brothers: all the while they saved to set up home themselves, their only disability Morley's tendency to spend money as soon as he earned it: he liked 'a good time', and the good time invariably involved him in getting rid of every coin in his pocket and moralizing afterwards on the simple precept that having 'a good time' was what 'life was all about', and if you didn't have 'a good time' what was 'the point of living'?

Yet Sarah's instincts were to conserve, to dig herself out, as she saw it, from the poverty of the houses by the river. For every shilling she saved, Morley, by the end of the following week, had managed to spend ten pence of it: week succeeded week and, by the end of three years, they had scarcely saved sufficient to buy the furniture. Still she persevered: she worked in a shop, and he worked, despairingly at first, then, when a baby became due, more hopefully, at Spencer's. They moved back to her parents' for the birth, lived there for a while, then moved out to a brother's, then moved back again and, finally, when the child was almost two years old, they were allocated the house on Stainforth estate.

*

21

Looking at the house had involved Sarah in feelings she had never experienced before: she ran her hand along the woodwork, along the plaster, she moved up and down its stairs and between its rooms and, from the windows at the front, gazed down across the slope towards the town and, from the windows at the back, towards the headlands of the valley. The air was fresh; the brick shapes strewn out across the slope were a new beginning; the old world of terraces and cobbles and gas-lit crevices, of smoke-ridden rooms and rat-infested cellars, of poverty and grime, had been discarded; not only was her own face set to the future, but the faces of everyone around her – couples like themselves, children like Alan, neighbours like Patterson: they were pioneers.

When she opened her eyes in the morning and saw the light on the curtains – the sun tracing in the material the thicker outline of leaves and flowers – she felt happier than she had felt during any previous day of her marriage. The rancour of the day before had vanished; her husband snored beside her, lying on his back, his mouth open and, but for the sound, she was reminded of the uncanny resemblance between the father and the son: she could hear Alan stirring in his cot, rattling the sides, talking his indecipherable language, laughing at one point as if the strangeness of the room were no strangeness at all but something he had been familiar with all his life.

It was Sunday morning; the estate was quiet: a dog barked, a child called out. Someone, closer, was chopping wood: a shovel scraped, a bucket rattled, coal tumbled against a metal screen. From the furthest distance came the tolling of a bell.

She got out of bed and went downstairs: she opened the curtains; sunlight came into the living-room. She made the fire, taking out the ashes, emptying them on the undug garden, and for a moment stood in the porch gazing out across the field to the uncompleted houses on the other side. Everything was still: the half-erected structures were strewn like ships across the slope, the chimney-stacks like reddened funnels: white clouds scudded from across the valley: the whole estate was in progress to the south.

Mr Patterson's wife came out and emptied ashes, a small, dark-haired woman, dressed in an apron, and, glancing across from the adjoining, half-dug garden, she nodded.

'Good morning.'

'Good morning,' Mrs Morley said.

Everything was fresh; through the air came the smell of paint, and of the dew, and the less discernible scent of the countryside beyond the houses.

'Isn't it nice?'

'Isn't it?' Mrs Morley said.

'Still sleeping?'

'He is.'

'Like mine.'

The ringing of a church bell was still audible from the summit of the slope.

'Have you got your linoleum yet?' Mrs Patterson said.

'Not yet.'

'Are you using Dobson's?'

'Hanley's.'

'Dobson's give free fitting.'

'I suppose they put it on the price.'

'No. No. I checked on that.' Mrs Patterson glanced round her at the garden: the spade had been left overnight in the upturned earth. 'I better get in and see to his lordship.'

'I suppose so,' Mrs Morley said.

The smell of cooking drifted down the slope. For a while, after Mrs Patterson had gone inside, Mrs Morley stood on the step and savoured the smell. Smoke trailed from the distant houses. They were a vast community, bound on a common venture, each household joined, yet each distant: she turned indoors with a feeling of pleasure.

She cooked the breakfast, then she went upstairs, brought down the child, dressed it, then woke her husband.

'Sithee, first morning,' he said, his hair tousled against the pillow. 'That's bacon I can smell, then, is it?'

'All ready.'

'By go. Worth coming home to.'

'I should hope it is.'

'Do'st get a kiss?' he added, reaching up.

'You'll get your breakfast,' she said, 'when you come downstairs,' yet she sat on the bed and stooped and thought, 'If I love

23

him now I shall love him for ever,' and kissed his lips. As she went downstairs she clapped her hands and, laughing at the child as it came, half-curious, to the foot of the stairs, lifted it and thought as well, 'We've set out on a journey. We've cast off from the past. We're going home at last.'

In the afternoon they walked out, through the half-completed roads, to the summit of Spinney Top. They came out, between two rows of pebble-dash houses, on the broad High Top Road which ran along the spine of the ridge and which was flanked, in turn, on the lower side by houses and on the other by the stone-built church.

Children were milling around the door.

'Send him up here when he's o'd enough,' Morley said. He glanced over an adjoining lane which separated the grounds of the church from the brick-built school. 'Theer an' all I shouldn't wonder.' He looked to the view, and added, 'I could fair step over to Spencer's from here,' pointing out, beyond the river and the hedged fields the other side, the curve of the lane, the line of trees by the hump-backed bridge and the thicker clump which marked the site of the farm itself. 'Like being on top of the world.'

They continued the walk: a path led off across the ridge, and down through the farm fields the other side; they crossed a stream, climbed up the valley slope and came out, finally, on a road of private houses which led back once more to the foot of Stainforth estate.

'It's a pretty place,' Mr Morley said. 'I think I shall like it here, tha knows.'

'If you don't, it's too late to complain,' Mrs Morley said, pushing the pram.

'Ne'er too late to change,' Mr Morley said.

'In all things?' Mrs Morley said.

'In all things,' Mr Morley answered, then added, seeing her look, 'Save one. I s'll never change in that.'

During the next few days, when he came home from work, Mr Morley dug the garden; he would stand out with Mr Patterson, their plots separated by a single strand of wire which, further along the road, was being replaced in the other gardens by a wooden fence. 'Nothing much'll grow in this,' Mr Patterson said, the first evening Mr Morley went out and made a start on clearing the builders' debris into the field. 'All clay up here.' He indicated the extensive patch he'd dug himself. 'I hear MacMasters,' he added, indicating his neighbour on the other side, 'has ordered a cartful of soil. I reckon I shall see if I can borrow a bit.' The MacMasters's garden had already been dug and the earth levelled off as if for a lawn.

'I can fetch you some manure, if you like,' Mr Morley said. 'We've any amount where I work.'

Mr Patterson had no children. When, sometimes, before he went to bed, Alan would come out to watch his father, and occasionally delve at the soil himself, Patterson would say, 'Tha wants to get him to give you a hand. He's got a bit of muscle on his arm already.'

'I shall, if he can stand up straight,' Mr Morley said, watching the boy fall then pick himself up. 'By the time I've been here a bit I s'll have him dig the lot, don't worry.'

Yet he had no great appetite for digging himself; it was too much like the work he did all day, whereas for Mr Patterson, who worked at a mill, it was always a change. He would watch the broad-muscled, bald-headed figure heave at the soil, stoop to his own task, then stand up to watch his neighbour once again.

'How about a shift down Spinney Moor Avenue?' he asked one evening, glancing at the house.

'I wouldn't mind,' Mr Patterson said. 'I s'll tell the wife. I shan't be a minute.'

Yet Mr Morley didn't go into his own house; he walked round the side and across the front and was already at Mr Patterson's gate by the time his neighbour came out.

'I don't suppose it'll run away,' he said to Patterson, indicating the garden. 'We're going to be here a long time, so I don't suppose there'll be any rush.'

They walked down the slope, their sleeves rolled, their hands in their pockets, glancing over at the other gardens: 'He's made a mess of that,' and, 'He's doing wonders with that,' they each observed, pausing here and there, where a privet hedge had already been planted, envisaging the effect of this civilizing feature on their

25

own front gardens, leaning on a gate and persuading another man, whom Mr Patterson knew, to join them. 'By go, we'll have a party afore we're through,' Mr Morley concluded, clapping his hands, laughing, and thinking that, apart from the army, his present life, on Stainforth estate, was turning out to be the best on earth.

It was after dark by the time he got back: the light was on in the living-room and when he tried the front door he found it locked.

He went round to the back: it was locked as well.

He knocked; for a while there was no response and he was on the point of going to the window to look into the living-room when he heard Sarah's footsteps cross the hall.

'Is anyone there?'

'It's me,' Mr Morley said.

'Is that you?'

'It's me,' he said again, lowering his voice.

'Is that you, Arthur?'

'It's me,' he called again and rattled the latch.

'Where have you been?'

'Let me in.'

He tried the latch; the door was still locked. From its firmness, at the bottom, he assumed it was also bolted.

'Where have you been?'

'I've been to the pub.'

He rattled the latch more fiercely.

'You never said.'

'O'ppen the door or I'll smash it.' When he tried the latch and the door still held he went to the window. That, too, was locked.

He went back to the porch.

'Do I have to bre'k the glass?' he said, yet he heard no sound from the other side. 'Sarah?' He pushed his weight against the door. The light which, through the keyhole and the cracks in the door, he had seen earlier had now gone out. He steppped back from the porch: the light had gone off in the living-room, too.

The house was in darkness.

He went round the front.

'Sarah.'

His voice echoed along the road and, since the houses opposite were in darkness, and a light was showing only in Patterson's scullery window, he called again, 'Sarah!' between cupped hands.

There was no response; despite the warmth of the evening, the windows of the house were closed.

The curtains, too, were drawn on Alan's room.

He sat down on the front step and gazed along the road; then, when a light went on in a bedroom opposite, he went round the back: he was in his shirt-sleeves and, despite the warmth of the evening, he could feel the dew as he walked about the garden.

Then, conscious of just how much he could see of the ground, he raised his head and saw, projecting above the nearest roof, the tip of the moon. Its light flooded into the field and gleamed, eerily, in the windows of the half-completed houses on the other side.

He ducked under the wire dividing his garden from the field and walked across the moonlit grass; he pulled down his sleeves, fastened them, and stood for a while with his hands in his pockets. He was'nt drunk; he'd borrowed money from Patterson to buy him a drink. Buy him two drinks to be exact, and two for his friend. He'd had a pleasant evening; he'd been very happy. She didn't wish to see him happy; she wished to see him tied to the house.

He gazed up at the moon: its shape was fully visible now from the centre of the field. The sky was clear: he was reminded of nights like this near Suez, gazing up at a myriad of stars so clear it was as if, sober or not, he could have touched them. Life was larger than Sarah imagined: she had never travelled further than the nearest seaside town, and even that she hadn't liked – not so much the place as the fact he'd gone there to enjoy himself. She didn't understand pleasure; she didn't, come to that, understand men; men were beyond her: feeling was beyond her.

Nevertheless, he concluded, she was still a gift. She was still the animal he was conjuring from its burrow.

He sat down in the grass; the fact was, as usual, he'd drunk more than he'd imagined. He knew, very soon, if he didn't do something, he'd fall asleep.

The moon loomed above the house; it appeared to grow smaller and more intense, its light colder: he was conscious of several stumbling footsteps, then a figure appeared, its arms outstretched.

'Arthur?'

27

The back door of the house was open.

'Are you all right?'

'I wa're having a rest.'

'Are you coming in?'

'Tha shouldn't have locked the door.'

'You never told me you were going off.'

'Do I have to tell you everything?'

'You could have said. Mrs Patterson will think you never tell me anything.'

'Nay, I can damn well walk down to the pub if I want to.'

'Aren't you coming in?'

'Nay,' he said, 'thy's locked the door.'

'You can come in now.'

'I'm damned if I shall.'

'Then don't,' she said. 'I've told you it was unfastened.'

She turned back to the house.

'She's more worried about being seen than ought I might feel,' he told himself. 'That's a rare game to play: alus under the eye of other people.'

He saw the back door close; a light was switched off in the landing window.

'Let her wait,' he thought, looking about him at the uncompleted houses. 'I can sleep over theer, if the worse come to the worst.'

He got up after a moment and walked over to the nearest shell.

But the houses that had a roof on had also doors and when he tried the first and then the second, and the windows, too, he found them fastened.

He turned back to the field; he had no facility for telling the time at night, and had taken his watch off earlier that evening when he dug the garden.

He opened the scullery door, half-expecting it to be locked, turned the key, fastened the bolt and for a moment stood in the dark, listening; then, taking off his boots, he went upstairs.

He washed in the bathroom, took off his clothes, his nightshirt having been laid on the landing rail.

She murmured quietly as he got into bed.

'Is that you?'

'Who else would it be?' he said. 'Or ar't thy expecting somebody better?'

She moved away.

'Why lock the door on your husband?' he asked.

'Let's talk about it in the morning,' she said.

'Let's talk about it now,' he said. 'I've been out theer for half an hour.'

'I'm tired.'

'We'll see what happens if I'm locked out again.'

'Yes,' she said.

'We'll see what happens to the back door, for a start.'

'Did you lock it when you came in?' .

'I did.'

'Well, then,' she said. 'We'll see in the morning.'

'So this is what it is,' he thought, lying on his back, gazing at the ceiling, at the faint glow of light which came in from the road outside.

'Have you any money left?' she asked.

'No,' he said.

'Well,' she said, 'that's one thing settled.'

'What's that?'

'I've none left either till the end of the week.'

Yet tiredness, too, enveloped his mind, and the last thing he thought of was a joke told him at the Spinney Moor by Patterson's friend, and he remembered, too, how Patterson had laughed and how the friend had slapped his back and had said, 'Have another, Arthur, before they throw us out.'

'Aye, another,' Morley said, already fast asleep.

THREE

The garden was dug; he planted flowers, vegetables and, in the lower half, he set a lawn: another he shaped out in the plot at the front. Workmen came and erected fences; a privet hedge was planted and a gate put up. Within a month most of the houses in the road were occupied.

The noise of the builders' lorries faded. In the house next to the Morleys' a policeman came to live; his wife was young: they had a daughter, the same age as Alan, and in the evenings, when the policeman came home from work, he would sit in the porch, the girl on his knee, bouncing her up and down and, laughing, throw a ball for a dog to fetch. A tall, bald-headed man, with dark-brown eyes and a flushed, thick-featured face, he would come out at these intervals between his shifts and dig the garden; soon he had overtaken Morley, and Patterson, and the MacMasters: he laid paths, erected a walk, planted roses, arranged a trellis, a rockery and a stepped terrace which led up to the top half of the garden. His name was Foster; occasionally he would come into the Morleys' house, tapping on the door – for the girl, nicknamed 'Pretty' by him, and called Alison, would often wander across the footpath between the houses and come into the scullery to play with Alan – 'Pretty?' he would call, his tall figure, with its gleaming, dome-shaped head, thrust round the door and, hearing the child's voice, he would add, 'Come to visit her boyfriend, has she? You can see where her thoughts will turn in two or three years' time.'

'Oh, a bit longer than that,' Mrs Morley would say, looking up from her washing, or from where she was cooking, shy at first with the uniformed figure, standing there, invariably without his tunic, blue-shirted, dark-tied, dark-bracered, big-booted, the geniality of the bald-headed man, and the way he strode through

30

the house to retrieve his daughter, setting her on his shoulder, or thrusting her with her blonde-coloured, dancing curls across his back, soon putting Mrs Morley at her ease: he would sit at the table and take a cup of tea. 'She's too much like her mother for me not to know: an eye for the lads from the age of dot.'

The girl would laugh; he would bounce her up and down: Alan, dark-eyed, would gaze up at the uniformed figure, with its heavy, laughing, red-cheeked face, at the laughing figure of the girl set on his knee and, scowling, tip one foot on its side, or, speculatively, put out a hand and endeavour to join in the bouncing up and down, and the laughter and the rolling of the blonde-haired girl from side to side in the policeman's heavy hands. Soon, the two of them would be bouncing up and down together, their shrieks and laughter filling the house, the policeman's wife, if the activity continued long enough, tapping on the woodwork at the side of the door and saying, 'This is where he's got to? Send him on an errand and it's another two hours before I see him.'

'Like mine,' Mrs Morley would say, offering her neighbour a cup of tea, the two women chatting at the side of the table while the tall, blue-shirted figure, set on a stool, bounced the children up and down, tickled one and then the other, slid one down then pulled it up, scratched the one's head and then the other's, and, still jogging, would sing, 'Here's two rabbits, fit for a stew; which shall we have: this 'un, or *you*!' chasing them finally into the other room, or up the stairs, Mrs Foster calling, 'Now, that's enough,' and, 'He never knows when to stop,' still chastising the blue-shirted figure, who was almost twice her size, as they returned to the house, the tiny figure of the girl set up on the policeman's shoulder where she shouted and laughed and tapped the tall man's head as, finally, swinging her down, he carried her inside their door.

'At least they're happy,' Mrs Morley would say when Morley, returning home, came upon these scenes.

'Why shouldn't they be happy? He's got a good job.'

'You could have one.'

'Nay, I've been in a uniform half my life, I'm damned if I'll step in another. Any road, I'm not the right man.'

'You're not a criminal, are you?' Mrs Morley would ask.

31

'I'm just not cut out for a bobby. You've to be the right sort of man for a job like that.'

'You don't begrudge him it?' Mrs Morley would ask.

'I begrudge him nought. I begrudge no one nothing,' Mr Morley would add. 'All I'm saying is, it's a damned easy job compared to some. You retire,' he would conclude, 'afore you're fifty.'

'Only if you've been in long enough.'

'He'll have been in long enough. He's been a bobby, I should think, since afore he wa' two year old.'

Yet, despite his misgivings, Mr Morley would talk to the taller man in the evenings across the fence and would sometimes cross over to his garden, examine his trellis, his crazy-paving, his bedding roses and his climbers, his border plants, the grass he had planted, the neat rows of vegetables already showing green, and would crouch down, too, and smoke a cigarette while the blue-shirted figure sat beside him in the porch, smoking a pipe, Morley returning later to report, 'His father wa're a policeman, tha knows,' or, 'He used to lake football for the City' or, 'He wa' telling me o' one chap they copped who'd had one hundred previous convictions. It makes you wonder what the world is coming to,' his manner deferential in the presence of the taller man, his head upraised, his face inflamed, as if, in courting the attention of Mr Foster, he were seeking ways to ingratiate himself with the law itself. 'You never know what they might pinch you for: a man like that can come in useful.'

'You haven't done anything you shouldn't, have you?' Mrs Morley inquired, this side of her husband's character a mystery to her.

'You never know if I shall.'

'I doubt if you'd get special privilege by knowing Mr Foster,' Mrs Morley said. 'They're not allowed to use the law like that.'

As it was, in the evenings and at weekends, Morley scavenged the half-completed houses for odd bricks and lengths of wood and shovelfuls of cement, which he brought back to the house in buckets, making paths, building a trellis himself, erecting a barrier to keep back the coal in the coal-house outside the back door.

'He'll not pinch me for that,' he would say whenever Mrs Morley complained about the amount of material he did bring back. 'It's

32

stuff they've thrown away, for one thing, and I gave him a bit of the wood, for another.'

'You didn't tell him where it came from,' his wife replied.

'No,' he said. 'But he's a good idea.'

Mr Foster never accompanied Mr Morley and Mr Patterson to the Spinney Moor Hotel and, largely because of this, Mrs Morley saw his influence as a more wholesome one on her husband than that of their other neighbour.

'He never drinks,' she would say. 'Yet he's perfectly happy.'

'His father wa're a great tippler,' Mr Morley said.

'How do you know that?' she asked.

'He told me.'

'At least he's learnt his lesson. Like Alan will, no doubt.'

'He's nought to be afeared of in me,' Mr Morley said.

'The amount you drink at times,' she said, 'he'll be bound to notice as soon as he gets older.'

Yet Morley had gone to some lengths to curtail his drinking; for one thing, once the household bills were settled, and their way of living more certain, he had very little money left to spend at the Spinney Moor, or at the Three Bells on his way home from work. Most weeks, from the Wednesday morning until the Friday evening, there was no money in the house, save a shilling for the electric meter and three pennies for the gas. 'Maybe I should have been a bobby,' he would say, looking over at the contented household on the other side of the garden fence. 'They're set, you can see, for a happy life.'

'At least, he saves his money. We never save a penny,' Mrs Morley said.

'What's the point o' saving?' Morley would inquire. 'Are you going to be happier in a fortnight than you are today by saving a couple of bob each week?'

'At least you'll know where you stand and you're not worrying from Monday till Friday that you'll have enough to see you through.'

'We'll have enough,' he replied, yet, at the end of the week, when he received his wage, he would be working out new ways of siphoning off a coin, if only a shilling, so that his evenings at the Spinney Moor should not be further curtailed.

'You're a family man. Not like Patterson. He has no children.'

'He'll be having some. Don't worry. Then he'll complain.'

'Are you complaining because you have a child?'

'I'm complaining about nought,' Mr Morley said. 'All I'm saying is, he'll get fastened up.'

'Is Mr Foster fastened up?' she asked.

'He has no need to be. He's content with what he has.'

'Aren't you content?'

'It's that I can't see the logic of waiting for tomorrow to enjoy what you can just as easily enjoy today.'

'It makes nothing of life,' Mrs Morley said. 'It makes it all spending, without thought and reason.'

'To me, it makes common sense,' Mr Morley replied. 'A second wasted is a second lost.'

'A penny saved is a penny wiser.'

'You'll be saying the same at eighty, if we live that long.'

'Everything we've got here is what I've saved,' she said.

'I've asked Spencer for more,' he told her for, prior to moving to the new house, he had asked Spencer for a rise, only to be refused, and to be offered, in recompense, the loan of the cart.

'Perhaps you should get another job.'

'What other job?'

'At Chatterton's: sheet-metal working. Engineering.'

'I could never work indoors,' he said. 'I'm used to being in the open. I've alus been in the open. I don't think there's ten week I've lived in barracks, for example, in the army: nearly all the time I wa're under canvas.'

'You'll get no money at Spencer's. There's no money in farm-work,' Sarah said.

'Maybe I'll look round for another farm.'

'No farm pays more than another. They have it settled,' she said, 'between them.'

'I'll think of something, don't worry,' he told her.

Yet it wasn't Mr Morley's nature to worry long, and it wasn't his nature to hold a grudge, or to remember the conclusion of an argument for more than twenty-four hours. By the end of the same week he was looking at his wage packet again and thinking of what excuse he could make to open it and extract a shilling.

*

Beyond Mr and Mrs Foster lived the Shawcrofts: a father and a mother and a baby in a pram, together with a second child a little older than Alan. Shawcroft worked at the coke ovens at the edge of the town, a slim, thin-featured man, dark-haired, his wife even smaller and darker than himself. The garden at the back was left unattended, weeds growing in profusion as far as the fence. In the evenings the couple often quarrelled, the child crying in the pram, the other child screaming, the voices of the father and the mother calling from the open door.

'At least we haven't reached that stage,' Morley would say, picking up Alan.

'Nor are we likely to,' Mrs Morley said.

'I suppose one morning we'll find he's killed her,' Morley said.

'Or she's killed him.'

'More than likely.'

Yet the unease caused by the Shawcrofts' arguments was absorbed by the greater feeling of confederacy which united the tenants of the estate, neighbours calling to neighbours once the first few days of strangeness had passed, a sense not only of being pioneers, occupying land which had never been lived on before, but the feeling that theirs was a common venture, uniting people who had never been drawn together before. Beyond the Shawcrofts came the O'Donalds, who owned a cycle shop, and, beyond the O'Donalds, with their two young children, were the childless Harrisons, of whom the wife worked in an office and the husband as a postman. Beyond the postman lived a cobbler and, next door to the cobbler, the Barracloughs, with four young children, the husband employed as a painter by the Corporation.

The houses, on completion, were steadily filled; the gardens were dug; children played in the field and brought back news to their parents. Sheds were built, hens appeared, a motor bike was tested in one of the gardens. At the bottom of Spinney Moor Avenue the row of shops was finally completed and, in the space between the shops and the Spinney Moor Hotel, the foundations of a cinema were being laid out. On Sundays the bell tolled from the church and each weekday morning crowds of children ran up the narrow roads to the school and in the evening came running down again: the sounds of their voices, calling, came out across the slope each

35

playtime, the flood of sound, ebbing and rising, marking the intervals of the day for the women in the houses.

Over the summer Morley was late home each evening as Spencer took in the harvest; he worked Saturdays and Sundays and, when he did come home, he would sit on the step and chide the tall figure digging in the adjoining garden, 'By go, I could be a bobby myself, the hours they have to work.'

'It's the responsibility, Arthur,' came Mr Foster's reply.

'I could have the responsibility as well, walking about all day wi' nought to do.'

'You'll soon be sitting back when you've done your stooking,' Mr Foster would add.

'It's threshing after that. Then ploughing. Then sowing. There's ne'er a day left free from now till Christmas. Aye,' he would call into the open back door, 'I think I've missed my profession, love.'

'Oh, he's always complaining, Sam,' Mrs Morley would call, more familiar with Mr Foster on these occasions than was her husband.

'Sam, is it, now?' Mr Morley would call. 'I can see I've been spending too much time away from home,' Mr Foster laughing, leaning on his spade, and adding, 'He's caught us out, Sarah. Might as well admit it.'

'That's the way the flag is flying, and I never saw it,' Mr Morley would add. 'By go, no wonder he's alus home. Hear that?' he would call to Mrs Foster. 'Never mind his stripes and his policeman's collar: just see which way his boots are turned.'

Yet, if the bantering scarcely concealed Morley's resentment, once inside the house and the door closed he would complain more vehemently about the hours he worked. Sometimes he wasn't home until after dark and, if not stopping at the Three Bells, by the time he reached the Spinney Moor he would be too tired to resist the temptation and, once inside, he would empty his pockets across the counter, arriving home to find his supper cold, and with scarcely enough energy to go to bed. One night he lay till morning in the chair by the fire and another morning he slept so late that by the time he got to work he had to feign an illness. He was back at the bar the following night.

One evening he arrived home to find the house in darkness.

36

Assuming Sarah to have gone to bed, he stepped into the scullery and took off his boots and looked round for his supper. There was nothing in the oven and the fire was out: all the pans were on the shelf.

He went upstairs, surprised to see the bedroom door still open.

The door to Alan's room was also ajar: he looked inside; the cot was empty.

The double bed in the front bedroom was still unmade.

He looked in the bathroom, in the spare bedroom at the back, returned downstairs, put on the lights, looked at the mantelpiece, the sideboard and the table, examined the cupboard in the scullery, re-opened the back door and looked out at the garden.

He knocked on the Fosters' door.

After an interval the lock was turned and the bolt drawn back.

Mr Foster appeared in his pyjamas, a raincoat over the top.

'You haven't seen Sarah?' Morley asked.

'I haven't, Arthur,' Foster said. 'I'll ask the missis.'

Mrs Foster came down; Alan and Mrs Morley had not been seen that afternoon.

'She must have gone to her mother's, or one of her brothers', and missed the last bus,' Morley said. 'I'm sorry to have got you up.'

'That's all right, Arthur,' Foster said, and gazed out at him as he went back to the house.

After waiting an interval he locked the back door and wheeled out his bike.

He rode slowly along Town Road, the street lamps lit above his head.

Close to the town, before the last steep rise to the central hill, he turned to his right along a thoroughfare which led, narrowly winding, between mills and factories, to come out by the river; the gas lamps here were more dimly lit. Passing the ends of several narrow streets he turned into one adjacent to the unlit structure of a mill and, propping his bike against one of the lamps, he knocked at a door.

A light showed in a window overhead.

A tousled head leaned out.

'Who's that?'

'It's Arthur.'

The window was lowered.

As he stood by the door to knock again a bolt was drawn and the door pulled back.

His mother-in-law, a small, grey-haired figure with, in the darkness, a grizzled face, gazed out. She hadn't put in her teeth and stood with one hand on the doorpost, barring his way.

'She doesn't want to see you.'

'Is she here?'

'She's asleep.'

'Is Alan here?'

'He's been in bed for three or four hours. So have I,' she added.

Below her shawl was a night-gown and, below the night-gown, a pair of slippers.

'She came because she's fed up with your drinking. I told her afore she wed but she never listened.'

'Nay, I'll come in,' Morley said, making to force his way in the door.

'You'll never,' the mother said. 'I'll call the bobby.'

'Call him,' Morley said and forced his way through his mother-in-law's arm. 'Where is she?' he added. 'In the room at the back?'

But already a figure had appeared on the stairs: she was in her night-gown and had evidently come prepared. Only her silhouette was visible, for the lights had not been put on in the kitchen into which the door of the house directly opened.

'I don't want to see you,' she said.

'You left no message,' Morley said. 'What am I supposed to think, wi' you and Alan gone?'

'You can think what you like.'

'I wa' never drunk.'

'As close as makes no difference.'

The door to the street had been closed by the mother. She said, 'I want him out of here, or you both go back together,' passing her daughter on the stairs and closing the door on the landing.

'Are you coming back?' Morley asked.

'I'm staying here.'

'In that case, I'll take Alan,' he said.

'You'll do no such thing.'

'I'm having him,' he said, yet he stayed on the stairs, craning up

38

at his wife whom, in the greater darkness, he could scarcely see.

'I want you out of here,' she said. 'I'll never forgive you if you wake him.'

'Are you coming back tomorrow?' Morley said, seeing no way out of the dilemma except by using force.

'No.'

'When are you coming back?'

'I'm not coming back.'

'What have I done, Sarah?' he asked.

'I've warned you. I've begged you. You drink every last penny you can get. You leave us with nothing. I'm not having it any longer.'

'I'll give it up.'

'I've heard that before.'

'I'll give it up definitely.'

'I'm not going to argue about it any more. If you try and take Alan I'll go to the police. Mrs Patterson knows how much you drink.'

'You've been talking to her about your husband, have you?'

'She can see enough as it is.'

'Aye, and I thought Patterson wa're a friend,' he added.

'He is. But he drinks in moderation, and only once a week.'

'Aye, we can't all be angels,' Morley said.

He turned to the door.

'In that case, I s'll go back home.'

He thought, 'I can go and join the army tomorrow and be damned to all of them. No more Spencer, no more wukking, no more nagging. I can drink as much as I like, for as long as I like wi'out anybody nor nobody butting in.'

Yet, once in the street, the smell of the malt-kilns and of the dark presence of the mill soon brought to him the realization that he couldn't go back: the army was a young man's game and, towards the end of it, he'd got sick of it and, Sarah apart, he'd wanted something settled.

In any case, he concluded, there was Alan: he couldn't leave someone, bearing his name, who was all the world to him, in a place like that.

He couldn't leave Sarah, either, for, as he got on the bike and looked back at the house, he thought of all the things he might have said: 'Haven't I done everything for her? Haven't I kept a job? Haven't we got a home? Haven't I looked after her like a husband should?'

He got back to the house and made some food, set the alarm and went to bed.

Yet he scarcely slept. He was up again at six and already on his bike by half-past, pedalling back once more towards the river, knocking on the door in Hasleden Street, waiting for it to be opened, this time by his father-in-law, a tall, willowy man who stepped aside and said, 'Nay, it's nought to do wi' me. She wa' warned afore she wed,' his overalls already on and his snap-bag packed, leaving the house for the mill only moments after Morley had entered.

He strode up to his wife's bedroom at the back and could hear her talking already to Alan.

When he opened the door she looked up in surprise: she was still in bed and Alan, in pyjamas, was sitting on the cover.

'Are you coming, or do I carry you?' Morley said, antagonized by the sight of the two of them together and by the cup of tea which, steaming, he saw had been placed on a chair by the bed.

'I'm not coming back, and you won't carry me,' she said. 'I'll report anything you do to the authorities,' she added.

But for the child, he might have grabbed her.

'Come on, Alan,' he said. 'We're going home.'

Yet the child continued to cling to its mother.

'Come on,' he said. 'Let's lift you.' He tugged the child and it cried in terror.

He heard his mother-in-law in the door behind. 'You'll kill her.' He felt the woman's fist across his back.

He went back to the door.

He wiped his face, watching his wife bowed over the child, she crying, the boy screaming.

'Tha s'll be home tonight, or I'll come again.'

He went to the stairs.

'You can tek him where you like. I'll find you.'

His legs tremored: he could scarcely mount the bike. He stopped at the end of the street and held his head. 'What have I done now?'

he thought. 'Does she want me to be like Patterson next door, or Foster? Nothing but a woman's man?'

His eyes full of tears he cycled from the town.

'What's up, Arthur?' the farmer called, seeing him enter the farmyard early. 'Clock got stuck?'

'Aye, Mr Spencer,' Morley said. 'Just about.'

In the evening he delayed returning home until it was almost dark. 'The light'll either be on or it won't,' he thought. He didn't raise his head until he'd dismounted at the gate.

The curtains were undrawn. No smoke came from the chimney: the scullery and the living-room were as he'd left them.

He made some supper and thought about going down to the Spinney Moor.

Finally, he went up to bed and lay in the darkness, gazing at the pattern of the street light on the ceiling.

He heard a knock on the door and when he went down he found his neighbour, Foster, standing there.

'Everything all right?' the policeman said. He was in uniform and had either just come off or was about to go on duty.

'Aye. All right,' Morley said.

'The wife all right?'

'Champion.' The policeman glanced past him into the scullery. 'She's staying at her mother's.'

'We thought she might.'

'Wi' the harvesting I've scarce time to go back'ard or forr'ad,' Morley said.

'Aye.'

The policeman stepped back from the porch.

'If there's anything we can do you'll let us know.'

'Oh, I'll let you know,' Morley said, nodding at Foster then closing the door.

He stood listening to the policeman's steps as they crossed to the adjoining house.

'Nay, he'll twig it,' he thought. 'But I s'll not care.'

Yet he lay in bed, his body curled to the shape of his wife.

He imagined her lying in bed by the river. 'Two more nights down theer, and she'll come crawling back,' he thought. 'I shall be the winner.'

But Sarah didn't come back the next day or the next; Morley, on the fourth night, called in at the Spinney Moor and stayed till closing time, coming home on the arm of a man he had never seen before.

'Can you see your way on from here?' the stranger asked.

'Let me tell you a secret,' Morley said. 'Never get wed.'

'Never,' the man acknowledged.

'Not ever.'

'Never.'

'Word from a wise man.'

'Correct.'

'Which way am I?'

'Uphill, Arthur.'

'See you tomorrow.'

'All being well.'

'May the sun always shine.'

Lurching from side to side he set off up the road.

The street lights reeled above his head and, when he reached his gate, he fell against the hedge.

For several seconds he struggled to pull himself upright and finally fell through the thin sheaf of privet and knelt for a while on the halfgrown grass the other side.

'All for nothing,' he thought. 'All for nothing-othing-o!'

He pulled himself up, found the path, went round the side of the house then hunted for several minutes in his pockets to find the key.

He looked about him; he retraced his steps: he got down on his knees and finally found the key beneath the hedge.

He returned to the door, unlocked it and, having staggered inside, collapsed in a chair and, thinking some time later he might get up, he turned, collapsed and lay there oblivious until the sunlight, streaming through the window, finally woke him.

He cycled to work with no money in his pocket and, on arriving at Spencer's, he went directly to the door of the house. The barking of dogs came from inside and Spencer himself looked out.

'I thought tha wa' poorly,' the farmer said, indicating that, whatever Morley might make of the rest of the day, he wouldn't count it as a full one.

'My wife's left me,' Morley said. 'I'm in a bit of a fix.'

42

It was the first mention he'd made of his private life, beyond the fact that he was married and had had a baby and had got a new house, and the farmer stood in the doorway uncertain what to make of it.

'Come in, Arthur.' He pulled the door wider and Morley stepped into the stone-flagged kitchen. Rabbits were strung up from hooks on the low-beamed ceiling: a fire burned in a black-enamelled grate.

The dogs, barking, ran into the yard.

'Fancy a cup of tea?'

'I wouldn't mind,' Morley said.

'How long ago has she gone?'

'A week.'

'A stiff 'un is it?'

'I think so,' Morley said. He sat at the large farmhouse table, at which he had only rarely sat before and, for no reason he could account for, began to cry: there was something enclosed about the gesture so that when the farmer's wife, a slender, delicately-featured woman with thin, fair hair swept sharply back, paused at the door she glanced in with consternation, gazing at the robust figure standing by the table who, shrugging, merely shook his head.

'Here go, Arthur,' the farmer said. 'Let's have a cup o' summat stronger.'

'Nay, I s'll never touch drink again,' Morley said. 'She left me for I could never ge' past the Spinney Moor without stopping off.'

Aware of Mrs Spencer, he dried his eyes, turning away, pulling out a handkerchief.

'I'm sorry to have troubled you.'

'Nay, it's no trouble to me, lad,' the farmer said, yet content to stand there, waiting for his wife to take command.

'I shall make a cup of tea, Arthur,' she said and Morley turned, blinking, rubbing his eyes. 'I tell Mr Spencer, but he never listens.' She gestured to the farmer as she made the tea. 'He's a Three Bells man, if ever there was one.'

'In moderation.'

'That's not how a wife must see it,' his wife replied.

'That's a fact.' Spencer glanced at Morley and winked 'Would you like the missis to have a word, and see if she can pull it through?' he added.

43

'If she won't listen to me she'll listen to no one,' Morley said.

'She might listen to another woman. Send a heifer in to butter another heifer up, but ne'er put in a bull,' he added, laughing and finally sitting as his wife, protesting, came up to the table.

'That's no way to talk about it,' she said when a child, crying, called from another room.

'She'll sort it. She can thread a needle from a tangle if you leave her long enough,' the farmer said, pouring the tea himself. 'Give her five minutes, and she'll soon have the wife back home.'

A child, scarcely more than eighteen months, was carried into the room: its pale-blue eyes, like those of Spencer himself, examined Morley gravely.

'Here's Margaret, fit for no one and nothing,' the farmer said, leaning over to squeeze the chubby leg and then the chubby cheek and running his hand finally over the mop of light-coloured hair. He laughed, leaning back, adding, 'Ought to eat with that, then, Arthur? I bet thy hasn't had a nibble. If the missis,' he concluded, ' 'll rustle summat up.'

That evening, when Morley got home, he could see from the angle of the curtains and the smoke from the chimney that the house was occupied, and as he came up the path at the side he could hear Alan playing in the garden and, rounding the corner, saw Sarah taking in washing from the line.

She said nothing, and he said nothing either, following her into the house, taking off his boots, hanging up his coat, avoiding the clothes, stooping to the sink and washing.

'Ought to eat?' he said.

'It's in the oven.'

He opened the oven door, getting out the plate, running with it, hot, to the table and thinking, 'She believes she's beaten me, and I suppose she has: nothing between us'll ever be the same again.'

When the child came in Morley nodded his head.

'How go, Alan?' he said, the child standing at the door. 'Ar't coming in?'

Yet the boy, instead of answering, turned to the hall and from there called to his mother who, coming through, said, 'Got everything you want?'

'Yes,' he said, for the table had been set.

'Mrs Spencer came to see me.'

'She said she would.'

'Pity you have to go telling everyone about it.'

'I've told nobody,' he said, 'apart from Spencer. I've told next door you were away for a while.'

He ate his food slowly, looking at the table, at the plate, at the window, occasionally glancing back at the boy.

'I've given up the drink.'

'So Mrs Spencer told me.'

'I swore Spencer I would.'

'I thought you said you had.'

'I have.'

'Well,' she said. 'We should be all right.'

'He's upped me another two bob a week.'

'Mr Spencer told me he had.'

'I'd never have thought he'd play, but he has.'

'It's hardly more than a farthing an hour.'

'Better than nought.'

'Next to it, I'd say.'

He didn't add anything further.

'Is your supper all right?'

'Champion.'

'I'll take your plate,' she said, 'if you've finished.'

He put out his arm to the boy and, after a moment, Alan came to him.

He lifted him to his knee; his hair smelled freshly from a recent bath.

'Now, then, how are we?' he said, and kissed his mouth.

The boy's head turned, listening to the sounds from the scullery.

Mrs Morley, in tidying the kitchen, had begun, faintly, to hum a tune.

'What did Mrs Spencer say?' he asked when she came back in.

The boy, already, had slipped from his knee.

'She said I'd done right.'

'Did she?'

He waited, but she said no more.

'Bed for you,' finally, she told the boy and her feet a moment later

45

came from the stairs, followed by the undressing in the bathroom.

'Normally she undresses him down here, but now it's suddenly i' private,' Morley thought, and for an instant the suspicion that perhaps she wouldn't be sleeping in their bed had crossed his mind.

When he went up, however, he found the cover of the bed turned back: he went into the boy's bedroom, kissed him in his cot, and drew the curtains, turning to him once again before he followed Sarah out.

'What else did she say?' he asked when the door was closed.

'I've come back, haven't I?'

'Aye, you've come back, love,' Morley said. 'And I'm glad. Though I feel for some reason, more, it's me that's come back home to you,' he added.

FOUR

The following spring Mrs Morley announced herself to be pregnant a second time. A change had come over Morley; at the news of the child he merely glanced up.

'Aren't you glad?' she asked him.

'Aye.'

'You don't sound it.'

'Nay, I'm glad.'

He had no way of showing it; even with the farmer he maintained his reserve: he pedalled more stoically to work, and he pedalled more slowly back. His purpose was to consolidate, to provision the fortress which, in his mind, their little house on Stainforth estate had now become. Never having worried about the future, the house had fallen into his lap; now that it was there it was a possession which, because of its value, had to be secured; not only had the garden to be dug but the house, six months after their arrival, had to be painted, the walls papered and, less than a year after, the paintwork once again retouched. The linoleum had been laid, a carpet added, a rug, a mat: utensils were bought to complement his bag of tools; coal, because of its price, had to be conserved; the vegetables grown in the garden were carefully rationed.

In one corner of his mind Morley was asking, 'What have we to be worried about?' but in the forefront of his mind he shared his wife's misgivings: life started in blackness and ended in blackness: darkness threatened it on every side. Not only had his youth departed but fresh burdens were being added to his back. He wasn't used to measuring, and each measure that he had to make was more painful than the last. 'Am I,' he began to think, 'to be condemned to live like this for ever?'

It was against this speculation that he protected Alan; and it was against this speculation, too, that he intended to protect the child to come. The measure of the protection he gave was seen in the number of times he never went near the Spinney Moor, and in the number of times he cycled to work and the number of times he cycled back, and the hours of overtime he could get, and in the number of wage packets he brought back unopened, pocketing the sixpence and occasionally the one shilling Sarah gave him after opening it on the living-room table.

The whole process of her campaign against life was revealed in the opening of the envelope which, each Friday night, he gave her – her examination of Spencer's careless scrawl which denoted the number of hours worked, and at what rate, and what deductions had been made, this calculation being confirmed before she poked her finger beneath the flap and tore it carefully along the edge in order not to disturb the writing; the drawing out of the money, the counting of the coins, then the division of the sums into what would be needed the following week: so much for rent, so much for insurance, so much for electricity and gas, so much for the Hospital Fund, so much to Morley, so much to be set aside for coal, so much, if possible, to be saved, so much for items of clothing she intended buying, a decision which had to be anticipated by several months, and so much, finally, for food. In no time the sum had vanished, most of it into her purse, each item finding a place in a separate compartment, the remainder into a variety of tins; in a separate tin, which had once held tea, she placed, as she had since the day they had married, the brown-paper envelope itself, securing it to a wad of similar envelopes by a rubber band.

Morley acquired a strange contentment from seeing this weekly ritual, for, once the money had been counted, and each sum assigned to its specific place, and he had had his wash, done what jobs had to be completed and seen Alan into his cot, he would set off on his bike to the fish and chip shop which had been built, like a miniature cottage, on the adjoining Moor Field Road. If his income had been sufficient he would purchase two fish, with the accompanying chips, or if not, two fishcakes, cycling back with the supper, wrapped in a newspaper, tucked inside his jacket, the warmth adding a feeling of achievement to the final day of the week.

'I s'll get used to living in a prison,' he would think, dismounting from his bike at the gate and looking up at the curtained window, at the coil of smoke from the chimney. 'Perhaps it's the only place where any of us live, for isn't Spencer, who has a car and a house like a palace, always complaining about how hard things are, and have I ever known anyone who didn't feel in some way fastened down and cheated?'

With the baby due he redoubled his efforts to help about the house, and redoubled his efforts, too, with the garden; he brought Major several times to the house, hauling on each occasion a load of manure, awarding due portions of it to Foster and Patterson, and even to MacMasters, a large, fat man who drove a lorry and who, in exchange, brought him one night a load of paving: he constructed a path down the centre of the garden to the field, and built a forecourt immediately around the porch. Plants, too, he got on occasion from Spencer, and these he also divided amongst his neighbours. In the evenings and at weekends the men played cricket: he joined them in the field, using shears to cut back the grass, the stumps set up from broken fences, the men, after the game was finished, lying in the grass, roaring amongst themselves, drifting off, finally, in ones and twos. In this way he got to know nearly everyone in the square of houses, for those who didn't play often came to the fences, called over, or stood and watched; in the winter, too, when the field wasn't wet, the same men climed over, set out a pitch, and kicked a ball from one end to the other.

'They play more than the children,' Sarah said, watching the young husbands running up and down, their voices calling, almost screeching, bursting into laughter, their coats tossed down, their shirt-sleeves rolled, then sitting, later, in shadowed groups as, the light fading, they lay back in the grass. 'More like children,' taking little account of the number of times Morley himself climbed over the fence, merely complaining whenever he came back, 'Somebody has to wash those: just look at your clothes.'

'Want me back i' the Spinney Moor?' he would ask, and she would add, 'I thought you'd made your decision. It's no account to me what you do.'

They preserved a peculiar silence between them; it was never more apparent than on the Friday evening: the division of the wage,

49

the clearing-up, the putting of the child to bed, the departure for the supper, the return to find the table set, the fire burning; afterwards, the table cleared, they would listen to the radio, a gift to them, second-hand, from one of Sarah's brothers, Sarah sewing, Morley reading the paper or sitting, abstracted, gazing at the blaze.

On Saturday mornings Morley worked but Sarah went into town to do her shopping, pushing the pram along Town Road, up the steep hill to the Bull Ring and the adjacent market. Occasionally, if she could be sure Morley would be back in the afternoon, she would wait for him to return and they'd go together, Morley pushing the pram, Sarah walking beside him, the bag for the shopping suspended from the handle.

Ever since her taking the child and leaving the house and returning to her mother's, a mark had been put on Morley's life – a wound which, if it had healed, had left a scar so deep that it had acquired the characteristics of a natural feature. On their silent walks to the town a vibrancy existed between them, like two people linked by a chain, the one unable to move without the other.

At the market they would push the child before them, drawing it aside or thrusting it through a gap in the crowd, the money they were to spend already allocated, an occasional indulgence allowed, after some discussion, when they forewent one commodity in favour of another, or Morley delved in his pocket and spent a few pence of his own allowance. Then, after the crowds and the shouting, came the journey back, the swinging of the bag in Morley's hand as he walked beside the pram, occasionally, as was his habit, calling to the child, 'See that?' at the train passing over the bridge that crossed the steep incline leading to the town, or lifting him sometimes from the pram to look in the beck that, for the first hundred yards or so, flowed alongside the Town Road before it separated up either flank of Stainforth estate itself.

Once back at the house came the sorting of the purchases – as carefully stored in the stone-slab pantry as were the various divisions of their weekly wage in the pockets of the purse – the bread into an earthenware bowl, the biscuits into a large square tin, the bacon on to a dish which in turn was placed beneath an upturned saucer, the meat on to an oval plate which was covered by a sheet of paper, the margarine and the butter, if any had been purchased, being placed either end of a wooden shelf. On the topmost shelf would be set the raisins and currants in their blue-coloured bags and, on the bottom stone shelf, a piece of dripping wrapped in greaseproof paper. The sugar was carried through to the living-room where it was kept amongst the plates and the cups and saucers in a cupboard by the fire.

The amount of food they bought was determined not only by what they could afford, but by how much Morley had brought home from Spencer's during the week, or, more particularly, at the end of it. On principle the farmer never allowed him any: 'If I gev it to you, Arthur, I shall have to gev it to the others,' which, presumably, meant the herdsman who looked after the cows and the others he employed. Nevertheless, occasionally, when Morley was leaving, having stayed behind in the evening or on the Saturday to finish the work, the farmer would call from the back door of the house and offer him a cut of pork, or slices of ham which his wife had boiled, or a piece of bacon, or, at harvest time, a rabbit. At Christmas he gave him a hen. But these gifts, spread over the year, were few and far between, and were accompanied, in their giving, by such an air of complicity that frequently Morley, had he had the choice,would have preferred to have gone without: he took them because he thought they were his due, and because, however obscurely, Spencer derived some pleasure, despite the sub-terfuge, from letting him have them; the gifts were invariably en-dorsed by his wife, who, slim-featured, would be glimpsed, smiling, in the kitchen behind.

Alternatively, and more often, Morley helped himself: on his way home he would stop by a field and lift a root of potatoes, a turnip or a swede, some Brussels sprouts, spring greens or a cabbage; he had little compunction in taking what, in one sense, he believed belonged to him and, because of the regularity of this habit, he acquired a degree of skill which gave him a certain amount of satis-faction, not merely at getting away with it but from the modesty of his claims upon the farmer from whom, quite easily, he might have taken a great deal more. Unlike the mill-hands who came out from the town at weekends, stepping over the hedge to help themselves, Morley always went some way into the crop, digging up a root where it wouldn't be noticed, removing a cabbage where the crop was thickest, taking out the swedes and turnips only where the uniformity of the rows had already been depleted. Similarly, he went into the orchard in the autumn and took up the apples and the pears which had already fallen and, later still, picked up nuts from the walnut tree; if, in his lunch-hour, he found the hens which thronged the yard had been laying in the barn, he took the eggs, too, always careful to take in to the back door of the farm more than he took himself; additionally, he had had the habit of leaving a little can in the sheds for the herdsman to fill with milk each afternoon, but this, on discovery, Spencer refused to allow the herdsman to do. 'Nay, tha s'll have to sup it, Arthur. I'll be skint if he gi'es it to the lads like this.'

'Has he given you these?' Sarah would ask whenever Morley turned out his bag and lifted a cabbage or half a dozen eggs or a turnip on to the table.

'How should I have them if he hasn't?' he would ask, the dis-ingenuousness of his reply reinforced by the occasional legitimate gift when there could be no doubt that the bacon had been cured, the ham cooked, the pork roasted or the rabbit shot: as for the Christmas hen, it had become a tradition and one Christmas, even, he was given two. 'What about the potatoes?' she asked on one occasion when, only the day before, he had reported Spencer's rage at the depredation of the crop by weekend visitors from the town.

'I lifted them on the way home,' Morley said.

'Did he say you could?'

'He didn't say I couldn't.'

'You've stolen them.'

'I sowed them. I've cared for them. I'll lift them next week, an' all,' he added.

'If there's any left.'

'Don't worry: he makes a fair whack. It's nought, what he pays, to the amount of work I put in.'

'It's his money.'

'And my work.'

There was no getting round the argument: without the occasional 'gift' they couldn't have managed; for large parts of the year there were no crops to lift, the 'gifts' being mainly confined to the autumn.

In any case, having made her protest, Sarah left it to him: it was his 'province', just as the house and looking after it were hers; neither, fundamentally, would have questioned the other. There were even days when, at Morley's instigation, in the early summer, they would walk out to the farm, the child pushed before them in the pram; he would show her the fields and the prospect of the farm as if, in many respects, they were his own creation, the burgeoning crops, the neatly laid hedges, the fat cattle: it was 'his' world, one where his power was undisputed. She liked to be re-assured she had no part of it: the neatness of the fields, the threading of the hedges, the sleekness of the cattle confirmed the domination of will over matter: 'nature' was as directed and as closely super-vised, as scrupulously defined, as was, for instance, the 'nature' of their marriage; nothing was more assertive than Spencer's grip on the land, just as nothing was more assertive in their marriage than her own determination that their life together should be shaped in the manner she desired; she bowed to her husband's will just as, in the house, he bowed to hers.

'Oh, don't go on about Spencer this and Spencer that,' she would say. 'If you want to say these things tell him yourself. Don't come home and complain to me.'

Without acknowledging as much, she approved of his stealing and, without saying as much, she washed her hands of it.

Morley, pedalling home with his 'swag', would frequently be driven to justifying his action, and had vividly imagined an en-counter when, in the midst of lifting a hand of potatoes, or the heart of a cabbage, Spencer himself would appear and ask him what he was doing. 'The fact is,' Morley reasoned, 'he doesn't pay me enough for what I do. He knows he doesn't pay me enough but doesn't want to admit it in case it opens a door which neither he nor anyone else could close. He lets me take the odd root because he knows, if I took some every day, which I never would, it still wouldn't make up the difference between what I do and what he owes me. Therefore,' he concluded, 'it pays Spencer to allow me to steal, and dishonesty on my part is only equalled by his own in never mentioning it.'

The solution to this problem he had never worked out; if, for example, the land were nationalized and he worked for no one in particular and for everyone in general he had a good idea he would take little if any pride in his work and, whereas he might be paid more, the 'pay' would become, as a consequence, the be-all and the end-all of his existence, and his pride in showing Sarah a field of growing corn, or a pasture of well-fed cows, would disappear with his incapacity to relate it to anyone in particular; the fact was, Spencer 'personified' the farm in a way which he respected: he admired Spencer's pugnacity, he admired his skill. His resentment only arose when Spencer's will was imposed upon his own: but without that conflict there was nothing.

He admired the farmer's independence, an independence that went down to the very roots of life, and contented himself with the thought that, at some point in the future, his son, or his sons, might be able to resolve his problem for him.

Their second child was born at the beginning of the new year. Alan was four years old and while Sarah was away at the hospital he was looked after by Mrs Foster. Morley would go in in the evenings to see how he was and found him peculiarly contented, playing with Alison, running through her toys, and provided with meals which were, on the whole, if not more varied, more plentiful than the ones he was used to: the regime of 'measuring' did not prevail in the Foster house and Mrs Foster was as subject to whims and fancies as were her husband and daughter. When it came time to take Alan back the boy expressed a desire, mortifying to Sarah, that he might be allowed to stay at the Fosters' longer and it was only by the persuasion of a new toy that he could be prevailed upon to allow Morley to carry him back and set him in his cot which, dismantled, had been re-erected in the tiny back bedroom. In a pram, in the front bedroom, crying, was placed the baby.

The Morleys called their second child Bryan. Small, black-haired, he struggled fitfully with illnesses the first few weeks, his grave-eyed look a curious echo of the gravity which characterized the relationship between Morley and his wife. He seldom cried and, despite his illness, lay on his mattress or in his pram gazing up with a peculiar look, if not of quietude, then of resignation. The child absorbed Mrs Morley completely; it was as if she examined it for a solution to their 'problem': it was the latest arrival from the blacknesses

54

which encompassed them on every side and, in its dark-eyed look (it had Mrs Morley's eyes and not her husband's), she gazed intently for a sign, an indication that, at least so far, they were doing 'right'. Morley, equally absorbed, would watch her with the child, envious of its complicity; he took to drinking once again: he called at the Mitre, an almost derelict pub which stood by the railway bridge he passed under on his way home from work. He took great care to measure the amount he drank. He knew no one at the Mitre, and the bar invariably, when he visited it, was deserted. The drink was a prize, a token awarded him for having got through each day.

And yet, one Saturday afternoon, having emptied his pockets in a manner familiar to him from his earlier days, he had found himself unable to mount his bike and had pushed it up the slope, past the Spinney Moor itself and, reminded by that building if by nothing else, he had asked himself, 'What am I doing now? Am I going back to what I was before?', arriving home and going upstairs and, after washing in the bathroom, going to the bedroom where, within no time, he was fast asleep.

He woke to find the room in darkness and, feeling in the bed beside him, found it empty. Getting up he went into the front bedroom and, switching on the light, saw the baby sleeping in its cot; he went downstairs. The living-room and the scullery were both in darkness: the front door was bolted; the fire still glowed in the living-room grate.

He returned upstairs: in the tiny back bedroom Sarah was sleeping in the single bed, Alan asleep beside her.

'Is anything up?' He gazed in at her, her figure lit by the light from the landing.

Stirring, she gazed up from the bed.

'I was sleeping in here tonight,' she said.

'What for?'

'I preferred it.'

'Isn't your own bed good enough?'

'It seems it isn't.'

'Isn't a man to be allowed any relaxation?' he asked.

'Is breaking a promise relaxation?'

'Promise. Promise.' He chanted the words. 'Haven't I stood by you? Have we ever done without?'

He went downstairs; he made some tea: he knew, having transgressed, she wouldn't forgive him, and he knew, in any argument, he could never win. He knew, too, her will was stronger than his: hers stuck to a point and never let go; his wandered aimlessly over everything; hers was ungenerous, his forgetful.

When he went back upstairs he paused, aware of her acutely behind the door.

'Sarah?'

No sound of any sort came from inside.

He went to their bedroom and closed the door.

He lay in the bed, the curtains still undrawn, and watched the pattern of the window outlined on the ceiling by the lamp in the road outside: a moment later, he got up off the bed and, creaking along the landing, opened the back-bedroom door.

'I'm sorry,' he said.

There was no answer from the bed.

'Do you hear? I'm sorry,' he said.

'Too late to be sorry,' came the quiet reply.

'What more do you want?'

'Actions speak louder than words.'

'Your actions could kill,' he said. 'I used to be happy until I met you.'

'You know what you can do in that case.'

'This is my house. I work for it,' he said. 'I work harder than any other man round here,' he added.

'As hard as some, but no harder than most. They don't come home drunk and sneak into bed.'

'What more do you want, Sarah? Do you want me on a lead and to live in a kennel?'

'You might as well,' she said. 'The way you behave.'

'Aye,' he said. 'You speak like that because you're a woman and come out with jibes and sit and primp yourself because you're always right. If it wasn't for me you'd still be by that river.'

'If it wasn't for you I wouldn't be tied here like a slave,' came the voice from the bed.

'Ah, you've more here than you ever had,' he told her.

'Oh, yes,' she said. 'And no redress when you come home drunk.'

'I'm a grown man,' he said. 'If you don't like the way I live

56

you'll have to lump it. I've told you I'm sorry. I am. If you come back to the bed we can both forget and go on as we were afore,' he added.

The boy, roused by the argument, had begun to stir. 'I'm staying here,' she said.

He closed the door. 'At least I've that,' he thought. 'Though she's scarce bigger than a mouse, she must be damned uncomfortable lying with Alan. What a woman.'

Passing the other bedroom door he opened it, gazed in for a moment, then went in and lifted the baby from the cot.

He carried it with him to the double bed and, folding it around with pillows, laid it beside him.

He had scarcely lain down than the door opened and the light came on.

'Have you taken the baby with you?'

He had scarcely seen her so enraged.

She picked the baby up.

'Never ever do that.'

'What do you want?' he called. 'What are you trying to do to me?'

He followed her into the other room: she laid the baby in the cot, then, as it began to stir, she picked it up again and rocked it.

'Now you've woken it.'

'You woke it,' Morley said. 'You whore.'

He hurled the door to and could hear the floor creak as the Pattersons got up in the house next door.

He went back to bed, curled up, and endeavoured to sleep.

In the morning he got up, dressed, and went to work without any breakfast. He didn't come back until late; he expected the house to be empty, yet the light was on in the living-room: smoke curled up from the chimney.

He felt relieved; all day, the terror of the empty house had matched the rage he felt at his wife.

When he opened the door he could hear the boy singing in the living-room, his voice faltering, however, as he heard his step.

Yet, as he took off his boots, the living-room door opened and the boy came out.

Morley held out his arms: the boy sprang up.

'How have you been, young 'un?'

'All right.'

'Tea ready for me?'

'We've eaten it.'

'Nought for me, then, I take it?'

The boy laughed; Morley swung him round.

'Do you want some, Dad?'

'I wouldn't mind.'

Beyond, in the lighted room, he could see his wife with the baby.

'Ought going?' he asked, casually, calling through.

She didn't answer and, as he stepped into the room in his stocking feet, the boy still in his arms, he said, 'Ought going?' again and she added, 'Your supper's in the the oven.'

'There, then,' he said to the boy. 'Some supper at last,' setting him on a chair beside him. He didn't glance at his wife, calling to the baby, kneading it as he passed it on his way to the table.

It was as if, on his return, nothing of the previous night had happened; later, Sarah came up to bed and he lay beside her, his hand, finally, creeping out, only to encounter the rigidity of her arm which, after clenching for a moment, he released.

'She's taken me again,' he thought. 'I'm as fastened up as ever.'

A quiet tyranny began: under it Sarah suffered intensely. She hated Morley, yet she bore his children; the whole house and everything in it was synonymous with his presence. She would gaze out from the front-bedroom window at the distant prospect of the town as someone might gaze out from the walls of a castle, knowing, as a refuge, it was a place they could never leave: from the back-bedroom window, she would see the hills beyond the valley, the wooded slopes and the undulating contours of the moorland, and think, 'At least, Bryan will escape,' for, in a curious way, she already saw the eldest boy, in his moods and energy, as belonging to his father.

Her power over Morley she maintained by refusing him her love. 'If I had lived in another street,' she thought, 'I would never have met him: there is something absurd in the fact that the whole of my existence is dictated to by someone I only met by chance.' It reduced everything to the level of that compulsion which, when she was hungry, told her she ought to eat, when she was thirsty she ought to drink, and when she was tired she needed to sleep; and yet everything in life proclaimed 'love' as something different. She looked at her youngest child and in its eyes recognized the same perplexity gazing out at her: 'Where am I? Who am I? What have I done?'

Now, at odd moments, when she looked at Morley, it was like gazing at a stranger; the things that seemed of greatest account in their lives – their marriage, the intimacy which bore them children – were the most superficial elements in their existence: Morley, the intangible spirit of Morley, the man who sat there, had as little to do with her as the man next door.

When, at other instances, she saw him talking at the door – to Foster, or to Mrs Foster, or to the Pattersons, or even to the neighbours in the gardens beyond – she would decide, 'Yes, he is different, he is separate, he is integral to himself, and has no part of me at all. Yet how he enjoys his separateness: he laughs and shouts.' And her rancour would rise at his independence just as, when she was younger, before they married, she had marvelled at it, felt frightened by it, and had thought it a challenge she ought to meet.

FIVE

'How can he get to every house?' Bryan asked.

His brother lay back in bed, his dark head circled by the sheet and blankets; in the faint light that penetrated the green-coloured curtains Bryan could see the darkness around his brother's eyes and the strange, bulbous protrusion of his nose. A frost had formed on the inside of the window: his father's coat had been laid on Alan's bed, and his mother's had been laid across his own.

'There isn't time.'

His brother's mouth was hidden and Bryan could only tell that Alan's eyes were open when, intermittently, they glistened within the shadow of the cowl comprised of the sheet and the blankets.

'He travels faster than light.'

Bryan glanced at the window; earlier, getting into bed, he had gazed up through the fern-like pattern of the frost at the expanse of sky above the town. It was lit by stars and crossed here and there by moonlit clouds: up there, when he was asleep, the figure would be passing, its task to visit every home on Stainforth in which a child was living. Not only did this figure ride a sledge drawn by reindeer but, in its bright-red costume, tinged with white, it was capable of descending the narrow chimney and emerging in the fireplace without getting its costume dirty, or its beard, or the white bobble on its hat, and carrying at the same time a bag full of the toys it intended leaving not only at their house but at the Fosters', the O'Donalds', the Shawcrofts' and the Barracloughs'. In the fireplace, by the ashy grate, still glowing when he came to bed, his mother had set a plate containing a portion of Christmas cake and a piece of cheese and, beside it, his father had set a glass of milk. 'If that hasn't gone by the morning,' he'd said, 'I shouldn't be surprised. He'll be feeling hungry by the time he gets to us.'

Several weeks before, supervised by his mother, he had written a letter and, like the plate of cake and the glass of milk, left it in the hearth to be collected: that, presumably, had now been read, his record checked and, somewhere up there, this benevolent spirit, this power which defied the forces of gravitation, would be travelling towards him, conscious of his name, of his address and even, specifically, of what he wanted: a train, a book and, if there was space to carry it, a tool set.

He listened to the house; his parents had gone to bed and the ashes had been raked so as not to impede their visitor's progress. He listened for the tinkle of the plate. Up there, this bountiful presence, who was conscious of who he was and of how well, throughout the year, he had behaved, was journeying towards him.

It was the scale of its task that most impressed him: beyond Spinney Moor Road lay Spinney Moor Avenue and beyond that lay an infinite number of roads; and beyond those were the houses of the town and, beyond the town, the houses of England.

From beyond the window came the sound of singing.

'O come, let us adore Him,
O come, let us adore Him,
Chri-ist the Lord.'

'What is it?'

'The church choir.'

The murmur, solemn, preceded by a pause, came from Alan's bed.

A moment later, sure enough, he could here the rat-tat as the collectors moved along the road.

His parents' bed creaked; his father got up and went down to the hall: he must have put on a coat and waited for, when the knocker rapped, his father opened the door and called, 'A Happy Christmas.' He heard the chink of money.

'Do you think he's come?'

Not yet.'

'When will he?'

'Go to sleep. He won't come until you do.'

He heard his father return to bed, the murmur of his voice.

His eyes closed.

'O come, let us adore Him,
O come, let us adore Him,
O come, let us adore Him,
                    Chri-ist the Lord.'

Lulled by the singing, he fell asleep.

In the corner of the room, on a plant-stand, stood the tiny Christmas tree with its silver-coloured bird and the stout, red-coated figure, white-lined, with its bobble-cap. The room was warm; from the oven came the smell of the chicken as it began to roast.

Bryan had watched the bird being plucked when his father first brought it home from Spencer's: some of the feathers still lay about the garden and others had blown over into Foster's, into Patterson's, and into the field. His preoccupation with the bird had distracted him from his more immediate preoccupation with his presents; he had gazed at its head and its lifeless eye and had thought that the bird were still alive. He had watched the exposure of its flesh with a feeling of horror, and had gazed at Alan, as he took over from his father, with a feeling of revulsion: that his brother could compound the suffering to which his father appeared to be aloof raised the speculation that his brother took a delight in causing pain.

He had wanted nothing to do with the bird: the disarray of its feathers, their blowing about the yard, the indignity of the creature's pimpled flesh, its helpless head with its tiny eye and its opened beak, appalled him more than ever.

As he played with his metal train by the fire, wound and rewound it, and set it going on its metal rails, and felt Alan's displeasure that he hadn't got anything as extravagant himself, his anguish at the bird subsided beneath the excitement and then the anti-climax of having a present. Even now, behind his back, and even as the thought arose, his mother opened the oven door and spooned fat across the bird. That morning he had examined the empty plate and the empty glass, and had even gazed at the crumbs on the plate and thought, 'Those crumbs have been touched by his hand. And those are the remains of the milk that he drank,' and having opened his pillow-case and examined his presents, he

62

had looked from them to the plate, from the plate to the glass, and back to the presents, at the hole in the fireplace, now lit by flames, through which this figure had passed, at the room itself which this figure, however briefly, had occupied, and thought, 'I must be good, otherwise he wouldn't have come,' and yet, with the chicken in the oven, he thought, 'Does he know about the bird?'

His brother's head was down: he was playing with a line of soldiers formed up before a wooden fort: the fort was roughly painted and to a nail driven into each of the turrets was attached a paper flag. His brother's hand was inside the portcullis, pulling up and down a brass-coloured chain.

The room smelled of cooking, and of the metallic, entrancing odour of the clockwork train and its two brown-painted coaches: he had wanted the train, he had wanted the shilling – wrapped up in silver paper – and had wanted the apple, wrapped up in its blue-coloured tissue, and the bag of sweets, two of which he'd already eaten: yet something was missing – it was as his mother opened the oven door and, her eyes narrowed against the heat, spooned on the fat, that he realized that what was missing was the bird.

He glanced at the window: children were playing in the field with a brand new ball; its bright leather shape flew up in the air.

'Everything all right?' His father came into the room to set a pan of water against the flames.

'Yes,' he said.

'That chicken smells grand.'

His father rubbed his hands; he knelt by the hearth and, when the engine had stopped, wound up the motor and set it on the rails. The carriages rattled round.

On the carpet were the wrappings from the sweets which his brother had eaten, and the silver paper which had wrapped his brother's shilling. Also there was the pillow-case with its piece of paper on which the one word 'Alan' had been written.

'Have they captured it yet?' His father lined the soldiers up inside the castle: tiny, square-shaped doors and windows gave access to the hollow box which supported the turrets. A cannon, a gift from an earlier Christmas, had been set at the castle entrance. 'If you put some soldiers in Bryan's carriage you can bring reinforcements.' An ash fell in the fire and his father, leaning over, placed a fresh piece of coal behind the pan. 'When it boils,' he added, 'give a shout.'

He went back to the scullery; they could hear his whistling, then singing, and the soft hiss of the steamer as the pudding cooked.

'Let's have a go.'

Alan wound the engine, set it on the rails, and watched the brightly-painted engine run round and round.

'You want to get some points, then you can have another track.'

His brother's hands were large and red; in playing with the soldiers he frequently knocked the figures down. His legs were bare, his feet tucked into his slippers, the soles of which had been worn through and the backs of which were flattened; his heels, too, were red, his ankles white, the muscle bulging across his calves, his knees scarred, the legs of his trousers drawn tight across his thighs: he put out his finger: the train, running into it, fell off the track. The metal chimney came off and the clockwork-driven wheels spun round and round.

'Dad.'

'Don't tell him.'

'Dad.'

'It was an accident.'

'Now, what is it?' came his mother's voice. She appeared in the door.

'He's broken it.'

'I was getting up,' Alan said, the engine in his hand.

'You shouldn't have touched it,' his mother said.

'He let me have a go.'

'Have you broken it?'

'The chimney's come off.' Two metal flaps, slotted into holes, secured it.

His father appeared: his hands wet, he re-attached the chimney. 'It's brand new,' he said. 'You shouldn't have touched it. It's his present. You've toys of your own to play with.'

He took the engine into the scullery; his tool-box rattled: a few moments later he came back in.

'It's only a twopence-halfpenny thing. Just look how poor

64

they've made it.' Having re-attached the chimney he wound the engine, set it on the rails and let it go.

'He's spoilt it.'

'You shouldn't have let him have it,' his father said. 'How would you like it,' he added to Alan, 'if he broke your castle?'

Alan returned to his fort; he knelt across it, standing up the metal figures: his heavy fingers toyed with the drawbridge. 'He can have it if he wants.'

'What good will that do?' his father said.

'He can have it.'

His brother overturned the fort.

He ran upstairs.

'You shouldn't have upset him,' his mother said.

'What have I said?' his father said. 'He only broke Bryan's train on purpose.'

'How do you know he did it on purpose?'

'Why else would he do it?'

His father returned to the kitchen.

'Is it broken?' his mother said.

'It'll be all right.'

'Won't it clip on tighter?' The chimney, loose, had rattled off.

'No,' he said.

'You shouldn't have let him have a go with it. And look at his fort,' she added.

She picked the soldiers up and attempted to re-erect the turrets, each of which, secured to the base by a wooden peg, had fallen off.

'I'll do it,' Bryan said.

'I should leave it,' his mother said and, a few moments later, after she'd returned to the kitchen, she went to the stairs, called, and finally went up.

Bryan could hear his brother crying.

Why, if the engine was a twopenny-ha'penny thing, had he been given it? He watched the engine running round and round, the wheels clicking regularly over the joints in the rails, the speed of the engine declining as the spring wound down.

He glanced at the red-coloured cardboard box from which the engine and the rails had been taken: he retraced the sensation of opening it, and, before that, of seeing the box itself, with the painting of the engine in the centre of the lid, and relived, vividly, to the sounds of his brother's voice complaining, wailingly, above his head, the moment when he had drawn it from the pillow-case.

He lifted the lid.

The pan behind him began to boil.

He called to his father, who, a few moments later, came in and, cutting up peeled potatoes, dropped them into the water.

'You shouldn't have let him touch it.'

'He asked to.'

'He has all his presents and it's worse than a day when he hasn't any.'

He placed a lid on the pan and set it against the flames.

He opened the oven door, closed it, and went back to the scullery.

A moment later he reappeared with a pan full of sprouts; he lifted the pan of potatoes from the fire, poured water on top of the sprouts, then set both pans against the fire.

'If you see them boiling give a shout.'

Bryan examined the declivities inside the cardboard box.

The children in the field had gone; he gazed across the bare earth of the garden at the railings and, beyond the railings, at the lank grass of the field and the windows of the houses opposite.

He got up from beside the railway and ate another sweet.

'He doesn't have to come down the chimney because Dad brings it,' Alan said, his head framed by the familiar cowl.

'Where from?'

'He makes them. Like the fort. He made that at work.'

'What about the soldiers?'

'He buys them. Like your train set.'

'What about the cake?'

'He eats it.'

Bryan lay back against his pillow, the blanket pulled tight beneath his chin.

'What about the letter?'

'They tear it up.'

As his brother spoke his breath rose in a cloud from the dark-

66

ness of the cowl, his bulbous nose visible beneath the edge of the blanket.

'Isn't there somebody who comes?' Bryan said.

'How can there be?'

'Why not?'

'Do you think he lives in Greenland?'

'You wrote a letter as well,' he said.

'They asked me to.'

'Why?'

'So's not to spoil it.'

He could see where his brother's hands were fisted beneath the blanket, drawing it up beneath his chin.

'It doesn't make any difference,' Alan added.

'Why not?'

'You still got what you asked for.'

'I still believe in it,' Bryan said.

His brother laughed; a fresh cloud of vapour sprang from the cowl.

'They wouldn't go to all that trouble if there wasn't something.'

'Why not?'

'There must be something.'

His brother laughed.

'You ask them.'

'They'll say you told me.'

'Tell them somebody told you at school.'

'I still believe in it.'

'You would.'

'Why shouldn't I?' Bryan said. 'They wouldn't go to all that trouble if there wasn't something.'

His brother's eyes had closed; only the bulbous nose remained on guard.

Bryan gazed at the curtains.

'Yes, I believe in you,' he said aloud.

SIX

They pedalled past the Spinney Moor Hotel, turned off the Town Road, passed under the railway bridge, and out across the canal and over the river. The fields were bare, the sky dark: Bryan pedalled in his father's wake, watching the tails of his father's coat as they flew backwards beside his wheel, and the bowed momentum of his father's back.

'Not tired?' His father, freewheeling, had turned his head.

'No,' he shouted back.

'We'll go see Spencer. We'll give him a surprise. He'll think his cows have died if he sees me knocking.'

The road rose over a hump-backed bridge; his father paused at a gate, flanked by a stone-built barn and a brick-built shed.

Releasing the catch on the gate, he opened it, waiting for Bryan to pedal inside.

'Better push it,' he said. 'Too muddy to ride.'

Barns and sheds and a house enclosed a rutted yard: directly opposite was a gate, closed, leading to a pasture. To Bryan's right the yard ran back to a low stone wall and beyond the wall, to a green-painted door flanked by square-paned windows.

Against the low stone wall his father propped his bike; Bryan laid his own beside it.

A paved yard fronted the door of the house, his father stepping across it and knocking and rousing, as a consequence, the barking of dogs inside.

A curtain moved in one of the windows; a latch was lifted and the door drawn back.

A tall, red-cheeked man gazed out; on his feet were a pair of slippers. His sleeves were rolled, his forearms thickly muscled. He glanced at Bryan. ''Ow go, Arthur?' The man scratched his fair hair and added, 'Anything up?'

68

'We thought we'd ride over, Mr Spencer,' his father said. He nodded back at Bryan, and then at the bicycles, visible over the top of the low stone wall.

The farmer shouted to the dogs behind. One animal rushed out, ran round Bryan's legs, then dashed off, barking, across the yard. The sound of hens squawking came from a barn. 'Look at this, Mary,' the farmer called. In the room behind, the light from the open door and the windows revealed a stone-paved floor in the centre of which stood a thick-legged table upon which at the moment stood several pots and pans.

A smell of baking came out to the yard.

A slender, thin-featured woman appeared in the kitchen door: her eyes were grey and her hair swept back: its fairness glittered in the light from a fire.

'If you don't hurry, love, he'll go away,' the farmer added, turning, as he heard her foot on the kitchen floor and calling, 'It's Arthur's young 'un. Though there's no more than threepenn'orth of him here at present.'

The woman smiled.

'This is Bryan, Mrs Spencer,' his father said.

'Are you feeling tired?' she asked him.

'No,' Bryan said.

'The Morleys don't feel tired,' the farmer said. 'Show 'em a spot o' work and you don't see it again until it's finished.'

'Would you like a cup of tea, love?' Mrs Spencer said. 'He looks half-frozen,' she added to his father.

'He won't say no to food, Mrs Spencer,' his father said.

'We can shove him i' Top End,' the farmer said. 'We've a few turnips up yonder could do wi' weeding.'

Bryan followed his father inside the kitchen: two dogs whirled round in front of a fire which occupied the centre of a massive range: its black-leaded ovens and alcoves reached to the ceiling; copper pans and basins hung from hooks and on a side-table stood several pieces of uncooked meat.

'By go, look at these muscles,' the farmer added, grasping Bryan's arm. 'There's nought much here but skin and gristle.'

'He's cycled all the way,' his father said, removing his cap.

'All the way, has he?'

'Every step, Mr Spencer.'

The farmer's thick fingers remained on Bryan's arm.

'The wind must 'a' shoved him.'

'It's been against us.' His father glanced at Mrs Spencer, who had placed a kettle against the fire.

'It must have whistled round him and not noticed he wa' theer. We could do wi' one or two like that round here.'

'Sit down, Arthur,' Mrs Spencer said, indicating a chair at the table. She held one out for Bryan. 'Don't be frightened of Mr Spencer,' she added. 'If he doesn't shout, he won't think you can hear him.'

'If I can't talk normal in my own house, I don't know where I can.' The farmer took a seat at the table himself, sitting sideways to it and, laying one clenched red fist on his knee, gazed at Bryan. 'What dos't think to your bike?' he added.

'I like it,' Bryan said.

'Do you?' the farmer said. 'Nought stronger than that?'

'He cleans it every day,' his father said.

'Does he? I can let him loose on the tractor. It hasn't seen a cleaning rag sin' the day I bought it. Not to mention,' he added, 'one or two carts.'

Mrs Spencer laughed; from a cupboard she took out a teapot and several cups. The dogs, after whirling round by the fire, lay down on a rug before it.

'We've had that bike here since Christmas.' The farmer got up from the table and crossed to the window, glancing out then returning to the table where he sat down once again, the chair creaking, his broad, thickly-muscled arm laid out before him. 'It wa' nought but bits and pieces when your faither brought it. I ne'er thought we'd see it together again. He's gi'en us a surprise, I can tell you that.'

A dog began barking outside the door.

'As daft as a brush,' the farmer added. 'Barks to go out, then barks to come back in again.'

He got up once more, opened the door and the dog rushed in: it circled the room, examined his father's boots, glanced at Bryan's, then crossed to the fire where it lay down with the others.

The kettle steamed; Mrs Spencer filled the pot.

'Would you like a piece of cake with your tea?' she asked.

'Like hhis father,' the farmer said. 'Ne'er say no to nought.'

His father laughed; Mrs Spencer crossed to the inner door of the kitchen. A polished wood floor was visible beyond.

'Margaret?' she called, her head to one side. 'Would you like some tea? We're having some.'

She came back to the cupboard. A cake was produced.

'All home-grown fruit in theer,' the farmer said, adding to his father as Mrs Spencer poured the tea, 'Want summat stronger i' that, then, Arthur?'

'No, thanks,' his father said.

'Still tee-total.'

'As much as can be.'

'They wa' telling me at t'Three Bells the takings are down this year.'

'Oh, there's nought worse than drink,' his father said, glancing at Mrs Spencer.

'There isn't,' Mrs Spencer said. 'I'm glad to hear it.'

The figure of a girl in a light-blue dress appeared in the kitchen door; for a moment she was silhouetted against the light from the room beyond, then she stepped inside, nodding her head at his father.

She had pale-blue eyes, like Mr Spencer, and the same light-coloured hair, her features, however, heavier than Mrs Spencer's, the cheeks broad, the mouth full-lipped, the jaw sharply projecting. Her hair, drawn back, was fastened in plaits, each secured at the end by a blue-checked ribbon.

'See here, Margaret,' the farmer said. 'We've a visitor fro' Stainforth. The owner of that blue bike we've heard so much about.'

The girl sat down at the table; she occupied the chair adjacent to Mr Spencer, who leaned across and laid his arm along the back of it.

'Hello, Mr Morley,' she said.

'Hello, Margaret,' his father said, half getting up from his chair. 'This is Bryan.' To Bryan he added, 'She watched me make your bike.'

The girl glanced across. 'You've cycled here, have you?' She reached for a piece of cake.

'Serve it to Mr Morley first,' the mother said.

The girl held out the plate; his father took a slice. She held it out to Bryan. He took one also.

'Not fancy a sandwich?' the farmer asked Bryan.

'Nay, he'll be having his tea when we get back home,' his father said.

'Take a bit of ham back with you.' The farmer got up from the table. 'I'll cut you off a slice.'

Mr Spencer returned to the table, handing several pieces of ham to his father wrapped in a greaseproof paper.

'Ought else we've got while they're here?' he added to his wife.

'He can take a few eggs.'

'Oh, this'll be champion,' his father said, nevertheless receiving a paper bag containing several eggs a moment later.

'Margaret's been cutting out,' Mr Spencer said when they were, once more, seated at the table.

'Cutting out what?' his father asked.

'Horses and film stars,' the farmer said. 'Though I can't tell one from the other, as a matter of fact.'

'She's interested in film stars, is she?' His father, until now, had sat formally at the table, his cap before him, his clenched hand resting on the table top. Now he leaned back, opening his jacket, for the room, with the heat from the fire, was hot. He glanced at the girl.

'Them and 'osses,' the farmer said. 'The front of one looks like the back of the other, and I won't say which road round,' he added.

The girl's eyes flashed towards his father who, laughing, leant back, his chair creaking. He had already begun to eat his piece of cake and the crumbs flew out from his mouth.

The farmer banged the table, laughing, and the cups and saucers rattled.

'You've got no romance, that's your trouble,' Mrs Spencer said.

'I've no time for romance,' the farmer said. 'Nor has Arthur.'

'You had when you were young, no doubt,' Mrs Spencer said, glancing at her daughter.

'I'm damned if I had time for ought but seeding and planting and mowing and hoeing and ploughing and reaping, and milking and kicking, maybe, one or two backsides.' The farmer glanced at Bryan and winked. 'You don't cut ought out, then, do you?'

72

'No,' Bryan said.

'Got more common sense.'

'Aye, he's a bike cleaner, at present,' his father said.

'Gave her one or two ideas when she saw your father putting your bike together,' the farmer said to Bryan. 'Got her own out and painted it and made it a damn sight worse than it wa're already.'

'Take no notice. He's always exaggerating,' Mrs Spencer said. 'Do you want another piece of cake?' she added to Bryan.

'Wrap it up,' the farmer said. 'He'll need that when he gets back home. Four miles on that bike is like ten on any other.'

A piece of cake was wrapped up and placed in a paper bag.

'Ought else have we got?' the farmer asked.

'He can take a bird.'

'Oh, this'll be ample,' his father said, getting up from his chair. 'We ought to be going,' he added.

'She cuts them out,' the farmer said, 'and sticks them in a book. She'll show you one if you ask her,' he added to Bryan. 'Do you want to show him one?' he asked the girl.

'No, thank you,' she said.

'If she offers you a smile,' the farmer said, 'I mu'n drop down deard.'

'She's not as bad as that,' Mrs Spencer said.

'She's a grand girl,' his father said.

'Should see her with her dander up,' the farmer added.

'Can I go now, Mother?' Margaret asked.

'Show Bryan round the fields. He hasn't been here before,' the farmer said.

'No, thank you,' she said.

'Won't you show us some of these 'osses you've been cutting out?'

'No, I shan't.'

'I shan't ask to see the film stars,' the farmer went on. 'I reckon Major looks a damn sight better. At least his hair's in better condition, and his teeth, too, I shouldn't wonder.'

'Good-bye, Mr Morley.' The girl put out her hand.

'Good-bye, Margaret,' his father said and shook it.

' 'Osses and film stars,' the farmer said. 'Gi'e me half an hour wi' each i' Top End and you'll not see either again for dust.'

73

'Have you said good-bye to Bryan?' Mrs Spencer asked.

'Good-bye,' the girl said.

'Good-bye,' Bryan said, getting up from the table.

The girl disappeared beyond the kitchen door; the sound of her feet came a moment later from a landing overhead.

'You shouldn't provoke her,' Mrs Spencer said to her husband.

'That's not provocation,' the farmer said. 'That's a statement of fact.' He handed the bag of eggs to Bryan. 'Carry these without breaking, can you?'

'I'd better take these,' his father said and took the bag himself. 'He can carry the meat,' he added, 'if he likes. And his bit of cake.'

'Say nought to nobody,' the farmer said, breathing into Bryan's face and pressing the cake inside his jacket. 'We don't want a queue out yonder.'

'Where's your other son, Arthur?' Mrs Spencer said as they went to the door.

'He wasn't up to coming,' his father said. 'His bike's brok', I think,' he added.

He stepped out to the yard, placing the eggs in the pannier behind his saddle.

'Come again, Bryan,' Mrs Spencer said, 'whenever you like,' stepping out to the yard and, as Bryan mounted his bike, running her hand across his hair. 'There aren't many children round here. There's hardly anyone for Margaret to play with.'

'Nay, Margaret's enough wi' her film stars and 'osses,' the farmer said, glancing up at a window where, as Bryan looked up, a curtain fluttered.

He cycled with difficulty across the yard. 'Mind he doesn't drown,' the farmer shouted as his father pushed his bike between the puddles, laughing and, as he reached the gate which Bryan had already opened, calling, 'I'll keep an eye on him, don't worry,' adding to Bryan, 'He doesn't mean half of what he says,' nevertheless waving his arm and calling, 'Thanks again,' as he closed the gate.

They cycled off in single file. Stooped, Bryan pedalled behind his father. 'Put a spurt on, if you like,' he called, waving him in front, so that Bryan was some distance ahead by the time they reached the house.

'Like a duck to water,' his father said when, after taking off his boots, he followed him inside. 'Once he gets up speed I never see him,' setting the eggs on the table, beside the meat and the bag containing the cake which were already there. 'They took to Bryan. I don't think they wanted him to leave. Asked Margaret to show him round.'

'Did she?' his mother said.

'Nay,' his father said. 'She wa' far too shy.'

'Of you?'

'Not me,' his father said, and laughed. 'Of Bryan.'

SEVEN

'Is that boy stopping you from working, Maureen?'

'Yes, Miss Featherstone,' Maureen said.

She was sitting in the desk beside him: she was short and stocky with coal-black eyes and coal-black hair – the hair cut symmetrically, like the crown of a flat-peaked cap; her cheeks and her lips were cherry red and her teeth were large and white.

'Come out here.'

Bryan got up.

'I would have thought,' Miss Featherstone said as he reached her desk and the two children standing there stepped quickly aside, 'you would have learned your lesson already.'

'I wasn't doing anything,' he said.

She glanced at Maureen. 'Was he stopping you from working?'

'Yes, Miss.'

'I have warned you before, and I shall not warn you again.' She raised her desk lid and brought out a wooden ruler. 'Hold out your hand.'

He held out his hand.

'Clench it.'

He closed his eyes; he simulated an expression of pain in the hope it might dissuade Miss Featherstone from carrying out her threat: it had never worked in the past and it didn't work now. He heard her grunt as, having stood up, she brought the ruler down.

The sharp edge rapped across his knuckles.

He winced. His fingers convulsed.

The pain, more sharply, ran into his wrist.

'Your other hand.'

He held up his other fist.

'Tighter.'

He heard the silence in the room behind and felt the rap across his knuckles.

'If I have occasion to call you out again I shall report you directly to Mr Swan.'

His hands beneath his armpits, he returned to his desk.

He glanced at Maureen then, bowed, drew his arms against his chest.

'I told you you should have looked,' Maureen said. She ducked her head, and added, 'Does it hurt?'

'Is Bryan talking to you again?' Miss Featherstone said.

'No, Miss Featherstone,' Maureen said.

Feet shuffled; a desk lid banged.

'Do you want to have a look?'

He shook his head.

Miss Featherstone's voice droned on; sensations other than pain returned to his hands.

Maureen had bowed her head to her desk; her tongue protruded between her teeth.

Bryan rubbed his hands: a broad weal ran across his knuckles. The circulation returned to his fingers and he picked up his pen.

'Look!' Maureen said.

Two short-fingered hands with their square-ended nails were holding aside the edge of her knickers.

'Are you interfering with Maureen, Bryan?'

Miss Featherstone stood up.

The blood pounded in his ears.

'Come out here.'

He got up from the desk.

'Would you mind telling me what you are doing?'

'Nothing.'

'Don't lie to me.' She glanced across the desks. 'Was he talking to you, Maureen?'

'No, Miss,' Maureen said.

'Are you sure?'

'Yes, Miss.'

'He wasn't speaking?'

'No, Miss.'

Maureen's red-cheeked face with its coal-black eyes was poised between the heads of the children in front.

'If I thought you were I would have taken you down the corridor in an instant.' Miss Featherstone raised her arm.

Her eyes followed him to the desk and remained fixed on him when, without looking up, he returned to his work.

'Let me look at yours.'

'No.'

'I let you look at mine.'

His head remained bowed, the point of the pen, soaked in ink, pinioned on the page before him.

'You looked at mine.'

'I didn't ask you.'

He heard a ruler slammed down on the teacher's desk.

'Is that boy talking?'

'No, Miss.' Maureen stood up.

Silence descended on the room again.

'You may sit down, Maureen.'

'Yes, Miss.'

Maureen sat down.

Bryan moved to the end of the bench.

A fist, clenched tightly, struck his wrist.

'I let you look at mine.'

He didn't answer.

'Do you want to look at it again?'

He gazed at his nib; he examined the blackness of the ink at the end.

'Bryan.'

The name, sharply delivered, distracted him.

He turned to see an empurpled mass exposed between the ends of Maureen's square-nailed fingers.

'Show me yours.'

A movement at the teacher's desk and in an instant Maureen's hands were on the desk: a pen was placed in her mouth.

Miss Featherstone had left her desk and was walking down the aisle.

She glanced over at the desks on either side then, opposite Bryan, she grasped his ear, twisted it, and said, 'Stand up.'

78

He let the pen fall.

'Has he got something under that desk?'

Maureen's black-capped head disappeared; a moment later it re-emerged.

'There's nothing there, Miss Featherstone,' she said.

'I shall have you stand at the front, young man.'

He was led from the desk to the corner of the room.

'Stand up.'

He stood with his back to the class, his ear stinging, gazing at the composition of the wall before him.

He heard Miss Featherstone return to her desk, the banging of Maureen's lid as she indicated her approval of Miss Featherstone's action, then the teacher's voice recommenced as two more children were summoned to have their work examined.

'Stand straighter. Hands behind your back. I don't want you leaning forward.'

He straightened his back; from the corner of his eye he could see the edge of the blackboard and, from the other corner, the glass pane in the upper half of the door which, partly obscured by paper, gave access to the corridor.

His legs ached; his knuckles burned.

Before him, vividly, was the image of what he had seen beneath the desk, a vertical incision distorted by the grip of Maureen's hands.

He shifted his feet.

'Keep still.'

A figure passed in the corridor outside; its feet echoed: a door closed, reopened, and the feet came back.

Outside the door of the classroom the footsteps paused; the handle was shaken, the glass vibrated: he had to step back to avoid the door and in doing so was brought face to face with Mr Swan: or, rather, he gazed at the button of the headmaster's jacket.

'Is this boy in trouble, Miss Featherstone?'

'He is, Mr Swan.'

A hand came down to indicate the corridor outside.

'Anyone else?'

'No, Mr Swan.'

The broad-shouldered figure remained with its back to the door.

79

After a pause, it turned and came out, closing the door behind it.

The glass rattled.

Without glancing at Bryan, Mr Swan strode off.

Bryan followed, watching the headmaster's gigantic hands with their thick, square-ended fingers clenching and unclenching, and observed the brief ducking down of the bulbous, close-cropped head as he passed each classroom: at one of the doors the headmaster paused, his features inflamed, waited, gazing in then, as the murmur of voices subsided inside, passed quickly on.

At the door to his study the headmaster paused. 'Stand by my desk.' He waited for Bryan to go in before him.

Bryan placed his hands behind his back.

The headmaster sat down; his fists were laid across his blotter.

'Bryan, is it?'

'Yes, sir.'

In a glassed-in cabinet to the side of the desk were several books and, fastened on hooks, horizontally, across the back of the cabinet, were several canes, the thinnest at the top, the thickest, bound with cord, at the bottom.

'Your brother was always in trouble.'

'Yes, sir.'

'Look where he is now.'

'Yes.'

Mr Swan stood up; his chair creaked: his shirt inside his jacket rustled.

'He's in the Seniors, when he might have gone to the Grammar.'

'Yes, sir.'

'Do you know why that happened?'

'No, sir.'

'He was fooling around. He failed his exam. He might have made something of himself. Now he'll make nothing.'

Tears came to Bryan's eyes; the thought of Alan oppressed him; and the thought of Alan, whom he loved, coming to nothing, oppressed him further: Mr Swan was disparaging someone closer to Bryan than he imagined.

'Do you want to make nothing of yourself?'

'No, sir.'

'You want to make something?'

'Yes, sir.' He added, 'My brother won't make nothing of himself.'

'What do you mean?'

Mr Swan's boots creaked; his shadow loomed across the room.

'He'll make something of himself.'

'In the Seniors he'll make nothing. He'll end up with a pick and shovel.'

The thought of Alan, with all his qualities, making nothing of himself was a thought that Bryan couldn't countenance.

'He'll make nothing, because he has made nothing. He even fools about where he is at present.' He gestured off to the opposite end of the building where, across an asphalt yard, stood the wing occupied by the Seniors. 'I've had reports of his fooling around already.'

He got up from the desk, inserted a key in the glass-panelled door of the cabinet and pulled it back.

'Why were you in the corner?'

'Someone was talking.'

'Was it you?'

'No, sir.'

'Do you always tell lies?'

'No, sir.'

'Miss Featherstone would not have called you out unless she was sure.'

He took out a cane, lifting it from the hooks.

'I don't like liars. Your brother was a liar.' He paused; the cabinet door swung to: the keys rattled against the glass. 'I don't like people who cry before their punishiment. Your brother never cried. He took his punishment like a man.'

Bryan examined the figure before him; all he saw, distorted, were disparate elements of the face itself, a glaring eye, a massive nose, a red-flecked cheek, a protruding lip.

'Hold out your hand.'

The tears, redoubled, obscured his view of the room.

'You're nothing but a whiner. You get up to mischief, cause trouble, say you never did it, then whine. Do you still say you were doing nothing in Miss Featherstone's class?'

'Yes, sir.'

'You're telling lies.'

'No, sir.'

'Half the battle is won with liars if they admit they are telling lies.'

'I'm not, sir.'

'Hold out your hand.'

He held it up.

'Higher.'

He felt the fingers of the headmaster flatten his palm.

The cane descended.

He gave a cry.

'I don't like cry-babies, either.'

He grasped Bryan's wrist.

'What's this?'

He looked at the back of his hand.

'Have you been caned by Miss Featherstone already?'

'Yes, sir.'

'And you have come to my room to be caned again?'

He looked at the back of his other hand.

'Was that a ruler?'

'Yes, sir.'

'I hope,' the headmaster said, 'you have learned your lesson.'

'Yes, sir.'

'What did Miss Featherstone call you out for?'

'She said I was talking.'

'Were you?'

'No.'

'If you weren't, why should she think you were?'

'I don't know.'

'That is the point at which you begin to tell lies.'

He laid the cane down.

'I can tell when a boy is lying. I haven't taught all these years without knowing when someone is not telling the truth.' He thrust his head towards him. 'Who sits in the desk beside you?'

'Maureen.'

'Does she do any talking?'

'No.'

He gazed at the button in the centre of the jacket.

82

Mr Swan reached down and grasped his wrist.

'Come with me.'

He opened the door and, still holding the wrist, led him back to the classroom.

Miss Featherstone, interrupted in mid-sentence, glanced up from her desk.

'Go back to your place.'

Bryan walked through the class to his seat.

'Maureen.'

The figure quivered on the bench beside him.

'Come to my room. Miss Featherstone, perhaps you would like to come with her.'

Instructions were given to the class, then Maureen, followed by Miss Featherstone, walked quickly to the door.

The clipping of their heels came from the corridor outside.

The door of the classroom had been left ajar.

'What did he do?' a figure asked from the desk in front.

'One on one hand.'

'Did it hurt?'

'Not much.'

'What about Maureen?'

He shook his head.

Some time later Maureen came back; she walked quickly to her desk.

'What did he say, Maureen?' someone asked.

'I haven't to talk to him,' she said.

'Did he hit you?'

She picked up her pen and bowed her head, and didn't look up when, a few minutes later, Miss Featherstone came in the room and closed the door.

'I'll be moving Bryan,' she said.

She indicated a desk adjacent to her own.

'If there is any more trouble, you know what the consequences are,' she added.

In the playground, Maureen said, 'Why won't you show me yours if I showed you mine?'

He felt the force of her fist at the back of his neck.

'Are you arguing again, Maureen?' the teacher on duty said.

83

'No, Miss.'

'Why don't you run along and play with the girls?'

'Yes, Miss.'

Maureen ran off; Bryan stood by the railings: he gazed off to where the fields began, sweeping down towards Spinney Beck.

In the adjoining playground his brother was running along in a crowd of boys; his life was simpler than his own, uncomplicated by anything that had gone before – a facing out of events, encountering each one for the very first time.

He glanced back at Maureen's figure, attracted by her raucous voice: she was gazing in his direction and shaking her fist.

'We wondered if you were coming,' Mrs Spencer said.

The dogs circled the interior behind her and, as Bryan entered, returned to the rug in front of the fire. The smell of baking came from the ovens and on the table, set on a wire mat, stood several loaves of bread. 'Not puffed?'

'No,' he said.

'It's a long way on your bike.' She ran her hand across his head.

'It's not too far,' he said.

'I think Margaret would find it far enough.' She called through to the wood-floored room beyond. 'Your friend has arrived.' To Bryan, she added, 'There are some slippers she's left out.'

He stooped in the door; a pair of woollen slippers had been left at the point where the stone paving of the kitchen gave way to the hall.

'We thought you were never coming.'

'I was late coming out of Sunday School,' he said.

Conscious of his darned stockings, he took his shoes off quickly.

'You hear that?' Mrs Spencer called into the hall and, from a door opposite, came the sound of Margaret's voice. 'She doesn't go, though we've often asked her.'

The door to the room opened and Margaret appeared; over a blue-checked dress she wore an apron.

Her hair was swept back and secured, as it had been before, in two ribboned plaits.

'I don't have to go,' she said.

84

'You don't have to go,' Mrs Spencer said. 'However, if you did, it would give you something to do on Sunday.'

'I have something to do on Sunday,' Margaret said.

'Not much.'

'All that I want to.'

'That's not what she tells me,' Mrs Spencer said, nodding at Bryan. 'You should hear her complaints.' To Margaret, she added, 'Will you be staying in, or going out?'

'Staying in.'

Margaret turned back inside the room; she held the door, formally, for Bryan to enter and as her mother called, 'Tea soon,' she closed it behind him.

'She's always having quarrels.' She indicated a table which occupied the centre of the room: a fire burned in a yellow-fronted grate. Chairs were set around the table; the firelight glowed from the polished wood.

Across the room, whose floor was relieved by a patterned carpet, two curtained windows looked out to the front of the house; flower beds had been dug and, between the beds, a lawn ran down to a low stone wall: beyond the wall a grassy slope descended to a stream which, below the house, had been dammed to form a pond: geese and ducks swam up and down and hens ran to and fro across the slope above it.

Beyond the stream the ground rose to a wood; cows grazed in a pasture.

The table had been covered by a cloth, one half turned down and covered, in turn, by a sheet of paper. A pair of scissors and a pot of glue were laid beside a grey-papered book.

'Do you want to cut out?'

'I don't mind,' he said.

He pulled out a chair.

From the kitchen, once more, came the barking of the dogs followed by the slamming of the outer door.

'She's always having arguments she can never finish.'

'Why?' he said.

'Because she's silly.'

He watched her tongue protrude as she applied the scissors to a magazine.

'Have you always gone to Sunday School?'

'No,' he said.

'I thought it dull.'

She glanced across.

'You can cut that out if you like,' she added. 'Do you go to the pictures much?'

'No,' he said.

'I go every Wednesday. Daddy comes up to town and meets me after school.'

The gruff voice of Mr Spencer could be heard a moment later coming from the kitchen, and shortly after that a door was opened.

'Have you seen *The Ghost Train?*'

'No,' Bryan said.

'*The Thirty-nine Steps?*'

Bryan shook his head.

'*The Love Match?*'

He shook his head again.

'What do you do at night?'

'Play out.'

'There's no one to play with round here.'

She leant back in the chair; its legs creaked: she turned her head to gaze out of the window, past the low stone wall with its wicket gate, to where the ducks quacked, the geese honked and the hens ran up and down. From the left of the grassy slope a pig appeared, its nose to the ground.

'What school do you go to?'

'Stainforth.'

'I go to one in town. St Margaret's. It's got my name.'

She pressed down the page.

Bryan handed over his cut-out shape.

'You haven't cut it very well.'

'It slipped.'

'That's the only one I have of Ronald Colman.'

'I can cut out the bit I missed and stick it together.'

'It won't look the same.'

She trimmed the edge of the shape herself.

'Do you like his moustache?'

'Yes,' he said.

86

She laid the photograph flat on her hand, stooped, and kissed the area of it which was characterized principally by the thin moustache. She closed her eyes.

'I think he's whoozy.'

'What are you two doing?'

Bryan looked up to find the figure of Mr Spencer standing in the door: the farmer was wearing a dark-blue suit, the jacket of which was open; on his feet were a pair of slippers.

'Not kissing these cart 'osses, is she?' he added to Bryan.

'I'm loving Ronald Colman, Father,' Margaret said.

'I'm glad he doesn't know about it,' Mr Spencer said, glancing once again at Bryan. 'Got you at it, has she?'

'Bryan hardly ever goes to the pictures,' Margaret said.

'He's got more common sense,' the farmer said. 'And has a better way to spend his money.'

'I don't ask to go,' she said.

'Not half,' the farmer said. ' "Aren't we going to the Regal, Daddy?" ' He mimicked his daughter's voice.

A flush of colour came to her cheeks and, after laying the photograph down, she began to cut round another figure.

'She'll have you as daft as she is,' the farmer said, coming into the room and gazing over Bryan's shoulder. 'How about the cowshed having a scrub?'

'We'll leave that to you,' the daughter said.

'Anything that involves a bit o' work.'

'Haven't you anything to do?' she asked.

'I'd better go and do it,' the farmer said and clasping Bryan's shoulder, added, 'Your bike still 'o'ding together, is it?'

'Yes,' he said.

'There's tea ready,' he said, 'in one or two minutes.'

He closed the door.

'Do you want to cut out Laurel and Hardy?' Margaret indicated their figures on a page torn from the magazine before her.

'Do you like them?' Bryan asked.

'Not as much as Ronald Colman.'

'Or Charlie Chaplin.'

'I don't like Charlie Chaplin,' Margaret said.

Bryan cut round the fat figure, had difficulty with the hat, then cut round the thin figure, removing the brim of its bowler and, he noticed, having released it from the paper, the toe of one of its shoes.

'You're not very good at it,' she said, taking it from him.

'What names are your dogs?' he said.

'Roger, Dodger and Sammy.' She leant forward on the table. 'My mother doesn't like them.'

'Why do you have so many?'

'You need them,' she said, 'on a farm like this.'

Bryan examined her more closely; she was glueing down a shape: her tongue protruded, her eyes expanded: she pressed the shape down with the edge of her hand.

'Do you believe in God?' she asked.

'Yes,' he said.

'What about the Devil?'

'Yes.' He nodded.

'Have they taught you that at Sunday School?'

'Yes.'

He gazed out of the window; he gazed beyond the rutting pig and the honking geese to the herd of cows across the stream: it was like gazing out from the walls of a castle.

'Is God in everything?'

'Yes.'

'How about the Devil?'

'He's in everything, too.'

The clamour of the geese penetrated to the room and a flutter of wings sent up a column of spray on the pond. The pig, which had been joined by several others, nosed against the wicket gate, then, having pushed against it for several seconds, its bright eyes gleaming, it turned away.

'There doesn't seem any point in it.'

'Why not?'

'What's the point, if they're both in everything, in doing anything? It's all decided.'

He examined the face beside him more intently: the snub-looking nose, the broad cheeks, the wide mouth, which was framed at either end by tiny dimples, the declivity of the chin, the smoothly drawn-back strands of hair which, framing the skull, ran back to the neatly threaded plaits: he gazed to the view beyond the window and, back from the view, once more, to the room.

'We've been give the freedom of choice,' he said.

'Why? Why does there have to be a choice?'

'I don't know,' he said.

'It's pointless,' she concluded.

'Don't you enjoy cutting out these pictures?'

'Sometimes.'

'What about now?'

'I have done. Until you came and spoilt it.'

He had never contemplated a world in which there wasn't a presence larger than his own; larger than everything he could see around him. At one time it had been the benevolent spirit which came at Christmas; from that had grown an awareness that nothing was what it seemed – fields led on to other fields, roads to other roads, towns to other towns, countries to other countries, but, finally, the world led on to heaven.

'Is anything the matter?'

'No,' he said.

'Why are you shaking?'

'I'm not,' he said.

'I'll put some wood on the fire.'

She got down from the chair; the wood crackled as the flames took hold.

'It doesn't give much heat, but it looks as though it should.'

'Why do you cut out all these pictures if they don't mean anything?' he asked.

'I like them.'

She tapped her hands on the table.

'Are you two ready?' came a voice from the kitchen.

The table, when they went through, had been laid with cups and saucers.

'How's he been with the scissors?' Mr Spencer stood with his back to the fire.

'He cuts off all the edges,' Margaret said. 'In addition to which, he shakes all over.'

'Is anything the matter, Bryan?' Mrs Spencer said.

'No,' he said.

89

He had, for no reason he could think of, begun to cry.

'He's frightened,' Margaret said. 'He's frightened of Daddy.'

'He's frightened of no such thing.' Mrs Spencer placed her arm across his shoulder.

'Then he must be a cry-baby,' Margaret said.

'Are you feeling unwell?' Mrs Spencer asked him.

'No,' Bryan said.

'Just look at his hands.'

His jaw, too, had begun to vibrate; he clutched his sides and tried to concentrate on the dogs by the fire, on the figure of Mr Spencer standing amongst them, on the flickering shadows, on the gleam of the firelight on the pots and pans.

'You'd better lie down,' Mrs Spencer said. She felt his brow. 'Let's put him in the front room,' she added. 'We'll lie you down for one or two minutes.'

They crossed the hall; a door, facing the room in which, earlier, he'd been with Margaret, was standing open: a couch was set before a fire.

He was covered by a rug.

A rose-patterned wallpaper covered the walls.

'Did you feel anything coming on as you cycled over?' Mrs Spencer asked.

'No,' he said.

'Has Margaret been saying something to upset you?'

'No.'

From the kitchen came the sound of Margaret's voice.

'Perhaps it was the rushing over.'

'Yes.'

Her hand stretched out to his brow.

'I'll get you a powder.'

He gazed, in the afternoon light, at an ochreish-looking print which was suspended on the wall before him: figures ran to and fro across a hill.

He looked to the fire which was shielded by a metal grill; he looked at the ceiling: around a central lampshade ran a plaster-of-Paris relief shaped in flowers. Roses, with cabbage-like petals, formed themselves, on the wallpaper, into vertical lines; soon he was deciphering the crevice of an eye, a brow, the curve of a cheek, a grimacing mouth.

He looked back to the fire.

Mrs Spencer came in.

She gave him a glass of liquid.

'Lie back and rest,' she said. 'It'll take effect in a minute.'

She resettled his head; apart from his mother he had never been touched by a woman before: he was aware of the pressure of her arm as she supported his back, and the strange delicacy of her fingers.

'Would you like me to sit by you, Bryan?'

'I'll be all right,' he said. 'I'll get up in a minute.'

He felt the pressure on the couch released.

The door closed.

The faces on the wall were spinning round.

He got up from the couch.

He fumbled with the door and went out to the hall; he crossed to the kitchen and, as the door opened, he said, 'I'm going to be sick.'

All he could think of was the farmer and his daughter sitting there, and, his eyes narrowed, he turned to the hall. His feet caught against the stairs, then, at the top, he was directed along a landing: a door was opened; he stooped above a sink.

Finally, when he raised his head, the dizziness had gone.

He washed his face.

A towel was presented.

'That feel better?'

'Yes,' he said.

'You've not been tasting Margaret's paste while you've been glueing down those pictures?' Mrs Spencer laid her arm around his waist.

'No,' he said.

Behind him, on the landing, he could hear Mr Spencer say, 'Perhaps it's the yard. A few whiffs of that can send you rattling. We're used to it, tha knows. He isn't.'

They returned downstairs.

'No doubt he'll feel like summat to eat,' the farmer added, surveying the table.

'I'd better get back,' Bryan said.

'We'll ask Mr Spencer to run you, there's no hurry. You sit

down,' Mrs Spencer said. 'Perhaps you'd like some tea now you've fetched things up.'

A cup was placed on the table before him.

'I'll be able to go on my bike,' he said.

'Oh, we couldn't let you, love,' Mrs Spencer said. 'It'll only take Mr Spencer ten or twelve minutes.'

It was dark by the time they left; Mr Spencer lifted his bike into the back of the car and Bryan sat in front.

Margaret, after an argument inside the house, squeezed in beside him.

'It won't stop you coming again?' Mrs Spencer said, leaning in the window.

'No,' he said.

'The next time should be better. It won't be a repeat of the first.'

She waved.

The faint tremor of the car as the engine started ran through his legs; a gate was framed in the glare from the lamps. The car turned: the hump-backed bridge appeared.

Beyond, as the car increased its speed, lay the darkening fields; they passed other vehicles on the road: he glimpsed a wall, a bridge and, finally, the lighted front of the Spinney Moor Hotel.

They turned up the road; by the time he had pointed out the house Mr Spencer had driven past: he reversed the car and lifted out the bike.

A curtain moved.

His father appeared.

'One wounded soldier,' Mr Spencer called out.

'He's not had an accident?' His father came down to the gate.

'He's fetched up his dinner. He's given us a fine half hour,' the farmer added.

Margaret, her hands clenched, gazed up at the house; his mother had appeared and called, 'Is anything the matter?'

'A funny tummy,' the farmer said. 'He's better now. All right now?' he added to Bryan.

Their figures were lit up by the lights from the car. Margaret, her hands still clasped, had climbed inside.

'I'm sorry it's turned out like this,' his father said.

92

'No bother, Arthur.' The farmer closed the door. 'See you to-morrow.'

'Are you all right?' his father asked as the red lights dipped down at the end of the road.

'I could have cycled back,' he said.

'Why didn't you?'

'They said they'd bring me.'

'You could see he wasn't pleased.' He turned to the bike. 'Is anything up with that?'

'No,' he said.

'Do you still feel sick?' his mother said as they went inside. She added, 'He must have something. He's lines like charcoal under his eyes.'

He was put to bed.

He lay there several days.

On the Monday his father brought some eggs. On the Tuesday he brought a cake. On the Wednesday he brought a rabbit, skinned it, cleaned it, and made a soup.

'I've never seen so many inquiries,' he said to his mother.

The doctor came, suggested flu, changed his mind, and put it down to something Bryan had eaten.

At the weekend Margaret came.

She brought a parcel from her mother.

Sitting in the living-room, her hands on her knees, she gazed at Bryan with her eyes expanded, her brow flushed, her lips compressed. His mother, having introduced her, retreated to the scullery: Alan was out, his father still at work.

'What do you think made you poorly?' she said. 'You don't look better now,' she added. 'Do you think it's your con-stitution?'

'No,' he said.

'Perhaps you're too nervous.'

She clasped her hands, looking at the range, at the walls, at the window. 'You have to accept things as they are. It doesn't have to add up to anything, does it?'

Bryan was only aware of the freshness of her figure, of the white socks turned down above the black-strap shoes, of the blue dress uniform of her school, of the brightness of her cheeks and eyes.

93

'I wondered if you'd like to go to the pictures.'

'When?' he said.

'Next Wednesday.'

'Which one?' he said.

'The Regal.'

'All right,' he said.

'I'll pay for the ticket.'

'It'll be all right,' he said.

'My mother said I had to.'

'I'll pay for it,' he said.

His mother came in and laid a cake on the table.

'Here you are,' she said. 'We can't let you go without having some tea.'

She brought in three cups; finally, when the table was set, they drew up the chairs.

The cake was cut.

'I've invited Bryan to the cinema,' Margaret said as she watched his mother pour out the tea.

'That'll be a treat.' She glanced at Bryan.

'On Wednesday. After school. Will he be able to get up to town by five o'clock?'

'Oh, he'll get there, I'm sure,' his mother said. 'What time does it finish?'

'Seven-fifteen.'

'He should be back before eight. His bedtime is half-past seven.'

'As early as that?' Margaret glanced at Bryan then back at his mother.

'What time do you go to bed?' his mother asked.

'As late as ten.'

'Ten.' His mother rearranged her plate. 'Why, we're in bed ourselves before then,' she added.

'Oh, I suppose it's different with us, Mrs Morley,' Margaret said.

'What film is it?' his mother asked.

'I don't know,' Margaret said. 'I always go on Wednesdays.'

'Well,' his mother said. 'That is a treat.'

'I suppose,' Margaret said when the cake was eaten, 'I ought to be getting back. Thank you for the tea.'

'Thank your mother for the cake,' his mother said.

'Good-bye,' the girl said as she mounted her bike.

'She's a strange girl,' his mother said as they watched her cycle off. At the dip in the road she turned and, seeing them still waiting, waved.

On the Wednesday he found her waiting on the marble-coloured steps outside the foyer. She wore a long, dark-blue coat and a beret to which an oval, light-blue badge was attached. Over her shoulder she carried a satchel.

'I've bought the tickets,' she said. 'I thought, if you were late, it would save us time.'

The money was hot in his hand and as he held it out she added, 'Don't be absurd. You can't afford to come to a cinema in town. I wouldn't have invited you if I knew you'd have to pay. I'm not stupid.'

Looping her satchel over her other shoulder she disappeared into the darkness beyond the swing doors.

Bryan followed; he made out the shape of her back silhouetted against the beam of a torch: he slid into a seat.

'Near enough?'

'Yes,' he said.

'Do you want a sweet?'

He felt a bag pushed by his arm: the paper rustled; he extracted a toffee.

'This is the end of the film,' she added. 'If you don't want to see what happens don't look.'

All day he had thought of his ride to the town, of the walk down Southgate from the Bull Ring, of the cinema entrance, of what he should do if she wasn't there – he'd been told to come home – of what he would see once he was inside the building, a vast, glass-fronted edifice, only recently constructed, and had wondered all day, too, sitting at his desk, if he would be in time and, finally, what the subject of the film might be.

'Don't look.'

He glanced beside him to see the eerily illuminated face shielded by a hand: beneath the hand he could see the masticating lips and, below the arm to which the hand was attached, he could see the knees of the light-coloured dress turned sideways in the seat and drawn towards him.

'You'll spoil it.' She covered her eyes again.

A woman screamed.

Bryan gazed about him in the darkness; accustomed to the light from the screen he identified several pallid faces.

The lights came up.

The curtains on the screen were drawn together.

The few figures in the rows about them, banging back the seats, got up.

An usherette moved down the aisle: a spotlight illuminated a tray about her shoulders.

'Do you want an ice-cream?'

'No.' He felt for the money in his pocket and wondered even now how he might, before he left, be able to give it to her.

'I think I'll get one,' she said. 'Are you sure?'

'No, thanks.'

He watched her walk off between the seats; she had left her satchel beside him and now she walked with her arms outstretched, half-running down the slope of the aisle, her feet thudding on the carpet: plaits protruded from beneath her beret, a blue-checked ribbon glowing against the darkness of the coat.

Then, coming back, she peeled off the top of the carton, the wooden spoon she'd been given already in her mouth.

Everything about her actions reminded him that all this, for her, was a regular routine: she came back along the row without raising her head, collapsing with a sigh, thudding back the seat, drawing her legs beneath her.

'Did you see the end?'

'No,' he said.

'It spoils it, knowing she'll be saved.'

'Who?'

'The woman.'

She licked the ice-cream from the wooden spoon. 'Are you sure you wouldn't like a taste?'

'No,' he said.

'Do you want another sweet? You can keep the bag.'

96

She handed him the sweets; every few moments a changing display of lights passed to and fro across the curtains.

'Adverts,' Margaret said, finally, as the lights went down, and added, 'Can I have another toffee?'

The street was in darkness when they emerged; a queue was standing at the door, curving off into an alleyway at the side of the building.

Margaret, having slung her satchel across one shoulder, and having arranged her beret to her satisfaction, gazed up and down the road.

A horn sounded as a car drew up against the kerb; the face of Mr Spencer stooped to the window.

'Jump in,' he said. 'I'll take you home.'

'It's all right,' Bryan said. 'I'll go on the bus.'

'Did you have a good time?'

'Yes,' he said.

'We saw the end first,' Margaret said, and opened the door.

'That's a waste of money,' the farmer said, and added, 'Sure about the lift?' He glanced across at Bryan.

'I know where the stop is.'

'Cheerio, then,' the farmer called.

Margaret nodded through the window.

'Good-bye,' she said as the car drew off.

Bryan walked up the road past the lighted shop windows; it was the first time he'd been in the town on his own.

Figures passed him on the pavement and, glancing back at the cinema, he saw the queue filing in.

When the bus came he sat at the front; above him loomed the driver, his face lit up by the glow from the dashboard.

Along the Town Road he saw the cluster of lights across the valley: a pale moon lit up a canopy of cloud.

The bus stopped, the engine rattled, the windows shook, then, once more, it moved into the darkness; people chatted in the seats behind: he gazed in at the house windows on either side, then into the blankness of the distant trees, and, finally, he got up and waited for the bus to stop.

The last people had gone into the Empire cinema at the bottom of Spinney Moor Avenue and the shutters were being placed on the sweet shop at the side: in the foyer the doorman in his long brown coat with gold epaulettes was walking up and down, clapping his white-gloved hands together.

Bryan ran up the avenue and, assuming it was too late to use the back door, knocked on the front.

The key turned; his mother looked out.

'Had a good time?'

'I didn't have to pay,' he said, smelling the food which had been cooked for his father's supper.

'Oh, you shouldn't have let her pay,' his mother said, coming into the living-room behind.

His brother was sitting by the fire.

'She wouldn't take it.'

'You should have forced her.'

'Aye, you should have paid,' his father said, sitting at the table and gazing at the money as Bryan laid it out. 'What have you spent?'

'Bus fare.'

'Didn't you buy her any sweets?'

'She already had some.'

'If he hasn't spent it, does that mean I can't go?' his brother said. He had already negotiated his own visit at the end of the week.

'You'll have to get somebody to invite you,' his father said. 'We can't afford these jaunts into town.' He laid his hand over the money and drew it to him.

'That's mine,' his mother said, grasping his arm. She took the money and, having counted it, put it in her purse and placed the purse in the sideboard drawer.

'Did Spencer pick Margaret up?' his father asked.

'He offered me a lift,' he said.

'You should have taken it.'

'He's taken enough from them already,' his mother said. 'Now, off to bed the two of you.'

'Does it mean I can't go?' his brother asked again.

'We shall have to see.'

'He always has the best of everything,' Alan said.

'We didn't arrange it,' his mother said.

'It always comes out that way.' His brother disappeared to the stairs: his feet pounded on the landing.

'I don't suppose it'll happen too often,' his father said.

'No,' his mother said.

'Once in a blue moon,' his father said. 'I reckon it's their way for saying sorry about Sunday.' To Bryan he added, 'Best not to encourage her. We can't keep up with people like that.'

'Oh, he'll be all right.' His mother gazed at Bryan who, frowning in the light, had turned to the stairs. 'We don't want to discourage her,' she added. 'It's just that we can't keep up,' she continued, 'if we haven't the money.'

He could still hear her voice when he got upstairs, and when he went in the bedroom his brother's voice came muffled from the bed. 'You always get the best.'

'I didn't ask to go,' he said.

'It always turns out that way.' His voice was low; only moments before, Bryan thought, he might have been crying. 'What was the picture like?' he added.

'All right,' he said.

He got into bed and lay on his back.

The interior of the cinema returned – the star-shaped lights, the glow from the screen, the concavity of the ceiling – and the image of the girl, the movement of her arm, the curve of her legs as she tucked them up beside him.

EIGHT

A plane appeared above the roofs and passed across the field.

He could see the insignia on its wings and imagined, perhaps even saw, the head of the pilot in the square-shaped cockpit.

'Did you see its bombs?'

'Did you see its guns?'

'Did you see the pilot?'

'I saw him wave.'

The crackle of its engines faded.

'Do you think it's crashing?'

'It's making for Fenton aerodrome.'

The grass had been removed from an oblong area of ground at the top end of the field: the soil underneath had been dug out and now, with spades, the older children were digging at the clay beneath.

Alan dug with their father's spade, his head and shoulders, from a distance, bobbing up and down, the rest of him invisible.

Bryan pushed back the pieces of clay as his brother tossed them up, ran after the other children as they threw pieces of clay at one another and, finally, having nothing else to do, he sat at the edge of the yellowish mound and fashioned figures, pressing in an abdomen, shaping an arm and finally a head. Having finished one figure he stood it up, completed a second, rolled a third, set the head on a flange of neck, attached the legs and the arms, flattened the feet, and stood it, finally, beside the others.

'What are you doing?' his brother asked.

He tapped his fingers against a head.

'That looks like Crossey.'

He indicated a dark-haired, pinched-cheeked boy who was digging at the bottom of the hole.

'Or more like Cloughie.'

A large, fair-haired boy, digging with a stick, came to the edge of the hole and gazed at the figure: he had a low brow, a thickly-fleshed nose and light-pink cheeks; his resemblance to a pig had earned him in the past the nickname 'Snout'. He was the eldest of the Barracloughs' four children, three of whom were digging in or around the hole; 'Crossey' was the elder of the Shawcrofts' two children, his nickname derived from the reputation his parents had acquired for quarrelling. Both boys were Alan's age, or older, Barraclough the leader: his hands covered in clay he dug his finger against the figure. 'That's good.' He flattened the head to the shape of a saucer. The children laughed.

Their interest, after being distracted, returned to the hole: pieces of clay were lifted up; steps were cut back and battened with wood.

Bryan took a fresh piece of clay across the grass and modelled a head, then a body and, finally, four legs. He attached a tail and a pair of horns. He made a second and then a third; amongst the four-legged figures he set a man. The noise from the hole, the shouting and laughing, the calling of instructions, faded; he sat with his legs outstretched, shaping the figures between his knees. Soon a herd of animals stretched out across the grass with the figure of the man behind.

Someone came across; a boy called out: a second shouted.

Soon the whole group was spread-eagled in the grass.

'Who's digging?' his brother called, only he and Barraclough being left in the hole.

Bryan took two lumps of clay and climbed into the garden; he sat in the porch and modelled the shapes again: he constructed a table, around it a number of block-like chairs. He fashioned a dog.

'Aren't you playing in the field?' His mother came out and, in-advertently, placed her foot on the edge of the table. 'What a mess you're making.' She stepped over the clay and shook a cloth. 'Keep it off the step or we'll have it in the house.' Striding over it again, she returned indoors.

He collected the pieces of clay and took them back to the field. Alison Foster was standing by the hole; Barraclough, O'Donald, Shawcroft and Alan, together with the other children, were leaning

101

on their spades: in the bottom of the hole was O'Donald's sister, a dark-haired girl, with glasses, her hair tied back in a single plait.

'You can't come out, Muriel,' Barraclough said.

The girl gazed up, the light, reflected from her glasses, concealing her expression.

Shawcroft and his brother laughed; the younger children danced up and down, one tripping up and falling. A moment later, as he scrambled up, Muriel took the opportunity to climb out herself.

She was pushed back in.

'Let her out, Cloughie,' Alison said.

She was a small, well-built girl, wearing a pinafore dress, her fair hair tumbled down across her shoulders: having leant down to take Muriel's hand she was pushed back, first by Barraclough, then by Shawcroft.

'You'll go in, Ally, if you let her out.'

'Push her in,' O'Donald said.

The boys jostled Alison at the edge of the hole.

'Push her.'

'Grab her.'

Alan had clasped one arm and Shawcroft the other: she was taken to the side, held there, then pushed forward to where the other girl knelt in the bottom.

'Take them off, or you don't come out,' Barraclough said, standing by the steps and pushing Alison back.

The dark-haired girl had begun to cry.

'If you don't let her out,' Alison said, 'I shall fetch my father.'

'How will you fetch him?' Barraclough said.

'Bryan, go and fetch him,' Alison said.

'Nay, let her up,' Alan said. He had played with Alison when he was younger and occasionally, even now, he would talk to her, brusquely, across the fence. He put down his hand and pulled her up.

'Take 'em off,' Barraclough said, more intent on the dark-haired girl than ever.

Her brother stepped back from the hole and glanced at the house.

'You have to take 'em off,' Barraclough said, 'or you can't come out.'

The girl stooped; from beneath her skirt she lowered her knickers.

'Lift it.'

Her gaze, obscured by the reflected light of her glasses, was turned, red-cheeked, to the figures round the hole.

'You have to bend down.'

'Lift it.'

'Bend down.'

'You have to bend down.'

The figures laughed; they danced up and down at the side of the hole.

'Higher.'

The skirt was lifted.

'Longer.'

The skirt was lifted again.

'I saw it!'

Barraclough stood at the side of the hole, his spade in his hand. Shouts sprang up on either side.

The girl pulled on her knickers; her sobs, stifled by the hole, muffled by the screams, were audible as the shouting died.

Alison stooped down and the girl, having pulled on her knickers, clasped her hand.

'She'll tell her mother.'

'No, she won't.'

'You won't tell her, will you?' Barraclough said.

Having been pulled up the side the girl cried in her hand.

'She's passed the test. She's one of us. When we've got the hole finished she can come inside.'

A guffaw of laughter came from the boys.

Bryan took a fresh piece of clay across the field, set it down, and, sitting, dug in his fingers: as the clay dried it cracked or, where it had caught up fragments of soil, it crumbled. He spat on his fingers, rolled the clay between his hands then, as the screaming and the shouting faded, he lay back in the grass and gazed at the sky.

He wasn't his parents' child at all: he'd been put out to live with the Morleys in order to make him realize what life was all about. He had nothing in common with the people around him although he was subject to them in every respect. His caning at school had been to test his courage; similarly, his invitation to the

Spencers', despite his falling sick, and the subsequent invitation to the cinema, were part of the plan conceived by the King whereby his experience of life should not be confined to Stainforth School.

As he examined his clay-ringed fingers he came to the conclusion that everyone with whom he came into contact was involved in his assessment: periodically they would attend a meeting and it would be decided how well or, conversely, how badly he was doing; the test, he assumed, was going well, otherwise, he calculated, he would have been sent back to the place from where he started.

He had both hands raised against the sky and was confirming within himself that it was the intensity of his feelings, together with their depth, that marked him out from other people, when he heard Alan's voice say, 'What are you doing?'

'What?'

'Come and dig.'

'I don't want to dig.'

Alison's voice came screeching from the hole as she was chased around its clayey edge.

'They won't let you in unless you dig.'

His brother sat beside him.

'I don't want to go in,' he said.

'It'll be a good den when it's finished. We're making a chimney.'

He indicated Shawcroft delving in a crevice some distance from the hole.

His brother's hands were larger than his own: he looked at his brother's feet, spread-eagled in the grass, at the thickness of his brother's legs.

'We can go in at night and cook some grub.'

'What?'

'Anything you like. We're going to have a signal.' He handed Bryan the spade. 'I should let Cloughie see you and dig a bit.'

Bryan took the spade and crossed over to the hole: it was deeper than when he'd last looked in.

He joined the two or three boys who, together with Barraclough, were digging in the bottom.

'Don't put it near the edge. It'll fall back in,' Barraclough said, rooting at a hole dug into the side and which, presumably, was to be the chimney.

'How deep are you going?' Bryan asked.

'Where's thy Alan? Has he gi'en o'er?'

Yet Alan was chasing Alison Foster.

'Are you coming, Ally?' Barraclough called. 'Gi'e your kid a hand?' adding, 'Shove it down harder,' to O'Donald who was digging the outlet to the chimney. 'Shove it down harder, and then we'll meet.'

Someone had stood the survivors from his earlier figures on a ledge at the side of the hole. Digging out a piece of clay, he crouched in the corner and shaped it into a face.

''Ow go, Bry?' came his brother's voice and a hand, streaked with earth, came down and squashed it.

'So this is the young man,' the woman said.

She sat at the kitchen table, a small, slim-featured woman with tawny-coloured hair. She wore a blue coat with large white buttons, and a dress made up of white and blue dots: a hat of the same light blue, with a white ribbon around its crown, was lying on the table before her.

On her feet, which were small and dainty, were shoes of a darker blue, the fronts of which were open.

Mrs Spencer, while not retaining her coat, had nevertheless retained her hat, a pink, broad-brimmed shape, not unlike the woman's: over her dress she wore an apron, while on the table before her stood several parcels.

'This is Bryan, Fay,' Mrs Spencer said. 'Bryan, this is Margaret's aunt,' and, moving to the door, called out to the passage, 'Could you help me in the kitchen?' waiting a moment, then calling once again before, from overhead, came a sound, first of the stamping of a foot, then of a muffled shout and, finally, of Margaret's voice: 'I've been helping out there already.'

The mother came back to the room.

'They've been out in the fields all day,' she added, cutting bread at the table. 'She makes it feel like a week.'

'How is my brother?' The woman glanced at Bryan.

'How is Mr Spencer, Bryan?' Mrs Spencer asked.

'He's driving the tractor,' Bryan said.

'Has he given you a ride?' the woman asked.

'I've been stooking,' he said.

'That sounds hard. Is it hard?' The woman smiled.

'Yes,' he said. He opened his hands.

'Look at his bruises!' The woman pushed back the sleeve of his shirt. 'And his arms.'

'Oh, Bryan's a soldier,' Mrs Spencer said. 'He doesn't mind one or two bruises.'

Bryan gazed steadily into the woman's face: most clearly of all he saw the blueness of the eyes, and most powerfully of all he was conscious of her scent. 'He seems so young to be doing rough work.'

'Bryan's older than his years,' Mrs Spencer said, and added, 'There you are, Margaret. You can butter the bread.'

Margaret had worn a skirt and a blouse in the fields and now she had put on a dress.

'You see how difficult it is to have even one day off,' Mrs Spencer said as Margaret took a knife and, glancing at Bryan and then at her aunt, dug it at the butter. 'It's resented by everyone. If her father came in now and saw those parcels I don't think he'd speak to me again.'

'You didn't have to go out shopping,' Margaret said.

'If I hadn't have gone today I wouldn't have gone at all.' Mrs Spencer glanced at the aunt. 'Aunt Fay and Uncle Harold offered me a lift. Something your father has no time for at present.'

'He's busy.'

'I know he's busy. So am I.'

'How do you like working with the men, Margaret?' The woman turned her attention to Margaret's face which glowed not only from the work she had done and the heat of the day but from the wash she had had upstairs.

'I've worked with them before,' she said.

'Have you?'

'Often.' She dug the knife at the bread. 'But not in company,' she added, indicating Bryan.

'It must be rough,' the woman said. 'Doesn't it do awful things to your hands?' She glanced at her own which were small and neat.

'I find it pleasant,' Margaret said, cutting the bread then count-

106

ing the slices. 'Why don't you come out, Aunt Fay, and join us?'

'Me?' the woman said. 'I don't believe I could. Exertions of that nature have been beyond me now for quite some time.'

'It would do your figure good, Aunt,' Margaret said.

'Do you think so?' the woman got up from the table and crossed to a mirror above the sink. 'I used to work here in the old days,' she added. 'But that was some years before your time.'

'Not so many years, Fay,' Mrs Spencer said.

'Not so many.' The woman laughed. She returned to the table. 'Do you think I look stout?' she added to Bryan.

'No,' Bryan said. He shook his head.

'What category would you put me in?'

'What categories are there?' Bryan asked.

'The slim, the medium and the fat.'

'The slim.'

'What a diplomat.' She laughed. 'I don't think he'd tell me if I wasn't,' she added. 'Although I'm quite sure that I am.'

Sandwiches were cut; tea was made and, together with the milk and the stirred-in sugar, poured into two enamel jugs. The sandwiches were wrapped in towels. Margaret and Bryan took one jug and one bundle of sandwiches apiece, and on Bryan's arm Mrs Spencer threaded a carrier bag containing metal mugs.

'Will you be back before I leave?' the aunt inquired.

'Probably,' Margaret said, already at the door.

'I won't say good-bye in that case.' She smiled, came to the door and watched them cross the yard.

'I'll stay out till midnight, in that case,' Margaret said.

'Why?' Bryan said.

'She's so conceited.'

'Do you think so?'

'I know so.' Cows were drifting across the pasture and the herdsman had come out from one of the sheds. 'Any of that for me?' he called.

'It's for the men, John,' Margaret shouted.

'What am I?' the man complained.

He was tall and thin, and wore a blue overall and a large, check cap.

'There's some for you at the house,' she shouted.

'Nay, they know where I am.' The man turned back to the shed. 'It's all for them out theer, then, is it?'

'Ask at the house,' she shouted again, but the man had already disappeared inside the shed from where, after a moment, came the sound of sweeping. 'Don't tell me you like her?' Margaret added as they started across the pasture to a wood the other side. 'Even Daddy doesn't like her, and she's his sister.'

Bryan didn't answer; the presence of the woman had taken him by surprise: the neatness of her movements, her gentleness, the brightness of her eyes.

'She's a terrible flirt.'

'Is she?'

'She can't help flirting with anyone.'

'I thought she was pretty.'

'With all that make-up?'

'Isn't she like a film star?' Bryan said.

'She is not!' She laughed. 'I think she's ugly.'

'Why?'

'Her nose is too long.'

'I never noticed.'

'Don't tell me,' she said, pausing, 'you liked her figure.'

'It was her eyes I noticed,' Bryan said.

'All that mascara.'

A man was walking out of the wood. He was tall and slim, and wore a grey suit; his hair, which was short and almost white, curled down in a fringe: from the top pocket of his jacket he took a handkerchief with which, as he approached them, he wiped his brow. His eyes were dark, his cheeks sallow, his nose long and sharply pointed, his mouth thin-lipped. 'Is that for me?' He gazed at the jugs.

'It's for the men, Uncle,' Margaret said.

'Aren't I one of them?'

'Have you been stooking?'

'I've been watching them.' He mopped his brow, wiped his hands on the handkerchief, and returned it to his pocket. 'Which is just as hot.'

'There's some for you at the house.' She added, 'This is Bryan.'

'Hello, Bryan.' The man glanced down. 'You're loaded.'

108

'Sandwiches and tea mugs,' Margaret said.

'I suppose I'd better get back.' The man stooped to look inside the carrier bag. 'Once your aunt gets started there's no catching up again.'

Margaret glanced at Bryan and nodded her head.

The man smiled; he glanced off along the track.

'What birds are those?'

A flock of black-and-white birds, with short, squared-off wings, started from the grass.

'Peewits,' Margaret said.

'Peewits.'

'Or plovers.'

'Are they the same?'

'Or lapwings.'

'This girl knows everything,' the tall man said. 'In addition to which, she's been to every film that's ever been made, as well as knowing all the actors.'

'Do you like Aunt Fay's dress?' Margaret said.

'I do.' The man nodded; he closed his eyes and nodded again.

'I think a warmer colour suits her,' Margaret said.

'I prefer the blue.' The man glanced down at Bryan.

'Nor do I like its pattern,' Margaret said. She turned to Bryan, and added, 'Spots.'

'Dots.'

'Spots.'

'I shall tell her,' the tall man said, 'and see what she says.'

'Don't say I told you.'

'I shan't.'

The man turned, his dark shoes covered in dust, and continued along the track; when, a short while later, they reached the wood, Bryan glanced back to see him approach the gate to the yard: he paused, gazing off to the flock of birds which, no sooner settled, rose up again.

'I much prefer him to her,' Margaret said.

'I like them both,' Bryan said.

'You like everyone.'

'I don't think so.'

At the opposite end of the wood a patch of sunlight shone on

109

the field where the men were working. The clatter of the tractor echoed beneath the trees and the smell of its fumes mingled with the more persistent smell of straw from the binder.

The air in the shadow of the trees was cool; pigeons fluttered in the branches: a dull echo came from the shuffling of his and Margaret's feet.

'You realize her figure is reinforced?'

'What by?'

'All that bosom. Even mother doesn't like her using make-up.'

'Why not?'

'It's a barbarous habit.'

'Is it?'

'Why do you never answer a question except by asking another?' The metal mugs jangled in the bag.

'I liked her make-up.'

'You've no taste. Even Daddy thinks she's vulgar, and he's her brother. Fancy her taking mother off to buy those clothes when she knows she's needed at home at present.'

Mr Spencer could be seen descending from the tractor as they came out from the trees; he walked round to the binder and the tapping of a spanner came a moment later as Bryan's father got down from the high seat and, stooping beside Mr Spencer, reached into the machine beneath the canvas screen.

Mr Spencer looked up; he waved his arm. 'Shove it under the hedge,' he shouted.

The men who were stooking threw down their sheaves; the sandwiches were unwrapped, the tea poured out.

'How are you faring, Bryan?' his father said as he came across. He was followed by Mr Spencer. 'Not taking too much out of you?' he added. The farmer lay back in the shadow of the hedge, the men sprawled out around him.

His father was invariably shy whenever he encountered Bryan with any of the Spencers; even after making the inquiry he glanced at the farmer before sitting down, taking his mug of tea from Margaret.

'Made these, have you?' he asked, taking a sandwich from one of the towels.

'With Mrs Spencer.'

110

'And Aunt Fay,' Margaret said, speaking to her father.

'We've had your Uncle Harold out here,' the farmer said. 'Ask Arthur. He gave us two minutes and ran away.'

His father laughed; the other men laughed as well.

'I said: "Come to give us a hand, Harold?" at which he shifted faster than a rabbit.' He indicated two dead rabbits lying by the hedge. 'I suppose he wa' still running when he reached the house.'

The field stretched out to an adjoining field and, beyond that, the slope ran down to the river.

A distant perspective of the town stood out across the valley, the intervening area of fields and copses giving way to an assemblage of roofs out of which, sharply focused in the light, rose the central hill with its silhouetted domes and steeple.

Bryan lay back; uncomfortable in his father's presence, largely because of his father's own embarrassment, he abstracted himself from the figures around him and gazed over to the town and, adjacent to the town, and directly across the valley, to the cluster of roofs which, together with the block-like structure of the church, the school and, beyond it, the hospital, marked the summit of Spinney Top. The whole area was laid out in a sun-lit vista, the haze of the afternoon only evident in the valley bottom where the river glowed between its shallow banks.

The voices droned on, dominated by that of Mr Spencer: 'It'll see us through till supper will this. She can make a sandwich when she wants to,' and, moments later, 'She's back from town with your auntie, is she? I hope we're not skint, or there'll be nought to pay these lads out here.' He spoke with a sandwich in his mouth and, after chewing it, swallowed it down with tea.

The curious thing was, despite their roles of employer and employee, Mr Spencer and his father were closer in spirit than Bryan himself was either to his father or to his mother: he half-imagined, as he listened to their voices, that if he had had a choice, he might have chosen Margaret's aunt to be his mother, or someone like her, someone whose distinction matched his own.

The smell of her perfume was still on his clothes and absently he raised the sleeve of his shirt and breathed it in: he lay with the cloth against his nose and reflected on the last moment he had seen her, framed in the kitchen door, waving, the blueness of her

111

dress highlighting the warmth of her features; above all, he had been affected by the movement of her arm, and the swaying of the hand above the wrist, a suppleness that suggested not merely a degree of spontaneity but a vulnerability as well.

'I've never seen a man shift faster, when he was offered a spot of work.'

Mr Spencer belched.

His father laughed.

The farmer stretched, stood up, and belched again.

'I reckon thy young 'un better be off.'

'Aye.' His father nodded. 'You'd better be getting back, Bryan. Tell your mother I'll be late tonight. Not to wait up.' He glanced about him. 'It'll be getting dark in one or two hours. I want you home by then.'

The men returned to the field; the tractor restarted: the clatter of the binder began again, cutting at the swathe of wheat that ran up to the summit of the rise beyond which, uncut, the fields rose higher still to the crest of Feltham Castle.

They picked up the metal mugs and put them in the bag.

'I think I'll stay out longer,' Margaret said. 'Tell my mother I'll be back before dark.'

Yet, when he was halfway through the wood, he heard her calling and saw her running after him.

Her face was red, gleaming and, having caught him up, she ran past, slapping his arm, pausing several paces ahead and calling, 'I'll go back with you. Do you want a hand?'

'No, thanks,' he said.

'What an independent person you are,' she said.

'I don't think so,' he said.

'You're always sulking.'

'I'm not,' he said, for he had worked beside her all day and, despite their difference in build, had not only stooked more quickly, but had kept up with the men: his hands and his arms were raw and although, as Mrs Spencer had suggested, this was something that was not only inevitable but which had to be accepted, he felt whatever injury he might have incurred, either to his feelings – by seeing his father's subservience to Mr Spencer, and Mr Spencer's seeming disregard of it – or to his body, the cuts and scratches

112

were worth it for his having met the one woman who, in appearance as well as manner, summed up all that he felt to be synonymous with his own position: a princess to his prince.

He quickened his step in the hope that, when they reached the house, she would still be there.

'I can never make out what you're thinking, Bryan.'

'I don't have to be thinking anything,' he said.

'Or feeling.'

'I don't know what you're feeling, either.'

'You've a good idea.'

'I haven't.'

The metal mugs and the jugs clattered on his arm.

'You have a purpose in life,' Margaret said. 'You won't tell anyone about it.'

'I don't know what it is,' he said.

'My mother likes you,' she said. 'My father thinks I shouldn't invite you.'

'Why?'

'It raises problems with your father.' She added, 'He doesn't mind you coming to the farm and doing odd jobs, or playing in the barn, but he's not keen,' she continued, 'to have you in the house.' She paused. 'My mother doesn't mind, but then, she doesn't have to work with the men. After all, my father is your father's boss and though he doesn't often show it, they could never be considered equals. You can't be someone's superior at work, and then not have that superiority reflected in your private life, however reasonable you're trying to be.'

'Perhaps he'd prefer it if I didn't come,' he said.

'Perhaps he would.'

'Then I shan't.'

'That'd be silly.'

'Why?'

'Because I've invited you.'

'I don't want to come if I'm not wanted.'

'You are wanted, but the other thing gets in the way.'

'She is only saying this,' he thought, 'because she is annoyed at my reaction to her aunt.' Nevertheless, he reflected, she wouldn't say it unless it were true.

'I'll leave these at the door,' he said, indicating the metal mugs.

'Don't be silly.'

'Your father's right.'

'He may be right for him, but he's not for me and my mother.'

'It's his farm.'

'We live on it,' she added.

Dust rose from the track and Bryan, having raised his eyes towards the farm, lowered them at the thought that he might not be coming here again.

'If I have a purpose in life,' he said, 'I'd like to be well known.'

'What for?'

He gazed ahead. 'For something that no one else could do. Otherwise,' he added, 'I don't think there's much point in living.'

'That can't be true,' she said. 'Think of all those people who haven't a gift.'

'It's vanity,' he said, 'that keeps them going.'

They reached the gate to the farm. Perhaps his remarks had echoed a not dissimilar sentiment in Margaret herself. Her father was an artisan; his manners were those of an artisan: the only civilizing element in the house came from Margaret herself and from her mother. And now, crowning that civilizing element, was her aunt.

Although Margaret had paused behind him he walked quickly to the door: the dogs which, earlier, had been in the field, had returned to the kitchen and their barking came from the other side.

'If they're barking like that,' he thought, 'I doubt if she can be there,' and as he knocked on the door and pushed it open, and the dogs ran out to the yard, he saw that Mrs Spencer was standing at the table, very much as he had left her, glancing up, half-smiling: only her hat had been removed.

'First back?' she said.

'My father thinks I ought to be going,' he told her.

'I'm sure he's right.'

He put the bag by the sink.

Margaret had followed him in the door, leaving it open, and sat at the table, her head in her hand.

'That's one it's tired out, at least,' she added.

114

'I'm not tired,' Margaret said.

'You look it, my girl.' The mother laughed.

'Has Aunt Fay left?'

'Just.'

'Bryan liked her.'

'I'm glad.'

'He thought her very pretty.'

'She is.'

'And knows it.'

'That's impertinent, Margaret,' Mrs Spencer said, and took the last of the plates to the sink. 'If there's one thing Aunt Fay knows about it's how to dress.'

'She's not the only one.'

'As far as she's concerned, she is.'

'And lets everyone know it.'

'That's her manner.'

'And unfortunate,' Margaret said.

'You can leave the mugs, Bryan,' Mrs Spencer said as he stacked them by the sink. She added, 'Did you bring a coat, or did you come without?'

'I came without.'

'Just as well, in that case, you're going now. It's chilly, cycling, once the sun goes down.'

She came with him to the door.

'Are you saying good-bye to Bryan?' she added to Margaret who was still sitting at the table, her head in her hand.

'Good-bye,' she said.

'Won't you see him to the gate?'

'If I have to.'

She got up from the table, sighing.

'I'm not sure it does Margaret much good having her friends visit her,' Mrs Spencer said. 'Or her relatives. She invariably shows them the worst side of her nature.'

'I'm fed up, that's all,' Margaret said.

'What with?'

'With him.' She indicated Bryan.

'I'm sure no one else could say that, in the light of all the help he's been,' Mrs Spencer said, standing in the door.

115

'It's not him,' Margaret said. 'It's Father. He doesn't like him coming.'

'He's never said that.'

'You can see it, without him having to.'

'It needn't affect your friendship,' Mrs Spencer said.

She stood in the door and Margaret, having come out from the kitchen, stood with her back to the wall, kicking her heel at the step.

'There has to be someone in charge,' Mrs Spencer added.

'And some with money, and some without.'

'Oh, we can't get into those arguments at this hour.' Mrs Spencer glanced at Bryan. 'Those are the arguments you should have had with your aunt,' she added. 'Rather than about her dress.'

'Aunt Fay's no different,' Margaret said. 'If anything, she's worse.'

'Her opinions are more clearly expressed,' Mrs Spencer said, still gazing at Bryan. 'Shall we see you tomorrow?' she added.

'I don't know,' he said.

'You're welcome. You know that. Don't let Margaret put you off.'

She turned to the house.

A moment later she reappeared, closing the door behind her. 'Just for the dogs,' she added.

'She wants us to have a private conversation, and make it up,' Margaret said.

She followed him to the gate.

'What's this unusual thing you're going to do?' she added.

'I don't know,' he said.

'You could marry me and then you could have the farm.'

She flushed.

'It's not a material ambition,' Bryan said.

'What is it?'

'A spiritual one.'

'To be a priest?'

'That's no more exceptional than being a farmer.'

'I see.'

'It has to be something special.'

She gazed at him intently; the earnest, boy-like look of earlier that afternoon had been replaced by one of indignation.

'Are you coming tomorrow?'

'Yes,' he said.

'I'm glad.'

She stood on the gate as he cycled off and he could still see her there, leaning out, as he reached the hump-backed bridge.

Standing on the grass verge at the side of the road was Margaret's aunt. She had just stepped on to the grass from the road, stepping back again as he approached.

His attention was drawn to her hair, more tawny-coloured than ever in the evening light, falling in a profusion of curls across her brow.

'Look what we've gone and done,' she said, her heels clicking in the road.

Standing under a tree at the side of the road was a blue-coloured car; it was tilted to one side, supported at the rear on a metal jack. The tall figure of Margaret's uncle, without his jacket, was stooping to the offside wheel. The boot of the car was open.

'I wanted to send back for one of the men, but Mr Corrigan wouldn't have it.'

Her husband straightened.

'Which one of us,' he said, 'would have had to go and fetch him?'

'Oh, I'd have gone,' she said, shaking her hat in her hand.

Bryan, from a distance of several feet, was conscious not only of her smile but of the strange effect of the evening light, for it appeared to silhouette her figure.

He gazed at her for several seconds during which her husband, having removed the rear wheel of the car, came round to the back and, having unscrewed it, lifted out the spare tyre.

'I'll help you,' Bryan said.

'That's kind.' He glanced at his wife. 'There's not much to do but fit it on.' He bounced the wheel beneath his hand.

Bryan, laying down his bike, helped him to lift it on to the bolts.

The underside of the car was covered in mud; in the open door, lying on a seat, was the tall man's jacket: beside it lay a pale-blue handbag: a light-coloured handkerchief was lying on top. The back seat of the car was covered in parcels.

'It must have been a nail in Freddie's yard,' the tall man said, and added, 'There were any number lying about.'

His wife stepped back to the verge to watch; Bryan was conscious of her dark-blue shoes, high-heeled and open-fronted: he was reminded of the moment when she had stretched out from her chair to take his hand and had revealed, beneath her dress, at the apex of her thigh, the outline of her stocking.

Her husband, stooping, inserted a spanner on one of the nuts.

'It's better to screw it on with your fingers,' Bryan said. 'And tighten the nuts when you've taken out the jack.'

'You know one or two useful things, Bryan,' the tall man said. He glanced at his wife.

'The moment I saw him I knew he was intelligent,' she said. 'I'm never wrong on first impressions.' She glanced at Bryan and smiled: he had already taken the handle of the jack and begun to lower it. The car sank down on the tyre.

Taking the spanner, he tightened the nuts.

'That's been useful.' The man felt in his pockets.

'That's all right,' Bryan said.

The man held out a coin.

'I'd like you to have it.'

'That's all right,' he said again. He collected the tools from the grass: he placed them in the boot of the car, disengaged the jack, and set it beside them.

'I'd like to give you some token of our appreciation, Bryan,' the tall man said, stooping, lifting up the hub-cap and trying, unsuccessfully, to fit it on.

'I'll do it,' Bryan said.

He sat by the car then, leaning back, pushed the hub-cap on with his foot.

Dusting his hands, he got up, smiled at the woman and picked up his bike.

A smell of perfume engulfed him.

'Perhaps you'd accept it from me,' she said.

'No, thanks,' he said.

'Not even to please me?' She offered him a smile.

'No, thanks,' he said.

'He's determined not to accept it, Fay,' the tall man said. Having pulled on his jacket he stood by the car door, reaching inside. 'Perhaps we can give you a lift?' he added.

'No, thanks,' Bryan said.

'We shall find some way of rewarding you. We're not used to being refused,' the woman said.

Bryan got on his bike.

'You shan't get away with it.' The woman laughed.

'Good night,' Bryan said.

'Good night, Bryan,' the tall man said.

They watched him cycle off. 'If she feels she owes me something,' he thought, 'there's the possibility she and I might meet again. If, for instance, she asks Mrs Spencer and on her advice sends me a present, I can always write back and thank her for it, or even,' he concluded, 'take a letter round: I wonder what sort of house she lives in?'

Absorbed by these thoughts he forgot that the subject of them was only a short distance behind him in the road and when, a few moments later, the car came past, sounding its horn, he swerved to one side and saw that, on the passenger's side at the front, the window had been lowered.

The brightly-featured face gazed out.

'Good night,' the woman called.

The car sped past and left in its wake a cloud of dust which, irritating his eyes, prevented Bryan from gazing after it.

NINE

'You've got a surprise,' his mother said one morning when Bryan came down to breakfast.

A brown-paper parcel, fastened with string, was lying on the table; beside it, ready, lay a pair of scissors.

His name and address were written in a script he couldn't decipher; only with his mother outlining the words did he make out his name and then the number and the name of the road. 'Stainforth' was printed in capital letters and the word 'estate' had been omitted.

'Open it,' she said, for he continued to hold it. 'See what it is.'

Alan was standing by the table and had taken the parcel once himself, read the address closely, then handed it back.

'Who's it from?'

'I've no idea.'

Bryan cut one string and then the other; a metal box, rectangular and flat, gleamed from the sheet of paper.

He drew it out.

'Open it.'

He was aware of his mother's hands, inflamed, as her fingers reached out to press back the lid.

A small metal catch released it.

In a white metal surround lay innumerable oblong blocks of colour: they varied through innumerable shades and were arranged in several rows; in a central well lay two black-handled brushes, together with several black-capped tubes.

'Bryan!'

He could feel his mother's excitement more clearly than he felt his own.

'Who on earth is it from?'

Having gazed at the paints and run her hand across their surface, each block upraised, she examined the sheet of wrapping paper and finally drew out a blue-tinted envelope on which his name, once more, was written.

'Open it.' Her head stooped down beside his own.

Inside was a sheet of blue-coloured paper folded once and inscribed with several words more carefully written than those on the cover.

'To our Good Samaritan. From a grateful Mr and Mrs Corrigan.'

His mother read the note aloud. Alan, leaning over to read it as well, gazed at the colours; he picked up one of the brushes, drew out the bristles, then pressed the brush, lightly, then more heavily, against the lid.

'Don't spoil it.' His mother took the brush herself, examined it, ran its bristles between her fingers, then returned it to the box. She picked up one of the tubes, read the label, 'White', then put it down, and gazed at the box again.

Finally, she leant down and smelled it.

'It smells very nice.'

She closed the lid, examined it, then opened it again: the inside was set with several panels.

'Those are to mix the colours in.'

She smelled the paints again.

'They must have cost a fortune.'

'How much?' Alan said.

'Over a pound.' She glanced at Bryan. 'And this for helping to change their tyre.'

He had told them, on the evening of his return, about the incident with the car.

'He couldn't have done much,' his brother said.

'He's obviously impressed them,' his mother said. 'Otherwise, would they go to all this trouble?'

She must have considered what to buy, he thought. Perhaps, even, had analysed what she knew of him, as opposed to what she might have learned from consulting Mrs Spencer.

Only now did he run his fingers across the lid, contemplate the turned-up edges, which formed a white line against the blackness of the box itself, and open it again: several shades of red gave way to several strips of orange, the orange to yellow, the yellow to blue, the blue to green. On yet another rank deep-purple gave way to violet, to brown, to ochre. Stooping, he read the labels: viridian, blue lake, cerulean, sienna. He picked up a brush, felt the fineness of the bristles, then, moistening them in his mouth, he painted a pattern on the inside of the lid.

'What a beautiful present.' His mother's head came down as she read the names herself. 'Lamp Black. Naples Yellow. Burnt Ochre.'

Alan had gone off across the room. He was pulling on his stockings, and putting on his shoes.

'They must have got the address from Mr and Mrs Spencer. You didn't give them it?'

'No,' he said.

'You'll have to write and thank them.'

'I shall,' he said.

'We'll have to get you some paper.'

'Oh, I'll find some,' he said.

'It has to be special paper. Perhaps we can buy a sketch-book.'

'How much do they cost?' Alan said.

'Oh, we'll find the money,' his mother said.

In the evening, when he came home, his father, too, examined the box; he did so, after his initial surprise, by turning it over and over in his hand, the blocks of paint, the paint-tubes and the brushes rattling inside. Finally, when he opened the lid, he gazed at it in silence; then, flush-faced, he glanced at Bryan.

'That's a good present.'

'It is.'

'You'll have to make sure you take care of that. Make proper use of it.'

'I shall.'

'Have you tried it out?'

'No,' he said.

'Make sure you mix it properly.' He ran his fingers across the colours. 'Make sure they don't run into one another.'

He had just come in from work and hadn't taken off his coat or his cap: his blackened hands had marked the lid.

'I s'll wash my hands,' he added, 'afore I look at it again.'

Having washed his hands, he wiped the lid clean, picked up the brushes, the tubes of colour, put them back, then laid the box on the table before him while he ate his supper, its lid up, gazing at the rows of paints, smacking his lips, shaking his head and occasionally glancing at Bryan, his face still red, not only from washing, but from the strange embarrassment if not confusion the giving of the present by the Corrigans to Bryan had aroused.

'Have you written back to thank them?'

'Not yet.'

'I've told him to,' his mother said.

'By go, it must have cost a bob.'

'Over a pound,' his mother said.

'More.'

His father had turned the box over, intending to discover a label and, having failed to find one, examined the lid more closely.

'More, far more. It's not a cheap 'un. It's got every colour that's been invented.'

'Two brushes,' his mother said.

'And tubes of paint, an' all.'

'We'll have to get him some paper to paint on.'

'By go, it comes expensive, does painting,' his father said.

'We can't have him wasting it,' his mother said.

'No. We can't waste it,' his father said, nevertheless gazing at the box with a deeper frown.

Bryan kept the paintbox on a shelf in the bedroom; even in the darkness he could see the blackness, gleaming, for the lid caught the light and, where it didn't, lay like a stark rectangle against the whiteness of the paint behind.

The shelf formed a box-like structure in the corner of the room, behind the door, and adjacent to the foot of Alan's bed. On it were one or two books and an embroidered cloth, creating the semblance of a table: the structure was fashioned from the intrusion, into the corner of the room, of the staircase ceiling. Half sitting up in bed he could gaze across at it and identify not only the shape of the paintbox but the outline of the embroidered cloth, and the books propped up by the wall in the corner. He could, he speculated, make that corner of the room his own: on the opposite side of the door, adjacent to the foot of his own bed, was a wardrobe, and the only clear space in the room was the area between the beds and the even narrower space between his own bed and the window.

The box dominated the room; even when he lay back and closed his eyes he was aware of it lying in the corner and, furthermore, aware of its smell, a strange combination of paint and metal. Every few seconds he breathed it in and, although some time had elapsed since he had last seen her, he tried, as he re-animated the smell, to imagine the processes involved first in thinking about, then in setting off and, finally, in buying the present itself. Perhaps she and Mr Corrigan had chosen it together; more likely, however, she had chosen it herself. He saw her enter the shop, witnessed, from a distance, her conversation at the counter, the picking out of the box, its actual purchase where she opened a bag and took out the money; then, in his imagination, he followed her out to the street and then, from that moment, the rest of the process became a blur, ending with a picture of her sitting at a table and writing the note on the blue-coloured paper.

At some stage she would have wrapped the paintbox up, first tucking in the note, then the box, folding them both within the paper; then the name and address would be written on, the string fastened and, later she must have picked it up and taken it to a post office.

He sat up in bed to gaze at the box again. He could just make out the whiteness of the line at the edge of the lid and the faint, symmetrical swellings which indicated the indentations for the mixing of the colours.

His head sank back against the pillow.

He was standing on a road which wound off between high hedges: standing on the verge was a woman in a light-blue dress; her features were half-concealed beneath her hat. Beneath the brim, as he drew closer, he was aware of the brightness of her eyes, half-smiling, and yet half-anxious – gazing out at him with such an intensity of expression that instinctively, he put out his hand.

He felt his fingers taken; the blueness of her dress engulfed him and, by some peculiar adjustment of their height, he found himself, a moment later, gazing not only at her eyes but at her lips.

'Are you still awake?'

His brother's bed creaked and his own bed jarred as, having waited for an answer, Alan knelt down to say his prayers.

124

Opening his eyes, Bryan saw his back and heard the faint murmur of, 'God bless Mother, Dad and Bryan, and make Alan a good boy. Amen,' then felt a fresh jarring as his brother curled up in the blankets, drawing them in a cowl about his head.

'Are you awake?'

Bryan closed his eyes; perhaps his brother had already seen them open: nevertheless, re-invoking that blue-clad figure, he kept them closed, adjusted his breathing and endeavoured to keep his body still.

'I know you're awake.'

His arm ached, pinned beneath his body.

'The paintbox indicates,' he thought, 'that Mr and Mrs Corrigan are aware of who I am.' The possibility that the tyre had not been punctured, that the Corrigans had been waiting there in order that he might encounter them on his own; that they, and the 'incident' were a futher planned step in his 'education', had already crossed his mind. From his mother and father's home he had progressed to the Spencers', and from the Spencers' he had progressed to the Corrigans'; or, specifically, if he had had a choice, to Mrs Corrigan. In his daytime speculations, he had already invented a scene whereby he heard of Mr Corrigan's death and, paying Mrs Corrigan a visit and finding her in tears, he took her hand, stooping to her and, discovering her to be as solicitous of his feelings as he was of hers, he kissed her cheek.

'You can't even paint.'

'I have done.'

'Where?'

'At school.'

'You've done nought here.'

'I hadn't any paints.'

Opening his eyes, he gazed at the box again: its shape was still visible, against the embroidered cloth, adjacent to the foot of Alan's bed.

'If you'd wanted some you could have asked for them.'

'I never thought of it.'

His brother was silent; his solemn rhythmical breathing came from the other bed, the sound muffled by the proximity of the blankets.

125

Bryan wanted to get up at that moment and bring the box a little closer; from a distance of several feet he thought he could still detect its smell. The paintbox was a message. It said: 'Have faith. I am with you here as well.'

'You can have a go, if you like,' he added.

'I don't want to,' his brother said. 'Painting's soft.'

'It isn't.'

'I think it is.'

Having decided to get out of bed and move the box, perhaps place it beneath his pillow or on the floor beneath the bed, he now lay back and gazed at it from a greater distance.

'Why did they send you it?'

'I've told you.'

'They could have sent you money.'

'They offered me some.'

'You should have taken it.'

'I didn't want to.'

'Or sent you a book.'

His gaze returned to the box.

'The paints,' he said, 'were what I wanted.'

'You could always send them back,' his brother said.

'No,' he said. 'They're what I wanted,' and, turning on his side, his head arranged on the pillow so that, when he opened his eyes, he could still see the box, he fell asleep.

First there was the red, then, beside the red, came the orange.

Beside the orange came the ochre and, beside that, the yellow.

Beyond the yellows came the blues.

He painted slowly. First the colour deepened then, when dry, it lightened. The figures, with their protuberant limbs, succeeded each other across the page.

'Is that the one you're sending?'

His mother looked over his shoulder.

'Yes.'

'Shouldn't you send them something pretty?'

'Like what?'

'A picture of a country scene.'

'I can't think of one,' he said.

126

He gazed at the massive figures, each straight, its head erect, a gun thrust diagonally across each shoulder. In the distance, against the cloud, was silhouetted the shape of an aeroplane and, beneath the aeroplane, a large explosion, with fragments flying off on either side.

'How about a ship?'

From the row of massive figures he gazed to the blank sheets of the sketch-book; its price having been calculated before he'd gone to fetch it, he felt reluctant to use it at all. For one thing, it contained twenty-four sheets of paper which, by simple calculation, meant that every picture he did, unless he painted on both sides, cost almost a penny.

'I'll finish this,' he said.

The colour flowed from the tip of the brush; occasionally it flowed into the one next to it: one smudged figure led on to the next.

Soon the sheet was a mass of indecipherable shapes and blotches; he looked from the neat rows of colours to the patches of separate colour mixed in the lid, and from the separate patches to the intermingled patches that now obscured the figures altogether.

'You're making a mess.'

His brother leaned across his shoulder.

'It's with everybody watching me,' he said.

'Nay, I'm not watching.' His brother, moments before, had come in from the field, reddened and panting, and now, still panting, stooped over the paper, his features swelling, his black finger poised over the sheet. 'What's that?'

'Soldiers.'

'Looks like a lot of blots to me. Doesn't it look like a lot of blots?' he added to his mother.

'It's only his first try,' she said, yet nevertheless gazing at the sheet with much the same expression.

'He's not roaring about it, is he?'

Bryan had turned away, flung down his brush and, lurching across the room, buried his face in a chair.

He heard his brother laugh.

'Leave him,' his mother said, and added, 'Perhaps it would be better, Bryan, if you did it upstairs.'

127

His arms ached; his hand ached: the restraint imposed upon him in holding the brush had constrained not only the movements of his arm but his feelings.

'I can't do it. I've tried,' he said.

'You can try again,' his mother said.

'It's all wasted.'

'It's not a waste.'

'It's all wasted if I can't use it.' He raised his head; through a blur of tears he saw the paintbox on the table and, worst of all, saw that his brother had picked up the brush and, mixing a colour in the lid, was preparing to paint. 'Leave it.'

He sprang across, missed the brush as his brother, laughing, snatched it away, and called, 'Leave it,' grabbing first at his brother's arm, then at his wrist.

'Let him have it, Alan,' his mother said, and added, as the jar of water spilled, 'Look at the mess you've made.'

'Look at the mess he's painted.' His brother laughed again.

Bryan snatched up the paper; he screwed it up.

'Do you know how much that paper cost?'

'I want the brush!'

'Give him the brush,' his mother said.

'Nay, he can have it,' his brother said.

The sound of a smack followed the movement of his brother's arm.

His mother, red-faced, stood over him.

'Go pick it up,' she said.

'I'll not pick it up.'

'Go get it.'

His brother went to the corner of the room, stooped, straightened and, from where he was standing, tossed the paintbrush back to the table.

'Leave his things alone.'

'I'm not touching them,' his brother said. 'He can make as many messes as he likes for me.'

Bryan closed the lid; he carried the box upstairs: from below came the sound of his brother's voice.

He closed the bathroom door and stood by the basin, one hand on the cistern.

128

He examined his face in the mirror; the dark eyes gazed out, caverned, his cheeks drawn in.

'He's alus crying. And he's alus getting presents. He alus gets the best of everything.'

Why, if things were always going his way, did he feel at a disadvantage? Why, despite all his efforts, had the picture come to nothing? The frustration that he felt he saw in the mirror merely as a tautening of the skin around his eyes, a grimacing of the lips, and saw how several streaks of paint were smeared across each cheek.

He opened the box, washed out the lid, filled one of the declivities with water and, opening the bathroom door, crossed to the bedroom.

He laid the paintbox on the cupboard top, closed the door, and tore a page from the front of the book.

Moistening the brush, he began again.

A lake gave way to a mountain; trees were reflected in the water.

In the foreground, a hump-backed bridge crossed over a stream.

He tore out another page; across the top he painted a hat, light blue, with a sweeping brim, across which dangled the end of a ribbon.

Beneath the brim he set a face, pink, gleaming, the eyes pale-blue, the teeth white, showing in a smile.

The reddened lips he painted when the teeth were dry.

Beneath the face he painted a neck, broadening into the collar of a light-blue dress.

Behind the figure he painted a car, a wheel lying on the floor before it; beyond the car he painted a man, tall, grey-suited and, beyond the man, a hedge and a tree. A bird flew overhead and, by the woman's feet, he painted a flower.

His name, prefixed by the word 'Master', was written on the envelope with the familiar scrawled writing underneath.

He smelled the paper.

A tang of perfume was mixed with the smell of ink.

Inside, the blue-coloured paper was folded twice.

'Dear Bryan,' he read. 'I'm sorry we haven't replied earlier to let you know how much we liked your picture. I wonder if you would like to come to tea? Saturday would be a good day for me. Perhaps you would like to come at four o'clock and I can show you where we have hung your portrait. Yours sincerely, Mrs H. Corrigan.'

'Alan ought to go with you,' his father said, having delayed his departure while Bryan read the letter. 'You've not been up to Chevet,' he added, reading the address at the top of the sheet. 'I don't think Mrs Corrigan has taken into consideration how young you are.'

'I don't want to go,' his brother said, having just come down. He rubbed his tousled head and yawned.

'Neither your mother nor me can take him,' his father said.

'Why not?'

'It wouldn't look right.'

'I don't mind him coming, if he wants to,' Bryan said.

'Tell them he can't come,' his brother said.

'How can I tell them he can't come?' his father asked.

'You can ring them up.'

'You'll take him. It's only on the bus.' He turned from Alan as his brother, yawning, went back upstairs. 'What sort of clothes will you wear?' he added.

'I'll be all right,' Bryan said.

'I don't know what your mother's going to think.'

'She won't mind me going,' Bryan said.

'Nay, she'll be very pleased,' his father said, taking the letter from Bryan and reading it again. 'It's just the expense that's all,' he added. When he left for work, finally, he called from the porch, 'We'll think of summat. Don't worry. We shan't miss out on a chance like this.'

TEN

Alan jangled the coins in his pocket: he glanced up Spinney Moor Avenue, he glanced at the arcade of shops, at the Empire Cinema, the foyer of which was lit for the children's matinée, at the Spinney Moor Hotel, in front of which several cars were parked. 'What's that you've got?'

'Pictures.'

A roll of paintings, covered by a sheet of newspaper, he carried in his hand.

'They want some more, then, do they?'

'I've done them some.'

'What's she like?'

'All right.'

'What's he like?'

'He's very tall.'

When, finally, a bus came into sight, his brother didn't move; it was Bryan who put out his hand and only when the bus slowed did Alan glance up in recognition.

They sat downstairs; his brother handed over the money for the tickets then gazed out at the houses and gardens before the larger buildings of the town began. Finally, as the bus reached the summit of the central hill, he got up and stood at the door, ready to jump off before it halted.

They walked through the narrow streets, crowded with afternoon shoppers, to a stop immediately below the gate of All Saints Church. The clock chimed out a quarter to four and, never having paused by the church, Bryan gazed up at its tall, dog-toothed spire, crowned, against the cloud, with a gold-coloured cockerel, and at the massive white, black-segmented, black-handed face of the clock itself.

'It'll take longer than fifteen minutes. Thy'll never make it.' His brother had never been out to Chevet himself and had asked someone in the queue if they were waiting at the proper stop. When the bus drew up it was already crowded.

They stood downstairs, hemmed in by shoppers.

'Can you tell us where to get off for Carlton Drive?' Alan asked the conductor who, taking the fares, answered over his shoulder.

'That's Corrigan's,' his brother added, indicating a façade of shops outside but, through the intervening heads and shoulders, Bryan merely caught a glimpse of a blur of faces.

The bus rattled on; they crossed the river, and started up the valley side: beyond the nearest roofs lay a stretch of woodland.

The bus emptied; soon, but for one other passenger, they were the only ones downstairs.

The conductor sat across the aisle, counting the money from his bag and checking his tickets.

'Is this Chevet?' his brother asked as the first of several houses came into sight.

'Chevet it is.'

'Where's Carlton Drive?'

'You the ones for Carlton Drive?' He reached up for the bell as the other passengers got up. 'Two stops on.'

The houses, each enclosed by trees, stood back from a central green.

The bus passed on, turned into a narrow lane, and descended the slope the other side.

'Here's Carlton Drive.' The conductor rang the bell.

'Is there a stop for coming back?' his brother said.

'We'll be coming back,' the conductor said, 'in ten or fifteen minutes.'

A stream passed beneath the parapet of a stone-walled bridge: it flowed through a narrow valley, shrouded with trees. At the side of the stream a road wound up the valley side.

They passed between a row of wooden bollards: houses looked out across the valley.

'Do you still want to go?' His brother gazed up at the massive windows. 'They must be millionaires up here.'

In one of the drives a car was parked; a man in uniform leaned over the bonnet.

'Which is the Corrigans'?' he added.

Bryan consulted the paper in his pocket.

'It's called "Aloma".'

'Let's have a look.'

His brother had read the address before setting off; now he examined it more intently.

'Don't they have a number?'

'It doesn't give one.'

They passed a house entitled 'Riviera', its name embellished in gold lettering on the metal gates: a drive curled off across a terraced lawn: at the front of a large stone façade stood several cars.

'You don't have to go if you don't want to.'

'They're expecting me.'

'Perhaps they thought you wouldn't come.' His brother gazed up at a stone mansion, shrouded by trees, the drive to which was approached by a pair of metal gates.

'This is it.'

A lawn swept up to a stone-built terrace; beyond, square windows were inset with leaded glass.

'It might have been politeness.'

'What politeness?'

'Inviting you. They wouldn't expect you to come.'

A metal-studded door was inset within a pillared porch.

'Are you going up?'

'I think so.'

He stepped past his brother and started to the drive.

'Do you want me to come up with you?'

His brother still stood at the open gate; something of the incongruity of his appearance struck Bryan at last: the ill-fitting coat, the trousers which, from a distance, appeared too large, the dishevelled stockings, the bent wings of his collar – his hair, which he had neatly brushed and which, by its neatness, lent an air of absurdity to his half-anxious figure.

'No.' He started up the drive.

His brother was still standing there when he reached the door.

A flight of stone steps ran up to the porch: to one side, in a brass surround, was a white-buttoned bell.

He knocked.

A key was turned and the door drawn back.

A woman in a black dress gazed out; she wore a small white apron.

Then, with narrow features and large brown eyes, she glanced over his head to the garden behind.

'Bryan? We thought you'd got lost.'

The door was opened wider.

'Come in.' She stooped to take his coat. 'Did you come on the bus?'

'We were late catching it,' Bryan said.

'Someone brought you?'

'My brother.'

'Is he outside?'

'He'll have gone now.'

'That was kind of him,' she said.

A broad staircase swept up to a banistered landing.

'You can look at a book Mrs Corrigan's bought you. Come into the sitting-room.' The woman led the way to a door at the end of the hall.

A grand piano stood beside a window; beyond the window a garden, enclosed by flower beds, stretched down to a clump of trees: the roofs and chimneys of another house were visible beyond.

Several chairs were arranged in front of a fire; on one of them, a settee, lay a picture book with a galleon on the cover.

Bryan sat down.

The woman closed the door; he could hear her voice calling from the foot of the stairs.

Feet echoed as they crossed a wooden floor.

The walls of the room stretched up to a decorated ceiling; a frieze of plaster leaves and flowers encircled the lampshade at the centre.

He opened the book, examined the drawings, of ships at sea, of figures fighting, read the heading to one of the chapters, 'Barnabus Strikes Back', and, stooping, smelled the ink.

Above the fireplace hung a picture of cattle standing in water

134

at the edge of a lake. Below it, on the mantelpiece, stood several photographs in wooden frames.

The fire crackled; it had been lit for some time, the redness reflected on the tiles of the hearth and on the stone projections enclosing the grate.

To the side of the fireplace, on a bamboo table, stood a wireless plugged to the wall.

The door opened; a woman dressed in a dark-green skirt and a dark-green jacket came in: her face glowed, its features caught by the light from the window and by the redness of the fire.

'Bryan.'

A smell of perfume filled the room.

'We thought we'd have to come and find you.'

'I came on the bus,' he said.

'And with your brother. You should have brought him in as well.'

She took his hand and, sitting on the settee beside him, added, 'What are those?'

'I've brought you some pictures.'

'You have been prolific.' She removed the elastic band. 'We wondered if it were the right thing to send.' She unrolled the sheets of paper. 'I shall have to look at these more closely.' After glancing at the top one she put them down. 'Have you seen your book?'

She picked it up.

'*Barnabus and the Pirates*. I thought I might read you a story. Mr Corrigan isn't home from work, but when he comes we can have some tea. Then, when you go, you can take it with you.'

Her head erect, her back straight, she turned the pages.

'Do you mind my reading?' she added.

'No,' he said.

'If Mr Corrigan isn't back, I can show you round the house.'

From a table beside the settee she picked up a pair of glasses.

' "Barnabus," ' she read, ' "was sitting at his desk and wondering what he could do at the beginning of the holidays. His parents were away and the house was in the charge of Mrs Kay." ' She paused. 'You've met Mrs Meredith? She was the lady at the door.'

'Yes,' he said.

'Did you like her?'

'Yes.'

'She has children of her own, who are now grown up.' She read again, ' "He stared out of the window to where the path ran down to the cliff." '

Her knees were turned towards him and glistened with the redness of the fire. On her feet, matching the greenness of her skirt, were a pair of green-coloured slippers: they were tucked beneath her so that the weight of her feet rested on her toes.

On the lapel of the jacket she wore a brooch and, beneath the jacket, a white-coloured blouse: a button secured its collar and a row of buttons ran down the front.

Above each blue eye was a smear of colour; her mouth was reddened; flecks of powder showed round her nose.

The curls of hair were shaped in ringlets and danced to and fro, her head raised then lowered to emphasize the effect of someone speaking.

Her forehead glowed.

At no point, while she read, did she glance in his direction; once she glanced at the fire, sideways, still speaking, and once, lifting her head, she glanced at her nails.

She closed the book with a snap.

A smell of scent was mixed with the smell of the ink and the paper.

'That was good!'

On the settee, beside her, were the rolled-up pictures and, dropping the book on top, she added, 'Anyone you recognize?'

She stood and, from the mantelpiece, lifted down a photograph.

A familiar face gazed out from beneath the peak of a riding hat. Margaret was wearing a pair of jodhpurs; in her hand she carried a crop.

She put the photograph down, picked up another, put it down, then picked up a third.

Again, the familiar face gazed out: this time, in the company of Mrs Spencer, Margaret was frowning; she wore a dress and her hair was parted in the middle and arranged in plaits, one of which hung over her shoulder. Mrs Spencer was smiling – her eyes so nervously alive, that, seeing their two figures together, he was

136

drawn to the conclusion that the mother and the daughter had little if anything in common and that, curiously, gazing at the shyness of the smiling face, Mrs Spencer was as much a child as the figure frowning beside her.

Yet, more than any of the photographs, more than any reassurance these glimpses of Mrs Spencer and Margaret might have given him, Bryan was conscious of the hand which held the frames, small, white-skinned, delicately fingered, the nails rounded – and painted so lightly that, at first glance, he assumed the pinkness to be their natural colour.

Inside the wrist he glimpsed her vein, ringed by a bracelet and disappearing beneath the buttoned sleeve of the blouse.

Her hand came down.

'Mr Spencer doesn't like having his picture taken. Nor did he,' she added, 'as a boy.' She laughed; an exhalation of perfume came down as she raised her arm. 'Nor does Margaret. She takes after her father, whereas Mrs Spencer likes it.' She paused. 'Do you like Mrs Spencer?'

'Yes,' he said.

'She's so hard-working. She has so much to do I can never keep track.' Having replaced the photographs on the mantelpiece, she added, 'She hasn't a minute to herself, which I suppose is the lot of a farmer's wife. I wouldn't like the job myself.'

Bryan glanced up at the red-cheeked face, at the lipsticked mouth, at the froth of curls above the green-coloured jacket, and Mrs Corrigan, catching his expression, smiled and said, 'I have no children of my own, otherwise there'd be someone here for you to play with.' She clasped his hand. 'I must show you where we've hung your picture.'

At the door she called across the hall, 'I'm just taking Bryan up, Rose. We'll give Mr Corrigan a few more minutes,' at which a voice called from a room at the back, 'Tea's ready, Mrs Corrigan, whenever you want it.'

The voice was replaced a few moments later by the sound of singing.

They mounted the stairs; doors ran off from the banistered landing: a stained-glass window cast a tinted glow across the polished floor on either side of a broadly-fitted carpet.

'This is my bedroom.' Mrs Corrigan turned to a door which was already open and pushed it back.

A double bed faced a pair of curtained windows; through the windows he could see the trees at the front of the house.

'I keep my clothes through here.'

She crossed to a door the other side; a small room was lined with cupboards, one of which Mrs Corrigan opened.

Dresses, in a multitude of colours, hung from a metal rail; in an adjacent cupboard, in varying colours and a variety of styles, hung a number of coats.

Beneath a window stood a dressing-table with a mirror, hinged at either end. A round mirror stood on a pedestal before it.

On the top of the dressing-table were arranged a number of boxes and bottles; several brushes were set side by side on a glass-bottomed tray.

'This is my den.'

Reflected in the mirror, and echoed in the wing mirrors at either end, he saw Mrs Corrigan smile.

'Where I put myself together, Bryan.'

She opened a second cupboard; skirts and dresses hung from a rail and, beneath the rail, arranged on metal racks, stood innumerable pairs of shoes.

She drew out a dress.

'Do you like it?'

'Yes,' he said.

'One of those I bought the day we met.'

She held it to the light, then drew it against her.

'Margaret is right. I'm putting on weight.'

'I don't think you're fat,' Bryan said.

'Don't you?'

She laughed, gazing down at him, and added, 'If there's one thing I'm looking for, it's praise. That's kind of you to say so.'

She put the dress back, closed the cupboard door, touched her hair lightly and, taking his hand, drew him back once more to the bedroom and out to the landing.

At a door adjacent to the stained-glass window they entered a room which was occupied by a single bed; a cupboard and a

138

wardrobe stood on either side of a window facing the bed and, beneath the window, stood a desk and a chair.

On the wall facing the door was a fireplace, surrounded by tiles and above which, pinned to the wall, was his picture of Mrs Corrigan.

'This is the guest-room. Perhaps you can stay here one day.'

She examined the picture herself.

'It's Mrs Meredith's favourite. She wanted to hang it in the kitchen but I thought the damp might spoil it.' She smiled. 'Everyone admires the likeness.'

She gestured to the room.

'Do you like it?'

'Yes,' he said.

The ceiling, because of its height, and the heavy curtaining of the window, was enclosed in shadow; a frieze of plaster leaves and flowers ran round the top of the walls.

Through the window he could see the garden, the trees and the shrubs and, beyond the trees, the rear windows of a house.

'You can see the moors from here.'

She drew the curtain aside.

Fields ran off from one side of the house and, beyond an intervening barrier of trees and the roof of an adjacent house, rose a darker, undulating line.

'That's Chevet Common. The line beyond is Chevet Moor. Have you ever been up?'

'No,' he said.

'It's wild. You'll like it. It's very pretty. Lots of lovely views up there.'

They returned to the landing.

'That's Mr Corrigan's room. This is the bathroom. You don't want to use it by any chance?'

'No,' he said.

'This is another spare bedroom. Mrs Meredith stays there if we're having guests and it's too late to go back to the village. Do you know Chevet?'

'No,' he said.

'We'll have to show you. It's got lovely houses. Mrs Meredith has a cottage there.'

The sound of a car came from the front of the house and a moment later there was a knock on a door.

'That'll be Lawson's. I've asked them not to drive up to the house, but they still insist on coming.'

She paused by a door at the back of the hall. A murmur of voices came from the other side: a door slammed; a few moments later a car engine was revved at the front of the house.

Mrs Corrigan opened the door and they entered a square-shaped kitchen.

A large table occupied the centre of the floor; a window, beyond it, looked out to the garden.

On the table stood a cardboard box from the top of which protruded a number of packets.

Standing at a stove across the room was the tall, black-dressed figure of Mrs Meredith.

She wore a coloured apron.

'I've told him not to drive up to the house,' Mrs Corrigan said.

'I've told him, Mrs Corrigan. He says it's too heavy to carry from the gate.' She turned to the sink and carried a bowl to the table.

Beside the cardboard box stood a pan of peeled potatoes, a pan of carrots and, on a wooden block, a cabbage which had been cut in half.

Mrs Meredith smiled at Bryan; she had begun cutting up the cabbage, first into quarters, then into eighths, then she placed the leaves in the bowl of water.

'How are you liking your visit, Bryan?'

'I've been reading him a story, Rose,' Mrs Corrigan said. 'And showing him his picture.'

'My favourite.' Mrs Meredith came round the table, pouting her lips and kissing his cheek.

She passed by him to a door, disappeared inside, and came out a moment later with a piece of meat.

'How is dinner coming on, Rose?'

'Another hour,' she said, 'and we'll be under way.'

She placed the meat on the table.

'Three hours from now, Mrs Corrigan, and dinner will be served.'

'Shall we have tea now, or wait for Mr Corrigan?' Mrs Corrigan asked.

'Oh, we'll give him a few minutes,' Mrs Meredith said. 'I thought it was him when I heard Lawson's van. I had the kettle on the gas and now I've turned it off again!'

She laughed, her gaunt face with its large brown eyes turned once more in Bryan's direction.

'Play him one of your songs, Ma'am, I'm sure he won't have heard them,' she added. 'As for tea, it'll all carry through.'

They returned to the hall.

'It's difficult for Mr Corrigan to get back on Saturdays,' she said. 'It's the busiest day of the week. On the other hand, he would have rung up if he couldn't get.'

She indicated a telephone standing on a table by the foot of the stairs.

'Let me show you his study.'

She opened a door with a large brass handle.

The interior was occupied by a large square desk, the top of which was inlaid with leather; two windows looked out to the front of the house.

The walls adjacent to the desk were lined with books; over a mantelpiece hung a framed photograph, several feet in length, across the foot of which was arranged a group of men in long white aprons, with a second standing group behind and, in the background, two large, bow-shaped windows above which, in large lettering, was painted, 'Corrigan and Sons'.

'This is Mr Corrigan's study.'

Mrs Corrigan rearranged a blotter; she rearranged a ruler, an ink-stand, a paper-knife and a rack containing pencils.

'And this is where we shall have tea,' she added, returning to the door, closing it behind them, and opening a door across the hall.

Beneath two curtained windows stood a long rectangular table.

One end of the table had been laid with a cloth: in the centre of the cloth stood several bowls, a cake, and a plate of jelly designed in the shape of a rabbit.

A fire glowed in a marble-fronted grate.

'Do you like salmon?'

'Yes,' he said.

'Those are the sandwiches Mrs Meredith has made. Also a jelly.'
She indicated the red-shaped mound standing by the cake. 'Mrs
Spencer was telling me when you went to tea at the farm you were
taken ill.'

'Yes.'

'I hope it's not a habit.'

'No.'

'If you'd like to look at your book I'll telephone Mr Corrigan
and see if he's left.'

They returned to the sitting-room and Mrs Corrigan went out
to the hall.

Her voice came a moment later from beyond the door.

He sat down, pulled up his stockings, and gazed at the fire.

Through Mrs Corrigan's voice came the more distant sound of
Mrs Meredith singing.

Then, from the front of the house, came the sound of a car.

'There he is now,' Mrs Corrigan called and, a moment later,
the front door was opened and he heard Mrs Corrigan add, 'I
was just ringing, Harold, to see where you were.'

'Delayed,' came Mr Corrigan's voice followed, after a further
moment, by the sound of a kiss. 'Has Bryan arrived?'

'In the sitting-room.'

'Have you shown him his book?'

'I've read him a story.'

'Seen his picture?'

'He has.'

'Not missed tea?'

'Not yet.'

The door opened.

'Here we are,' Mrs Corrigan added.

Mr Corrigan followed her in.

'Here he is, is he?' he said. 'Found us without too much trouble,
did he?'

'His brother brought him up.'

'Did he?'

Mr Corrigan wore a dark-grey suit in the buttonhole of which
was a large red flower: his tie, also red, protruded conspicuously
from a stiff white collar.

'We thought of meeting you in town and giving you a lift,' he added, shaking Bryan's hand, his features lightened in their gravity by the glow from the fire. 'Then, at the last moment, it proved too late to write you a letter. We trusted you'd find your way, after the initiative you showed in mending our tyre.'

'I told you we'd get our own back, Bryan,' Mrs Corrigan said, and added, 'When Mr Corrigan is ready we can have some tea.'

'Oh, I shan't be a moment,' Mr Corrigan said. 'I've been looking forward to this tea all day. I've been saving up for it, as a matter of fact.' One dark eye was closed while the other remained fixed on Bryan. 'I don't often have tea,' he added. 'So I thought I'd miss out on lunch.'

He disappeared to the hall.

'And these are your pictures,' Mrs Corrigan said, retrieving the roll from the settee. 'Mr Corrigan and I can look at them later. Do you want to take your book with you, or will you leave it here?'

'I'll take it with me,' Bryan said.

As they turned to the door Mrs Corrigan laughed, and said, 'I meant, take it in to tea. Mr Corrigan hasn't seen it yet.'

'I'll take it with me,' he said, confused, and they returned to the hall and from there to the room where the tea was laid.

Mrs Corrigan took her own place facing Bryan, the chair between them, at the end of the table, left for Mr Corrigan.

Mrs Meredith came in.

'See he leaves none of it behind. I don't want to see any left,' she said. 'Nor any of that jelly.'

'We've waited long enough, Rose,' Mrs Corrigan said. 'I'm sure he'll do it justice.'

'Justice is all I ask.' Mrs Meredith smiled and, after the door had closed, Mrs Corrigan said, 'Rose has a charming sense of fun. She can't resist a joke, and is especially fond of children,' and added, 'You're the first young person we've invited to tea for a very long time.'

The door reopened, Mr Corrigan came in: he took his place at the table, bowed his head, placed his hands together and, waiting for Bryan and Mrs Corrigan to do the same, said, 'For what we are about to receive may the Good Lord make us truly grateful.'

'Amen,' Mrs Corrigan said.

'Amen,' Mr Corrigan and Bryan said together, the former handing the plate of sandwiches to Mrs Corrigan, then to Bryan, and adding, 'Now, then, let's see if, between the three of us, we can't make a hole in this.'

ELEVEN

He ran up the path and, thinking the occasion warranted it, knocked on the front door, tested the handle and found it fastened.

He ran round to the back, glimpsed the trail of smoke from the chimney of the den, heard the shouts of several of the boys and, opening the back door, called, 'Mother!'

The scullery was empty and when he went through to the living-room the fire was out.

'Dad?'

He went to the stairs, called, waited, then went out to the garden.

His father's bike was missing; his own and his brother's were thrown against the fence.

He glanced out at the field; the sun was setting beyond a bank of cloud: a faint mistiness, interspersed with smoke, overhung the houses.

'Alan?'

He heard someone shout, 'Thy kid's back, Ally.'

No one appeared from the den.

He went back in the house and closed the door.

He looked in the pantry; the Saturday's shopping was arranged on the shelves, but not in a manner, he knew, which would have pleased his mother.

Returning to the living-room he sat by the fire.

He opened the book, glanced at the pictures, following the sequence through from the coloured frontispiece to the black-and-white drawing of a galleon, silhouetted, sailing into a sunset, at the back, then got up from the chair and took off his coat.

He went out to the garden again; the air was chill: avoiding the clay he climbed the fence and crossed over the field to the mouth of the den. Only as he ducked down to gaze inside did a face peer out.

145

A moment later the face was replaced by that of his brother.

'Where's my mother?'

'She's gone to our Granny's.' His brother had changed back to his older clothes and wasn't wearing his jacket: his face was blackened; a thin drift of smoke came up from the entrance as well as the chimney.

'Where's my dad?'

'He went with her.'

'What for?'

'They went to show off.'

'What about?'

'The Corrigans. My dad came back. He got on his bike and went down to the pub.'

'When's she coming back?'

His brother shrugged. 'I've no idea.'

He stepped back from the hole.

'They've given me a present.'

'What?'

'A book.'

His brother's face disappeared.

''Op it, Kipper,' Barraclough said. 'We don't want any young 'uns here.'

A murmur of voices came from the darkness of the hole then someone called, 'Gi'e o'er,' then his brother's voice called, 'Has he gone, then, Cloughie?'

In addition to the smell of the wood smoke came the smell of cigarettes.

Bryan returned to the garden, climbed the fence, and went back inside the house.

He sat down once more in front of the fire, gazing at the ashes, rooting at them finally with the poker and, finding no glow, sat back again.

He looked at the clock.

Beside it, propped up, was a sheet of paper.

On it, in his father's writing, was printed, 'Gone out. Back soon. Dad.'

He turned on the wireless; he was still listening to it when the back door opened and his brother came in.

146

'Are they back?'

Bryan shook his head.

'Have you let the fire out?'

'It was out already.'

His brother's hands were grimy, his face black; his shoes and his stockings, his knees and his elbows, his trousers and his pullover, were covered in mud.

'They said to keep it in.'

His brother poked the ashes and added, 'I'd better light it,' then, glancing up, he asked, 'Is that the book they give you?'

He took it from him, turning the pages.

'You'll mucky it.'

'I'll not.'

Having looked at the illustrations, then at the cover, he gave him it back.

'They said you should have come in,' Bryan said.

'It was you they asked for.' His brother went through to the scullery. 'Have you had some tea?' came his voice.

'They gave me some.'

His brother came back with a bucket and a shovel.

'What wa' the house like?'

'Big.'

'Wa' both of them theer?'

'Mr Corrigan came later.'

'Have they got any kids?'

'No.'

His brother, having filled the bucket with ashes, went out again.

Bryan heard the bucket clank in the garden, then came the rumble of the coal in the coal-house as his brother filled it.

The back door closed and he came back in.

'I'm not doing all of it. Tha can go outside and chop some wood. I'll not ge' it lit wi'out.'

Bryan went out to the porch; he got the wood from the coal-house and chopped it on the step.

When he went back in his brother had crumpled up the paper and swept the hearth: he laid the pieces of wood on top of the paper, then put on pieces of coal, tipped the bucket over it and, having poured half of it on, added, 'You can go out and fill it.'

147

When Bryan came back the fire was burning behind a piece of newspaper propped up on the shovel.

They gazed at the blaze, Alan sitting forward on his chair, his arms across his knees.

'They've invited me again.'

'When?'

'I don't know.' He shook his head.

'What did they think to your pictures?'

'They said they'd frame them.'

'All of 'em?'

'One or two.' He paused again. 'They're giving one as a present, at Christmas, to Mr and Mrs Spencer.'

'Thy's moving on.' His brother's hair was disarranged and his shirt was grimier than ever. His jersey, too, was torn at the waist, and there were holes in each of his elbows. 'What did they give you for tea?'

'Salmon.'

'I' sandwiches?'

'And jelly.'

His brother nodded; from the darkness of the field came several shouts and, looking out of the window, Bryan saw the outline of figures running past.

'I mightn't go back.'

'Why not?'

Bryan shook his head.

'They might do summat for you.'

'What?'

It was his brother's turn to shake his head. 'You never know. They might come up wi' summat.'

The glow reddened and the sheet of paper began to burn; Alan reached forward and drew the paper off.

The flames licked up around the coal.

'I suppose he'll say we should have used wood i'stead o' coal. But there's not much heat in a bit of wood.' He added, 'I'd go, if they invited me.'

'Why?' he said.

'What chance do you have round here?'

'To do what?'

'Anything.'

Bryan's hand crept out to feel the smoothness of the book and for the first time, too, he felt a sense of reassurance, not merely in his brother's tone, but in the fact that Mr and Mrs Corrigan existed, that they had given him a present, and that the book, like a credential, lay beside him, an indication that there were forces in his life that were stronger than those in the lives of anyone around him.

'I'll do summat,' Alan said.

'What will you do?' Bryan asked.

'Nay, I'll do something,' Alan said. 'I'll make something of my life. I'll not be like all the rest round here. Cloughie's going into decorating like his father and Shawcroft says he's off i' the mill, and I suppose Donny'll work in his father's shop.'

'But what will you do?' he asked again.

'I s'll be a boxer.'

Bryan saw that perhaps his brother had been talking about this to his friends in the den: the declaration came, not so much with an air of resolution, as in a reflective, almost inquiring tone of voice, as if the decision, though made, had already been questioned. He could imagine Barraclough saying, 'Thy can't beat me,' and laughing. 'So how's thy going to be a boxer?' and yet he thought that, although Alan never had, his brother could beat Barraclough in a fight and that it was because he could beat him that he allowed Barraclough's authority to prevail.

'When will you start?'

'I do some now.'

'What sort of boxing?' Bryan asked.

'There's only one sort. I s'll turn professional. Tangey,' his brother added, referring to a teacher at the school, 'says he'll teach me.'

Bryan picked up the book again, glanced at it in the faded light, and asked, 'Shouldn't they have been back by now?'

'I don't know about my dad, but my mother should.'

'Did they have a quarrel?'

'Don't ask me.' His brother shrugged; he leaned forward, picked up the poker, and lifted the coals at the front of the fire: the flames, dying down, were re-ignited.

'If they don't come soon we can make some supper.'

Having put down the poker, he leant back in his chair.

'How did you come back?'

'In a car.'

'What kind wa're it?'

'An Alvis.'

'My dad says Spencer's is a Wolseley.'

'Mr Corrigan's is bigger.'

'Did you sit i' the front?'

'Yes.'

The elation of returning from the Corrigans' had begun to fade; it had begun to fade, initially, with his returning to the house to find no one there, the fire out, and to see the plates from the dinner washed but not dried on the draining-board by the sink – something his mother normally would never have allowed.

More certainly, however, the elation was being replaced by a feeling of unease; Mrs Corrigan disturbed him: she was not at all like she had been at the Spencers', nor on the roadside when she'd watched him help to change the tyre, nor how she'd been when she'd waved to him, in passing, from the window.

'If they invited me again, I'd go,' his brother said.

It was the first disinterested attention Alan had shown him and he wondered, after recognizing it as such, if there wasn't another motive.

'I might.'

'Are they posh?'

'They have a servant.'

'What's she do?'

Bryan paused; he had liked Mrs Meredith despite her appearance which, at first sight, might have discouraged anyone from liking her at all. When he was leaving and he had gone down to the car she had come to the door and had stood there, waving.

'She brings in the food and serves it.'

'Tangey reckons I should be a heavyweight when I'm fully grown. He reckons I should have a build like Harvey.'

'Who's Harvey?'

'Have you never heard of Harvey?'

His brother glanced across.

'Harvey's the best boxer we've ever had. Middleweight, light-heavyweight, heavyweight. There's nought he hasn't fought at.'

As he spoke they heard the rattle of his father's bike as it was propped against the fence and a moment later his feet sounded at the door.

The sneck rattled.

His brother stood up.

The back door opened, his father coughed then, calling, 'Alan?' he coughed again.

A moment later came the sound of someone falling.

The room shook.

Alan crossed over to the hall and stood in the threshold of the scullery, gazing in.

His father was lying on the floor, sprawled out towards the sink.

'Dad?'

His father groaned; he had still got on his cycle clips and was dressed in his suit, the soles of his shoes turned up to the light.

'Dad?'

Alan stepped into the scullery and his father stirred.

One set of his father's false teeth had fallen out and lay on the floor beside what looked like a pool of spittle.

'Wheer's the light?'

His father spoke with his mouth compressed against the carpet: his cheek was cushioned underneath and from the corner of his mouth came a stream of bubbles.

Alan stooped down; all Bryan could see were the backs of his brother's legs, the swelling of his calves as he took his father's weight.

'Gi'e us a hand, Bryan.'

Bryan caught his father's arm and, with Alan tugging at the other, tried to lift him.

'What's up, Dad?'

'What?'

'What's up?'

His father closed his eyes.

151

'Wheer's the light? Who left it off ?'

'Is he ill?' Bryan asked.

His brother gazed down at his father's teeth, at the curve of the plate that fitted his father's mouth, and at the pool of blood-flecked spittle.

'Should I fetch Mr Foster?'

His brother shook his head.

'Or Mr Patterson?'

'I shouldn't.'

His brother's fear, curiously, dispelled any fear in Bryan himself. He thought, 'If Alan is frightened there's no need for me to be frightened, too,' and he wondered in that instant, as he gazed down at the figure of his father and then looked up at his brother standing, helplessly, with his legs astride it, if he didn't despise his brother to the exclusion of everything else: 'And yet, why should I?' he thought, for he couldn't help but feel that his father lying there and his brother standing astride of him, that they were, for some reason, curiously united.

'Shall we lift him again?'

'Aye.'

'Wheer's the light?' His father moaned as they lifted him together.

'Can you get up, Dad?' Alan asked.

Bryan lifted the teeth and, feeling the slime on the plate, dropped them in the sink.

'He's drunk.'

'I thought he was ill.'

'Can't you smell it? He's had too much to drink.'

His father moaned.

It was inconceivable to Bryan that his father should be drunk. As he gazed at the figure on the floor and recognized a growing relief in Alan that his father wasn't ill, Bryan felt that he had been cut off from his father for good; he could never imagine him to be again the father that he had known before, nor could he imagine joining in his brother's relief that what his father had done was not important, and, going by his brother's reaction, could even be condoned.

'By go,' his brother said, 'he's plastered.'

Alan gazed at his father with a look of respect; then, in the back of his throat, he began to snigger.

'Let's get him up.'

They stooped to his father again.

'Come on, Dad,' his brother said.

'I s'll be all right,' his father said.

'Come on, Dad,' Alan said again, and added to Bryan, 'Grab 'o'd of his legs.'

Half-carrying, half-dragging, they drew him into the living-room and on to a chair, his father's head subsiding against one arm, his legs thrust up on the other.

'I'd better wash his face.'

His father, his eyes closed, had begun to snore.

'I'd leave off the light,' Alan said. 'We'll let him sleep.'

Liquid gurgled in his father's throat.

'I'd better put a bucket here in case he's sick.'

Bryan fetched a flannel from the bathroom; his brother, when he came down, had taken off his father's shoes.

'Can you get us a towel?'

Alan stooped across his father's face.

'Will he be all right?'

'He'll be all right. He might have brok' his nose when he fell. He won't know,' he added, 'until he wekens.'

Bryan brought the towel through.

His brother, stooping over his father, had begun to laugh. 'Would you believe it?' he said, and added, 'have you got the bucket?'

Bryan went through to the scullery, poured water into the bucket and brought it in: he stood it by his father's head.

'I'll be all right,' his father said. He echoed, 'All right,' his chest and his jacket streaked with spittle.

'Wheer's our mother?' Alan asked.

'She's gone back home.'

'What home?'

'Thy Granny's home.'

'Is she coming back?'

'I've no idea.' His father paused. 'We had a quarrel.'

'What about?'

'The Corrigans.' He closed his eyes.

'I s'll fetch a coat and cover him up.' His brother wiped his father's jacket and added, 'That'll need washing. What a smell,' and took the towel and the flannel through to the kitchen.

Bryan gazed down at his father sprawled with his feet on the arm of the chair, at the fringe of hair which had fallen across his brow, at the strange animation of the face which came with the flickering of the fire, and was suddenly conscious that his father's eyes were open.

'Are you all right?'

From the scullery came the sound of Alan washing his hands.

His father's chin was compressed against his chest, his head forced forward by the arm of the chair: his mouth didn't move, and in the one eye only the firelight flickered.

'Can I get you anything?'

'Nothing.'

'Do you want to go upstairs?'

'I'll lie down here.' A moment later he resumed his snoring.

'What wa're he saying?' Alan said, bringing with him his father's overcoat from a peg in the hall.

'I think he's awake.'

'Do you want to get up, Dad?' Alan said, and though he stooped over him and added, 'Do you want to go up?' his father didn't reply. His brother laid the coat over his father's legs. He began to laugh. 'It doesn't half smell. It smells in here, an' all,' he added.

Bryan went through to the scullery: there was the outline on the carpet of his father's head.

He opened the back door to clear the air.

His brother had gone upstairs.

Voices called: feet sounded on a path.

He went into the living-room and got his book: it was lying on the floor where, in putting his father down, his brother had dropped it: he glanced at the strange symmetry of his father's feet thrust up beneath the coat and, hearing his brother come downstairs, went out to the hall, closing the door of the living-room behind him.

'Will you be all right on your own?' his brother said.

'Where are you going?'

'I' the field.'

'Can I come with you?'

'They won't have you.'

He crossed to the door.

'You're not frightened, are you?'

'No,' he said.

'He'll be all right in yonder.'

He looked at the book in his hand.

'You can read your book.'

The back door banged.

The thudding of his brother's feet was followed by a shout, 'Donny!' as he climbed the fence.

He put the book down on the mangle.

Not wanting to go upstairs, he picked up the tea-towel and began to dry the pots; he banged the plates, then the cups, stacking them on the mangle top, then he clattered the two pans, reaching up to put them on the scullery shelf, hoping the sound might waken his father.

Through the closed door of the living-room came his father's snores and, at one moment, when they paused, and an intense silence filled the house, he waited, the tea-towel in his hand; then, with a snort, the snoring began again.

He went into the pantry; on the stone shelf was the piece of meat for the Sunday's dinner.

The biscuit tin was empty.

In the bread bowl was a loaf his mother had bought that morning.

He came out, picked up his book, put the light out, and went upstairs; he wondered if he should lock the door: on the other hand, he could take the pots through to the cupboard by the fire, and stack them in their usual place and, perhaps, with the noise, his father might wake and, feeling better, get up and go to bed.

He put on the bathroom light: his brother had laid his pyjamas over the cistern in order to get them warm, and it was with something of a shock that he realized his own were still downstairs in the cupboard next to the fire.

He washed his face and cleaned his teeth and, still holding the book, went back downstairs.

He opened the living-room door; his father's arm had fallen to the floor, the hand upturned: his head, too, had been turned towards the fire and the light of the flames danced across his features.

A crust of blood had formed around his nose.

As Bryan crossed the room his father stirred; his breathing faltered.

He opened the cupboard door, got out his pyjamas, and re-crossed the room in front of the fire.

His father, suddenly, flung out a hand: his breathing then his snoring recommenced; a strand of saliva glistened from his mouth.

He closed the door and went upstairs.

He undressed in the bathroom, put his clothes on the banister then, glancing along the landing, crossed to his bedroom door, felt inside, switched on the light, glanced in, closed the door behind him and, reluctant to allow his fear to persuade him to look inside the wardrobe, got into bed.

He laid the book on the counterpane, closed his eyes, and thought, 'No one will kill me while I'm saying my prayers, nor will anyone kill me while my father is snoring,' and, after praying, 'God bless Mother, Father and Alan, and make Bryan a good boy, Amen,' he added, 'Will my mother come home soon? Amen,' and wondered, as he glanced round the room, if angels would guard his father if he were drunk, or whether, even, they might abandon him and the family altogether, gazing at the tasselled lampshade then at the cover of *Barnabus and the Pirates*, then getting out of bed and laying the book beside the paintbox on the wooden projection behind the door.

He drew the covers up and listened intently to the sounds of his father.

Only a faint murmur, periodically, came from the room downstairs.

What would the Corrigans think if they could see him now? What would they have thought of him that afternoon if they had known what was going to happen that evening? He recalled the ten to

156

fifteen minutes sitting in the car, the smell of the petrol; and recalled, too, the strange mixture of excitement and apprehension
evoked by Mrs Corrigan herself.

The back door opened. A moment later came the sound of his
mother's step.

The woodwork creaked: having started on the stairs his mother
paused; then, after an interval of silence, the steps came on again,
mounting to the landing.

'Bryan?'

He raised his head.

'Are you all right?'

'Yes.'

A light came in from the landing.

'Where's Alan?'

'He's out.'

'At this time?'

'He won't be long.'

'Who put your father on the settee?'

'We did.'

'What happened to him?'

'He must have tripped.'

'Where?'

'In the scullery.'

She came into the room.

'How did you get on at the Corrigans'?'

'They gave me a book?'

'Another?'

'It's the only one they've given me.'

'I mean,' his mother said, 'another present. Did you come back
on the bus?'

'They brought me in their car.'

'Did they?'

His mother's hand had grasped his shoulder.

'Were they pleased with your pictures?'

'They said they'd frame some.'

'That's good.'

Her fingers squeezed his arm.

Then, releasing him, she added, 'I'll see to Alan.'

She lurched against the bed, dislodged it, drew it back, then continued to the door.

'Good night,' she said.

'Good night,' Bryan said and, from within the shield of his blankets, he saw Mrs Corrigan's face silhouetted in the door before his mother closed it.

TWELVE

'You can have another one. I don't have to save any until after.'

His hand crumpled the paper inside the box, drew out another chocolate and, not familiar with the shape, he bit it, tasted something soft, sucked it quickly, then swallowed it.

The light flickered in its passage through the smoke-filled air.

'Do you like Ginger Rogers?'

'Yes,' he said.

'She's pretty.'

'Yes.'

Periodically she pulled herself upright, depressing the back of his seat as well as her own, pushing her legs sideways, their knees colliding, at which, sharply, she whispered, 'Sorry!'

He didn't like the dancing figures; yet the warmth of the cinema was sufficient to distract him and, on each occasion that the screen was filled with a gigantic head in which the mouth opened like a cavern and the lips tremored and the teeth were bared, he gazed up at the larger orifice of the stage itself. In addition, there were the chocolates and the intermittent bustling in the seat beside him, the hissed, 'Sorry!' and the occasional, 'Do you like her dress?' Perhaps it was the smell of the perfumed box of chocolates which reminded him of Mrs Corrigan but, in each made-up face, bright with lipstick, powder and rouge, with its sparkling, pencilled-in eyes, he struggled to identify her features.

'You didn't have to come if you didn't want to,' Margaret said as they came out to the foyer.

'I wanted to,' he said.

'You were wriggling all the time.'

'You were.'

'I was wriggling, if I was, because I was excited.'

159

'I didn't know I was wriggling.'

'You were.'

He saw how her mouth was streaked with chocolate and he wondered, as he wiped his own, at the propriety of pointing it out to her, or whether it might be better if she discovered it herself.

'You've got chocolate on your mouth.'

'Have I?' Instantly a handkerchief was taken from her pocket and she rubbed her cheek. 'Why didn't you tell me?'

'I have told you.'

'Earlier.'

'I've only just seen it.'

'Is it off?'

He examined her mouth.

'I think so.'

'Honestly!'

She returned the handkerchief to her pocket.

'Where did you get the chocolates?' he asked.

'Mummy knows someone who keeps a shop.'

She was gazing about her, still standing on the steps.

'Is your father meeting you?' he said.

'No.' Having pulled on her beret, she added, 'He says I have to show you to your stop.'

'I know the way.'

'It's what he said.'

They walked up the hill which led past the church to the Bull Ring. Over her shoulder she carried her satchel and in her hand the box of chocolates.

The invitation to go to the cinema had been brought by his father, and the money to go had been saved for over two weeks. However, the coins were still in his pocket and all he had spent was his fare on the bus.

'That's Uncle Harold's shop.'

Two plate-glass windows, bevelled outwards, flanked, between them, a glass-panelled door. Bryan identified, inside the panes, the shape of a table.

'It's very expensive.' Margaret breathed on the glass. 'Even Daddy can't afford it.'

160

'Who can afford to buy it?' Bryan said.

'Only the best.' She raised her head. 'There's an upstairs as well.'

'Have you been in?'

'Once or twice.' She indicated a passage at the side. 'That goes down to the workshop. They make the furniture as well.'

They continued up the hill.

'How did you like Aunt Fay?' she added.

'I like her,' Bryan said.

'She's very nervous.'

'Why nervous?'

'Mummy says she's nervous. She's very tense.'

'I hadn't noticed,' Bryan said.

'She's like a child.'

They walked in silence; vehicles edged up and down the hill, the headlights casting glimmerings on the road which were reflected in the panes of the shops on either side. A figure passed them on the pavement.

'She likes you,' she added.

'Why?'

'You tell me.' She hummed a tune from the film, then added, 'Daddy says I shouldn't have invited you to the cinema and Mummy says I should.'

'Why shouldn't you?'

'He says I shouldn't encourage you.'

They were almost opposite her stop; the outline of the church dominated the slope at the top of the hill.

'Perhaps she can't have children,' Margaret added.

'Why not?'

'Some women can't. It's to do with their insides. Why else,' she added, 'should she invite you?'

It was a thought which had preoccupied Bryan himself and the only conclusion he had come to was that Mrs Corrigan was aware of who he was.

'Do you like going to see her?'

'Yes.'

'Are you hoping she'll leave you something when she dies?'

'Is she going to die?'

161

'*When* she dies.' Margret added, 'Uncle Harold wouldn't allow it.'

'Why wouldn't he?'

'He thinks she's making a fool of herself.'

She stepped aside to allow someone to pass; a moment later a voice said, 'Why, Margaret! What on earth are you doing here?'

'Hello, Aunt,' Margaret said. 'We've been to the pictures.'

Mrs Corrigan's face was invisible beneath the brim of a hat. 'What film have you been to?' she asked.

'The Regal.'

'I was meeting Mr Corrigan there,' she said. 'I've just come up to town on the bus.'

'We went after school.' Margaret glanced down the hill as if, despite the coincidence of their meeting, she were wishing her aunt to go.

'Is it worth seeing?'

'I enjoyed it very much. Bryan didn't. Except for the news.'

'Are you on your way home?'

'I'll catch the bus when I've seen Bryan to his stop,' Margaret said.

'That's kind of you.' Mrs Corrigan stooped to Bryan to see him more closely.

'I was told I had to,' Margaret said.

'I'm wondering whether I shouldn't see you on to yours,' Mrs Corrigan said. 'Wandering around in the dark at this time. I'm surprised your mother allows it.'

'I've done it before,' Margaret said.

'Did they know it would finish as late as this?'

'Mummy suggested it,' Margaret said.

'And you've been into town on your own before?'

'Often.'

'It can't be often.'

'If I have to stay behind at school it's often dark by the time I get back.'

'Only in winter.'

'I like it darker.'

'Do you?'

Still she stood there.

'I'd still better see you to your bus.'

'I don't mind,' Margaret said. 'There's one coming now, as a matter of fact.' As the glow of the vehicle appeared from behind the church and its headlights focused on the cobbled slope, she added, 'What about Bryan?'

'I'll see him to his,' Mrs Corrigan said.

Bryan was conscious of Margaret's gaze as she turned to the bus and, the next instant, Mrs Corrigan had grasped their hands and was leading them across the road.

'Good night, Aunt,' Margaret said once they'd reached the other side. 'I'll tell Mother I saw you.'

'Take care the other end,' Mrs Corrigan said.

'I shall.'

Margaret mounted the bus: her white stockings flashed against the metal steps then, with a run, she disappeared to the upper deck.

'That's one girl where charity goes astray,' Mrs Corrigan said. 'Where's your stop, Bryan?' she added.

'It's in the Bull Ring.'

'Stainforth estate. Which do you have, the Town Road or the Moor Top bus?'

'The Town Road.'

She turned along the pavement, holding his hand. 'I used to travel by bus a great deal when I was younger. The Moor Top bus especially.'

'Did you live at Moor Top?' Bryan asked, for this was the area beyond Stainforth, beyond the church, the school and the hospital, where several larger houses stood.

'I travelled up there almost every day. But things have changed a great deal since then.'

They passed round the darkened edifice of the church and, by a shop-enclosed lane, entered the triangulated area of the Bull Ring. A bus from the Town Road stop was pulling out.

'There, then, that's a nuisance,' she said. 'How long to the next one?'

'I can wait,' Bryan said. One or two other people, running up to the stop, were gazing after the bus themselves.

'I can't leave you on your own,' Mrs Corrigan said. 'Now you're

163

in my charge.' She stepped back into the doorway of a shop: its glass panes enclosed them in a narrow porch.

Her hand came down and drew up his collar.

'I'm sorry the picture wasn't much fun.'

'Perhaps you'll like it,' Bryan said.

'Oh, I shall. Anything that's gay and happy.' Mrs Corrigan laughed, and added, 'We'll miss the second feature, but that doesn't matter.'

They stood in silence; other people joined the queue or stood like them against the shop. He was conscious not only of the warmth but of the pressure of her hand.

'How thin your coat is. Is that the only one you've got?'

'Yes.'

She gazed across the street to the illuminated windows of the Buckingham Hotel: balconies looked out to the street below; figures moved to and fro behind the panes. A faint sound of music came from an open door.

'Did you enjoy your visit?' she asked.

'Yes,' he said.

On his mother's advice he had written to Mrs Corrigan to thank her for the tea and for the present of the book.

'Mr Corrigan and I have been wondering how, in the future, we might help you.'

'How?' he said.

'For one thing, with your education. For another,' she continued, 'with your clothes.'

He felt the warmth of her breath on his face.

His hand was squeezed more tightly.

Then, as the bus drew up, she added, 'We'll have to see what the future holds,' and, drawing him to the bus door, she called, 'Good night,' and, walking several steps along the pavement, her figure illuminated by the streetlamps, waved as the bus drew out from the stop.

The letter, held in his mother's hand, had a serrated edge and the writing which occupied it had been set out neatly down the centre; a second page had been completed and a third page had been written halfway down. He recognized the scrawl unfamiliar

164

only with the straightness of the lines and the neatness of the setting out.

His mother, having read the letter, read it once again.

'Who's it from?' his brother asked.

'The Corrigans.'

His brother stood up.

'They want him to go to Peterson's.'

'What's Peterson's?' Neither Alan nor his mother had glanced at Bryan since the letter had arrived.

'It's a private school.'

'What do they want him theer for?'

'They're prepared to pay the fees.'

'Does he have to live theer?' his brother asked.

'They've suggested he stays at Chevet, and comes back home at weekends.' She folded the letter up. 'Have the Corrigans mentioned it to you?'

'No,' Bryan said. 'I haven't even heard of Peterson's.'

'It's a private school. In town.' She added, 'I suppose the idea of your going there is to give you a better start, and the idea of you living at the Corrigans',' she paused, 'is to give you a better address. They'd hardly expect a pupil to come from Stainforth.'

'Why not?'

'In summer,' his mother said, 'they wear a straw hat.'

His brother laughed.

His mother replaced the letter inside the envelope, held it in her hand a moment, then set it on the mantelshelf, behind the clock.

'Did they mention another school?' she asked.

'No,' he said.

His brother pulled on his jacket and stood in the door.

'Are you going to let him go, then, Mother?'

His mother shook her head. 'I might. What will you feel like?' she added.

'I don't mind.' His brother shifted his weight from one foot to the other.

'Why not?'

'If they've offered him a chance, why should he turn it down?' His brother clenched his fists. 'He can alus come home at the weekends,' he added, 'if thy doesn't want to see him i' uniform up here.'

His mother stood over the fire; finally, she glanced at Bryan.

'Any road,' Alan said, 'that's what I think,' and, having drawn on his coat, he called, 'I'm off,' and was out of the door before his mother could answer.

'So much for his thoughts,' she said.

Bryan went out to the hall to get his coat.

'Do they criticize the way we've brought you up?' she asked.

'No,' Bryan said.

'Her letter is considerate enough, but I don't think she's aware of the complications. Not all of them.' She followed him to the scullery.

'I wouldn't mind going to a better school,' he said.

'Wouldn't you?'

'I could be an artist,' Bryan said.

His mother laughed. 'What does an artist do?' she said. 'Can you imagine an artist on Stainforth estate? How, when you leave school, would you earn a living?'

'By selling pictures.'

She laughed again.

'You'll sell none round here. Nor anywhere else. You've to have a job to earn a living. Being an artist,' she concluded, 'isn't one.'

At the door, she added. 'We can't give to one child what we don't to the other: that's something Mrs Corrigan, with not having any children, fails to understand.'

She watched him from the scullery window as he walked down the path and he imagined her still watching as he set off along the road.

Ahead of him, halfway up the hill, he could see his brother walking with an arm on Barraclough's shoulder and his own, in turn, supporting Shawcroft's.

Walking up the other side of the road was Alison Foster and a group of girls; he could hear their shouts and the occasional call from his brother, from Barraclough and, also walking with their group, from O'Donald.

At school he gazed at his teacher, Miss Mitchell, and transposed her features into those of Mrs Corrigan. Miss Mitchell was an 'old' person: she was past the age when she might have married but was nowhere near as old as Miss Walters who was the deputy

166

Headmistress, and who had hair bristling in clusters from her chin; nor was she, he suspected, as old as his mother nor even as old as Mrs Corrigan herself, whom he didn't think of as 'old' nor, indeed, as of any definite 'age' at all.

Miss Mitchell wore glasses, whereas Mrs Corrigan did not; but she had the same full-lipped mouth, and the same pink-tinted cheeks and similar, though not as clearly marked, blue eyes. Unlike Mrs Corrigan, she didn't wear make-up but, in the slanting, down-ward-projecting light of the room, this was scarcely noticeable: even her hair, though roughly groomed, was comprised of the same profusion of tawny-coloured curls which, like Mrs Corrigan's, fell forward in a fringe across her brow.

If he were to stay at Stainforth Miss Mitchell was the teacher he would have like to have stayed with; if he were to leave she was the person he would miss the most. As he listened to the transposed Mrs Corrigan mark the register and watched her laying out the work for the lesson, he wondered what his mother might be doing at home, whether she might not, having glanced at the letter, be reconsidering her decision in the light of what his brother had said.

What Alan had said took him on to speculate on what his father would have to say; which in turn took him on to conclude that Mrs Corrigan's suggestion, so casually executed – he could imagine her stooped to Mr Corrigan's desk and writing the letter without raising her head – had, with his father, less chance of succeeding than it had with his mother.

'Have you heard that, Bryan?'

An exercise book had been placed on his desk: across his shoulder he felt the pressure of Miss Mitchell's hand.

'What did I say?'

'Page nine.'

'You haven't looked at it,' she said.

'No, Miss Mitchell.'

'I often wonder if you're with us half the time.'

Miss Mitchell seldom lost her temper; her pale-blue eyes would widen with alarm if something were done which she disliked: the alarm was not her own but reflected the apprehension she felt on behalf of any child who might have done something to displease her.

167

This look of alarm she extended to Bryan.

'You appear to be paying attention and gazing at me like everyone else, but I feel, for most of the time, your thoughts are not in this room at all.'

'Yes, Miss.'

'Perhaps you could tell me where they go to?'

Bryan shook his head.

'Are there pirates?'

'No, Miss.'

'Brigands?'

He shook his head again.

'Soldiers and aeroplanes?'

'No, Miss.'

'Ships and tanks?'

'No.'

At this catalogue of distractions the class had laughed.

'Where, then? Where,' she inquired, 'does your imagination wander?'

'All over.'

'All over where, Bryan?'

'The countryside, Miss Mitchell.'

'What do you see in the countryside?' she asked.

'A house.'

'A house in the countryside.' She glanced at the class. 'What sort of house?'

'A large one.'

'A large one.' Her eyes expanded. 'Who lives there?'

'A woman.'

'A woman.'

'And a man.'

'A man and a woman.'

'They haven't any children.'

'Haven't they?'

'They decide,' he said, 'to have one.'

'Do they have one?'

'They go to a poor family who haven't any money and ask for one of theirs.'

'Do they get one?'

168

'I don't know.'

'Do you know anyone like that?' Miss Mitchell asked.

'Yes,' he said.

Miss Mitchell's back was turned towards the class and she was gazing down at him directly.

'Perhaps tomorrow, or the day after, Bryan,' she said, 'you can tell me more about it.'

'There isn't anything else to tell,' he said.

'I see.'

Still she gazed down.

'If there's anything troubling you,' she added, 'you can always come and tell me.'

Miss Mitchell taught in the Sunday School, across the road, and, although she wasn't his teacher on the Sunday afternoon, she superintended the singing of the hymns and spoke the prayers, and read the lessons before the children broke up into separate groups.

'Meanwhile,' she concluded, 'you'd better get out your pen and pencil.'

He looked at the date inscribed on the board, and at the heading to be given to the work and, opening his desk, took out his book.

Through the window he could see the lane which wound across the fields and, where the land dipped down across the valley, the darkness of the woods at Feltham.

'Bryan?'

'Yes, Miss Mitchell?'

'Are you dreaming again?'

'No, Miss Mitchell,' and, stooping over the desk and opening his book, he dipped his pen in the ink and set to work.

'It puts us into a pickle as much as ought,' his father said.

'It's what I told him,' his mother said, yet she didn't indicate whether the 'him' she referred to was Alan or Bryan. The content of their discussion that morning had been repeated by his mother as his father was about to have his tea, the letter and its envelope laid on the cloth before him.

'I don't think she's thought about it,' his father said.

'She can't have.' His mother nodded her head.

169

Alan sat upright on a chair beside the fire, gazing at his father with a disinterested look.

'Peterson's.' His father shook his head.

'I've heard of one or two who have gone there,' his mother said.

'Who?' his father said.

'Chatterton's, for one.' She mentioned the family-owned engineering works at which Mr Morley's father and his brothers at one time had worked. 'They had two sons at Peterson's.'

'So you can see how ridiculous it is,' his father said. 'The fees alone come to more than I could earn in a year.'

'We wouldn't be paying,' his mother said.

'Would you let someone else pay for the education of your son?' his father asked.

His mother glanced away. 'What's best for Bryan is what we have to think about,' she said.

'What's best for Bryan is for him to believe, because it happens to be true, that he has been brought up by parents who love him, and Alan, too,' his father said. 'And to believe that they are parents who don't go back on their word.'

Bryan was standing in front of the fire and, although Alan periodically drew him aside, indicating he was shielding the heat from the room, because of his agitation he invariably drifted back again, gazing over at his father, examining each gesture he made with his hand as he picked up the letter and, having read it a fourth time, put it down again.

'The principle,' his mother said, 'is to bring him up the best way possible. And the best way possible is to equip him to live his life when we aren't here any more. The same with Alan. If somebody came along and gave Alan a chance like that we'd not think twice about it.'

His father glanced at Alan.

'We'd think,' his mother continued, 'how we could do the best for Bryan.'

'I'd have thought we'd do the same for both of them,' his father said.

'We would.'

'How could we do the same for both if one's got a chance the other hasn't?'

170

'They're not going to come out equal, anyway,' his mother said. 'They've different natures. One will do one thing, and the other,' she continued, 'will do another.'

'We'll give one a chance that the other can't have?' his father inquired.

'We'll give them an equal chance,' his mother said. 'We can't stop a chance that comes from somewhere else.'

'It's not the Corrigans' responsibility to bring up our children.'

'It's our responsibility,' his mother said.

His father, having started his tea, had now abandoned it: he was waiting, Bryan assumed, for his mother to decide it for him.

'And he'll go to live at Chevet?' he asked.

'He'll live here at weekends,' his mother said. 'And holidays, too,' she added.

'You think he ought to go?'

'I'm not saying he ought to go,' she said. 'All I'm saying is there's another side to the question.'

'We don't even know the Corrigans,' his father said.

'We've seen them once or twice.'

'How much knowing is that?'

'She's Spencer's sister,' his mother said.

'And think how much you respect Mr Spencer.'

'I don't say that he treats you right, though he has at times in the past, as you know yourself, as well as Mrs Spencer,' his mother said. 'He's always pulled round when the going got rough. There's no farmer round here who's a better employer. Which isn't saying much, I know, but it happens to be true. He's fair according to his lights. Even if you don't happen to agree,' his mother continued, 'that his lights are anything to write home about.' She picked up the letter. 'He's even invited Bryan over. They've taken him to the pictures. I'd never see him doing the same for Jack Woolgar's boy, or Finnegan's, and they've both been there for as long as you have.' She glanced at Bryan. 'How's he going to thank us later when he comes up with a dead-end job?'

His father glanced at Alan who, in turn, glanced at his mother, and kicked his heel at the rug.

'In your opinion he should go,' his father said, when it seemed his mother had nothing more to add.

'We have to consider what's best for Bryan.' She glanced at Alan herself. 'What do you think, Alan?'

'He ought to go.'

'Should he?' his father said.

'He'd be daft not to,' Alan said.

His brother sat upright, watching his father intently.

'Wouldn't you feel your nose put out wi' having a brother at Peterson's?' his father asked.

His brother shook his head. 'I wouldn't want to go,' he said. 'Not even if they asked me.'

His father waited.

'You might regret it later, Alan.'

'I shouldn't. There's nought for me at Peterson's, fro' what I reckon.'

'You can't see it from our angle,' his father said, stooping from the table.

'I'm saying what I think. I reckon there's nought theer, Dad, for me, whereas I can see summat theer for Bryan.'

'She says they specialize in art. Which is why they brought it to our attention,' his mother said, taking up the letter. ' "Bryan's particular talent would be nourished in a sympathetic environment." ' She glanced at his father before continuing. ' "Sensitivity is something that can easily be destroyed by an environment which is not receptive to it." '

'He's not sensitive,' his father said.

'Other people think so,' his mother said.

'There are lots of sensitive people who've had a harder life,' his father said.

'So you want him to do without this opportunity. You want him to give it up?' his mother said.

'I'm thinking about fairness,' his father said, so vehemently that his mother looked away. 'What do'st thy think, Bryan?' he added.

'I'd like to go,' he said.

'Would you?'

'I can always come back at weekends.'

'Better-off children of his age go to boarding-school,' his mother said. 'He wouldn't even be away for more than five nights.'

'You want to leave us?' his father said.

172

'I wouldn't be leaving,' Bryan said.

'It's a chance in a million,' his mother said. 'There's everything out there for him to work for. There's nothing for him here. Why,' she continued, despite his father turning away, 'if someone came along and said, "I can turn Alan into a champion boxer but he'll have to come and live in my gymnasium," you'd say, "Go ahead, grab your chance! You'll not have another like it!" And he'd go. I know he would. And with Bryan: I know you'd say the same.'

'You want to go to the Corrigans'?' his father asked.

'I'd like to go to Peterson's,' Bryan said.

'Aren't you happy living at home?'

'I am,' he said.

'Why do you want to leave?'

'I'm not leaving,' Bryan said.

'He could come back each Friday night,' his mother said. 'And go back Monday morning.'

'He could never wear his uniform round here,' his father said. 'He'd have to stay five nights at least.'

'We'd work something out,' his mother said. 'It'd be no different than a lot of families who send their children to school for three months at a time. Why, there were the Aitchisons in Hasleden Street who came into money and sent their children away to school and none of them were older than Bryan.'

His father stood up.

'Have you decided to send him?' he asked, going to the door as if the argument were now resolved and he couldn't delay his going any longer.

'We have,' his mother said.

'In that case,' his father said, 'we'll do what we always do: make the best on it we can.'

He closed the door behind him.

'I knew he'd want the opposite,' his mother said as the sound of his father's footsteps came from the stairs. 'If he knew I'd be against it he'd be for it. He'll soon get over it,' she added, taking up the letter, re-reading it then laying it down once more before smiling and gazing down at Bryan as he started to eat his tea.

THIRTEEN

Throughout the journey she chatted to his father, as well as to Mr Corrigan, the two men sitting before them, the tall figure of Mr Corrigan and the shorter figure of his father silhouetted against the lightness of the road ahead.

His father sat upright, nodding, half-turning but never actually glancing round, looking up once only, at Mrs Corrigan's indication, as the car turned into the drive, the gates of which were already open, and the house was revealed, beyond the copse of trees, at the summit of the rise.

As the car drew up, the front door of the house was opened and the white-aproned figure of Mrs Meredith appeared.

His father got out, uncertain at first how to release the door.

'Here we are, Rose,' Mrs Corrigan called. 'All safe and sound,' and introduced his father.

Unsure of Mrs Meredith's function, his father extended his hand. 'Pleased to meet you,' he said.

'Oh, we'll look after him, Mr Morley,' Mrs Meredith said. 'We'll keep an eye on him, don't worry.'

Bryan, in getting out of the car, had gone round to the boot but his father, stepping past him, took his case and, turning, fresh-faced, to the house, gazed up at it and said, 'This is a grand place, Bryan.'

'Look at the view, Mr Morley.' Mrs Corrigan took his arm and indicated the area beyond the garden which dipped down to the narrow valley and, beyond, expanded to a broadening vista of the river and the slope of the hills above the town. 'You can see to Spinney Top. It's not so far away, after all,' she added and, turning him to the door, she called, 'Let's see if Bryan's room is ready.'

'All ready,' Mrs Meredith said, indicating to his father that he might go ahead.

They entered the hall and Mrs Corrigan inquired, 'Shall we have tea first, or go upstairs?'

'Oh, go up and look, Mrs Corrigan,' Mrs Meredith said. 'I'm sure Mr Morley is dying to see it.'

'Nay, I know he's in good hands,' his father said.

He had scarcely glanced at Bryan, and not once had he looked at him directly; now he went ahead, the suitcase in his hand.

Bryan, his hand held by Mrs Corrigan, followed.

At the top of the stairs Mrs Meredith went ahead, opening the guest-room then stepping aside for his father to go in before her.

'This is a grand room,' his father said as Bryan and Mrs Corrigan, followed by Mrs Meredith, entered.

'Perhaps we should leave the two of you together,' Mrs Corrigan said, glancing at his father and then at Bryan. 'Say your farewells, though it shan't be for long.'

'Oh, no time at all,' his father said.

Mrs Corrigan went out, followed by Mrs Meredith who, nodding at Bryan, closed the door.

'It's a grand room, Bryan,' his father said.

'It is.'

'As cosy as ought.'

His father crossed to the window.

'Who lives in that house?' He indicated the roof of the adjacent house above the clump of trees at the end of the garden.

'I don't know,' Bryan said.

'It's bigger than this.'

'I think so.'

'What do'st think to it?' he gestured round.

'I like it.'

'Thy's seen the room afore?'

'Yes.'

Smaller pieces of furniture had been added to it; an electric fire stood in the yellow-tiled hearth; a lamp had been placed on the bedside table; the bed had been covered by an eiderdown. Fresh curtains, with a floral design, had been draped at the window.

'By go,' his father said, 'it's grand,' gazing at the plaster surrounds which circuited the ceiling. 'Do'st want to unpack?'

'I'll do it later.'

His father was wearing his only suit; his face gleamed from where he'd shaved, his hair greased down and combed, leaving a stark white line at the parting.

'Is there ought else you want?'

'No,' he said.

'I hope you'll make the best of it.' His father, for the first time, glanced at him directly.

'I shall.'

'We're alus theer. You can come home as often as you like,' he added.

'I shall.'

'Shall I give you a kiss?'

He didn't wait for an answer but stooped, grasped his shoulder, and kissed him on the cheek.

'I'd better be getting back.'

He turned to the door.

'There's nought else I can do?'

'No,' Bryan said.

'It's what you wanted?'

'Yes,' he said.

'Right.' His father clapped his hands.

Downstairs Mrs Corrigan came out from the sitting-room at the back of the house and his father called, 'I'll be getting back, then, Mrs Corrigan, if that's all right.'

'Oh, but you'll have some tea, Mr Morley,' Mrs Corrigan said. 'Mrs Meredith's made it specially.'

'Nay, I'd better be getting back,' his father said. 'Mrs Morley wa're a bit upset afore I left.'

'Well,' Mrs Corrigan said. 'I hope we'll see you soon.'

'Oh, you shall,' his father said, and added, 'We appreciate very much the chance you're giving Bryan.'

'We're only too glad to help. It's to our benefit as much as Bryan's.'

His father went directly to the front door which, after fumbling with the latch, he opened himself.

176

Mrs Meredith emerged from the kitchen.

'Aren't you staying for tea, Mr Morley?' she asked.

'I'd better get back, Missis,' his father said from the open door. 'I think Bryan'll make a hole in it,' he added.

'Oh, I'm sure he will,' Mrs Meredith said, coming forward and, together with Bryan and Mrs Corrigan, gazing down to where his father, the door held for him by Mr Corrigan, was getting into the car.

'See you soon, Bryan,' Mr Corrigan said as he got in behind the wheel and, as the car dipped down the drive, his father's hand appeared, waving from the window.

'What do you think to it?' Mrs Corrigan said.

She opened the wardrobe door.

Inside were several sections of wood secured by straps and wooden wedges.

'If you unfasten the straps and release the screws you have a collapsible easel.'

On the floor, beside it, lay a wooden box.

Metal clasps secured the lid.

'Oil paints,' Mrs Corrigan said. 'have you ever tried them?'

He shook his head.

'You can use the lumber-room to paint in.'

She indicated a rug beside the bed.

'I want you to keep it tidy.'

'I shall,' he said.

'I'm sure it's what you're used to. You can try your easel out, if you like.'

He released the canvas straps and unfolded the wood: Mrs Corrigan held one end, he arranged the other.

'At the back of the wardrobe, if you look, there's a further surprise.'

He drew out a paper parcel; unfolding it he extracted a canvas mounted on a stretcher, and several pieces of board with canvas stretched across.

'The boards are to practise on, and the canvas to use when you feel more confident,' she added.

'Mrs Corrigan,' came Mrs Meredith's voice. 'Do you want tea now or later?'

'Oh, we'll come down now, Rose,' Mrs Corrigan said, and added, 'I'm sure that Bryan is hungry.'

And downstairs, sitting by the fire, with the tea arranged on a tray between them, she said, 'I have a great respect for your parents, but a change of clothes is essential. Our next appointment is to go into town.'

She watched him eat.

'I hope you're going to be happy, Bryan.'

'I will be,' he said.

'You don't look happy at present.'

'I feel it,' he said.

'You're missing home.'

'Not much,' he said.

'Oh dear. I hope it's going to work,' she said. 'Let's do some-thing jolly.'

She led him to the piano, raised its lid and arranged several sheets of music on the stand above the keyboard.

She began to play.

'There!'

She glanced up at him and smiled.

'Can you sing?'

'Not much.'

'Let's try something together.'

She rearranged the music, turned a final sheet then, stabbing it with her finger, said, 'Can you see the words?'

He read the first line out.

'I'll play the tune. We'll sing together.'

She played the music through, turning the pages, indicating the words; then, with a flourish, she added, 'When I say "three".'

Occasionally Mrs Meredith's voice called from the hall outside; at each response Mrs Corrigan would nod her head and, raising her own voice, indicate that Bryan should join in, too.

'How about a jolly one?'

'Wasn't that one jolly?'

'This is jollier.'

Her fingers raced across the keys, her shoulders swelling: she sang the first verse through herself.

'When I say "three".'

178

Answering responses came from the hall outside.

'That was a good one!'

She finished with a flourish; her hands flew up: she replaced the sheets of music on the stand, selected a new song, examined it closely then, practising the notes, she added, 'This is even better!'

Some time later Mr Corrigan appeared at the door: the grey-haired figure stooped with his head inside and called as they came to the end of a song. 'What a jolly sound to come in to,' adding, 'Supper's ready whenever you like.'

'Come and join us!' Mrs Corrigan said.

'Oh, I'll only spoil it,' Mr Corrigan said, still standing at the door.

'We don't mind,' Mrs Corrigan said, running her hands across the keys, and added, 'The more the merrier for Bryan and me!'

Mr Corrigan came inside: a flower had been added to his button-hole.

'Did Bryan's father get back all right?'

'Safe and sound.' He stooped from his vast height and examined the music. ' "The Centipede",' he said. 'My favourite. "So many feet, and so many toes, that everyone hears him, wherever he goes!" ' He laughed, glancing down at Bryan, and added, 'Ready!'

By the light of the fire they sang songs which only Mr and Mrs Corrigan knew; the room darkened: Bryan watched the movement of her hands and endured the strange intimacy which came from the movement of her arm as, in the darkness, she drew herself more closely to him.

'Everything to order?'

'Yes.'

He was already in bed.

From below came the sound of Mrs Meredith's voice and the additional sound, a moment later, of her feet as she came up-stairs.

When a knock came on the door Mrs Corrigan called, 'Come in, Rose, he isn't sleeping,' and Mrs Meredith put her gaunt-featured face inside and said, 'All tucked up and cosy?'

179

'I think so, Rose. I was just,' Mrs Corrigan added, 'kissing him good night.'

'We don't want to spoil him, do we?' Mrs Meredith said, advancing into the room herself.

'I shan't spoil him, Rose.' She stooped towards him and, for Mrs Meredith's benefit, kissed his cheek.

'I'll say good night, too,' Mrs Meredith said. 'I hope dinner was all you wanted.'

'Perfect, Rose,' Mrs Corrigan said, smiling at Bryan and squeezing his hand.

'Mr Corrigan has said he'll run me home.' She kissed Bryan's cheek. 'You won't mind an old woman kissing you good night,' she added.

'You're not old, Rose!' Mrs Corrigan laughed.

'Not really. Only feel it,' and, returning to the door, she added, 'See you tomorrow.'

Mrs Corrigan drew up his quilt.

The light went out.

The door was left ajar.

Later, the front door downstairs was opened and he heard, once more, the sound of Mr Corrigan's voice.

'Everything all right, Fay?'

'All right, Harold,' came Mrs Corrigan's cheerful answer.

'We'll go to Bennett's first,' she said, pausing by a nearby window, examining the draped figures displayed inside and adding, 'Do you think the brown would suit me? Perhaps, if you wouldn't mind, I could try it on.'

When they entered the shop an assistant glanced at Mrs Corrigan, glanced at her again, and called, 'Why, Mrs Corrigan, I didn't know you.'

'Why on earth not?' Mrs Corrigan laughed.

'You look so young,' the woman said. 'Younger than I've ever seen you.'

Having disappeared behind a counter she returned with a costume.

The costume was followed by a dress, the dress by a skirt. On each occasion Mrs Corrigan emerged from the curtained-off alcove within which she tried on each garment, she glanced across her shoulder and called, 'What do you think?' adding to the assistant, 'He is, I might tell you, my severest critic.'

The assistant smiled; other clothes were brought: a bill was produced. 'I shall ask Mr Corrigan to call this evening,' Mrs Corrigan said and, after the assistant had followed them to the door where, blinking, they re-emerged in the morning light, she added, 'Your turn now, I think.'

Three plate-glass windows gave access to Bennett's shop, the two entrances placed on either side of a central window. As in the previous shop, an assistant came directly out from behind a counter, complimented Mrs Corrigan on her appearance and, having been introduced to Bryan, shook his hand. Measurements were taken; a suit was produced: alterations were suggested. He tried on a blazer; stockings and shirts were laid on a counter; a tie was selected. Shoes were bought. 'Mr Corrigan will call before this evening,' Mrs Corrigan said and, outside the shop, she added, 'How about paying Mr Corrigan a visit?'

As they entered the bow-windowed shop a figure detached itself from a group of assistants waiting by the door.

'Mrs Corrigan?' the figure said, to which Mrs Corrigan inquired, 'Is Mr Corrigan in?'

'He is, Mrs Corrigan,' the figure said and, bowing, led the way to a flight of stairs.

Halfway up, Mrs Corrigan straightened Bryan's collar, ran her hand across his hair, and asked, 'Are you all right?'

'Yes,' he said.

'If you'd rather we didn't go up you only have to say.'

'I want to,' he said.

'Well,' she said, glancing up the stairs. 'Try and look happy.'

'I am,' he said.

'In that case,' she said, 'happiness with you must look like misery to most other people.'

She laughed; from behind a glass-panelled door at the top of the stairs came the sound of Mr Corrigan's voice.

'Mrs Corrigan to see you, Mr Corrigan,' the assistant said, thrusting his head inside.

'Come in, Fay,' Mr Corrigan said, emerging from behind a desk.

'And come in, Bryan.' He shook Bryan's hand and, as the door closed behind them, stooped to Mrs Corrigan and kissed her cheek. 'What a surprise.'

'We've just been shopping,' Mrs Corrigan said. 'If you'll call at Bennett's and Charlesworth's before you come home this evening.'

'I shall.' Mr Corrigan held out a chair and indicated that Bryan should take a second.

The office looked out to a tiny yard; a van, with 'Corrigan and Son' painted on the side, was visible through an open window.

Their two chairs were drawn up in front of the desk.

'Coffee?' Mr Corrigan inquired.

'Oh, we'll have coffee out, Harold,' Mrs Corrigan said.

She glanced at Bryan and smiled.

'Or tea, if you'd like,' Mr Corrigan added.

'Oh, we'll have it out,' Mrs Corrigan said again, and added, 'I hope you'll like his clothes.'

'I'm sure I shall.' Mr Corrigan smiled. 'His Peterson's uniform.'

'That's right.'

'I can't wait to see it.'

Mr Corrigan clasped his hands; his desk was littered with files: a telephone and a calendar occupied one corner and, mounted in a silver frame – and almost hidden amongst the files – a photograph of Mrs Corrigan: she was dressed in a light-coloured suit and was sitting formally, half-turned towards the camera, in a high-backed chair: a look of extraordinary sadness characterized her features.

'Swainley show you up?' Mr Corrigan added.

'That's right.'

'Never misses a turn.'

'He doesn't.'

A door on the opposite side of the office opened.

A woman, with short, tawny-coloured hair, appeared; she was wearing a blouse, a dark skirt and carried a sheaf of papers in one hand and a handbag in the other.

'I didn't know you were busy, Mr Corrigan,' she said, and glanced at Bryan.

'Come in, Clare,' Mr Corrigan said. 'Meet Bryan.'

182

The woman was younger than Mrs Corrigan, although she wore more make-up. 'Hello, Bryan,' she said, and added, 'Is he looking for a job?'

'He's here to be introduced,' Mr Corrigan said and, taking the papers from the woman, added, 'By now he's met so many he must be feeling confused.'

Bryan stood up.

'This is Miss Watkinson, Bryan,' Mr Corrigan continued. 'Miss Watkinson is my secretary, and Mr Swainley, whom you've met already, is the manager of the shop.'

'Tea or coffee?' Miss Watkinson said, shaking Bryan's hand.

'Neither, Clare,' Mrs Corrigan said. 'We've already been invited but I'm taking Bryan to Fraser's.'

'That's a nice place,' Miss Watkinson said. 'Do sit down,' she added to Bryan.

He indicated the chair, however, and stepped aside.

'Oh, secretaries don't sit down,' she said. 'They have to work.'

Mr Corrigan laughed.

'Not all the time,' he said.

'No,' Miss Watkinson said, 'but most of it.' She glanced at Mrs Corrigan intently. 'You're looking very well, Mrs Corrigan.'

'Thank you, Clare.'

'I've never seen you look more lovely.'

'I've never felt so well,' Mrs Corrigan said.

'Not for a long time, Clare.' Mr Corrigan glanced from his secretary to his wife then back to his secretary again.

'How long is Bryan to be with us?' Miss Watkinson said, the chair still empty between them. 'What wonderful manners he's got.'

'He's about to attend,' Mrs Corrigan said, 'Peterson's School, and is staying with us during term-time.'

'That's a grand school,' Miss Watkinson said. 'He'll have to have his brains screwed in to stick in there.'

'Was it anything important, Clare?' Mr Corrigan asked, resuming his place behind the desk.

'I'll come back later.' Miss Watkinson smiled at Bryan and then at Mrs Corrigan and, returning to the door, she added, 'See you again, no doubt,' closing it behind her.

'Would you like to see the shop, Bryan?' Mr Corrigan said.

'We'll see it another day, Harold.'

Mrs Corrigan stood up.

'What about the workshop?'

'We'll see that another day, too.'

Something about Mr Corrigan's behaviour had suddenly displeased her.

'Drop in any time,' Mr Corrigan said.

'We shall.'

Mr Corrigan got up and opened the door and, moments later, at the entrance to the shop, he asked, 'Is there anything more you'd like me to do?'

'Nothing,' Mrs Corrigan said.

'I can drive you home if you like,' he said.

'No, thank you.'

'After you've been to the Fraser Café.'

'We may not go to Fraser's. I'd like some fresh air,' Mrs Corrigan said.

Already she was moving off and Mr Corrigan, after gazing after her, called, 'I shan't forget Charlesworth's and Bennett's,' gazed after her a moment longer, waved, and disappeared inside the door.

'Don't you like the shop?' Bryan asked.

'Not much.'

'Why not?'

'I don't dislike it, Bryan,' she said. 'But,' she continued, 'I don't like it as much as Mr Corrigan. At least, not enough to indulge myself.'

'Is looking at the shop indulgence?' he said.

'Not really,' she said. 'But at the moment we have better things to do.'

Intermittently, passing a shop window, he caught a glimpse of Mrs Corrigan's reflection – a pale figure, wearing a lilac suit and a lilac hat, her animated face hidden beneath its brim – and thought, 'What on earth made her change her mind?' and as they threaded through the crowds and came to the market with its confusion of stalls and its even more thickly-congested pavements, and he caught sight of several children moving to and fro in the company of their parents, he reflected, 'If it wasn't that I'd seen it happen I'd have thought the two of us were mad,' and yet, a

184

moment later, he was consoling himself with the thought, 'All this is planned: it was bound to happen. She has no more say in it than I have.'

They were walking aimlessly through the market when, some distance ahead, he caught sight of his mother; she was standing at a stall, feeling in her purse, examining its contents and, a moment later, glancing up at the stall itself.

He couldn't help but compare her shabbily-coated figure with that of the woman by his side – her hand clasping his, if anything, more tightly – and he decided in that instant not to point his mother out, turning Mrs Corrigan across the street and into a thoroughfare which led, by a series of yards, back to the road from which they'd come.

'Where are you taking me?'

'Nowhere,' he said.

'We're walking in circles.'

She probably wouldn't have recognized his mother, he thought, even if his mother had been pointed out. He even speculated on the possibility that his mother might have seen him – that, moments before he'd glimpsed her himself, she had turned aside and busied herself with her purse in order to avoid him. If anything, that glimpse of the shabbily-coated figure with its familiar stoop and the anxious, bird-like cocking of its head, reassured him that, even if there had been something to unite them in the past, there was nothing now.

'I saw someone I knew.'

'Who?'

Mrs Corrigan's regular habit, in walking past a shop, was to examine her reflection; having returned to the main road that ran below the church, and having emerged into it some distance below Mr Corrigan's shop, she paid no attention whatsoever either to the windows or – another medium by which she judged the effect of her appearance – to the other passers-by, but walked with her eyes fixed firmly ahead, her look, if anything, abstracted.

'My mother.'

She released his hand.

'Where?'

'In the market.'

185

'Did she see you?'

'No.'

She glanced behind.

'Why didn't you stop?'

'I didn't think you'd want to meet her.'

'Why not?'

She glanced behind her again.

'I didn't want to talk to her.'

'I see.'

Grasping his hand more firmly, they continued in the same direction; they passed Bennett's, and the couturier's, passed the Regal Cinema, and continued down the road to the river.

'I have a confession to make as well.'

'What is it?'

'It wasn't the shop I didn't like.'

'What was it?'

'Someone there.'

'Miss Watkinson?'

She shook her head. 'Why do you say Miss Watkinson?'

'I thought you might be jealous.'

'Why should I be jealous?' She laughed, squeezed his hand, and added, 'It's when you say things like that I like you more than ever.'

'Who was it, then?'

'Someone.'

'Who?'

'I don't have to submit to your questioning, Bryan. I am merely telling you something I wish you to know.'

'You've only told me half,' he said.

'I wish you'd told me about your mother.'

'Would you have gone up to her?' he asked.

'She might have come to the conclusion we'd decided not to acknowledge her.'

'I don't mind.'

'That's cold-hearted.'

'Is it?'

His own grasp on her hand had tightened; he felt the pressure of her ring.

186

'You have to acknowledge your mother,' she said.

On either side narrow streets opened out on to cobbled thoroughfares and yards: from beyond the nearest roofs came the hooting of a tug.

'I used to live down here,' she said. 'It was an exciting place in those days.'

'My mother used to live down here as well,' he said.

'What was your mother's maiden name?'

'Wolmersley.'

'I never heard of it.' She glanced up one of the brick-lined yards: children were running to and fro; their screams echoed between the houses. 'How awful,' she said, and added, 'Not that I knew many people. I was determined to get out of it as soon as I could.'

'I thought you enjoyed it.'

'Whatever gave you that impression?'

'You said it was an exciting place to live.'

'It was,' she said, 'for a girl, and at an age when I didn't know any better.'

'When did you know better?' he said.

'Quite early, Bryan.' She added nothing until, emerging from beneath a railway bridge, they came out by the river: water cascaded over a concrete weir and barges were moored to a crane-lined wharf. 'We can walk back home from here,' she said.

They passed the Chantry Chapel and, with Mrs Corrigan leading, descended a flight of steps to a footpath which, paved with flagstones and flanked by a fence, followed the bank on the opposite side.

'I used to play down here,' she said. 'I used to come down with Mr Spencer. He had lots of friends. There were always lots of fun.'

'If you were poor, and had no money, how did Mr Spencer become a farmer?'

Mrs Corrigan paused where the path broadened and was joined, at a lock-gates, by a stone-banked canal. Beyond stretched a vista of fields crowned, at their summit, by the houses of the village. 'He was employed as a farm-labourer,' she said, 'and fell in love with his employer's daughter.'

'How did *you* get out of it?' he asked.

'That story,' she said, 'will have to be told another time.' She

187

extended her hand towards the village. 'What a wonderful view. I can't tell you how my heart used to rise when we got to here and we crossed the lock-gates and the town and its dirt had been left behind.'

'You don't like dirt,' he said.

'Throughout my life,' she said, 'I've always learnt that dirt and indifference go together. Where there's apathy,' she added, 'there's always filth.'

She stopped by the lock-gates.

'You go across first. I haven't come this way for ages.'

Holding to the metal rail, he crossed to the other side.

She followed, pausing where the gates came together, and called, 'When I got to here my brother's friends would often threaten to throw me in.'

'Did they ever do it?' he said.

'Mr Spencer would never allow it.'

'Why do you call him Mr Spencer?' he asked.

'He is Mr Spencer to you,' she said.

'He's your brother.'

'You can't be informal at your age, Bryan.' She indicated a footpath which led off through what, at one time, had been an orchard; the stumps of several trees, arranged in rows, were covered in ivy. At one side, behind a stone wall, stood the ruins of a cottage. 'This is Morgan's Place,' she said. 'A man used to live here who always chased us. He looked after the lock and didn't like people coming across. Particularly children.'

'What shall I call you?' Bryan asked.

He felt the tug on his arm as she came to a stop.

'You could call me "Aunt".'

Already she was walking on.

'Shall I call Mr Corrigan "Uncle"?' he asked.

'That's right.'

A stile came into veiw at the end of the path.

She held his hand.

'We ought to get something straight,' she said, as they regained the footpath the other side. 'Because I take an interest in you, you don't have to be,' she paused, 'familiar.'

'I'm not,' he said, not sure what the word implied.

188

'You talk to me at times,' she flushed, not having taken his hand again since crossing the stile, 'as if I were a friend.'

'You are,' he said.

'I hope you won't forget that I am also someone who is responsible for your welfare.'

'No,' he said.

'You were right about the shop.'

'What about it?' Bryan asked.

'I don't like seeing Mr Corrigan there.'

'Why not?'

'It's the way I am. I can't tell you why.' She clasped his hand. 'You don't mind the way I am?' she added.

'No,' he said.

'Well,' she said, 'so that's all settled,' and, clasping his hand more tightly, her eyes brightening, the colour lightening in her cheeks, she led him up the slope.

FOURTEEN

The building stood up a cobbled sidestreet opening off a main thoroughfare of the town. The room they waited in was occupied by a secretary seated at a desk. Her hair was fastened in a bun, one strand of which she leant back in her chair to fasten.

Mr Corrigan was dressed in a dark-grey suit with a high-winged collar: from the top pocket of his jacket projected a handkerchief and, intermittently, from beneath his jacket, he extracted a watch, wound it, then returned it to his waistcoat pocket.

'Mr Berresford won't be long.' The secretary smiled. A bell rang on her desk. 'Mondays are always busy,' she added.

She got up from her desk and crossed the room, opening a door the other side.

'Mr Corrigan, Mr Berresford,' she called inside.

A man stood up behind a desk; strands of dark hair grew out, like wings, from the back of his head, the brow of which projected heavily above a pair of dark-brown eyes. Large nostrils were underlain by a dark moustache: a mouth, thin-lipped and scarcely visible, ran down into a circle of fat which, projecting outwards, was compressed against a stiff white collar.

The man wore a dark-brown suit and – like Mr Corrigan, and contrasting strangely with its colour – a pale-blue tie.

'Hello, Harold,' he said, and shook Mr Corrigan's hand.

'This is the gentleman in question.' Mr Corrigan indicated Bryan.

The man shook Bryan's hand, indicated two chairs which had already been placed in front of the desk, and asked, 'What do you think to our building, Bryan?'

'It's old.'

'Very.' Teeth, tinted yellow, were revealed within the thin-lipped mouth. Opening a drawer, the man took out a pipe. 'Mind if I smoke?'

'Go ahead.' Mr Corrigan crossed his legs and, having done so, glanced at Bryan.

'Two old boys.' The headmaster gestured at his pale-blue tie, and then, with the stem of his pipe, at Mr Corrigan's. He laughed, Mr Corrigan laughed, and each, in turn, once more, glanced down at Bryan.

'What are we to make of him, Max?' Mr Corrigan laughed again.

'Another Petersonian?' the headmaster said.

'I think so.'

The headmaster, having struck a match, applied it to his pipe.

'His report gives grounds for hope.'

'Considerable,' Mr Corrigan said.

'From rougher wood than this.' The headmaster exhaled a cloud of smoke.

Along one wall ran a case containing books; a second, glass-fronted case was occupied by silver cups: above it, suspended from the wall, hung a wooden plaque bearing, in relief, a painted coat of arms beneath which, in black, was inscribed the one word, 'Independence'.

The headmaster, following Bryan's look, glanced up. He exhaled another cloud of smoke. 'Any questions before we cast him to the wolves?'

'He hasn't his books,' Mr Corrigan said.

'Been ordered, have they?'

Mr Corrigan nodded. 'Nor his uniform.'

'Being altered at Bennett's?'

'Correct.'

The headmaster stood up; he opened the door to the outer office. 'All under control, in that case,' he said, and added, 'You'll find it different from what you're used to, Bryan. We'll make greater demands, despite our lack of the State's resources, and also, as a consequence, look for better results.'

The secretary, typing, looked up from her desk.

'I'll be downstairs, Mrs Fletcher,' the headmaster said.

'Right-o, Mr Berresford,' the woman called out.

A flight of stone steps led down to a hall: a door opened off

191

on either side; a front door, at the opposite end, opened to the street. Here, after calling, 'Good luck, Bryan,' Mr Corrigan put on his hat, turned, waved, added, 'Cheerio, Max,' and disappeared, closing the door behind him.

'Down to business,' the headmaster said, knocking on one of the two doors and, thrusting his head inside, called, 'One more for the chopping-block, Mr Waterhouse.'

'Come in. Come in, Mr Berresford,' came a high-pitched voice. 'I'm ironing out,' the voice added, 'one or two creases.'

A group of heads, each surmounting a pale-blue blazer, was turned in Bryan's direction: large, wooden desks faced a larger desk, behind which stood a blackboard on metal castors and in front of which, his arms folded, leaned a small, bald-headed man, with stocky shoulders, bow-legs and a bright-red face: within the bright-red face were set a pair of pale-blue eyes, a protuberant nose and a similarly proportioned mouth which, as Bryan came into the room, was opened in the configuration of the letter 'O'.

'Mr Waterhouse,' the headmaster said to Bryan, and added, 'I believe we have a desk for Bryan.'

A desk was pointed out at the front.

'The uniform is forthcoming. Books and utensils forthcoming, too,' the headmaster said.

'*Compris.*' The teacher glanced down at Bryan.

'Any problems?'

'None.'

'Any problems, Morley?'

'No,' he said.

'"Sir" is the normal suffix, Morley.'

'No, sir,' Bryan said.

'Correct.'

The headmaster, having run his hand across Bryan's head, glanced round him at the class, nodded, placed his pipe in his mouth and went over to the door. 'Carry on.'

His footsteps sounded from the stairs outside.

'Morley, initial "B",' the teacher said, stepping behind his desk and mounting a stool. 'No other initial?'

'No, sir,' Bryan said.

'B.M.,' he wrote with a pen taken from the top pocket of his jacket. 'Not B.O.M., or B.A.M., or even B.U.M., but simply,' he wrote silently for several seconds, 'B.M.'

A murmur of laughter came from the room.

'Have you got a pen?'

'Yes, sir.' He took one, like the teacher, from the top pocket of his jacket, a fountain pen given him that morning by Mrs Corrigan.

High overhead a gas candelabra, unused, hung from a stuccoed ceiling.

The window beside him, and one other, looked out to the street: a house, of similar proportions to the one he was in, stood directly opposite, a brick-built structure with seven windows on the first floor, seven smaller ones above, and five dormer windows in the attic roof.

'You will find your exercise books inside your desk. The red is for English, the blue is for French, the green is for Science, the orange for Maths, the purple for History, the pink for Geography, and the grey,' he concluded, 'is for General Studies, including,' he raised his head, 'Religious Instruction.' He glanced round him at the class. 'Perhaps you'll do us the favour of inscribing your name, together with "Class 3", on each of them.' He returned his gaze to Bryan. 'And then we shall all get down to work.'

Voices echoed in the room; feet shuffled on the ceiling: the building, he decided, had once been someone's home. Behind the blackboard, on its metal castors, was the sealed-in fireplace with it high mantelshelf and voluted surrounds, and beside each window, folded back, were the original wooden shutters.

The walls, like the ceiling, were cracked, the cream distempered surfaces pocked here and there by the outline of a football and, in one spot, above the door, by the marks of someone's foot.

The teacher's voice droned on; at intervals, having descended from the stool and resumed his position, standing, in front of his desk, he glanced at Bryan and called, 'Is that understood?' crossing to his desk and inquiring, 'Have you got the subject "English" written on the red book?' or, 'It's orange for Maths,' or, 'The darker green, by the way, is Latin. I may have missed it off my list. If you've any inquiries raise your hand.'

That morning he had kissed Mrs Corrigan good-bye, she stooping in the porch then watching him descend to the car in which Mr

Corrigan was already waiting, her figure still visible on the steps as they reached the end of the drive and the car dipped down to the road, and, in glancing across at the gaunt-featured figure beside him, he had thought, 'This is part of the plan. She might not even be his wife.'

'Morley?'

'Yes, sir?'

'Do you agree with that?'

'With what, sir?'

'Weren't you listening?'

The tiny mouth was pursed.

'Yes, sir.'

'Sit up.'

'She'll be sitting in the dining-room,' he thought, 'or playing the piano. Or might even be coming into town, or be walking past the school.'

'Do you always sit in a day-dream, Morley?'

'No, sir.'

The teacher, after waiting for the class's laughter to subside, stepped closer. 'Have you inscribed your books correctly?'

'Yes, sir.'

'Let me see.'

He handed up each book in turn.

'Ever done Latin?'

'No, sir.'

'Do they teach French where you come from?'

'No, sir.'

'This will be a new adventure.'

'Yes, sir.'

'A new start.'

The pale-blue eyes examined him intently.

'Why are you trembling?'

His arms and his legs had begun to vibrate; he could feel the disturbance inside his chest.

'You're not frightened of me, are you?'

'No, sir.'

Glancing round at the uniformed figures, the teacher said, 'I'm not a frightening person, am I?'

194

'No, Mr Waterhouse,' the class as a single voice replied.

'Far more,' he continued, 'it's the other way round. They,' he gestured at the class, 'have a far greater capacity to frighten me, one which they exercise without compunction. The hours,' he concluded, 'I have shivered at this desk.'

The class laughed; they banged their desks: the majority, however, gazed at Bryan.

'Parkinson.'

A tall, thin-featured boy stood up; he had bright-red hair and his pale face, particularly around his nose and across his forehead, was sprinkled liberally with freckles.

'Parkinson is the worst boy in the class and he will bear me out as to how much he and his co-conspirators can frighten me.'

'We don't frighten you at all, sir,' Parkinson said, closing his eyes and stammering before he added, 'You frighten us.'

'That can't be true.'

'It is, sir.'

'I, Algernon Hardwick Waterhouse, frighten this class?'

A hand was placed above Mr Waterhouse's breast pocket, the top of which was lined by several pens.

'It can't be true.'

'It's true, sir,' came a chorus of shouts.

'I, who have never raised my voice in anger.'

'You have, sir!'

'When, ever, Parkinson, have I raised my voice to you?'

'Every day, sir.'

'Every day?'

'Yes, sir.'

The tall, red-headed figure bowed its head and a crimson flush rose across its freckled brow.

'I can't believe it.'

'Your name isn't Algernon,' a voice called out.

'If it isn't Algernon,' Mr Waterhouse replied, 'may I lose every hair on my head.'

'You have, sir!'

The hand from the breast pocket of Mr Waterhouse's jacket was raised to the top of Mr Waterhouse's head. 'And this morning, in the mirror, I looked so pretty.'

The class laughed. Desk lids were banged. Feet stamped on the floor.

'You'll have to bear me out in this,' Mr Waterhouse said, raising his hand, at which the banging of desks subsided. 'Have I ever frightened anyone?'

'Yes, sir,' Parkinson said.

'Who?'

'Everyone, sir.'

'Including you?'

'Yes, sir.'

'I see little sign of it.' He glanced at Bryan. 'You will have to believe me when I say I was not aware I frightened anyone. If I do,' he added, 'I apologize.'

The desk lids were tapped, the feet were stamped; the laughter in the room broke out again.

'I am an ogre. What am I?'

'An ogre,' everyone in the room replied.

'A tyrant.'

'A tyrant,' everyone in the room responded.

'I terrify everyone, as Parkinson can attest. No one sleeps at night who has spent the previous day in my classroom. Why, no one sleeps at all,' he concluded, 'if ever I catch them at it.'

The laughter broke out more loudly.

'If Parkinson will sit up we'll all get down to work,' the teacher said, glancing round the room, and adding, 'Everyone suitably frightened, are they?' glancing down at Bryan, smiling, and calling, 'When I say "three" take out your pens. One, two,' pausing, his hand raised, 'two and one half, two and three-quarters, two and seven-eighths, two and fifteen-sixteenths, two and thirty-one thirty-seconds, two and sixty-three sixty-fourths,' and, beaming at the room in general, 'two and one hundred and twenty-seven one hundred and twenty-eighths,' and, finally, '*three!*'

'Why did you come here if you didn't have to?' Parkinson said. He walked beside Bryan in the tarmacked yard, his hands in his pockets, his tall figure stooped, his freckled face turned down to watch his shoes. A tennis ball rose, bounced off the windowed wall of the school, fell back to the yard and was pursued, still bouncing, to a chorus of shouts.

'I was invited to come here,' Bryan said.

'Who invited you?'

'My aunt.'

'Who's she?'

'Mrs Corrigan.'

'Never heard of her.'

'They own a shop in town.'

'Oh, that Corrigan,' Parkinson said.

'Do you know them?'

'I've seen the shop. My father gets most of his furniture there.'

'Does Waterhouse really frighten you?' Bryan asked.

Surprisingly, at a window overlooking the yard, the figure of Mr Corrigan was gazing down; a moment later it disappeared to be replaced by that of Mr Berresford.

'We call him "Watty",' Parkinson said. 'I once made him cry, as a matter of fact.'

'How?'

'I have my means.'

A tall, red-haired figure had come out from the glass-panelled door at the back of the school and stood for several seconds, picking a scab on its cheek, gazing down the flight of steps at the figures in the yard below: the tennis ball rose against the wall of the building, rattled a window, and came down again. The red-haired figure, after raising its arm, called, turned, and went back inside.

'Have you a brother at Peterson's?' Bryan asked.

'Clive.'

'What's your name?' Bryan said.

'Gordon.'

At the window overlooking the yard the figure of the head-master had disappeared.

'Why did your aunt send you,' Parkinson said, 'and not your parents?'

'They haven't any money,' Bryan said.

Parkinson examined the toe of each shoe.

'Why not?'

'My father works on a farm,' he said.

'Which one?'

'Spencer's.'

Parkinson's head came up. 'My father knows Spencer.'

'How does he know him?'

'By way of business.' The tennis ball passed by. Parkinson took a kick, missed, and, but for Bryan extending his hand, might have fallen.

'Ronald!' someone shouted.

'Saunders!'

'Victor!'

'Who's Ronald Saunders Victor?' Bryan said.

'Me.'

'I thought you said your name was Gordon.'

'My nickname. R.S.V.P.' He nodded his head, kicked at the ground, and added, 'Why did you come here if you didn't have to?'

'I wanted to come here,' Bryan said.

'If I had a choice I wouldn't.' Parkinson flung out his hand. 'I don't often come, in any case,' he added.

'Why not?'

'I don't like it.'

'Where do you go?'

'Reggie's.'

'What's Reggie's?' Bryan asked.

'Reggie's is Reggie's,' Parkinson said. 'Don't tell me you've never heard of it?'

'I haven't.'

'I'll take you one day.'

'Aren't you ever found out?'

'They don't mind.'

'Why not?'

'My wadjers wanted me to come so here I come and here I stay and here I take a day off whenever I like.'

'What's a wadjer?' Bryan asked.

'A wadjer,' Parkinson said, 'is a parent. Don't tell me you don't know what a wadjer is?'

'No,' he said.

'R.S.V.P.,' came a shout behind.

'Rotters,' Parkinson called across his shoulder.

'Morley moccasins,' came another shout.

'That'll be your nickname,' Parkinson said.

'Mocky,' came a further shout.

'That'll be the one they've chosen.'

'Why's that?' Bryan said, glancing at the figures cascading across the yard behind.

'Don't ask me,' Parkinson said. 'I've only been here three years, and I know less about the place than when I started.'

'I enjoyed it,' Bryan said.

She took his arm and, glancing to the main entrance of the school – a metal gate which led round to the yard at the back – she said, 'I set off over an hour ago and have been walking up and down for the past ten minutes.'

She'd been standing across the cobbled street, adjacent to the door of the building opposite which, like the entrance to the school itself, was approached by a flight of steps, lined by metal railings – and to the pavement end of which was attached a bracketed gas lamp: it was beneath the lamps, palely illuminated by their yellow glow, that she'd been waiting.

'You didn't have to wait,' he said.

She laughed. 'If I hadn't have decided to meet you I couldn't have got through the day,' she said.

Mr Waterhouse came out from the front door of the building, drew a white raincoat about his stocky figure and, glancing across at Bryan and then at Mrs Corrigan, came quickly down the steps, raised a hat in Mrs Corrigan's direction, and set off down the street towards the thoroughfare at the opposite end.

'Who's that?'

'Mr Waterhouse glanced back, nodded, raised his hat, and hurried on.

'He's my teacher.'

'He shows a great interest in you,' she said and tightened the grip on his arm.

'In you,' he said.

She laughed. 'I'm sure it must be you.' Yet even as she spoke

199

Mr Waterhouse glanced round again, stumbled against a flagstone, retrieved his balance, drew his white raincoat more closely about him, glanced back once more, then, breaking into a run, disappeared around the corner.

'What on earth have you said to him?'

'Nothing.'

'You must have said something, Bryan.'

She was wearing a light-brown hat and, beneath the hat, a costume.

'Mr Corrigan came at playtime,' Bryan said.

'I wish you'd call him Uncle.'

'Uncle came at playtime.'

'He rang me up to say he'd been across to see how well you'd settled.'

'Why?'

'I asked him to.' She drew him across the street. 'I don't suppose,' she said, 'you've thought of me all day.'

'I have.'

She brushed back his hair, and said, 'I thought we'd go to Fraser's.'

'Why Fraser's?'

'I thought we'd celebrate.'

A rush of voices came from the opposite pavement.

'I'm glad you came,' Bryan said.

'Are you?'

'I'd have been unhappy if you hadn't.'

'Well,' she said. She glanced about her. 'That's nice,' and, clasping his hand more firmly, led him down the street.

The interior of the shop was lit by lamps.

Halfway up a flight of steps she paused at a mirror, examined her make-up, then her hat, then, glancing at Bryan, smiling, she said, 'You needn't look so scared.' She laughed, turned to the remaining flight of stairs, took his arm, glanced back at the mirror, in which – wanly, grim-visaged – he caught a glimpse of his own dark eyes, spectral, expanded, seemingly distended, and added, 'Nothing's as bad as it seems.'

Numerous tables, the majority of them occupied by women,

heavily coated and brightly hatted, stretched across a carpeted interior illuminated, from the centre of the ceiling, by a dome of coloured glass and, from the opposite end, by several plate-glass windows across one of which, in an arc, reversed, was printed, in gold, the one word 'Fraser's'. A hand was waved, Mrs Corrigan called out, called out a second time and, not pausing in her progress, crossed to where a waitress in a black dress and a small white apron was standing at a table recently vacated. 'Thank you, Phyl,' she said, and added, 'This is Bryan. You'll be seeing a lot of him in the future.'

'Hello, Bryan,' the woman said, her appearance not dissimilar to that of Miss Watkinson in Mr Corrigan's office. 'What can I get you?'

'Cakes and tea, Phyl,' Mrs Corrigan said, taking off her gloves. 'It's been his first day at Peterson's,' she added.

'Then he will be hungry,' the waitress said and, smiling down, in turn, at Bryan, called, 'I shan't be long,' and disappeared across the room.

'Phyl's nice,' Mrs Corrigan said, and added, 'She worked at the shop and when she got married she only wanted a part-time job. She always saves me a table.'

His hand was clasped beneath the cloth.

'Isn't it cosy?' Beneath his hand he could feel her skirt and, beneath her skirt, the smoothness of her stocking. 'Most of my friends come here,' she said and, as a woman in a brightly coloured hat called, 'How are you, Fay?' she added, 'We could come here each Friday, at the end of the week, and celebrate, and probably on Mondays, too,' turning, as the waitress reappeared, holding a tray, swinging between the tables, and asking, 'I don't suppose Peterson's is very different from what you're used to?' and, once the food had been laid out and, with a smile at her and one at Bryan, the waitress had disappeared across the room, concluding, 'The teachers, I imagine, are much the same?'

'Peculiar,' Bryan said.

'How peculiar?'

'They put on more of an act,' he said. 'On top of which the children are different.'

'Because they're boys,' Mrs Corrigan said. 'You've been used

201

to girls as well until now.' She clasped his hand more firmly. 'And now,' she concluded, 'you've only got me.'

A moment later, after watching him eat, she said, 'You've no regrets, I take it?'

'None,' he said.

'You see how silly I am.'

'Yes,' he said.

'Am I silly?' She laughed.

'Very.'

'I hope not.'

'At times.'

'Can everyone see it?'

'No,' he said.

'You'll have to tell me if they can.'

She acknowledged several waves.

And later, before they left, several women, who had been on the point of leaving, came over to the table. 'Bryan is my recent charge. It's been his first day at Peterson's,' Mrs Corrigan explained.

'That's a good school,' the majority said, shaking Bryan's hand or, in one or two instances, clenching it tightly and asking, 'How did it go?'

'I enjoyed it,' Bryan said, varying his responses by adding, 'I think I'll be happy,' or, 'I'm going to like it,' implying by his look that his circumstances previous to his attendance at Peterson's had not been all he might have wished for.

'How charming he is,' several of the women said, one of the older, more soberly attired turning to Mrs Corrigan and adding, 'Is he adopted, Fay?' Mrs Corrigan, flushing, glancing back and answering, 'It's far too early to say,' laughing, still flushed, and nodding her head at a further remark, the woman turning, and calling, 'See you do everything Mrs Corrigan asks!'

'That went well,' Mrs Corrigan said as they crossed the room, acknowledging several further inquiries, and introducing Bryan at two further tables, and on the stairs she added, 'That didn't frighten you, I take it?'

'No,' he said.

'It frightened me. But then,' she added, 'I frighten easily,' pausing at the entrance, gazing out at the street and calling, 'It's begun

202

to rain. We'll take a taxi,' allowing him to precede her up the hill and to open the door of the first of the line of cars waiting in the Bull Ring and, in the process of climbing in, concluding, taking Bryan's arm, 'I think we can tell Mr Corrigan that the day, as a whole, has been a huge success.'

FIFTEEN

'Is it better than Stainforth?' His brother's head was cowled within the blankets.

'Different,' Bryan said.

'How different?'

'All the teachers are men.'

'It's changed your voice.'

'How?'

'It's posh.'

From below came the murmur of his parents' voices and the occasional rooting of the poker against the fire.

'How is it posh?'

'It's smarter.'

'How smart?'

'A lot.' The blankets and the counterpane were bunched where, beneath them, his brother held them in his hand. 'I don't suppose you like coming back.'

'I don't mind.'

'I bet.' The voices droned on in the room below. 'My father's taken it worst.'

'How?'

'The way he goes around.'

Some distortion of his brother's face was evident beneath the bedclothes.

He had arrived home, as it was, as late as he dared, insisting on travelling on the bus alone rather than Mr Corrigan bringing him in the car, and even refused Mrs Corrigan's offer to accompany him as far as the Bull Ring.

No doubt, below, they were discussing his return, his clothes, the change in his behaviour, particularly in his response to them.

'What's Mrs Corrigan like?'

'All right.'

'Does she kiss you good night?'

'Sometimes.'

'How often?'

'Once or twice.'

'Has she got good legs?'

'Why?' He asked.

'You ought to look,' his brother said.

'Why?'

'I'm interested in everything you do,' his brother said.

'It doesn't concern you,' Bryan said.

'You could give her a grope.' His brother paused. 'You know what a grope is?'

'No,' he said.

'You know what a quim is?'

'No.'

His brother waited.

'What about jess?'

He shook his head.

'Jess,' his brother said, 'are a woman's breasts. A quim is what she has between her legs. A grope is when she lets you feel her.'

There was no connection between what his brother was telling him and what he knew of Mrs Corrigan, just as there was no connection, any longer, between his brother and himself.

'You know Muriel O'Donald? She let Cloughie have a look at hers. Her tits are a couple of beauties. One neet last week she got hold of his cock. You know what a cock is?' His brother raised his head.

'Yes.'

'Does she kiss you on the lips?'

'Who?'

'Mrs Corrigan.'

'Why do you keep on about her?' Bryan said.

'I suppose all your time you have to spend working.'

'Yes.'

'School-work.'

'That's right.'

205

'Harder than Stainforth?'

'Yes.'

'Do they talk very smart?'

'I suppose so.'

'I suppose they laugh at you.'

'Not much.'

'Have they bought you a uniform?'

'Yes.'

'Have you brought it with you?'

'No.'

His brother's head returned to the blankets.

'I'll go to sleep now,' Bryan said.

'See you in the morning.'

'Right.'

'Don't forget,' his brother said. 'You can tell me about it when you come next week.'

Bryan closed his eyes: he listened to his brother's breathing and, lulled by the sound, he fell asleep.

The church was a brightly-illuminated interior; if he had agreed to come at all it was to reassure his mother: she had examined his suit with pride and he had thanked himself for his foresight in having brought it with him. 'Is it Bennett's?' she had asked, examining the label. It was the first time a Bennett item of clothing had been inside the house: he had had to stand about the room while she called his father's attention to it several times — to the coat as well as the trousers, to the stockings as well as the shoes, her excitement fading only when she saw Alan's expression, adding, 'Newness isn't everything,' pulling down his brother's jacket, straightening his tie and concluding, as Alan complained, 'We want you to look as neat as one another. It's tidiness alone that counts.'

Now, sitting in church, he could see his brother in the Senior pew, the Crusader emblem of a knight's head fastened to a shield on the wall behind, and, looking round at the plain-glass windows, at the ochreish-looking walls, he thought, 'If Mrs Corrigan is my instructress what is her relationship to the spirit which resides above the cross?' gazing up at the largest of the plate-glass windows and wondering, 'If the benevolent spirit, in which I still believe, exists in a world beyond our own, what is its relationship to this other spirit which exists inside this building?'

In tracing the origin of his belief to that benevolent spirit which came at Christmas, Bryan glimpsed the means by which his personal destiny as a prince was connected to that invisible presence which emanated from the area of the church above the cross – and specifically from that space where the patch of blue disappeared into a brightness animated only by the sun itself.

As he knelt for the prayers and stood for the hymns and listened to the talk of the vicar, walking up and down between the pews, this final thought absorbed him entirely.

And later, although his mother insisted on coming with him to the bottom of Spinney Moor Avenue, he had felt an immediate relief to see, on mounting the bus, the cinema then the Spinney Moor Hotel pass by, the bus rattling on towards the town and, watching its darkening contour approach, he had thought, 'I am going back to her, and she, I know, will be just as glad to see me.'

'Watty always picks on you,' Parkinson said. 'If he doesn't pick on you in the morning, he will in the afternoon.'

'On me?' Bryan said, for Mr Waterhouse had seldom had the occasion, since his first day at Peterson's, to speak to him directly.

'On me,' Parkinson said, quickening his stride. To their right appeared a tree-enclosed square: tall, terraced houses, with balconied first floors, looked out to a patch of grass encircled, in turn, by metal railings; the fourth side of the square was overlooked by a building Bryan had never seen before. At the top of a flight of yellow-tiled steps three pairs of glass-panelled doors opened on to a red-walled foyer: figures in black dresses were moving to and fro; a more conspicuous figure, in a dark-brown coat and a red peaked cap embellished with gold braid, was standing at the top of the steps themselves: a pair of yellow gloves was threaded through the tasselled strap on the shoulder of the coat, and a pair of large brown boots was conspicuous beneath the bottoms of the turned-up trousers.

Above the steps several cream-coloured columns rose to an

entablature within the blue-painted recesses of which were arranged a number of white-coloured figures; the frieze itself, surmounted by a cornice, was overlooked in turn by a large glass dome: coloured panes of glass gleamed and glistened in the afternoon light.

'The Phoenix,' Parkinson said. His tall, pale-cheeked, red-haired figure swayed as he surveyed the lighted foyer, the lettering above and, more specifically, the tall, brown-coated man who, raising a hand, waved in their direction, indicating, as he did so, a sandwich board propped on the steps which read – in yellow lettering on a blue surround – 'Matinée 2.30'.

'How are you, Gordon?' the man called down.

'We're all right, Tommy,' Parkinson called up.

'Where's your brother?'

'At school,' Parkinson called out.

'Why aren't you?'

'Lunch-hour.' Parkinson was already moving off. 'Come on,' he added, scarcely glancing at the man again.

'Come and see the show.' The man gestured to the foyer.

'Come on,' Parkinson called again to Bryan.

'Cater for all sorts,' the man called down. 'Long 'uns, fat 'uns, short 'uns, thin 'uns. Him an' all,' the man added, gesturing at Bryan.

'Who's that?' Bryan said, catching Parkinson up.

'A friend of my father's.' Parkinson paused.

'How does he know him?'

'By way of business. Though he knows my brother best,' he added.

'How does he know your brother?' Bryan said, intrigued by the uniformed figure as well as by the square itself – its balconied houses, its overhanging trees, the flight of yellow-tiled steps, the red-walled foyer – and by what he could see now were the frosted panes of a public house, standing at the corner of the square and separated from the theatre by a cobbled yard.

'He comes to the Nelson.' Parkinson indicated a sign above the door on which was depicted a one-eyed, one-armed figure in a nautical costume, a telescope beneath its one good arm and a sailing ship, firing its guns, at sea, in the background.

Half-way along the yard, protruding from the wall of the theatre, was an illuminated sign which read 'Artistes' Entrance'.

Directly opposite stood a green-painted door on which, after glancing through a pane of bottle-green glass, Parkinson knocked; having received no answer he rattled the latch, opened the door and, calling, 'Anyone at home?' descended a flight of steps inside.

An interior, paved by flagstones and illuminated by a single window adjacent to the door itself, was occupied by a black enamelled range and, in the centre of the floor, by a large square table. Hanging from a number of wooden beams were a side of bacon, several rabbits, a hare, an unplucked hen and what looked like, in the furthest corner, the carcase of a sheep.

A roar of voices, intermingled with the sound of glasses, came from beyond a glass-panelled door.

Sitting by the fire was a figure covered by a shawl who, at Parkinson's inquiry, 'Is Reg in, Mrs Brierley?' called, 'He won't hear you, sonny. He's far too busy,' glancing across at Bryan and adding, 'If you ask me, he's as daft as his brother.'

Parkinson crossed to the glass-panelled door but, before he could reach it, it was pushed open from the other side: a small, square-shouldered man with a balding head, glistening with sweat, and dark-brown eyes, a broken nose and a rugged jaw, came bustling in. 'Anything up?' he said, catching sight of Parkinson as a burst of laughter came from the bar the other side. 'What's this, then, Gordon? Not at school?'

'It's lunch-hour, Reggie,' Parkinson said.

'Bit of the usual?'

'I wouldn't say no.'

'Shan't be a sec.' The man disappeared once more to the bar, his reappearance beyond the door greeted by a burst of shouts.

'Reggie's popular,' Parkinson said. 'He used to be a boxer,' and sat down at the table, indicating that Bryan might do the same. 'This is Reggie's mother,' he added.

'How do you do?' The woman, having turned to scrutinize Bryan, laughed, soundlessly, her mouth – bereft of teeth – wide open.

'She's eighty-two.'

'Three,' the woman said.

'I knew it was over eighty,' Parkinson said.

'Who are you?' the woman said.

'This is Bryan, Mrs Brierley,' Parkinson said.

'Who?'

'Morley.'

'Never heard of him,' the woman said.

'He's a friend of mine,' Parkinson insisted.

'I never knew you had a friend.' She returned her gaze to the fire.

The surface of the table was covered by sheets of newspaper; half the sheets were coloured pink, and the other half green: several bottles and a miscellaneous collection of glasses, together with several patterned plates and a pile of knives and forks, were stacked along one side.

'The actors come over,' Parkinson said. 'Some of them have digs upstairs.'

'They're not here now,' the woman said. 'They're over for the matinée.'

'Have you been to see it?' Parkinson said.

'I haven't. I've never been, nor will I ever,' the woman said, glancing at Bryan just as the door opened from the bar and the square-shouldered, bald-headed figure of Mr Brierley reappeared.

'Who's this?' he said, catching sight of Bryan.

'His name's Morley,' the woman said. 'He's a friend of Clive's.'

'Gordon,' Parkinson said, and added, 'This is Reggie, Bryan.'

'Glad to meet you.' The man extended his hand, clasped Bryan's, shook it, and added, 'I suppose you'd like a drop yourself,' and returned to the door the other side.

'To your good health, Mrs Brierley.' Parkinson raised the glass Mr Brierley had brought him.

'Good health and fiddlesticks. I'm old and poorly,' Mrs Brierley said.

'You look well enough to me, Mrs Brierley,' Parkinson said, wiping his mouth on the back of his hand, belching, and adding, with a glance at Bryan, 'Grand.'

'Do you know his brother?' the woman said to Bryan.

'No,' he said.

'His name is Gordon.'

'I'm Gordon,' Parkinson said.

210

'So you're Gordon,' the woman replied, 'I thought you were Clive,' glancing at Bryan again, and winking.

The door from the bar reopened; several bowls and a plate were pushed aside and a glass set down. 'Anything else while I'm here?' Mr Brierley asked.

'This'll do fine, Reg.' Parkinson raised his glass and drank, lengthily, in illustration.

The man turned to the woman, adding, 'I'll be in the bar if you want me, Mother,' and closed the door, once more, behind.

'That's Reggie,' Parkinson said. 'He's a jolly good sort. I often come at lunch-times and sometimes, if I've had enough of Watty, I come in the afternoon. We sometimes play darts and have a sing-song. I come at weekends, too.' He glanced at Bryan's glass. 'I'll finish it off, if you like. Like nectar to the gods, is this.'

Bryan passed across his glass.

'You ought to let him drink it. Puts hairs on your chest.' The old woman laughed. 'Takes everything he can that doesn't belong to him. Like his brother. He's just as bad.'

The brown liquid disappeared down Parkinson's throat: he gulped, belched, said, 'Excuse me,' and, gazing at Bryan with a glazed expression, added, 'Worth every penny.'

'You don't pay for it, that's why,' the woman said.

'How much should I leave behind, Mrs Brierley?' Parkinson asked.

'We're not allowed to sell to juveniles,' the woman said. 'You're worse than your brother Gordon.'

'I'm Gordon, Mrs Brierley,' Parkinson said. He got up from the table, staggered, paused, then added, 'We ought to be going. It's Heppy this afternoon and he always tells Watty if I don't turn up.'

'Leaving us, are you?' the woman said.

'We've school,' Parkinson said, 'in one or two minutes. We'll have to be going.'

'I'll school you when I see your brother Gordon.' The old woman glanced at Bryan, winked and, indicating the rafters overhead, asked, 'Do you want a rabbit?'

'No, thanks, Mrs Brierley,' Parkinson said.

211

'Don't let him lead you into mischief. He's worse than his brother.' The old woman stooped, picked up a poker and stabbed at the flames.

Parkinson mounted the steps to the door, called, 'We're going now, Reggie,' and, getting no response, added, 'We're going now, Mrs Brierley,' and, waiting for Bryan to precede him, stepped outside.

'How did you come to know them?' Bryan said as, emerging from the entrance to the yard, they passed in front of the theatre.

'They're friends of my father.'

'Not too late to come in, boys,' the uniformed man called down.

'That's Tommy,' Parkinson said. 'He knows everyone in town.'

'How?' Bryan said.

'He makes it his business.' Parkinson glanced across. 'He's as bad as Watty.'

'Does Watty know everyone?' Bryan asked.

Parkinson coughed. He cupped his hand to his mouth, swayed, held his hand to his forehead, and said, 'He knows your aunt.'

'How does he know her?' Bryan said.

'He said it was every man's privilege to know one beautiful woman and his privilege had been acceded to when he first set eyes on Mrs Corrigan.'

'Where did he see her?' Bryan said.

'In the street.'

'He hasn't spoken to her,' he said.

'How do you know?'

'She would have told me.'

'Does she tell you everything?'

'Almost.'

Red double-decker buses were lined up at their stops in the Bull Ring.

'Just like Watty to say he knows her. He said he knew my father before he met him.'

'What does your father do?' Bryan asked.

'He's a book-maker.' Parkinson set off up the road to the school.

'What sort of books does he make?' Bryan said.

'He doesn't make books, he keeps one,' Parkinson said.

'What sort of a book?'

'For backing horses.' Parkinson flushed. 'Reggie owes him money but my father doesn't make him pay because he takes bets for him at the Nelson and gives us drinks. Watty bets as well,' he added. 'And Tommy, the doorman at the theatre, he takes bets as well. So does my brother,' he continued. 'So do I, as a matter of fact. Why, everything,' he concluded as they neared the school – and emphasizing the word 'everything' by slapping one hand against the other – 'in the last analysis, Mocky, comes down to money.'

'I've already moved it once,' Mr Hepplewhite said.

He indicated the blackboard on metal castors which had been swung round from his desk to face, at an oblique angle, the two windows across the room.

'The light shines on it, Mr Hepplewhite,' Parkinson called out.

'A moment before,' Mr Hepplewhite said, wiping one chalk-dusted hand on the other, 'it didn't shine upon it quite enough.'

'It hides what's written on it,' Parkinson said.

'There's nothing written on it,' the master said. 'It is,' he added, 'a drawing of a scientific experiment which you should by now have copied in your book.'

'I can't see the blackboard,' Parkinson said, his eyes matched in their gravity only by those of the teacher himself.

Mr Hepplewhite was a tall man; his skin was pale, and his hair, which was dishevelled as a result of his efforts to copy on to the blackboard a drawing from a black-bound book, was streaked here and there with flecks of dust. Patches of white chalk also marked his cheeks, and additional patches the sleeves and the collar of his jacket.

He moved the blackboard in Parkinson's direction.

'I can't see it, sir,' a voice called from across the room.

'Move your desk.' Mr Hepplewhite examined once more his black-bound book before, with a cry of vexation, he amended the drawing.

The legs of a desk scraped against the floor; its lid banged.

213

'I can't see because Williams has gone in front of me,' another voice said.

'Move your desk,' Mr Hepplewhite said.

Another desk lid was banged; the legs of a chair were scraped against the floor.

'I can't see it, sir.'

'Move.'

'I can't see it, sir,' another voice said.

'I expect this drawing to be finished by this afternoon.'

'Charlesworth's gone in front of me, sir.'

'Move.'

Fresh clouds of dust rose from the blackboard: a chalk-dusted arm was raised; fresh lines were drawn across the greyish surface.

'He's not even qualified,' Parkinson said, speaking behind his hand. 'He gets it from a book then comes in here as if he knew it.'

'You've pushed it back, sir,' another voice said.

'I shall move it for the last time.' Mr Hepplewhite glanced at the room: his blue eyes, the brows and lashes of which were laden with dust, expressed surprise at the disorder of the desks before him. 'Who gave you permission to move all those?'

'You, sir.'

'I shall listen to no further excuses about the light.'

He turned, drew on the blackboard, rubbed vigorously at an inadvertent line, drew again, consulted the black-bound book, drew, consulted the book, rubbed out, then drew again.

'Sir?'

Mr Hepplewhite's head remained bowed to the blackboard.

'I can't see it when you stand in front of it.'

'I shall go immediately and fetch Mr Berresford.'

'Yes, sir.'

The tall, white-haired figure strode quickly from the room.

Several desks were drawn hurriedly together.

Parkinson leaned back in his chair; he stretched his arms, belched, caused a ripple of laughter to pass across the room, yawned, belched, yawned, then belched again.

The door opened. A black-suited figure came inside.

His hair was plastered smoothly to the back of his skull; he wore, beneath his suit, a clerical collar and, beneath the collar, a black vestment.

His physique was large, his eyes expanded, his nostrils flared, his thick lips drawn back into the coruscations of flesh on either side.

'Who?' he said, standing in the door.

Mr Hepplewhite appeared from the hall behind.

'That.' He pointed at Bryan.

'Stand up.'

The sound of traffic was audible from the street outside.

Bryan stood up.

'Not him,' Mr Hepplewhite said.

'Who?'

'The one behind.'

'Parkinson.'

'Yes, sir?'

'Stand up.'

Parkinson stood up.

'Sit down,' the black figure added, indicating Bryan.

'I didn't do anything,' Parkinson said.

'He has done nothing but complain about the light,' Mr Hepplewhite said.

'I haven't,' Parkinson said.

'In addition to several others moving their desks in imitation of the same complaint.'

'Out.'

The black-clad figure stepped aside and one arm was raised to indicate the hall.

'I shall deal with this individual,' he added, 'myself. Mr Berresford is not available at present.' He gazed round him at the room. 'Is there anyone else?'

'Parkinson is the chief culprit,' Mr Hepplewhite said.

'I don't mind half a dozen,' the black-clad figure said. 'If anyone makes a whisper I shall require his presence in Mr Berresford's study where the traditional method of correction will be employed.'

'I shall send anyone else up directly,' Mr Hepplewhite said.

The black-clad figure went out, closing the door behind.

215

'Mr Berresford is not available, so anyone who misbehaves will have to be dealt with by Doctor Beckerman,' Mr Hepplewhite said, returning to the blackboard.

The castors squeaked; several desks were realigned: no further sound came from the room save an occasional gasp from Mr Hepplewhite, a corresponding gasping from the children, and the subsequent scratching of the master's chalk.

Four symmetrical patches of light fell directly on the table, isolating the sheets of paper laid there and intensifying further the shadows where the attic roof disappeared behind a line of cupboards.

'One of our number is missing,' Miss Lightowler said.

She examined the three other figures, in addition to Bryan's, and added, 'Gordon.'

'He's gone to see Doctor Beckerman, Miss Lightowler,' one of the figures said.

'What for?'

'Misbehaviour in Mr Hepplewhite's class,' the figure said.

Miss Lightowler flushed.

'I trust we shall have no repeat of it here.'

'No, Miss Lightowler.'

The four figures seated themselves on stools and stooped to the table.

'You have a natural facility, Bryan,' Miss Lightowler said, watching Bryan's pencil move across the paper then, as a consequence of her scrutiny, come to a halt. 'If you've achieved eighty, I shall expect you,' she added, 'to aim for a hundred.'

'A hundred what?' one of the other three said.

'The proverbial hundred,' Miss Lightowler said. 'Which is what,' she concluded, 'we all aspire to.'

Her eyes were cast in shadow from the attic window which in turn looked out to a chimney protruding from the roof of the adjoining buildings; tins of paint were assembled on a nearby table and, after examining each sheet of paper, Miss Lightowler began mixing colours in a variety of jars.

'I want you to get on to paint,' she said from the shadow of the room.

216

They drew in silence; periodically from below came the sound of someone shouting, the occasional slamming of a door, while, from outside, and across the adjoining roofs, came the distant roar of traffic.

A spire was visible beyond the window; clouds of smoke loomed across the sky. The woodwork of the rafters creaked.

Thin strands of dust gyrated in the pool of light which fell from the four-paned window.

'My parents, Miss Lightowler, wanted me to do Greek,' one of the figures said, its arm stretched out across the table.

'I understand art was recommended, Phillips,' Miss Lightowler said.

'Yes, Miss.'

'An unexpected bonus,' Miss Lightowler concluded.

Her eyes glowed from the darkness; disproportionately positioned over the corners of her thin-lipped mouth, their size ensured they were the most prominent feature of her thin-boned face. Her hair, dark-brown, was swept back from a central parting and tied with a ribbon at the nape of her neck.

'I'd prefer to do Greek, Miss Lightowler.'

'Doctor Beckerman's selection of classicists is invariably restricted,' Miss Lightowler said. 'Whereas art,' she continued, 'is accessible to all. It is not technique alone that counts, but feeling.'

The door of the attic room reopened and Parkinson's half-bent figure came inside.

Miss Lightowler paused.

'I trust Doctor Beckerman has given you permission to come up,' she said.

'Yes, Miss Lightowler,' Parkinson said, his head thrust forward. 'He said I could.'

'I hope you are in a suitable condition for sitting down.'

'Yes, Miss.'

'I understand,' Miss Lightowler said, 'you have been subjected to chastisement by Doctor Beckerman.'

'He telephoned my father,' Parkinson said.

'What did your father say?'

'He said he'd see me when I got back home.'

217

'Of the two chastisements, I imagine the domestic rather than the pedagogical will be the more severe.'

'Yes, Miss,' Parkinson said and, stooping to the table, thrust his legs beneath it, dislodging, as he did so, a tin of paint.

SIXTEEN

The light from the fire illuminated the low-ceilinged room and Mrs Spencer, who had been dozing by the flames, got up, yawning, then looking about her in some confusion. 'Oh, it's you,' she said to Margaret, glancing at her as she took off her boots, and adding, 'Look at his shoes,' as Bryan stooped in the porch and scraped off, on a metal grill, the mud around his heels. 'I thought you'd walk on the roads at least.'

A cloth was already set on the table; bread stood on a board and, beside it, a dish of butter and a bowl of jam. Several scones, recently baked, stood on a wire-mesh tray: a smell of baking filled the kitchen.

'If God doesn't exist, and there is no ultimate purpose, what's the point of living?'

Margaret stood at the sink, washing her hands, and directed this inquiry to the mirror hanging on the wall before her.

'That's not a problem to solve on a day like this,' Mrs Spencer said. A kettle was simmering on the fire and, as she poured the water into a teapot and the steam rose in a cloud about her head, she added, 'Certainly not at tea-time, either.'

'Why not?' Having washed her hands and dried them, Margaret added, 'When the light is fading, and the fire dying down, and the cows come in for milking.'

The lowing of the cattle came from the yard outside.

Bryan washed his hands at the sink; beneath his raincoat he was wearing his light-blue blazer and light-grey trousers: a uniform neither Margaret nor her mother had seen him in before. After cleaning his shoes he had taken them off at the door and now stood on the stone paving of the kitchen floor in his stocking feet.

Perhaps it was this transformation in his appearance that

distracted Mrs Spencer, for she was gazing across at him as if, having expected one person to come in the door, someone entirely different had entered. 'Who's this?' her look inquired while, wearily, she asked, 'What's so special about this time of the day that questions like that have got to be answered?'

Margaret sat at the table; having taken off her coat she was wearing a roll-necked jumper: it made her look older, as if she, and not the mother, were running the house. 'Don't you remember when you and Daddy first moved here?' She glanced round her at the room. 'You were told there'd been a farm on this site for a thousand years and, previous to that, in Ten Acre bank, they'd found arrow-heads from when the fields by the river were still a lake and neolithic men, after the last Ice Age, hunted along its shore.' She glanced at Bryan. 'Beneath this kitchen, men with only hair for protection sat, like we are, and had a meal.'

The bread was being cut: the impression created by Bryan's light-grey shirt, his blue-striped tie, his blue blazer with its yellow beading, by the badge with the one word 'Independence' embroidered underneath, was reflected in the bright-eyed gaze of Margaret; her cheeks flushed from the walk, her forehead, with her drawn-back hair, more boldly marked than ever, her blue eyes, so much like her father's, gleaming in the light from the fire, she examined him for a while in silence: 'Who is this?' her look inquired.

Mrs Spencer's eyes were animated not only by a look of curiosity but, he thought, by apprehension; the pot of tea trembled as she filled the cups, Margaret taking over the task of slicing the bread. 'How many?' she asked, and passed them on the knife, adding, 'So not only is it the time for speculation, but also the place.' She pointed the knife first at the stone-paved floor and then at the ceiling.

Mrs Spencer sat down at the table. 'Mr Spencer's out, Bryan,' she said. 'There's just the three of us at present.'

'No one comes back from the dead to tell us there's a life here-after,' Margaret said. 'Since the last war anyone can see that the whole of human life could be wiped out without God, if there is one, intervening; so what value do we put on anything and, if there is a value, why do we go to the trouble of doing anything about it?'

220

'Self-interest,' Mrs Spencer said.

Margaret bit her lip: 'I don't see why, if we're here like animals, we shouldn't do anything which expands our lives in whatever way we choose,' she said.

'With the proviso,' Mrs Spencer said, 'that it does no harm to others.'

'Irrespective of whether it causes harm.'

'You can't murder someone,' Mrs Spencer said.

'Why not?'

'The law wouldn't allow it. Nor,' she added, 'would your conscience. It would tell you you were wrong.'

'What if your conscience says you should?'

'Common sense,' Mrs Spencer said, 'would intervene.'

'Common sense,' Margaret said, 'is only a substitute for a lack of courage.'

The fire crackled in the grate: the lowing of the cattle in the yard had faded. Two dogs, lying by the hearth, got up, stretched, then, after glancing at the table, lay down again.

'If you abandon law, then there's nothing to stop anyone doing anything.' Mrs Spencer, gazing at her plate, drew several crumbs together.

'Not everyone would abandon law, and most people would struggle to uphold it,' Margaret said. 'But there must be people in every age who question what their lives are for. With people like that,' she concluded, 'anything is possible.'

'What do you think, Bryan?' Mrs Spencer asked.

'I don't know what she means,' he said.

'Of course he understands,' Margaret said. 'It's him I'm talking about,' she added.

Mrs Spencer smiled. 'The scones are for tea,' she said, moving the metal tray towards him.

'He's ideally placed.'

Mrs Spencer smiled again.

'He has ambition, he has ability when he wishes to use it, as you have pointed out yourself.'

'Bryan has everything to gain by upholding values which people rely on,' Mrs Spencer said and, reaching across, placed a smaller bowl in front of his plate. 'There's cream to go on the scones as well.'

221

'Bryan has everything to lose by upholding accepted values,' Margaret said. 'It's people like us who gain by behaving in the same old way. After all,' she concluded, 'he doesn't wish to end up like us.'

'Why not?'

'He wants to be someone special.' She glanced at Bryan.

Mrs Spencer took a scone herself. 'Aunt Fay is doing her best by Bryan, very largely for reasons you despise,' she said.

Margaret laughed. 'Whatever the motives of Aunt Fay, the fact remains that Bryan has the means as well as the ambition to do anything he likes.'

'Within reason.'

'Excluding reason.' Margaret clattered her knife against her plate as, suddenly, rising in the hearth, the dogs began to bark.

'There's your father,' Mrs Spencer said, yet a moment later only a knock came on the kitchen door and when Mrs Spencer went to open it the figure of a labourer was standing there, a cap in his hand, his jacket open, a torn pullover and a collarless shirt visible underneath.

'We'll be off now, Mrs Spencer,' the man said, calling inside and glancing in, as he did so, at the table.

'Right, Finnegan,' Mrs Spencer said.

'Good night,' the man called.

'Good night, Finnegan,' Mrs Spencer said. 'I'll make a note of the time.'

The man nodded into the open door then turned and walked back across the yard.

A draught of cold air and the smell of the cowsheds came in before the door was closed.

For a moment Bryan had thought it might have been his father.

'You're making too much of Bryan,' Mrs Spencer said, glancing at the clock then taking her place once more at the table.

'Only because others make too little of him,' Margaret said. 'Your instinct is to protect him, whereas mine is to encourage him all I can.'

'This comes from watching too many films,' Mrs Spencer said. 'Was she like this on your walk?'

'We were talking about Mrs Corrigan,' Bryan said.

222

'She and her aunt have never seen eye to eye,' Mrs Spencer said.

'We get on handsomely,' Margaret said. 'Each of us sees,' she added, 'what the other is about.'

Mrs Spencer got up from the table. 'You won't mind if I sit by the fire?' she said. 'The two of you go on without me.'

Margaret, too, got up; she began to collect the plates.

'There's so much I ought to do,' Mrs Spencer said, 'yet I've scarcely energy to do anything today.'

'What has the doctor said?' her daughter asked, splashing water at the sink.

'To rest. But how can you rest,' she added, 'in a place like this?'

'I'm surprised you have so much sympathy for Aunt Fay when she has nothing to do with her time but waste it.' Margaret held out a tea-towel and called, 'Will you dry these, Bryan?'

The dogs stirred by the fire and, a short while later, from the bowing of her head, Bryan assumed that her mother was asleep.

'She isn't well but no one does anything about it,' Margaret said. 'Least of all my father.'

'Am I disturbing you?' came Mrs Spencer's voice, dreamily, and Margaret called, 'You rest, Mother. Bryan and I are only talking.'

The table was cleared and the pots put away.

'I'll walk with you to the stop,' Margaret said. 'She'll be all right on her own.' She got their coats; outside, the yard had darkened.

'Are you going, Bryan?' Mrs Spencer called.

'I'll walk with him to the bus, Mother,' Margaret said.

'I hope tea wasn't disappointing, Bryan,' Mrs Spencer said, without raising her head. 'Come again, won't you, whenever you like. We're always glad to see you.'

In the yard, with a yellowish glow from the opaque glass panes in the cowsheds illuminating the mud and the pools, Margaret said, 'She takes medicine which makes her sleepy but I think, although she doesn't say so, she suffers a lot of pain.'

As they got to the road a car pulled up. 'That you, Bryan?' the farmer called. 'Don't see much of you these days.'

'He's just leaving, Father,' Margaret said.

'Stay and have some tea,' the farmer said.

'We've had some.'

'Is your mother in?'

'She's fallen asleep.'

The balding head gazed out at Bryan.

'You're looking smart.'

'He is smart, Father,' Margaret called, already several strides away. 'Come on,' she added. 'You'll miss the bus.'

'Come down sooner,' the farmer called. 'Give Aunt Fay our love.'

'I shall.' He nodded.

The car turned into the drive and disappeared.

'Why do you argue with your mother?' Bryan said as they walked up the lane to the road beyond the farm.

'I don't do it to upset her,' Margaret said. 'But I believe in what I told her.'

'That certain people,' Bryan said, 'can do anything they like.'

She looked away; the lane rose circuitously up the slope to the castle: something of the outline of the lake was visible below, like a misty imprint across which, in a thicker band of mist, coiled the broadening strand of the river.

'Ruthlessness,' Margaret said, 'doesn't exist, except for people like my mother.'

'There's such a thing as love,' Bryan said.

'What love?'

'The love of another person that stops you from acting in the way that you describe.'

'You wouldn't let love stop you from doing what you wanted?'

The lights of the main road appeared. A bus, in the far distance, was rattling down the slope towards them.

'Not someone who wants to do something which he knows no one else can do.'

He began to run.

'You're not going back on what you said?'

'When?'

'Ages ago.'

He reached the stop.

'This special destiny you have, which licenses everything that happens.'

'I haven't given it up,' he said.

'Well?'

She was panting; the light from the street lamp illuminated not only her features but the vapour from her breath.

'I have to do it my way,' Bryan said.

'Oh, your way,' she said. 'Well, there's only the one way. I might have known you'd cover it up. Though why with me,' she added, 'I've no idea. With me especially, Bryan.'

The bus drew up, its lights amplifying the glow from the overhead lamp: she frowned, then said, 'Give my love to my aunt. Tell her,' she added, 'I think of her,' and as he mounted the bus she called, 'As for you, I'm not sure what you're really up to,' standing there as the bus drew off so that, glancing back, he could still see her in the pool of light, gazing after him, and then – as he raised his arm – reminded, raising her hand and waving.

'I don't think I've ever seen anything like it,' Miss Lightowler said. 'Have you modelled with clay before?'

'Yes,' he said.

She turned the block of wood on the table before him to an angle at which the figure modelled on it might catch the light.

Above the chest the shoulders rose to the curve of the elongated neck, above which, in turn, was suspended the minutely featured head, surmounted by a froth of sculpted curls, the face animated by what, even from a distance, could be identified as a smile – slight, unmistakable and – framed between two dimpled cheeks – beguiling.

'Have you modelled a figure before?'

'No.'

'It's a considerable achievement.' Miss Lightowler's hand extended itself above the figure. 'I like the features.'

'Yes.'

'And the smile.'

Chairs creaked.

'Is anything the matter, Gordon?'

'No, Miss,' Parkinson said.

'Don't you think it good?'

'Yes, Miss.'

His blue eyes gazed out, blankly, from beneath his freckled brow.

'Has anyone any comment?'

'It's naked, Miss.'

'Any objection?'

'No, Miss.'

The faces were turned in her direction but the eyes in each face were cast towards the figure reclining on its wooden block.

'The angle of the hips I like,' Miss Lightowler added, 'and the way,' she continued, 'the one shoulder is subtended from the other. The whole depiction,' she extended her hand, 'is true to art as well as life.'

She raised her head.

'We can cast it.'

'How?' he said.

'We can make a mould. Meanwhile,' she added, 'we must keep it damp.' She glanced at Bryan and smiled. 'What do you usually do with your figures in order to preserve them?'

'I throw them away.'

'We won't throw this away,' Miss Lightowler said. 'And once you've cast it,' she continued, glancing at the boys, 'you can regale us with some other evidence of your skill. Perhaps an animal,' she concluded.

Only on the way down did Parkinson say, 'That was a close shave, Mocky. I thought it was footer, from now on, on Thursdays.'

'Why?' he said.

'I didn't think she would wear it.'

'I don't see why.'

'Clothes, or no clothes?' a voice called out and, as they descended the stairs to the floor below and, from there, to the hall, his mind went back to the amorphous mound of clay and, with the same detachment with which he had watched the shape manifest itself beneath his hands, he speculated on whether he might have made it larger or, if not larger, standing up. Running down the last steps, he called, 'Shall we go to Reggie's?' and was already in the street by the time his friend appeared, standing at the door before, finally, gazing down at Bryan and laughing.

'If you find the line that marks the furthest outward projection,' Miss Lightowler said, indicating with her finger the contour of the hip, 'you can insert each strip to form a continuous edge,' inserting the film of tin herself, then handing him the rest and adding, 'You do it now. You have to learn.'

Disinclined to damage the figure, he nevertheless constructed across the profile of the hip, the arm, the shoulder and the head, a barricade of tin which divided the front half of the body from the back: a filament of tin he inserted in the orifice between the legs.

At the central table the boys leaned on their boards, the tins of paint set out beside them.

Miss Lightowler's arm, its sleeve rolled to the elbow, was inserted in a bowl of plaster; a handful having been lifted out and held in such a position that not only Bryan but the boys might see it, it was dropped, with a downward extension of her fingers, on to the figure: its thighs and then its abdomen disappeared. Engulfed, the further extremities of the feet and head succumbed to the repeated dabbing, the scraping inside the bowl and the irregular flicking out.

Soon, only a mound of plaster remained, its two halves separated by the projecting layer of tin. The horror that she might have destroyed the figure, obliterating the clay for good, was displaced in Bryan by a curious sensation which came from watching the figure disappear, the thighs, the hips, the waist, the breasts, until, finally, only the smiling head remained, tilted back: then that too was enclosed by the dome of white and, for good measure, one or two lumps more were flicked across the surface, touched in here and there by Miss Lightowler's whitened fingers. Turning to the tap to wash her hands, she said, 'Next week we can remove the clay and clean it. I can't wait to see the final result.' Her back to the room, her hands in the sink, picking at the drops of hardening plaster which had coagulated around her wrist, her smock – flower-patterned and buttoned down the front – flecked with plaster, too, Miss Lightowler glanced at Bryan and then at the tin-divided plaster and, smiling, added, 'You'll have to think of a title,

Bryan. It could be a name.' Having washed out the bowl she turned it upside-down. 'Anything in mind?'

'No,' he said.

'Not a goddess?'

He shook his head.

'It could be both real, as well as mythological. Like Helen.'

He shook his head.

'Or Diane.'

Miss Lightowler smiled a second time.

'My name is Diane, as a matter of fact. I'm not sure, in the circumstances, I would welcome its use. How about Penelope?'

'No,' he said.

'We'll have to think.' Miss Lightowler glanced round the room. 'Anything the matter, Gordon?'

'No, Miss.' Parkinson's guffaw, aroused by the revelation of Miss Lightowler's name, had been followed by a snort.

'Remember the motto of the art-room.'

'Yes, Miss.'

'Concrete and specific.' She indicated the words written on a notice which hung on the wall above what was the only permanent fixture in the room: a sealed-off fireplace. 'C and S.' She indicated that Bryan might return to the table.

'Diane,' a voice interceded from the end of the room, followed by a snigger.

'It must be cold on the sports field this time of the year.' Miss Lightowler moved around the table, glancing over the backs at the wooden boards, each mounted centrally by a piece of tinted paper. 'I'm sure it must be preferable, however, to those who have no intention of understanding the disciplines of art.' Passing by Parkinson's back, she added, 'What are the disciplines of art?'

'I don't know, Miss.'

'I've read them on the notice, Gordon.'

'Concrete and specific.' Parkinson raised his head.

'To be specific and to be concrete. To the point,' she concluded, glancing at Bryan, 'and to be exact.'

'First,' she said, 'we'll detach it from its base,' and handed the heavily-weighted board along the bench, together with a piece

228

of wire, to either end of which was attached a wooden peg. 'Slice it like a piece of cheese,' she added.

He slid the wire towards him, felt it grate against the plaster and, towards the middle, against the softness of the clay beneath.

'Turn it over.'

He lifted the plaster from the board.

'We'll scrape it out.'

'Won't it spoil it?' Bryan asked.

'This is the easiest part,' she said and, taking the spatula, began to dig out the clay herself.

Nothing of the model now remained, its surface only distinguishable as the inner cavity of the plaster was suddenly revealed. An inverted image of the figure appeared, the abdomen, the legs, the arms and, finally – its features echoed in the recess of the mould – the head.

'We'll wash it out.' Miss Lightowler parted the piece of plaster, along the line of the metal foil, into two uneven sections.

She rinsed each section beneath the tap; within the wedges of plaster he could discern more clearly the lineaments of the figure, the abdomen cut along its length, the features of the face on one side, the back of the head on the other.

'We'll cast it this afternoon,' she said, and laid the pieces to dry, face upwards, by the sink. 'We'll paint the inside of the mould with clay, to make sure the plaster doesn't stick.'

He gazed at Miss Lightowler's hands as she took the spatula to mix the plaster, and said, 'Shall I paint the mould myself?'

'Oh, I'll do that. It has to be light. Merely a smear.' She turned to the sink, extracted clay from the bin beneath it, mixing it with water. She painted the inside of the separated halves: the inverse of the figure showed more clearly, the details of the eyes, the lips and, below the shoulders, the configuration of the chest. 'The consistency has to be right. Not too thick. Nor must it be too thin,' taking a length of coloured ribbon after painting the inside of the mould and adding, 'We'll join the halves together.'

She arranged the mould with its base upturned, its two halves coated along their adjacent edges with a layer of clay and fastened by the ribbon. 'Into the mould it goes,' she called finally, the head and the upper extremities disappearing first, the whiteness

229

expanding upwards from the neck, across the shoulders, around the abdomen and into the crevices that formed the toes.

Into the central cavity of the body Miss Lightowler inserted a length of wire.

'Stiffening.' She inserted the wire more firmly, inserted a second, shaped the plaster into a rectangular base and added, 'We'll put it on the shelf to dry.'

'We'll chip it first,' she said, 'to see if it'll take the pressure,' holding the chisel against the joint and, with a wooden mallet, tapping the handle, a thin crack appearing in the mould, whereupon she raised her head, glancing down at him, and added, 'It's coming,' running her finger along its edge. She tapped the crack again.

The boys glanced up; some leant forward, the drawing-boards propped up before them: with the tapping of the mallet the table shook.

The mould split; she prised the halves apart, loosening one side and then the other.

'If we can get it off in two pieces we can use it again. Even if it cracks into three or four, we might still patch it up,' she added.

She tapped at either end with the chisel, tapped again, and laid the mallet down.

Stooping, she drew one half of the mould away.

Loosening the other half, she drew it off: the head, white-dusted, was revealed inside, its features intact, the abdomen curved to the line of the hip, the toes extended at the end of either foot, the knees subtended, one from the other, drawn apart, the pelvis turned upwards from the angle of the hips, the supporting arm running up to the flexed white shoulder.

No one spoke.

'The mould hasn't cracked,' Miss Lightowler said.

The clay-lined interior of each half lay on either side of the figure.

'We can smooth the mould-line off,' she added, running her hand along the roughened edge.

She produced a piece of sandpaper and, stooping, removed the rim of protruding plaster which crescented the head.

'Your job.' She handed him the paper. 'Take it off gently without damaging the rest.'

The boys got up from the table; they ran the tips of their fingers along the legs, over the hips and, in Parkinson's case, across the shoulders so that, in drawing it aside, Bryan said, 'I haven't finished,' removing the protruding rim of plaster so that finally, no longer blemished, the figure reclined beneath him on its plaster mount.

'Shall we give it a bronze colour, like metal, or ebony, like wood?' Miss Lightowler said, having inverted the moulds on the table to dry.

The boys went back to their places: the murmur of voices resumed, the rattle of paint-tins, the scraping of chairs.

'How do we colour it?' Bryan said.

'Polish is best,' Miss Lightowler said, running her finger along the figure.

'What kind of polish?'

'Boot.' Miss Lightowler laughed. 'Paint will merely be absorbed, whereas polish,' she added, raising her head, 'can always be polished, and always,' she concluded, opening a drawer and getting out a tin, together with a rag, and addressing the room in general, 'comes up with a shine!'

A large crowd had collected around the table; at first, approaching it, he was unable to see between the bodies: only when he had completed a circuit of the room did he catch a glimpse, not of any shape, but merely of a colour, and realized that the cause of all the pushing and jostling, the shouting and the laughter, was his brown-polished figure, lying on a box or plinth set on a table in the centre of the floor.

Typed on a sheet of paper beside it was the cryptic message, 'RECUMBENT FORM. EXECUTED BY BRYAN MORLEY'.

The table on which the figure was arranged was one which was used to display objects of an archaeological nature: one week a key had lain there, found in the garden of an adjoining house; on another occasion a collection of fossils had been exhibited inside a showcase and, previous to that, Bryan recalled, a number of artefacts from the local museum. On the wall opposite the table it

231

was customary to display the latest composition from the attic art-room.

The room was the province of Doctor Beckerman; here he held classes in religious studies, in Greek and Latin, and here, too, he marked his books away from the distractions of the staff-room on the floor above.

A second piece of paper caught Bryan's eye: it was fastened by pins to the corner of the table and, jostled to and fro by the figures behind, he could only decipher the words, 'form' and 'content' and, finally, 'content being synonymous with form, and form synonymous with content', underlined.

The voices behind him quietened: he turned to find a figure wearing a Homburg hat, a black raincoat and carrying a half-rolled umbrella standing in the door.

The umbrella was shaken, the Homburg was removed: specks of rain were visible on the figure's shoulders.

'Is anything the matter, Parkinson?' Doctor Beckerman inquired. He raised the umbrella in the direction of the nearest boy.

'No, sir,' Parkinson's brother said.

'Why is everyone in here?'

'I don't know, sir.'

'Why are you in here?'

'I came to look at the statue, sir.'

Parkinson's brother pointed at the table.

'What statue?'

'The one on exhibition.'

'What exhibition?'

'On the table.'

Several tables, standing in bays, and each enclosed by chairs, occupied the room. The table in question stood adjacent to the one normally occupied by Doctor Beckerman himself.

His gaze settled on the statue; only after an interval of several seconds did it move to the piece of paper pinned beside it: after perusing the name inscribed beneath the title he read the second sheet pinned to the corner of the table itself.

'Who put it here?'

'Miss Lightowler, sir.'

'Could you take everyone's name? I've made a mental note of

everybody present. If any name is missing I'll need to know the reason why.'

He glanced at Bryan.

'Your name is Morley.'

'Yes, sir,' Bryan said.

'Did you have permission to come inside?'

'No, sir,' Bryan said.

His arms and his legs had begun to tremble.

'Go back to your room until I call you.'

A figure scampered off along the landing; names began to be called in the room behind.

Downstairs, in the classroom, he sat at his desk for several seconds conscious of the faces in the desks behind turned in his direction.

Mr Waterhouse appeared; he mounted his stool.

'I hear,' he called, 'there's been a commotion.'

'Yes, sir,' several voices said.

'Doctor Beckerman is taking names.'

'Yes, sir.'

'No one's name in here, I trust?'

Bryan, after glancing round, put up his hand.

'Your name was taken, Morley?'

A burst of laughter was followed, at the back of the room, by the banging of a desk.

'Yes, sir.'

'I saw your figure in the library.'

'Yes, sir.'

'By your figure I don't mean your figure *per se* but your representation of the female form.'

'Yes, sir.'

The room was silent.

'Commendable.'

'Thank you.' Bryan nodded.

'I relished in particular,' he got down from his stool, 'the modelling of its features.'

A murmur of laughter passed across the room.

'Also the feet.'

Bryan nodded.

233

'Not to mention,' he continued, 'several of the toes.'

The laughter, no longer suppressed, burst out at the back.

'Also the hair.'

The laughter spread to the front.

'No other part I missed?' He waited. 'One would have thought, from the expression, that there was someone in particular you had in mind. The whole figure,' he continued, 'is so specific.'

The tapping of desks increased.

'Though whether it is appropriate to mention it I've no idea. Art is inimical to this building. At least,' he concluded, 'it has been in the past.'

The door opened: a figure came inside: his tie dishevelled, his remaining tufts of hair pushed back, his suit rumpled, Mr Berresford called, 'Could I see you outside, Mr Waterhouse?', the master adding, 'Carry on from where we were. I'll be with you in a minute, boys,' crossing to the door, peering out before, with a backward glance, he closed the door behind.

The ceiling shook.

'What's happened?' someone asked.

The door opened as one of the boys went out; another followed.

Feet ran past. The windows rattled.

'He's had a fit.'

A figure in a dishevelled uniform appeared at the classroom door.

'Berry's called a doctor.'

'Who for?'

'Becky.'

'What's the matter with him?'

'He's jumping up and down.'

A weight was drawn across the ceiling.

A voice called out.

'Who's with him?'

'Heppy and Watty.'

A crowd of boys moved out to the door; other figures appeared from the opposite classroom.

Voices called from the top of the stairs.

Feet ran down from the floors above.

The ceiling shook.

'Not in here,' a voice called out.

A door slammed.

'Not in here,' the same voice called again. 'Not in this room. Ever.'

'Did he dislike it because it had been placed in the room without his permission?' Mrs Corrigan said, sewing more quickly.

'On principle,' Bryan said.

'I take it the figure's nude?' Mr Corrigan leant back.

'I haven't seen it,' Mrs Corrigan said.

'I was asking Bryan,' Mr Corrigan said, folding his evening newspaper on the arm of his chair.

'It's lying on its side,' Bryan said. 'Its head propped up on its hand.'

'It was the point I made to Max,' Mrs Corrigan said. 'If there is someone in the school who can lead,' she glanced at Bryan, 'he should seek to support and not discourage.'

She pulled out a thread, snipped it with a pair of scissors – the handles ringed neatly on her thumb and finger – and, taking up another skein, selected a length, drew it out, and, licking one end, held it to the needle. With one eye closed, she threaded it.

'When did you talk to Berresford?'

'This afternoon.'

'How?'

'On the telephone.'

'What did he say?'

'He has ambition, Harold, like everyone else.'

'Ambition to do what?'

'To please me, for one thing,' Mrs Corrigan said.

'Did Miss Lightowler suggest the subject?' Mr Corrigan asked Bryan.

'No,' he said.

'What did she say when you modelled it?'

'She offered to help.'

'I'm surprised Berresford has come to agree with her,' Mr Corrigan said. 'He's got the Governors to think of.'

'Are we to discourage someone with a gift,' Mrs Corrigan said, 'because of the prejudices of a religious bigot?'

'Propriety is one thing, bigotry is another,' Mr Corrigan said. 'Whether Bryan's figure should have been done in the first place, and whether, once done, it should have been exhibited in the manner in which it was, comes under Max's province, not ours.'

'Have you seen the figure, Harold?' Mrs Corrigan said.

'Have you?' Mr Corrigan said.

'I've spoken to Mr Waterhouse who described it as a remarkable work of art which he was proud to have had produced by someone in his class.'

Mr Corrigan stood up.

'You didn't mention that before.'

'I wondered how far you would go in supporting Beckerman,' Mrs Corrigan responded.

'I don't support him,' Mr Corrigan said. 'I'm merely anticipating his point of view.'

'His point of view,' Mrs Corrigan said, 'is one your friend Max is anxious to get rid of. If Peterson's remains embalmed in moral attitudes that have no relevance to the world as it is at present then Max, your old friend, Harold, has no future there at all.'

Bryan didn't hear Mrs Corrigan's voice: his gaze was fixed on her figure, on the downward curve of her cheek with its tint of rouge and its layer of powder, on the outward curve of her lashes as she blinked over her sewing and, beneath this attenuated profile, on the projection of her hips, the bunching of her thigh, the extension of her ankle, and the insertion of her foot inside her heelless slipper.

'Doctor Beckerman isn't married. He lives in Church House and has a housekeeper who looks after him.' She glanced at Bryan and smiled.

'We ought to call up Church House and inquire how he is,' Mr Corrigan said.

'It was a lunatic asylum he was taken to,' Mrs Corrigan said.

'Find out which one, in that case. He bought his furniture at the shop,' Mr Corrigan said and, reaching to the mantelpiece,

236

took down his pipe, lighting it slowly, glancing from the flame to Mrs Corrigan, then to Bryan, then – with a look Bryan had never seen before – back to Mrs Corrigan again. 'In addition to which,' he concluded, 'he's a member of my club.'

SEVENTEEN

The interior of the foyer glowed, its light reflected on the dampness of the steps outside. A rain had been falling when they'd left the house and now they had had a chance to walk through from the Bull Ring to the square in front of the theatre the last drops were splashing from the eaves of the building, rattling on the glass canopy above the steps, the damp pavement below flecked here and there by the light from the façade which glistened in the puddles.

From the red-walled foyer they passed down a flight of carpeted stairs. A bar opened out at the end of a passage: in a rectangular mirror he saw Mrs Corrigan's figure, her hat trimmed with fur, the fur collar of her coat drawn up – and saw what must have been a familiar alarm in his own expression, his mouth tight, his lips compressed, his eyes sunk in the shadows thrown out by the lamps.

'Are you all right?'

'Yes,' he said.

'You take everything so seriously, Bryan. Why don't you see the amusing side?'

'Has everything an amusing side?' he asked.

'If this evening hasn't one then I don't know what has.'

Despite her continuing to clasp his hand she glanced about her, stooping at one point, releasing his hand, and introducing herself to someone who had failed to recognize her, reclaiming Bryan's hand only when the figure, a man accompanied by a woman, disappeared through a pair of doors at the opposite end of the bar.

They entered the auditorium: seats, enclosed on either side by red-walled boxes, rose to the recesses of the coloured dome;

238

gold-embellished curtains, tasselled, and drawn in symmetrical folds, hung across the stage.

Sinking down, she loosened her coat and, glancing about her, her face more brightly lit than ever, said, 'We forgot to buy a programme.'

'Shall I get you one?' he said.

She opened her bag. 'I seem to have forgotten everything. What about a box of chocolates?' She produced a pound note and called, 'Excuse me,' to the people in the row as he made his way to the aisle.

From the rear of the theatre he watched her face: one eye was visible as she turned her head and, with a child-like gesture, looked up at the dome, at the rows of seats, and at the lamp-lit, curtained recesses of the red-walled boxes.

Having bought the programme and a box of chocolates, he paused at the end of the row to gaze at her again: her look traversed the curtains, the dome, the other figures seated beside her: the light glowed, beneath her hat, on the fringes of her hair.

'There you are,' she said, her face turned up. Taking the programme and glancing down at it she added, 'I've heard of her. She was here years ago when I came with Harold.'

The lights faded; the curtains parted: a knock came at a door. A figure entered: Mrs Corrigan reached down and took his hand.

'Am I mad?' he thought. 'Can't I experience anything unless, first of all, it comes through her?'

He was conscious of her laughter, of her involvement with the actors on the stage, with their passing to and fro from doors to windows and back to doors, from chairs to tables and back to chairs, her head drawn back and slightly raised, her mouth open, her eyebrows lowered, her eyes gleaming.

When the lights went up it was not her, however, of whom he was conscious but a figure wearing a bottle-green dress of knitted wool.

'This is a surprise,' Miss Lightowler said, leaning down in the seat beside him.

'This is Miss Lightowler,' Bryan said, recovering from his

239

surprise more quickly than Mrs Corrigan. 'This is Mrs Corrigan, my aunt,' he added.

Miss Lightowler leant across; Mrs Corrigan shook hands.

'Miss Lightowler teaches art,' Bryan said. He added, 'She helped me cast the figure.'

'I hope you defended Bryan,' Mrs Corrigan said.

'I defended the figure,' Miss Lightowler said. 'Bryan I defended by imputation.'

'After all, we're not living in the Middle Ages,' Mrs Corrigan said. 'If Peterson's has been led to assume that it is then it's our duty to disabuse them. How is Doctor Beckerman?' she added.

'Recovering.'

Miss Lightowler glanced down at Bryan.

'Do you come here often?' Bryan asked.

Miss Lightowler laughed; she shook her head. 'I work here, Bryan.'

'What as?'

She gestured at the curtains.

'I do the costumes.'

'Bryan never told me,' Mrs Corrigan said.

'It's not as grand as it sounds. Most of the shows are on tour and I touch up the scenery and do repairs. It's why I'm here this evening. This show has just arrived.'

Bryan turned in his seat to examine her more closely; her hair, instead of being drawn back with some severity and fastened in a pony-tail, was combed down smoothly on either side.

'Perhaps,' she added, 'you'd like, afterwards, to come backstage and meet the cast?'

'I'd like that,' Mrs Corrigan said.

'I'll collect you after the Anthem,' Miss Lightowler said, and disappeared up the gangway.

'What a charming woman,' Mrs Corrigan said. 'She certainly stood up to the school over the fuss about your statue.'

Something of the intensity of Bryan's feelings evaporated in the second half of the evening; the prospect of sharing Mrs Corrigan was not something that he welcomed: 'She is not here to be admired by other people,' he thought, for, if Mrs Corrigan had enjoyed the first half of the evening, she enjoyed the second half

240

more – breaking into applause, her applause expanding into laughter, her laughter accompanied, in turn, by indecipherable moans and cries only, a moment later, for her laughter, followed by her applause, to spring out once again.

Standing to the sound of the Anthem, the applause faded, the music trickling on in distant corners to be replaced, once the recorded sound was over, by a burst of conversation.

'That was good,' Mrs Corrigan said as Miss Lightowler appeared in the gangway. 'I haven't enjoyed an evening more. I can't tell you how much we've enjoyed it.'

She turned to Bryan.

'It wasn't bad,' he said for the noise around them made it difficult for him to hear Mrs Corrigan's voice – as difficult to hear it, or Miss Lightowler's, as it was to suppress his instinct to get out of the building and take her away from it for good.

'We can cut through here,' Miss Lightowler said, directing Bryan to a door marked 'Private'. 'Lead the way,' she added.

A narrow passage opened on to a faintly illuminated area adjacent to the stage; a flight of stone steps led up to a landing: doors opened off on either side.

Knocking on one of the doors Miss Lightowler pushed it open, put her head inside, withdrew it, and said, 'He won't be a minute,' when a voice called, 'Come in, Di. Come in, sweet dove,' at which she opened the door wider and indicated that Bryan and Mrs Corrigan might go in before her. 'Bring her in,' came the voice again and Bryan entered to find a figure in a dressing-gown standing in front of a mirror: reaching past him to clasp Mrs Corrigan's hand, he called, 'Bring in a chair, Di,' as Miss Lightowler said, behind Mrs Corrigan's shoulder, 'Mrs Corrigan, may I introduce Felix Pemberton. Felix, this is Bryan.'

'Bryan,' the figure said, glancing at Bryan. 'Mrs Corrigan,' he added, glancing at Mrs Corrigan. 'Come inside. We'll get a chair if Di can fetch one.'

Two further chairs were handed in the door and the sound of several voices came from the corridor outside: names were called, doors banged, laughter burst out in an adjoining room.

'We've enjoyed it so much.' Mrs Corrigan sat down.

'I'm sure I've seen you somewhere before.' The actor clasped her

241

hand more firmly. 'Your mother is a beautiful woman,' he added to Bryan.

'Bryan isn't my son.' Mrs Corrigan flushed.

'Too old. I can see that,' the actor said. 'You'd never have a son his age.'

'We've so enjoyed the show.' Mrs Corrigan flushed more deeply. Conscious of her hand being clasped, she sat upright in the chair.

'So rare for anyone to come round and say so,' the actor said. 'Particularly someone so attractive.' He joined his one free hand to the other and secured Mrs Corrigan's between the two. 'I've been to this town so often I thought I'd met everyone worth meeting. All this time and I never knew.'

'We come so rarely to the theatre.' Mrs Corrigan smiled at Bryan.

He observed the actor's knees, and the black curled hair on the front of his legs, and observed, too, the make-up which had not been completely removed from around the eyes and about which he appeared to be indifferent: he had a fleshy face and square-shaped hands.

'More the loser that you haven't been more often.' The man released one hand to indicate the mirror.

'The dialogue was charming.' Mrs Corrigan endeavoured to remove her hand from such close proximity to the actor's knees.

'Oh, the dialogue,' the actor said. 'Superb.'

'And the acting.'

The actor shook his head. Reclaiming Mrs Corrigan's hand, he glanced once more to the mirror.

'Wonderful.'

'The set was so attractive.'

'We have Di to thank for that,' the actor said.

'Are you coming to the Nelson, Felix?' a voice called from the corridor outside.

'I shan't be a minute,' the actor replied, raising his head, listening to a receding burst of voices, a clattering of feet down a flight of steps, then adding, 'Perhaps you'd come over, Mrs Corrigan? We can't let this opportunity go without offering you a drink.'

'I'll take them over, Felix,' Miss Lightowler said.

'Unless Mrs Corrigan doesn't mind if I dress,' the actor said.

242

Mrs Corrigan rose quickly, her knees, as a consequence, catching the back of the actor's hand.

'Where is the Nelson?' she asked.

'Di can show you. She spends more time in there than I do. We have an arrangement with the landlord. Mention my name,' he added to Miss Lightowler. 'I'll be over in a jiffy.'

Mrs Corrigan followed Bryan out, the dressing-gowned figure appearing at the door, smiling, glancing out, and calling, 'Don't let her go. Entertain her. Don't let her escape,' raising his hand in Mrs Corrigan's direction before she followed Bryan to the flight of steps.

'Do we have to go?' he said.

'I said we would.' Mrs Corrigan spoke with her hand on his shoulder.

'We don't have to,' Bryan said. 'You weren't given a chance to refuse.'

'Oh, Felix won't be long,' Miss Lightowler said, as if the inconvenience to the actor were Bryan's concern. 'He's such good company, too,' she added.

A passage and a further flight of stairs brought them out at the side of the theatre.

Directly opposite stood the side-door to the Nelson, already open.

'It needn't take long,' Mrs Corrigan said. 'It's only politeness not to refuse,' pausing, however, on the step and gazing inside.

'Are you sure we ought to go in?' Bryan said. 'I've been here before. I know what it's like.'

'When have you been here before?' Mrs Corrigan said.

'With a friend from school.'

Her hand was clasped to his arm.

'Lead the way, Bryan,' Miss Lightowler called from the yard behind.

'Who are all these people?' Mrs Corrigan said, gazing about her at the crowded kitchen: a smell of cooking came from the room.

'They're the actors.' He indicated a group of figures around the central table.

'Two sherries and a lemonade, Reggie,' Miss Lightowler called as the face of the landlord appeared at the bar-room door.

Glasses were set down from a metal tray. Mrs Corrigan was introduced.

From the table came a shout as the actor appeared at the top of the stairs.

Dressed in a check-patterned overcoat with pouch-like pockets and a fur-trimmed collar, with a tasselled white scarf and a trilby hat, flush-faced, dark-eyed, he surveyed the room before, with a wave, he slowly descended.

'Here you are. Not gone away. What can I get you?' he asked Mrs Corrigan after shaking the hand of someone at the table, embracing a seated figure and receiving a kiss, and coming across the room to take Mrs Corrigan's hand between his own.

'We already have one,' Mrs Corrigan said, indicating her own drink on the corner of the table, adjacent to which she had been found a chair.

Bryan sat beside her.

'Another, landlord. Another for Mrs Corrigan.' The actor waved to the perspiring figure of Mr Brierley. 'Good evening, Mrs Brierley.' He waved simultaneously to a figure by the fire.

'We shall have to go shortly,' Mrs Corrigan said.

'Nonsense.'

'My husband is coming to collect us.'

'I'm sure he'll wait.'

The pinkness which had characterized Mrs Corrigan's cheeks while they were in the actor's dressing-room had given way to a sudden pallor: the sallowness of her cheeks added to the impression that she no longer knew what she ought to do, as confused by the bustle, the screams and the bursts of laughter that came from the room as she was by the manner of the actor himself.

'We shall have to go,' she said again.

'Say you're delayed.' He laid his hand on her shoulder, whispered in her ear, withdrew his head to examine her expression, and added, 'You never told me your name.'

'Mrs Corrigan.'

'Your first name.'

'Fay,' Mrs Corrigan said.

'Fay.'

Bryan waited: he made an attempt to take her hand but found

244

it obstructed and contented himself with sitting as close to her as her preoccupation with the actor might allow.

Another glass of sherry was brought; a glass of a similarly coloured liquid was set in the actor's hand: a glass of lemonade was set on the table by Bryan.

'Is it always so busy?' Mrs Corrigan asked.

'Reggie's is a popular place,' the actor said. 'And more popular still to have someone here who is a cut above the rest. Not that they,' he continued, with a wave of his hand to indicate the crowded kitchen, 'aren't of the very highest.'

Across the room Bryan could see Miss Lightowler in her bright-green dress sitting on the knee of somone by the fire.

By the fire itself the shawled figure of the elderly Mrs Brierley rocked to and fro, the dark eyes periodically raised to examine the figures around her.

'Most of the time, Fay,' the actor said, 'we feel forgotten.'

'I'm sure you must have many distractions,' Mrs Corrigan said. 'So often on the move.'

The actor lowered his head. 'But so seldom someone we can really talk to.'

He glanced at Bryan.

'Is this a nephew?'

'A friend.'

'Perhaps he'd like to step outside to see if Mr Corrigan is waiting.'

'No, thanks,' Bryan said.

'Why not?'

'I've no desire to,' Bryan said.

'Would half-a-crown induce you?' The actor felt in his pocket.

'No, thanks,' Bryan said. To Mrs Corrigan he added, 'We ought to be going. I'm not sure I'm keen on this place at all.'

'Come another evening, Fay,' the actor said.

'I've seen the show already,' Mrs Corrigan said.

'A second time you'll see more in it.'

'I doubt if I've another evening free,' Mrs Corrigan said.

She began to rise.

'Come to a matinée.'

'I shall have to think about it.'

245

'You're not deserting me, Fay?' the actor asked. 'I can't stand broken promises,' he added.

'I haven't promised anything,' Mrs Corrigan said.

Her arm was taken as she turned to the door, the actor moving with her. 'Promise at least you'll try,' he said, drawing her to him. 'The matinée would give us an opportunity to meet before the evening performance.'

'I'll see,' Mrs Corrigan said.

'There's a great deal in this town I've never seen before,' the actor said, allowing her to precede him and, finally, as they reached the door, he added, 'I'm at the Buckingham Hotel.'

Bryan followed Mrs Corrigan out to the yard; behind him Miss Lightowler was swinging her legs on the knee of the seated figure, waving her arm and, to Bryan's surprise, blowing a kiss.

'Until tomorrow,' the actor said.

'Tomorrow?' Mrs Corrigan glanced round at Bryan.

'At the Buckingham. Any time can get me.' Without any further pronouncement the actor turned, stepped briskly to the door, waved, and disappeared inside.

'That was a pressing individual,' Mrs Corrigan said.

She took his hand.

'Will you see him tomorrow?' Bryan asked.

'Until that man has gone I shan't come to the Phoenix again,' she said. Yet he could feel even now the tremoring in her arm, an agitation that hadn't ceased by the time they'd found a taxi. 'I suppose you admired his performance,' she added.

'Which one?'

She laughed.

'The first of the two,' she said, and laughed again.

'I didn't notice,' he said.

'He's performed in London. Several times. And has appeared, I understand, in one or two films. There's a profile in the programme.' She opened her bag. 'I must have dropped it.'

'Good,' he said.

'It wouldn't have been unusual,' she said, 'if you'd asked him for an autograph.'

'No, thanks.'

'I'm sure that's what he wanted.'

246

'I thought,' Bryan said, 'it was something else.'

'It must be later than I thought.' She flushed. 'It's a good job we didn't ask Harold to meet us. We must have been at the Nelson longer', she concluded, 'than I imagined.'

'It seemed long enough to me.'

'You were very patient.' She squeezed his hand.

'There wasn't a great deal I could do,' he said.

'As I say,' she said, 'he's a pressing man.'

The house was in darkness when they arrived.

A light had been left on above the door: a glow flooded in from the drive outside.

He had never felt so glad to get back to the house itself, nor had he ever felt more conscious of its quietness.

'Do you feel like supper?'

'No, thanks,' he said.

She went to the kitchen. He heard a kettle being filled and the gas turned on.

He went into the sitting-room; the fire burned brightly behind a metal guard.

'Are you sure you don't want anything?' she called.

She appeared in the door, her coat unbuttoned.

'No, thanks.'

'You're not sulking?'

'No,' he said.

'I shan't allow it.'

'How would you stop me?'

'Oh, I'd find a way,' she said and, without glancing in his direction, returned to the kitchen.

He listened to the running of a tap and, finally, the kitchen door was closed; then came the sound of her going upstairs.

He listened to the creaking of the floor as she moved from the bathroom to her bedroom.

'Can you bolt the front door before you come up?' she called, waiting for an answer.

He got up from the fire, damped it down, went to the front door, drew the bolt, looked back at the sitting-room fire, then went upstairs.

Her light was on.

He went into his own room and got undressed.

When he came out her light was off.

He went to her door and knocked.

'Do you want me to come in?' he asked.

'I have a headache, with that awful drink.'

'Shall I kiss you good night?'

'I should leave it till the morning.'

'It won't be good night in the morning,' he said.

'You can kiss me good morning instead.' Her voice was scarcely a murmur.

'Good night,' he said.

'Good night,' she said. 'And thank you for the evening.'

'Why should you thank me for it?' he said.

'Thank you especially for this evening.' She turned on the bed.

'Good night,' he said again and, to show his displeasure, closed the door with a bang.

'There you are,' she said. 'I didn't see you.' She straightened his collar and glanced off along the street. 'I'd made an arrangement to meet a friend. I came in early, so I've only myself to blame if I have to wait.'

'I'll wait with you,' Bryan said.

'I've an appointment at the Fraser.'

'I'll come with you,' Bryan said.

'I'm perfectly capable of going to the Fraser without you escorting me.' She laughed, glanced down, and straightened his cap.

'You've welcomed it before,' he said.

She glanced back the way he'd come. 'Why are you out of school so early?'

'I'm not,' he said. 'I'm late.'

She examined a watch on her wrist. 'Is it as late as that?'

'There's that actor over there.'

'Where?'

He pointed across the street; the figure was waiting on the opposite corner.

'I can't see without my glasses.'

He might, in different circumstances, have been entertained by her attempts to conceal her interest: her cheeks were flushed, her eyes bright and her make-up, he thought, more garish than ever.

'The one in the dark-brown overcoat two sizes too big, and the trilby hat pulled over his eyes.'

'It doesn't look like him at all.'

'I'll go across.'

'I'd prefer you not to.'

'Why not?'

'I'd prefer you not to encourage him, Bryan.' She took his arm. 'You can walk me to the Fraser and leave me at the door.'

'I'll come up with you,' Bryan said.

'No, thank you.'

'Why not?'

'It'll be all right as far as the door.'

They set off in the direction of the café.

'I don't suppose he's got in touch,' he said as she held his arm to cross the street.

'I see no reason why he should,' she said.

He glanced behind.

'Are you sure you wouldn't like me to come up with you?'

'You'd better get off home. I'll see you this evening. I shan't be late.'

She stepped inside the shop and mounted the stairs.

Bryan crossed to the opposite pavement. When the bus came he climbed upstairs and, as his feelings of misery increased, imagined, in the adjoining street, their two embracing figures.

He could hear a clock striking beyond the village when Mrs Corrigan came back.

He didn't hear the front door open and assumed that, if she had returned by car, it had dropped her some distance from the house and she had walked to the gate, and up the drive, and let herself in without making a sound; it was only the creaking of the landing that disturbed him, and the clicking of her bedroom door.

A short while later he heard Mr Corrigan's door, then the light tapping on Mrs Corrigan's bedroom door, followed, after an interval, by his asking, 'Fay? Are you all right?'

The murmur of her voice replied.

249

Bryan, getting out of bed, looked through his own open door and saw the chink of light beneath Mrs Corrigan's. A corresponding chink went out as he watched beneath Mr Corrigan's. After waiting several seconds, he tip-toed back to bed.

No sound of any sort came from the house.

The clock struck once more beyond the village; perhaps she was sitting up in bed or, more likely, having undressed, was sitting in front of her mirror.

Or, perhaps, he thought, she was kneeling by her bed, something she did each evening – he had gone into her room on several occasions, ostensibly, if he'd been up late, to say good night, only to find her by the bed, her hands clasped, her head stooped, not stirring until she had said, 'Amen' in an instructional voice, her eyes blinking – unmascaraed – and the pale face smiling before she inquired, 'Is there anything you want?'

'Bryan?'

Her voice came from the door; she was standing there, however, not coming in.

'Are you out of bed?'

'No,' he said.

'I thought I heard you moving.'

'I was wondering if your light was out.'

'I'm sorry if I woke you.'

'That's all right.'

'Good night.'

He lost her figure against the darkness then, from along the landing, came the clicking of her door.

The following morning, by the time he got up, she'd already left: her bedroom door was open and Mr Corrigan was downstairs, lighting the sitting-room fire.

He came out in a dressing-gown, carrying a bucket.

'There you are,' he said. 'Sleep well?'

'All right,' he said, glancing to the kitchen as if he suspected Mrs Corrigan might well be there.

'Fay's out,' Mr Corrigan said. He hurried on to the kitchen, unlocked the back door, and went out to the garden.

He didn't go to school that day; nor did Mr Corrigan go to

250

work: when Mrs Meredith came Mr Corrigan sent her home. 'Mrs Corrigan's out,' he said. 'Take the day off, Rose. It's not often that Bryan and I have the chance of a chat,' indicating that this was an arrangement that he and Bryan had come to together.

It was midday when Mrs Corrigan came back; as she hurried past, wiping her hand at her face, he could see from the smudged mascara, the smeared lipstick, the distortion of her mouth as she endeavoured to control her voice, that she'd been crying. 'I shan't be a minute,' she called, running to the stairs. A weird cacophony of wails and cries expanded in the silence which followed the closing of her bedroom door.

'Shall I go up to her?' he asked.

Mr Corrigan shook his head. He was wearing an apron, one normally used by Mrs Meredith, and, shaking his head a second time, he returned to the kitchen, a pan in one hand, a cloth in the other, and called, 'I'll go up in a minute, Bryan.'

A quarter of an hour had elapsed, however, before Mr Corrigan finally went up, not knocking on Mrs Corrigan's door but going directly in and closing it behind him.

Bryan waited in the sitting-room; after a while he went through to the kitchen: pans were on the gas; meat was roasting in the oven.

He washed up the cooking utensils and cleared the table.

He had never taken much regard of the Corrigans' garden: the broad lawn, flanked by flower beds, led down to a summer-house; with nothing else to do he wandered down the path and looked inside.

Deck-chairs were folded against a wall.

He glanced back at the house: above the sitting-room, the hall and the kitchen windows were, respectively, the windows of the guest-room, the landing and of his own room, with the dormer window of the lumber-room, where he did his modelling, and occasionally his painting, above.

'Bryan?'

Mr Corrigan had appeared at the kitchen door.

He came into the garden, pulling on his jacket.

'Mrs Corrigan's on the telephone.'

'Who with?'

251

'Her brother.'

For a moment he wondered who her brother was; only slowly did the thought occur: 'The farm, the kitchen, the blue-eyed man.'

'Mrs Spencer died this morning.'

Bryan glanced at the house.

'Is that where she's been?'

'She's only just heard.'

'I thought she was upset before she came in.'

'She was.'

He wondered what on earth Mrs Corrigan could say.

'Why was she upset?' he said, turning to the house.

'I'll drive her over to Feltham,' Mr Corrigan said, not answering the question. 'Lunch is cooking. Perhaps you'd keep an eye on it. I may leave her there,' he added, 'and come back myself. We could get something to eat, if you like, together.'

Mrs Corrigan came down a little later; she had re-done her make-up and changed her clothes.

'Isn't Bryan coming?' she said, seeing him waiting behind in the hall.

'I thought it better he didn't,' Mr Corrigan said, already on the steps outside.

'He'll have to come,' she said. 'There's not much more I can say to Freddie.'

Mr Corrigan returned to the kitchen to turn off the gas.

Mrs Corrigan got into the back seat of the car and indicated that Bryan should get in the front, waiting for Mr Corrigan to lock the front door.

'I hope you've not been troublesome,' she said.

'No,' Bryan said.

'That you've helped Mr Corrigan.'

'I have.' He didn't glance back.

A light was burning in one of the ground-floor windows when they reached the farm; Mrs Corrigan tapped on the front door and, without waiting for an answer, went inside.

Upstairs, on the landing, there was the sound of footsteps then, from the kitchen, Margaret appeared.

'There you are, Aunt,' she said, turning her cheek to be kissed. 'Hello, Bryan,' she added, and led the way to the kitchen.

252

A fire burned in the tall, enamelled range: the dogs stirred, growl-ing, then sank by the hearth.

Mrs Corrigan sat down at the table – on the same chair on which she had been sitting the first time Bryan had seen her. Her look contrasted strangely with that previous occasion; not only was the table itself not occupied by parcels and the rudiments of a farm tea, but her manner as well as her expression were those of an older woman: she struggled to contain her feelings and Margaret, examining her aunt's dark eyes, ringed beneath by lack of sleep, the sallowness of her cheeks, her strangely puckered lower lip, asked, 'Shall I get you a cup of tea?'

'Is your father upstairs, Margaret?' Mrs Corrigan asked.

The strange force that now controlled her, compelling her to latch on to one grief in order to distract herself from another, caused her to get up from the chair and, stepping past Mr Corrigan, she ascended the stairs.

They heard her voice call, 'Freddie?'

'Anything we can do to help?' Mr Corrigan asked Margaret, who had turned to the sink where she was washing up.

'No, thanks,' Margaret said.

She stood for a moment with her back to the room, looking out to the yard: hens and geese moved to and fro amongst the ruts and, faintly, from the dairy, came the sound of sweeping.

Gas burned beneath a kettle.

Mr Corrigan sat down; he sat at the table, in the chair vacated by Mrs Corrigan: as Bryan picked up a tea-towel he called, 'I can do that, Bryan. You do the washing,' rising once again and taking off his jacket.

'It's finished, Uncle,' Margaret said, glancing round.

'In that case,' he said, 'I'll make the tea,' crossing to the cup-boards on the wall and opening several before finding the cups and saucers.

Bryan wiped the pots; no sound, other than those of the kitchen, came from the house: the methodical ploughing of Margaret's hands in the water, the clattering of the crockery as she laid each piece down, the clattering as Bryan picked each item up, the dripping of the water, the crackling of the fire, the odd sounds made by Mr Corrigan as, his jacket back on, he moved around

253

the table, emphasized rather than distracted their attention from the absence of any sound from above their heads.

'You didn't have to come over,' Margaret said.

'I wanted to,' he said.

'What about school?'

'I took the day off.'

'There isn't much washing-up to do, as a matter of fact. We haven't had any breakfast.' Having dried her hands she crossed the room, found the tea-caddy for Mr Corrigan and, having handed it to him, moved over to the door, glanced to the stairs, and said, 'I'll go up and see if Aunt Fay wants one.'

Her feet faded to the landing.

Mr Corrigan sat down.

'This is a to-do.' He glanced at Bryan. 'So early on in life.'

'I didn't know she'd been seriously ill,' Bryan said.

'For a long time,' Mr Corrigan said. 'She said little to anyone about it because, I suspect, she thought it was fatal.'

'Hasn't she been to hospital?'

'We thought whatever it was had been contained. Why,' he added, 'I was going to call this morning to see how she was. Then other things intervened.'

He glanced away.

From the stairs came the sound of the farmer's voice; a moment later Mr Spencer stood in the door: he was in his shirt sleeves and his stocking feet.

'Bryan.' He came into the room as Mr Corrigan stood up. 'We've summat in to eat. Gone lunch-time, has it?'

'We're not hungry, Freddie.' Mr Corrigan shook his hand. 'We've a pot of tea on, if that's all right.' He crossed to the kettle as it began to boil.

'How's thy faither?' Mr Spencer said, aimlessly, to Bryan.

'All right.'

'Good worker.' He glanced at Mr Corrigan. Having laid his hand on Bryan's shoulder, still grasping it, tightly, he added, 'Is Fay all right?'

'Fay?' Mr Corrigan placed the lid on the teapot and brought it to the table.

'She's looking under the weather.' To Bryan, he added, 'She

254

wa're alus emotional when she wa're a lass. Up one minute, down the next. She lives for the present and has ne'er a thought for what comes after.' He sat down at the table, his legs apart.

'Shall I go up to her?' Mr Corrigan said.

'Margaret's wi' her. She mu'n be all right. She's more common sense than Fay,' he added.

A goose honked; the sound of Margaret's voice came from the stairs.

Water was run in a basin.

Mr Corrigan began to pour the tea.

Steam rose above each cup.

A moment later, Margaret came in; she came directly to the table, poured the milk, gave out the sugar, went to a cupboard, came back with a tin.

'She's getting a wash,' she said. 'She won't be a minute,' and, in that instant, Bryan was possessed of the absurd notion that she was referring not to Mrs Corrigan but to Mrs Spencer and that, the next moment, the mother herself would appear at the door, grey-eyed, slim-featured, her hair drawn back and, with her habitual smile, inquire about their visit, comment on Mr Corrigan's appearance, and invite them all to lunch.

The fire crackled; the hens clucked and from further afield came the lowing of a cow.

A cup of tea was placed by Mr Spencer's elbow; he gazed towards the fire. Another was set by Mr Corrigan as he too took his place at the table, raising the cup, holding the saucer, drinking.

Mrs Corrigan appeared in the doorway; she had taken off her coat and folded it across her arm.

'I wouldn't mind a cup,' she said to Margaret who had raised the teapot in her direction, setting down her coat, moving to the table. 'Harold?'

'I've got one.' He lifted his saucer.

'Are all the arrangements made?' she asked Mr Spencer who, gazing at the fire, appeared not only not to hear but to have abstracted himself from the room entirely. 'Are they made?' she said again, this time to Margaret.

'Dad?'

'It's all been done,' Mr Spencer said.

His look was raised to the ceiling.

'Would you like me to stay, Freddie?' Mrs Corrigan asked.

'There's no need to, Fay,' Mr Spencer said.

'It's a lot for Margaret to handle.'

'She's handled it afore.' The farmer glanced at his daughter. 'She's been a big support these last few days.'

The forehead of his daughter gleamed; the boyish intensity of the face, its pale-blue eyes expanded, was heightened by the drawn-back hair: her cheeks glowed.

'I'd gladly stay.'

Mr Spencer glanced at Bryan. 'How about you lad?'

'What about him?' Mrs Corrigan said.

'He could kip down if he liked.'

'To stay?'

'There's room for a little 'un,' the farmer added.

'Would you like to stay, Bryan?' Mrs Corrigan asked.

'I wouldn't mind,' he said.

'He can 'a' a go on the tractor.' The farmer smiled.

'If Bryan doesn't mind.' Mrs Corrigan's mouth had fallen.

'Send his things o'er. Margaret'll find a sheet and a blanket.'

'He'll need nore than a blanket,' Mrs Corrigan said. 'Are you sure you want an additional burden?'

'It's not a burden to me,' the farmer said.

'What about school?' Mrs Corrigan asked.

'He can go to his school from here. Margaret'll take him with her pals.' The farmer glanced at his daughter. 'What do'st think to 'a'ing this rabbit?'

'It's all right by me.' The daughter flushed.

'I knew she'd leap at it.' Mr Spencer laughed.

The sound reverberated in the kitchen, and was echoed, eerily, by the noises from the yard outside.

'Are you sure I shouldn't stay as well?' Mrs Corrigan said.

'We'll be as well as ought,' the farmer said.

A moment later, his boots pulled on in the porch, the dogs at his heels, he clumped out to the yard. His figure was visible, briefly, as he walked on to the distant sheds.

'Are you sure your father wants Bryan here, Margaret?' Mrs Corrigan said. 'He's not quite sure what he's doing.'

'He wouldn't have asked if he wasn't sure, Aunt,' Margaret said. 'There'll be plenty for him to do. It'll not be a holiday,' she added.

'We can fetch his things over this evening, Fay,' Mr Corrigan said.

Mrs Corrigan drew her fingers against the cloth. 'I don't know what your father wants. Adding responsibilities to those he's got already.' She began to cry. 'I only spoke to Mary a day ago. She said she felt much better. Why didn't she tell me she'd been so ill?'

'She preferred not to make a fuss.' Margaret, lamely, glanced at Bryan.

'She was such a stoical woman.' Mrs Corrigan felt for her handbag, drew out a handkerchief, and blew her nose.

'She'd hate to see you crying,' Margaret said. 'She was always making an effort not to indulge her feelings.' She glanced at Bryan again.

'If you ever wish to stay at Chevet,' Mrs Corrigan said. Her fingers, once more, moved about the cloth, massaging one starched end of a broken thread then another.

'If there's anything we can do, Margaret,' Mr Corrigan said, 'you'll let us know.'

'Oh, I'll let you know, Uncle,' Margaret said, glancing to the window. They could see Mr Spencer now as he crossed the yard, wheeling back to the sheds a bale of straw on a barrow.

'Let me help you with lunch,' Mrs Corrigan said, wiping her eyes.

'I doubt if we'll have lunch today,' Margaret said. 'I couldn't eat anything. Neither could Dad.'

'Perhaps we ought to get back, Fay,' Mr Corrigan said. 'Margaret has enough to deal with at present.'

'You will ring us this evening?' Mrs Corrigan said, getting up. 'Mr Corrigan will come across with Bryan's things. Perhaps I could see you outside,' she added to Bryan.

He followed her to the hall then out to the garden where the path ran down to the wicket gate and, beyond the wicket gate, to the grass slope above the dammed-up stream: pigs were rooting in the earth by the bank.

'I don't think it was a wise thing to agree to Mr Spencer's whim.

It's not as if I didn't care about what you're doing.' The tears reappeared at the corners of her eyes.

'What about the actor?' Bryan said.

She glanced at the house: the curtains of a room upstairs were drawn and, perhaps for the first time, she saw the light burning in the lower window.

'If I've made a fool of myself,' she said, 'you don't have to rub it in.'

Mr Corrigan had appeared at the front door of the house; he made a pretence of talking to Margaret, smiling at one point and nodding his head.

'I don't think I could bear it if you stay here for very long.'

'Why not?'

'I need you at Chevet. You don't know how I feel at present.'

She gestured towards the house.

'Are you two finished?' Mr Corrigan called.

'I'm asking Bryan to do his best,' Mrs Corrigan said. 'I'm sure he'll manage,' she added to Margaret, stooping to her, finally, when they returned to the door, embracing her, and, moving to the car, she called, 'Tell your father I'll call this evening.'

Margaret walked with her arm in Mr Corrigan's, not glancing back as they reached the car and, after Mr Corrigan and Mrs Corrigan had got inside, stood in front of Bryan, waving, as the car pulled out from the drive.

EIGHTEEN

His room looked out to the yard: it was here, on the Monday, as he was about to leave for school, that he met his father; he saw him walking out towards the fields and called, waving, seeing the hesitation in his father's step as if, for that instant, his father couldn't understand who, in the dark raincoat and the blue-beaded cap, was calling.

'What are you doing here?' he asked.

'Didn't you get my letter?'

'Which one?'

'I posted it Friday.'

'It mu'n have come this morning,' his father said. 'Afore I left.'

'I'm staying here this week,' he said.

His father glanced at the house.

'How's Mr Spencer?'

'All right.'

'I heard about his wife.' He gestured to the sheds. 'I thought I'd go in later and say I wa' sorry.'

'I'm off to school,' Bryan said.

'I might see you tonight, in that case,' his father said.

Bryan watched him walk off but only when he called did his father wave, turning, and walked on more quickly towards the fields.

Bryan stayed at the farm for the next five days. He avoided meeting his father whenever he could, and, if he happened to glimpse him, he refrained, for some reason, from calling out, reluctant to remind his father either of his own position in the house, or of his father's subservience to Mr Spencer.

The greater part of his time Mr Spencer spent in town, returning home each evening relaxed, slumping in a chair where he smiled and talked about his work, or the weather or, more interestedly, inquired about Bryan's school: 'These statues we hear about,' listening with a sidelong look, dazed, as he might to a voice from another room.

Mrs Corrigan came on two occasions, both time, travelling by a local train which by-passed the town, circuiting it to the south and, after several stops at intervening villages, called at the tiny Feltham station.

It was approached by a lane which ran below the surrounding fields and, but for a distant glimpse of Feltham Castle and its ruined walls, was enclosed by hedges, like the bed of a stream. He came here one evening, when he had nothing else to do, and leant againt the wall of the tiny, brick-built booking-hall and watched the rails and the occasional train that thundered through.

It was here, on both her visits, that he saw Mrs Corrigan into her carriage; in the walk from the farm to the station they spoke very little: only the sight of the slate roof and the soot-flecked brickwork prompted her to ask about the school and he, in turn, to inquire about the actor. 'The show has moved on to another town,' she said. 'I don't know why you bring it up.' The gaslight of the station, set on a slight embankment, glowed above a distant hedge.

'How do I know,' he said, 'you won't be seeing him again?'

'How could I possibly see him again?'

'You could write to him,' he said.

She walked with her hand in his; or, rather, since he resisted, with his hand in hers.

'I've had no contact with him. Nor have I tried to get in touch,' she said.

'Does Mr Corrigan know?' he asked.

'What occurs between Mr Corrigan and me is not your concern,' Mrs Corrigan said.

She walked along more quickly, drawing him with her. Yet with only a gas lamp to illuminate the lane, half-way along its length, she wasn't sure of her step and stumbled, clutching his hand, drawing him to her: yet, having regained her balance, she thrust him away.

At the station, as they waited, she added, 'I don't understand why Mr Spencer invited you to stay at a time like this. He's keeping his grief to himself. It's self-defeating. He needs all the help he can get.'

'He wants me there as a distraction,' Bryan said. 'He can't bear to be alone in the house with Margaret, and can't stand the friends she has from school. I'm the next best thing to a dog. Like I am at Chevet. Something that can be called on or ignored, whenever anyone chooses.'

'Your life at Chevet hasn't been like that at all,' she said. And, after pacing up and down the deserted platform, she asked, 'Is there any reason why I shouldn't be attracted by another man? Do you want me to be absorbed in you entirely?'

Her expression was hidden by the brim of her hat and the shadows flung out by the station lamp.

The train appeared.

'Last week was more than I could stand,' Bryan said.

'Was it any different for me?' she asked.

'It was all your doing,' Bryan said.

She climbed into the carriage.

'You don't know what my feelings are,' she said.

A whistle blew.

Her last words were lost as the train moved off.

All Bryan caught was the sound of his name.

On the Wednesday morning Mrs Spencer was buried; Bryan drove with the Corrigans in the car behind the one in which Margaret and her father were sitting: he could see the suited figure of the farmer sitting upright, stiff-necked, the straight-backed figure of his daughter beside him, her gaze, like her father's fixed to the front.

At Feltham Church the coffin was lifted out, taken inside, brought out again, and buried in a clay-lined pit.

Bryan and Margaret, after a lunch at the Castle Inn, departed for school.

In the evening, when Bryan got back, the farmer talked not about the funeral, nor about his wife, nor about the Corrigans, not even about his life, but, curiously, about Bryan's father. 'He's a funny man,' he said. 'He can't say no to a pint, which doesn't go against a man in my book,' he raised his finger, '*necessarily*, but it went against his. I've seen him leave the Three Bells i' the evening and many a time I've wondered if I'd see him back and Mary has said, "Shouldn't you gev him a lift?" and I've said, "Gi'e him a lift and he'll want it every neet."' The farmer laughed, leaning back from the table; he'd laughed, too, at the Castle Inn, and he laughed in much the same way now, and added, 'he's been late for work a time or two. I ne'er tipped a wink. I've watched him set off along that road, and thought, "He'll be lucky if he gets home toneet," and taken my cap off when he's turned up next morning. "How's thy do it, Arthur?" I've asked, and he's said, "Do what, Mr Spencer?" bright as a penny, and never blinked an eye though I've known that he's known that I've known he wa' tippled the night afore. Remember the day thy pedalled here? He spent two months o' lunchtimes on that bike, sanding it down and painting it i' yon shed. If he'd worked as hard for me as he worked for hissen we wouldn't be sitting here at present.'

Each time that he verged, in these reminiscences, on mentioning his wife, his gaze would turn to Margaret and, seeing an acknowledgement in her half-attentive face, he'd glance away and add, 'He wa're a good man. There wa're alus summat behind him you could never put a finger on,' leaning back, only, at the last moment, to draw himself forward, thrusting his arms at the table.

At the weekend he went back home to Stainforth; Alan was in the house, reading the morning paper, sitting in a chair with his legs across the arm: he looked up in surprise and said, 'Kicked you out for good, or come back on a visit?'

'I've come back for the weekend.' He could see his last letter to his parents on the mantelpiece behind the clock, the torn lip of the envelope and the formality of the address, with the folded edge of the paper protruding from inside.

'My mother's out. My dad's at work.' Still his brother's look persisted. 'My mother was saying you were at the funeral.' The newspaper dropped from his brother's hand.

'I went with the Corrigans,' Bryan said.

In an adjoining chair was a carrier bag: as Bryan lifted it down he saw it contained a rolled-up towel, his brother's boxing-boots and a packet of what looked like sandwiches, together with a flask.

'Are you fighting?'

'A little 'un.' His brother laughed.

'A little fight, or a little opponent?'

'Both.' He laughed again, straightening his body across the chair. 'Did they have a beano after the funeral?'

'They had a meal.'

'Wheer?'

'At the Castle Inn.'

Having set down his case and removed his brother's bag, Bryan sat down, facing the fire which, from the freshness of the coal, had just been lit.

'The Corrigans went?'

'That's right.'

'How is she?'

'All right.'

'She wrote my mother a letter.'

'What about?'

'Putting her in the picture.'

Bryan's gaze went back to the clock.

'It's in her handbag, if you want to see it.'

'No, thanks.'

'She talks glowingly of you and says what a pillar of support you've been.'

The room was cold; he wondered why, in the circumstances, he'd troubled to come back: far better, he realized, to have gone to Chevet.

'I slept in your bed last night,' his brother said.

'Why?'

'I thought I'd have a change. You can sleep in mine, if you want,' he added.

Bryan got up from the chair; he picked up his case and went to the stairs: he heard his brother poke the fire and, a few moments later, as he sat on his unmade bed and wondered which one of the two he ought to sleep in, his brother came in and stood in the door.

In the corner of the room, on the cupboard-top construction which marked the rising of the stairwell, was the first box of paints given him by Mrs Corrigan: something in the faded texture of the lid reminded him of the slightness of her build, of her querulous eyes, and in this featureless room – as austere in its own way as the one he had slept in at the Spencers' – the feeling that he didn't belong anywhere intensified.

'How's Spencer now his wife is dead?'

'I don't think he's thought about it,' Bryan said.

'Did you see her?'

'When?'

'Afore she died.'

'No,' he said.

'Did you see her after?'

His brother gripped the board at the end of the bed.

'No.'

It was the tiny suitcase that absorbed his attention, absurd in its reproduction of the details of a larger case – the handle, the catches, the rectangular proportions, the sewing along the edge: a present from Mrs Corrigan at the beginning of his stay at Chevet.

'My mother wa're upset.'

'Why?'

'She used to know her.'

'When?'

'When my dad first worked theer. Mrs Spencer came to see her and give her some advice.'

The sneck sounded on the door below and he heard his mother's step in the scullery, the setting down of a basket, a sigh, then a slow movement to the hall as she hung up her coat. 'Alan?' came her voice from the stairs.

'We're up here, Mother,' Alan called.

'Is Bryan back?'

'He's up here,' he called again, still leaning to the bed.

'Is he coming down?'

He got up from the bed. His suitcase he stood on his brother's bed.

His mother – a sign of her displeasure, since she didn't wait to greet him at the foot of the stairs – had gone through to the living-room and was sitting in the chair he'd been sitting in himself, his brother's carrier bag beside it.

'How's Mr Spencer?'

'He keeps himself busy.' He sat down in the chair in which his brother had been reclining.

'And Margaret?'

'I don't think they've got used to it yet. At one time Margaret called out, "Mother," looking up from the table when she wanted to know where something was.'

'She once did me a very good turn. I shan't forget. She was very good to me. She gave me advice I've never forgotten.'

Later, when his father came back and had eaten his dinner, Alan and he left for the boxing – inviting Bryan to come but not disappointed when he refused, his father pulling on his coat in the door and calling, 'You'll still be here tonight?' his feet clipping on the path outside, his figure visible beyond the hedge as, fastening the buttons of his overcoat, he hurried after Alan.

Bryan went for a walk in the afternoon; he walked to the phone box at the foot of Spinney Moor Avenue and rang up the Corrigans', getting Mrs Meredith first: then came the sound of Mrs Corrigan's footsteps crossing the hall, and her voice inquired, 'Is anything the matter?'

'I was calling you,' he said.

'What about?'

'Does there have to be a reason?'

'Where are you calling from?' she asked.

'From Stainforth.'

'Is your mother ill?'

'I've missed you,' he said.

'I'm glad to hear it, Bryan,' she said.

'I'll have to put another coin in,' he said, and heard the gasp of impatience, then, as the clicking subsided, he added, 'What are you doing this evening?'

'Mr Corrigan and I are giving a dinner.'

'Who for?'

'One or two old friends. We've both been feeling low this week.'

'I'll see you tomorrow night,' he said.

'That's the arrangement, Bryan,' she said.

'How many are coming?' he asked, gazing out of the telephone box at the bleakness of the house opposite.

'Quite a few,' she said, and added, 'Twelve.'

'Anyone I know?'

'Not really. One or two faces from the Fraser.'

'Will you be entertaining tomorrow night?'

'Tomorrow night I shall be in bed. I shan't see you until the following morning. Providing you're not staying at Feltham.'

There was the sound of Mrs Meredith calling.

'I shall have to go,' she said. 'Thank you for ringing.'

The telephone was replaced the other end.

His mother was coming downstairs when he reached the house; she had washed her face and her cheeks were shining: pulling down the sleeves of her dress, she stooped to the fire, poked it, then called, 'Can you get some coal?' She felt the kettle, reassured herself it held some water, and set it against the flames. 'I've just had a sleep,' she added.

He made her some tea; she appeared content he should move about her, her back propped against a cushion, examining the fire, taking the tea, concluding, after she'd drunk it, 'It's so peaceful, Bryan, when everyone's out.'

The fire crackled, the ashes fell, the flames burned fiercely in tiny jets.

'Shall I close the curtains?' he asked.

'It'll be all right,' she said. 'Mrs Corrigan wrote in her letter the house seemed emptier than ever without you.' When he didn't reply, she added, 'She wanted us to feel how valuable you are.'

She flicked down her skirt.

'Certainly when your father and I got married I never dreamt we'd have a son out there.'

'I don't want to be content with what I've got,' he said. 'I want to create something which, without me, could never have existed.' He watched her look and, beyond her silhouetted head and shoulders, in the darkened window, he watched his firelit figure.

'What does Mrs Corrigan think?' his mother asked.

'I haven't mentioned it.'

'People can't be exceptional,' his mother said, 'unless it's in their natures.'

'What about Alan? He's trying to be special,' Bryan said.

266

'That won't last. If he isn't beaten senseless he'll grow too old to fight. How can that be special?'

'If we give in before we start there doesn't seem to be any purpose in doing anything,' he said.

'You can choose a profession. That's what Peterson's is for.'

He moved over to the fire and saw his shadow, projected by the flames, rising and falling across the wall.

'There's no limit to what I can do,' he thought, watching the expansion of his shadow on the wall behind. 'That's why the Corrigans are so important.'

It wasn't the feeling he wished to express and, glancing down at her, he asked, 'Don't you want me to be something special?'

'The only thing I want,' his mother said, 'is for you not to have to live like we do.'

'Alan is no different from her,' he thought. 'It's only a temporary flickering which will die down the moment his energy subsides.'

Yet later, when his father came back – opening the front door without a sound – he stood in the threshold of the room and, with an exuberance Bryan had scarcely seen before, he called, 'He's beaten him, Sarah!' stepping into the room and pressing on the light to reveal, in its sudden glare, the smiling, red-cheeked figure of his older brother.

NINETEEN

A cream-coloured van was parked in the drive; its side was embellished by the painting of a cow, above which was inscribed, in a rising arc, the legend, 'S. Proctor, Purveyor of Meat and Pork Specialist'.

Mrs Corrigan was sitting in the kitchen, together with a man in a brown-check suit; Mr Spencer wasn't there: the sound of Margaret calling came from a room upstairs.

The man stood up; in addition to the suit he wore a brown-check tie folded inside the collar of a red-check shirt: a check-patterned handkerchief protruded from the top pocket of his jacket.

Mrs Corrigan's legs were crossed, her skirt drawn up above her knee.

'The culprit in question.' The man was fat: a florid face, jowled and thickly creased – with a square moustache, a thick-lipped mouth and pale-blue eyes – was overtopped by a fringe of short fair hair. 'She's been waiting here for hours. Come to fetch you back and you've been walking i' the fields.'

'This is Mr Proctor,' Mrs Corrigan announced.

The man's nostrils flared.

'I've been hearing about your statue, Bryan.'

'What about it?' Bryan asked.

'How it sent this teacher mad.' Having grasped Bryan's hand he turned him to the light. 'There's not much more than a sparrow inside this jacket, Fay,' he added.

Mrs Corrigan glanced down at Bryan and added, 'Mr Proctor's an old friend of the family, Bryan.'

'Not so much of the old, Fay. Tha's only as old as you feel and, in present company,' he released Bryan's hand, 'I scarce feel o'der than this 'un.'

Mrs Corrigan uncrossed her legs; she drew down her skirt and, as Margaret shouted again from upstairs, 'Dad?' she crossed to the door and, leaning against the post, called, 'He's out, Margaret. You father's not here.'

'Where is he?'

'He's in the yard.'

The slamming of a door was followed, from behind Mrs Corrigan, by a burst of laughter.

'By go, Fay, you must have a way of speaking to her that I nor her father could muster.' The check-suited figure turned to Bryan and added, 'There's a flat hand behind every word she says.'

Mrs Corrigan returned to her chair; she hesitated from sitting down: a pile of plates stood beside a pile of saucers in the centre of the table. 'We were staying to tea.' She glanced at Bryan. 'I'm not sure whether Margaret has abandoned it, or is hoping you or I will do it.'

'Oh, we'll do it,' the check-suited figure said. 'Freddie'll be back, and she,' he gestured overhead, 'has only gone up to put on a dress.'

'You're invited, too?' Mrs Corrigan said, beginning to distribute the plates and saucers.

'I am.' The man drew up his sleeves; on the table, adjacent to where he'd been sitting, lay a bowler hat. 'Is this woman's work?' he added.

'There's no such thing as woman's work,' Mrs Corrigan said. 'Not inside a house.'

'What did I tell you?' The man laid out the cups. 'Spoken like a Spencer. Where one leads,' he added, 'the other follows,' glancing up as the sound of feet came from the stairs, a rapid descent followed by a thud: Margaret, wearing a dress, appeared in the door.

She also wore make-up.

'I didn't know there were going to be so many,' she said, glancing at the check-suited figure.

'Mr Proctor has no intention of staying if he's not welcome,' Mrs Corrigan said, removing a kettle from the ring and turning off the gas.

She retreated across the kitchen.

'Nay, I'm not one to force a hand.' The check-suited figure

winked at Bryan. 'If I'm not being asked to play it.' He winked at Bryan again. 'I can take my hook. And here I've come with an olive branch.' On the table he indicated a dish of boiled ham, the lid of which he raised. 'Nowt but the best and I'm shown the door.'

'Is there something the matter with your eye?' Margaret adjusted the cups and the saucers which had already been adjusted once, if not twice, by the check-suited man himself.

'I can see as true this minute as I could when I first set eyes on your aunt, who is as pretty now as she was in those days.' He winked at Bryan a third time. 'It's not often I get the privilege of being in a room with two such beautiful women.'

Mrs Corrigan mashed the tea; steam rose from the pot and, turning to the table, she covered it with a cosy and set it down.

'Is your father coming?' she asked. Something in the check-suited figure's manner had displeased her more than it had her niece.

'I'll call him,' Margaret said, and went to the door, Mr Proctor's gaze following her as she disappeared to the yard outside: he winked at Bryan again.

'Dad?' came the shout, then, 'Dad?' again, followed, after an interval, by a response from the yard for she called, 'Are you coming in? We're ready.'

'What a performer.' Mr Proctor glanced back at Bryan. 'If independence and strength of character are still considered virtues in a woman, Fay.'

'Are you staying or leaving?' Mrs Corrigan inquired.

'Staying. I'll not give in so easy. Past history,' he concluded, 'will have told you that.'

'I'd have thought Mrs Proctor would be expecting you,' Mrs Corrigan said, sitting at the table.

'We've been married long enough for her not to expect me until I get back,' Mr Proctor said.

'That sounds convenient.'

'If she doesn't know me now she never will.' Mr Proctor took a seat beside her. 'What a girl.' He nodded at the door. 'It runs in the family, and always has. Take a leaf out of my book, Bryan. Where one woman has trod, the other follows.' With a motion of his head he indicated the figure seated beside him.

270

'On his way, or is he staying out?' Mrs Corrigan said to Margaret as she came back in.

She handed Bryan a cup.

'He's coming,' Margaret said. 'Strange to come into your own home and find someone having tea with you.'

'We've no time to sit and argue,' Mrs Corrigan said. 'If you're quarrelling with Mr Proctor you can take it up the moment we've left. I don't wish to hear any more about it.' She handed Margaret a cup. 'I like your dress.' She made no reference to the make-up.

'Seen my new van?' Mr Proctor smacked his lips.

'I noticed the lettering.'

'When?'

'I saw you in town,' Mrs Corrigan said.

'You never told me.'

'You never asked.'

Mrs Corrigan smiled at Bryan.

'If I'd have seen you I'd have stopped,' Mr Proctor said, moving back from the table.

'I'm glad you didn't.'

'Why's that?'

Mr Proctor watched her with a frown; he might have winked, too, no doubt, only Mrs Corrigan refused to look in his direction, concentrating her attention, when not on the sandwich she was eating, and for which she showed no appetite, on Bryan and, finally, at the sound of her laughter, on Margaret herself.

'A butcher is a butcher. As for "specialist in pork", how can one specialize in that?'

'I specialize in lots of things,' Mr Proctor said. 'That's the one I'm on with at present.'

Both his hands were laid on the table, the fingers, square-ended, stretched out across the cloth.

'Why not "Pork Butcher"?' Mrs Corrigan said.

'I'm no more a pork butcher than Harold is a furniture salesman,' the check-suited figure said.

Mrs Corrigan continued eating; then, reaching for the teapot, she lifted it and said, 'More tea?'

Bryan passed her his cup.

'Margaret?'

271

'No, thanks,' Margaret said.

'Harold is a retailer of household furniture,' Mrs Corrigan continued, 'because that happens to be his business.'

'I'm a purveyor of meat,' Mr Proctor said.

'A retailer of household furniture is a fact,' Mrs Corrigan said. 'A purveyor of meat is an affectation.'

'If Harold retails, I purvey. I also retail, myself, and if I retail then Harold must also purvey.'

'If Harold were a furniture salesman then that is all that Harold would do,' Mrs Corrigan said. 'He is, however, a manufacturer. He hires salesmen, but is not a salesman himself.'

'I purvey meat,' Mr Proctor said, smiling at Bryan, 'and I specialize in pork. Pork comes from pigs.' He winked at Margaret. 'And pigs are my speciality and always have been, ever since I was so high.' He extended one hand to the height of the table.

'Precisely.'

'Mrs Corrigan laughed.

'When you were on your hands and knees at the Corrigans', washing floors, before Harold came into his fortune, I don't think we'd have had an argument of the sort we're having now. You'd have been glad I was a purveyor, as, indeed, you were at the time, and you wouldn't have minded what I specialized in as long as I specialized in summat.'

He clapped his hands and laughed himself.

'I was never on my knees in anyone's house,' Mrs Corrigan said.

'Why hide where you came from?' The check-suited figure directed the question, as he had the laugh, at Bryan. 'I never do.' He nodded his head. 'Nor does Freddie. We've each made our way in the world. Yours in a woman's way, ours in a man's.'

He offered Mrs Corrigan a look.

'No side on me.' Mr Proctor laughed. 'You'll know that from the past.' To Margaret, he added, 'Ask anyone about Stan Proctor.' To Bryan, he concluded, 'We both started out with nought and see where we both end up.'

'I've finished eating.' Mrs Corrigan stood up. 'We ought to leave. I'd like to get home before it's dark.'

'I'll give you a lift,' Mr Proctor said.

'I'm sure Freddie is capable of doing that,' Mrs Corrigan said

272

as Mr Spencer appeared in the door and stood there, for a moment, gazing in.

'There's not a piece of meat in it, Fay,' Mr Proctor said, 'apart from the ham I brought over for Freddie.'

'If Stanley's a brand-new van you ought to take up his offer,' Mr Spencer said, crossing to the sink and washing his hands. 'I've to be out in the fields in a couple of seconds.'

Turning to dry his hands, he winked at Bryan.

'We'll walk, in that case,' Mrs Corrigan said. 'We've walked before,' she added. 'No doubt,' she concluded, 'we'll walk again.'

'You're not above riding in a commercial van, Bryan?' Mr Proctor asked.

'No,' Bryan said. 'I've got my case.'

'You've carried it before,' Mrs Corrigan said.

'I'd prefer to have it carried for me,' Bryan said.

'Outvoted, Fay. What do you say, Margaret?' Mr Proctor asked.

'I say Aunt Fay should do exactly as she pleases,' Margaret said.

'If Bryan has something heavy to carry then Mr Proctor can carry it for him,' Mrs Corrigan said. 'There's nothing to stop us walking. It's a fine evening. If we set off now we can be at the station in time for the train.'

'I'd prefer to go in the van,' he said.

'Why?'

'I don't see why we shouldn't.'

She crossed the room to the door. 'I'll be outside when you're ready,' she called, and closed the door behind her.

'Is she going, or isn't she?' Mr Proctor said, gazing from Mr Spencer to Margaret, then back again.

'We'll go in the van,' Bryan said. 'I'll get my case.'

When he came back down Mr Spencer and Margaret were standing in the drive with Mrs Corrigan and Mr Proctor; neither of the men looked happy: Margaret was digging her shoe against the gravel. Another quarrel, he assumed, had taken place: Mrs Corrigan's eyes were dark, her nostrils flared.

Opening the passenger door, Mr Proctor indicated that Mrs Corrigan might get inside.

Her response was to draw her skirt behind her and, the eyes of the check-suited figure fixed firmly on her knees, to slide in sideways, easing herself back and drawing her skirt across her legs more fully.

'Bryan.' Mr Proctor closed the door and opened the one at the back. His case was lifted in.

Mrs Corrigan glanced back.

'Are you comfortable back there?' she asked.

'I'll be all right,' he said, sitting – the case beside him – on the metal floor.

Mr Proctor got in behind the wheel.

'Are you all right, Fay?' he asked, and started the engine. 'All right, back there?' he added.

'All right,' Bryan said.

'See you, Bryan,' Mr Spencer said, and added, 'You, too, Fay, whenever you care to come.'

'Cheerio, Freddie,' Mr Proctor called and, lowering his window, shouted, 'Don't I get a kiss, then, Maggie?'

'No thanks,' came Margaret's voice behind.

'I may change my mind about coming back.'

'I hope you will.'

'I hoped I'd get some encouragement,' the butcher announced, but already Margaret was moving back to the house and it was her father's laugh that came from the window.

'Are we leaving now,' Mrs Corrigan said, 'or are you stopping?'

'Cheerio,' Mr Spencer called and his figure was framed against the window as the van pulled out of the drive.

'I wish I'd brought the horse and trap, Fay,' Mr Proctor said. 'Remember the old days? There wasn't a gymkhana we didn't visit. More than once,' he added.

'Do you normally drive at this slow speed?' Mrs Corrigan said. 'Or can we get there quicker?'

'I'm running it in, Fay,' Mr Proctor said.

The speed of the van increased.

'Not that I'd hear a word against Harold,' the butcher continued. 'The best man won. I said it then and I say it now. Before witnesses,' he added. 'Do you remember that day at Snaresbrook? You looked a cracker. Everybody thought so.' He glanced at Bryan. 'The judges couldn't take their eyes off her. Never mind the horse and trap. If we'd walked round that field we'd have come in first. I don't

274

think there'd have been a man objected. There might have been a woman, mind.' He laughed, straining his bulk against the seat. 'Mrs Corrigan was the prettiest woman for miles around. And everybody knew it. She wasn't much more than a kitchen maid in those days but there wasn't anyone theer who would have known it.'

'I was a housekeeper,' Mrs Corrigan said. 'I trained,' she added, 'in household management.'

Mr Proctor raised his hand. 'You started as a scullery girl, Fay, at Spinney Top. I met a woman you worked for the other day. She still remembers. "That girl," she said, "had the pick of the barrel."'

The van drew into the station yard; the moment it had stopped Mrs Corrigan got out.

Mr Proctor, opening the rear door, lifted out the case.

'What a woman,' he said, helping Bryan down: when they crossed to the platform Mrs Corrigan was already standing at the opposite end, gazing off across the fields.

'Millinery was her first ambition.' He set Bryan's case by his feet. 'After she left this woman I was telling you about. She worked in a shop, a chemist's, then, after a while, old Corrigan took a liking to her, after his wife had died. Purely platonic. She took one look at Harold, who was as shy in those days as he is at present, and thought, "If that isn't a cloud with a silver lining, I don't know what is." Harold, in those days, being one of the best-known bachelors in town. Best known, tha knows, because he'd been around so long.' He laughed, took out a handkerchief, and mopped his brow. 'He's certainly not half the man his father was. Corrigan's has gone downhill since he took o'er.'

Mrs Corrigan came back along the platform.

Mr Proctor, surveying her figure, nodded as she passed, while Mrs Corrigan, reaching the opposite end of the platform, turned, paused and, conscious of his inspection, gazed off to the woods across the track. 'She won't mind me telling you this,' he added, 'but not many years ago I took a shop in town, not three or four doors above Corrigan's, for she was in the habit of coming in each day, just after they married, to see old Harold. It cost a pretty penny, and I lost a fortune by keeping it open, but I stood at the

275

window each morning, just to see her pass. I can't tell you how much I looked forward to that moment, and I can't tell you the pleasure it gave me, as it gives me now.'

Mrs Corrigan tapped her toe against the platform, the shape of her extended ankle outlining the slenderness of the calf behind.

'To watch your money drain away and the cause of it to pass your window every morning of the week would drive most men that I know mad. To me it wa' worth every penny. Until she realized why I wa' standing at the window, then she took to coming into town from the opposite direction. I sold up within a month and moved out to where I am at present.'

Mrs Corrigan came down the platform: the sound of a whistle and a plume of smoke announced, beyond a belt of trees, the arrival of the train; she made an attempt to take Bryan's case but Mr Proctor stooped down before her. 'I'll bring it along,' he added.

The platform reverberated as the engine passed.

Most of the carriages were empty.

Mr Proctor put down the case to open the door, indicating that Mrs Corrigan might go in before him.

'Anything else I can do?' he asked and shook Bryan's hand. He was about to do the same with Mrs Corrigan when the station clerk came past.

His case was lifted in. The door was closed.

A whistle blew.

The engine started.

'Any time,' he called through the window.

His stocky figure disappeared.

Mrs Corrigan crossed her legs.

'The man's a fool.'

'He said he bought a shop,' Bryan said, 'in order to watch you pass.'

'It's the sort of thing he would do.'

'It cost him a lot of money.'

'I'm glad.'

'Didn't you mind him as a friend?'

'He wasn't a friend,' she said, and added, 'Why did you encourage him?'

'I wanted to know what he thought of you.'

'Like most men did in those days, Bryan.'

'You drove in his horse and trap.'

'I drove in lots of traps.'

'Were you really a maid at Chevet?'

After contemplating the fields outside she took his hand, glanced down, then, securing his hand more firmly, returned her gaze to the fields and laughed.

TWENTY

'We could stay in town,' Mrs Corrigan said. 'I've looked at the designs in Maplethorpe's window.'

'You never mentioned it,' Mr Corrigan said.

'I've mentioned it now.' Mrs Corrigan smiled.

'Do you have a place in mind?' Mr Corrigan asked.

'The Buckingham,' Mrs Corrigan said. 'I've always liked it.'

'You're not thinking of our moving there?' Mr Corrigan said.

'Temporarily.'

Mrs Corrigan smiled again.

The light from the candles, which had been lit for the evening meal, was reflected in Mr Corrigan's eyes: the colour in his cheeks had deepened.

'It sounds as if it's decided, Fay,' he said.

In the kitchen a plate was dropped and sound of Mrs Meredith's singing was interrupted.

'There's a green I'd like for the bedrooms.'

'Upstairs as well?' Mr Corrigan glanced at Bryan.

'If we are to be at the Buckingham for several weeks, they might as well do the whole of it,' Mrs Corrigan said.

'Several weeks.'

'That was Maplethorpe's suggestion.'

'I thought you only looked in the window,' Mr Corrigan said.

'There's scarcely any point in my looking in the window if I don't go in and get an estimate,' Mrs Corrigan said. 'You could go in tomorrow yourself and ask to see the colours.'

'I shall.'

'There's a yellow that would go well in here and an ochre in the study.'

'I see.'

278

'With brown paintwork and a white relief.'

'There's little left for me to choose,' Mr Corrigan observed.

'These are only suggestions, Harold. They're easily changed.'

'We can't afford it.'

'Nonsense.'

'I'd say so.'

'There's no point in sulking,' Mrs Corrigan said. 'The house needs doing. I'm sure you'll agree.'

Mr Corrigan glanced at the unblemished paintwork, at the unblemished ceiling, at the unstained wallpaper: finally, he glanced at Bryan.

'The sooner it's done the better, Harold.'

'I'll look in tomorrow.'

'I've rung the Buckingham and booked a suite.'

'Already?'

'The Wellington,' Mrs Corrigan said. 'It has a central view and is least affected by the traffic.'

Two weeks later they moved out of the house and into the Wellington Suite at the Buckingham Hotel. Bryan had a single room adjacent to the central sitting-room on the other side of which were the doors to the bathroom, to a dining-room, and to Mr and Mrs Corrigan's bedrooms.

On his first day there, when he came home from school, he stood on a balcony outside the sitting-room window: odd figures passed below, Mr Waterhouse, Miss Lightowler, Mr Berresford; he called out to one or two pupils from the school, Parkinson included, but none of them heard him above the roar of the traffic.

A fire burned in the sitting-room grate and, shortly after his return, tea was served by a maid.

'Isn't it cosy?' Mrs Corrigan said, as stimulated by the noise of the traffic as she was by the room itself – the flower-patterned chairs, the flower-patterned wallpaper, the flower-patterned draperies and carpets and curtains. 'It's like being at the seaside, or in a foreign city. We must travel, Bryan, when we get the time.'

Yet Mrs Corrigan was scarcely ever there; when he left in the mornings she was invariably in bed and, if not asleep, disinclined to greet him and, when he came home in the afternoons, she was invariably in the tea-rooms below where, in an alcove opening off the central lobby, she entertained her friends.

One afternoon he came home from school to find the check-suited figure of the butcher sitting by the fire. 'There you are, Bryan,' he said in a voice loud enough to be heard in the adjoining bedroom. A moment later Mrs Corrigan appeared, her make-up freshly done, and said, 'There you are. You've just missed tea.' A tray stood on a table by the window. 'I have to go out. If you want tea, ring,' indicating the telephone as she drew on a coat.

'Are you coming back soon?' he asked her.

'I may be late,' she said. 'Mr Proctor dropped by. He can see me down.' Not once did she look in his direction. 'Don't wait up,' she added while outside, on the landing, Mr Proctor wheezed.

Without glancing back, she closed the door.

It was long after Mr Corrigan had gone to bed that he heard the closing of the outer door; by the time he'd got out of bed Mrs Corrigan had gone through to her bedroom and though he walked slowly up and down, creaking the floorboards, and switching on the light, she didn't come out: only once, faintly, did he hear, as if yawning, or singing, the murmur of her voice.

'How is that great oaf?' Mr Corrigan asked the following morning.

'As usual,' Mrs Corrigan said. 'He was only here for three or four minutes. By coincidence, at tea-time. If Bryan hadn't have arrived he'd have insisted on staying longer. The two of us soon got rid of him.'

'How did the meeting go last night?' Mr Corrigan asked. 'Anything of interest?'

'The usual,' Mrs Corrigan replied.

'Anyone I know?'

'One or two. I doubt if I'll go again,' she added.

'How did Proctor know we were staying here?' Mr Corrigan asked.

'He frequents the bar and saw you passing through.' Shadows darkened the skin beneath each eye: her cheeks were sallow, the corners of her mouth turned down.

'I thought you'd been drinking when you came in.' Mr Corrigan, who was standing at the window, glanced down at the street.

'These meetings wouldn't be complete without refreshment,' Mrs Corrigan said.

'Much?' Mr Corrigan said. 'Or little?'

'We called at the Settle.'

'The Settle?' Mr Corrigan raised his head from his inspection of the street below.

'A club that one of the members belongs to.'

'I see.'

'Nothing the least improper.'

'I'm sure it isn't,' Mr Corrigan said.

'I did feel tired, as a matter of fact.' She glanced at Bryan. 'It was nearly midnight by the time I got in.'

'Aren't you enjoying staying here, Fay?' Mr Corrigan asked.

'I am enjoying it.' Mrs Corrigan flushed.

'We're not obliged to stay,' Mr Corrigan said. 'The decorators could work around us.'

'I'd prefer to stay, Harold,' Mrs Corrigan said, and added, 'I thought I might go out this evening.'

'Where?'

'To a friend's. It was just a suggestion.'

'Will you be late?'

'I might.'

The panes in the window rattled; a coal fell in the fire.

'It makes very dull company in the evening, Fay,' Mr Corrigan said.

'I thought it would be a change to have dinner by yourselves.' She indicated Bryan.

'I thought you were feeling tired,' Mr Corrigan said.

'I'll brighten up when I get some fresh air.' Mrs Corrigan flushed more deeply.

'And dull company, too, for Bryan,' Mr Corrigan continued.

'I'm sure one evening, or even two, won't upset Bryan unduly,' Mrs Corrigan said. 'Why not go down to the bar? There's bound to be someone you know.'

'No, thank you,' Mr Corrigan said.

'With living so far out at Chevet you've forgotten what sociability can do,' Mrs Corrigan said. 'You'd be surprised whom you'd meet, if you went this evening.'

'Stan Proctor.'

She crossed to the bedroom.

'There's bound to be someone you know. The Buckingham is a place where everyone meets.'

'Will you be there?' Mr Corrigan asked.

The bedroom door was closed.

'Perhaps you'd like to go out, too?' Mr Corrigan asked Bryan that evening. 'I could give you the money for the pictures.'

'No, thanks,' he said.

'Are you going to bed?' Mr Corrigan asked.

'I thought I'd go for a walk,' Bryan said, having opened his door and taken his coat.

'Like me to come with you?' Mr Corrigan asked.

'I don't mind,' he said.

'I don't fancy this hotel,' Mr Corrigan said as they went down in the lift. 'Let's try my club.'

They walked through the darkened streets together.

'It's called the Liberal,' Mr Corrigan added, 'though there aren't many Liberals left. Only one or two like me.'

Stone steps led up to a stone-flagged hall; wood-panelled doors opened off on either side. 'At one time a businessman in this town could spend half his working day in here. On that side a restaurant, on the other a library. Offices now,' he added.

They ascended a flight of stairs; a room opened out beyond a pair of double doors: chairs, the majority upholstered, were arranged along its length. At the far end, surmounted by a mirror, stood a stone-flanked fireplace. There was a smell of damp, of cigarette smoke, and a faint aroma of coffee.

A man in a white jacket and black trousers moved amongst the chairs: in one a man was sleeping, in another a figure looked up as Bryan entered; a man was playing cards on a folded table.

Mr Corrigan ordered a drink; a glass of lemonade was brought for Bryan.

'It used to be the legal district.' Mr Corrigan waved his arm to the tall, framed windows. 'Dentists came in next. Even a barber. After that,' he waved his arm again, 'it went to pieces.'

He turned in his chair, finished his drink, and ordered another.

'The first time my father brought me here I wasn't much older

282

than you. A Minister had come up from London to explain the extension of the franchise. All I remember is a crowd of men who seemed at the time on the verge of a riot.' He raised his glass. 'It was the centre of enlightenment in those days. All it is now is an evening's retreat for,' he counted up the figures, 'six men and a boy who have no home to go to.'

He consumed his second drink and ordered a third. He asked for another. A man called out across the room; Mr Corrigan laughed. After the fourth drink Bryan decided he had never seen Mr Corrigan look so happy.

'Have you ever had the feeling you'd like to run away?'

'Where to?' Bryan asked.

'Anywhere.'

Bryan shook his head.

'I often felt the temptation when I was young. I got up one morning, bought a ticket for the first train that turned up at the station, and set off for a place I'd never heard of. A seaside town.' He raised his glass, finished it, and gave indications to the white-coated figure across the room that he'd like another. 'One place is very much like the next. You take your problems with you and, in the vacuum of an unknown place, they only multiply and become more insoluble than they were before.'

The empty glass was taken away and replaced a moment later; a figure stirred across the room. In the darkened panes Bryan could see his own reflection.

'For you,' Mr Corrigan said, 'the future is an open book, with the pages, as yet, unwritten on. For me, at your age, I knew what I would have to do, whether I cared for it or not.' He finished his drink. 'My father's son. Whereas for you,' he concluded, 'everything is different.'

The door opened; a figure came inside: dressed in an overcoat, a hat in its hand, it glanced round, noted the several faces, glanced at Mr Corrigan and then at Bryan, then at Bryan again, and went back out.

Mr Corrigan smiled; having drained his glass he didn't ask for it to be replenished: he examined his shoes, one foot raised above the other.

The leather shone, the laces neatly fastened.

In the window Bryan examined their two faces and, for the first time, realized that, superficially, he might easily have been mistaken for Mr Corrigan's son: the same gauntness, the same dark eyes, the same sallowness in the evening light.

'I wondered whether, in the past,' Mr Corrigan said, 'you were ever aware of the amount of tolerance you have to show when dealing with other people.'

'Yes,' he said.

'Mrs Corrigan isn't always aware of what she is doing, which comes as a shock, even to someone who has known her as long as I have.'

'Mr Proctor told me how they went to gymkhanas together,' Bryan said, anxious to introduce the name of the man with whom, at the moment, he was vengefully preoccupied, and to learn, also, what it was in Mrs Corrigan that Mr Corrigan had been attracted to, if not inspired by, in the past.

'I suppose my experience of Mrs Corrigan is not all that different from Mr Proctor's,' Mr Corrigan said, glancing about the room. 'She was eccentric, even in those days, though most people gave her the benefit of the doubt.' He paused. 'She was very high-spirited. I could never keep up. Nor could Mr Proctor. Though I shouldn't doubt it didn't stop him trying.'

He fingered his glass; his gaze, too, had caught the reflection of their two faces in the darkened window: he glanced across and laughed.

'It needs a lot of understanding. She's something of a child.' He paused again. 'If you have to show discretion from time to time you'll have to realize that, in the end, it's to your benefit as well as hers. If you feel you'd like to help her,' he gazed at a point above Bryan's head, 'I'd be very grateful. There's a great deal to be said for her.' He pressed his fingers together, the knuckles interlocked, and pushed them for a while beneath his chin. 'She was a revelation when she was young. I'd never seen anyone like her. My father took to her straight away. He thought he could tame her before he died. He never succeeded.' He tapped his chin again.

They walked back through the darkened streets together; Mr Corrigan walked slowly: he called, 'Good night,' to a figure in the

284

doorway of the club as they came out, but in such a spontaneous manner that the man, who had been about to enter, had not replied; and at the entrance to the hotel he called out again in a similar manner to the uniformed doorman who, showing something of the same reaction, saluted Mr Corrigan's swaying figure and gazed across the foyer as they approached the lift to signal to the receptionist behind her counter.

'She has a sense of style,' Mr Corrigan said as they ascended to the first floor above. 'A vision. Which is very rare in a place like this.' He paused at the door of the suite to insert his key but, after several attempts to do so, allowed Bryan to do it for him. 'Like your gift. Unusual. And expressed, in her case, amongst other things, by her choice of clothes.'

He gazed into the lighted sitting-room at a figure who, wearing a dressing-gown, had just emerged from the bedroom.

'Don't tell her I told you,' he concluded, blinking his eyes.

'Don't tell Bryan what?' Mrs Corrigan said.

'I thought you were out,' Mr Corrigan said.

'I was.'

'We went to the club.'

'What club?'

'The Liberal.'

'You haven't been there for years.'

'I used to go each weekend.'

'And now you're taking Bryan.'

Mrs Corrigan had been crying.

'Is there anything wrong with my taking Bryan?' Mr Corrigan said. 'We are left so often on our own that it's surprising we aren't there every night.'

Having entered the room, stepping around Mrs Corrigan, he collapsed in a chair, his legs splayed out.

'You're drunk.'

'Not much.' Mr Corrigan glanced at Bryan.

'Has he walked through the streets like that?' Mrs Corrigan asked.

'I haven't flown through them,' Mr Corrigan said.

Mrs Corrigan sat down.

'Is anything the matter?' Mr Corrigan frowned.

'I thought you might have been here,' Mrs Corrigan said.

'We were.'

'You weren't when I got back.'

'We were before.'

'How was I to know where Bryan was?'

'You appeared indifferent until now,' Mr Corrigan said. 'Out each evening. A new gown every night. Afternoons in the tea-room. Evenings in the cocktail lounge. Mornings in the coffee lounge. Nights,' he extended his hand, 'I know not where.'

'Is anything the matter?' Bryan asked.

'Nothing.'

'You've come back early,' Mr Corrigan said.

'I came back when I wanted.'

Mr Corrigan spread out his hands. 'As for me, one evening off in twenty.'

'I don't feel well.'

Mrs Corrigan bowed her head.

'Proctor not arrive?' Mr Corrigan asked.

'It's got nothing to do with Stan,' she said.

'Hasn't it?'

Mrs Corrigan had removed her make-up: her skin was greased, her cheeks puffy, her eyes red. Her feet, beneath the hem of her dressing-gown, were bare.

'It's something you've eaten.' Mr Corrigan drew back his head, his chin thrust down against his collar.

'You don't understand,' Mrs Corrigan said. 'I don't suppose you ever will. Not ever.'

'I've given you Bryan,' Mr Corrigan said.

Mrs Corrigan flushed.

'Even though you've had him with you, it hasn't stopped you,' he paused, 'with other men.'

'What other men?'

'Do I have to itemize each one?'

'It's all been innocent,' Mrs Corrigan said. 'It's innocent now. No one means anything to me as much as you.'

Mr Corrigan glanced down at his jacket.

'I'm more aware than anyone else of what I've done,' Mrs Corrigan added.

286

'You draw attention to it,' Mr Corrigan said, 'as if you wanted everyone to see it.'

'I show restraint. I've always shown restraint. Don't you think I'm not aware of what people think?'

'Didn't Proctor turn up tonight?' Mr Corrigan said. 'Is that why you're unhappy?'

'He means nothing to me,' Mrs Corrigan said. 'He meant nothing to me in the past. He means nothing to me now.'

'If you can't discuss it honestly then there's no hope for any of us, Fay,' Mr Corrigan said. 'Bryan should have been enough if you'd only controlled your appetite for creating a sensation with other men.'

'How can Bryan satisfy everything, Harold?'

'He satisfies enough.'

Mr Corrigan counted the buttons on his jacket, confirmed that each one was there, then said, 'You can send him back.'

'Where?'

'To Stainforth.'

'I can't send him back. He can't go back,' Mrs Corrigan added.

'I've done all I can, in that case,' Mr Corrigan said. He got up from his chair. 'Are you going to bed?' he added.

'I shall be,' Mrs Corrigan said.

'Good night, Bryan,' Mr Corrigan said. 'I'm sorry tonight has ended so badly,' and adding, 'If there's anything else I can do, no doubt you'll let me know,' he closed his bedroom door.

Later, Bryan heard them quarrelling from Mr Corrigan's bedroom, but the following day Mr Corrigan himself came into his room, standing in the door, reassuring Bryan by his manner that everything was exactly as it was before, and announcing, 'I enjoyed last night at the Liberal.'

'So did I.'

'Perhaps we'll go again.'

'I'd like to.'

And with the same inclination of his hand with which he had come into the room, he smiled at Bryan and left.

TWENTY-ONE

They returned to the house one Saturday morning to find the interior transformed: the rooms looked larger, the ceilings higher, the staircase broader, the windows brighter and, recalling that the choice of colours and wallpapers had been Mrs Corrigan's alone, Bryan's admiration for her increased by leaps and bounds. As he watched her move from room to room, appearing at one door and then another, passing across the hall, pausing on the stairs, he thought that, despite the ordeal of the past six weeks, he had never loved her more: their love had been transformed from the familiarity of the past into something more demanding.

A few days later Mr Corrigan fell ill; he was brought home from work in the afternoon but, by the evening, unable to resist the need continually to ring the shop, he was taken away to hospital. The following morning, when Bryan and Mrs Corrigan visited him, he appeared to be asleep, murmuring slightly when Mrs Corrigan spoke to him and opening his eyes only when Mrs Corrigan took his hand.

'I've told him repeatedly,' she said in the taxi back. 'He needs to relax. He takes the shop too seriously. The excitement of the past few weeks has been more that he could stand. Why,' she continued, as they reached the house, 'I tried to teach him the piano once, even to sing, but he had no voice. The hours I played accompaniment!'

Bryan lay awake that night wondering what, in future, his life with Mrs Corrigan might be: perhaps Mr Corrigan would die; he imagined a life with Mrs Corrigan and himself living in the house together.

The following evening, when he returned from school, he discovered she was out: his tea had been prepared. 'Mrs Corrigan

288

rang to say Mr Corrigan was feeling better,' Mrs Meredith said, sitting in the kitchen to watch him eat.

It was late in the evening by the time Mrs Corrigan returned.

'Are we going to the hospital?' Bryan asked.

'I've been there already,' she said.

She might easily have come in from a game of tennis, relaxed, her make-up freshly done.

'Are you going out again?' he asked.

'I might.'

She sat across the room, her back straight; her hair, too, he observed, had been freshly done, giving her face a slimmer look, the hair piled up at the top of her head and secured by a black silk ribbon.

'You didn't tell Mrs Meredith.'

'Why should I tell Mrs Meredith?' she asked.

'She stayed behind tonight because she doesn't like me being in the house alone.'

'You're not frightened, are you?'

'I resent you going out.'

'Why shouldn't I go out? I can't make Harold better. Nor,' she concluded, 'would he wish me to stay inside and mope.'

'You don't have to mope.'

'What else can I do?'

'We could listen to the wireless.'

'I'm going out in order to distract myself,' she said.

'From what?'

'From you.'

'Why me?'

'I think I ought to.'

'Why?'

She picked at her skirt.

'I have to think of the future. It's my job to see more clearly than you.'

She lowered her head.

Foreshortened, he didn't recognize her face at all: it might have been that of an older woman.

'I've always,' she added, 'been attracted by other men. By what they are like with one another. I always played with boys when

289

I was young. I always found men more interesting than any amount of women. I can't help it. It's the way I am. I like their company. Even when I know they're being coarse. One thing you have to believe. I've always been true to you.'

'Stay in tonight,' he said.

'I can't.'

'Why not?'

'I said I'd go.'

'Are you going to go out each night?' he asked.

There came a ring at the door; perhaps she'd heard the sounds preceding it, a car door, or the gate at the end of the drive.

He had reached the landing when he heard her in the hall, the release of the front-door catch and sound of a voice, cheerful, followed by a vague inquiry.

He closed his door.

He heard her come upstairs and change, and heard the man humming to himself in the hall below.

A man's voice called; Mrs Corrigan's voice replied; the man's voice called again.

His door was opened.

'I'll see you later.'

'Depends what time you get back in.'

'There's supper in the kitchen.'

She remained in the door, her face no longer young but bloated.

'Leave the door unbolted,' she added.

'I shall.'

'Good night.'

The sound of her footsteps faded; after an interval came the sound of a car engine starting in the road outside the house.

Some time later the door to his bedroom opened.

'Are you awake?' she asked.

'I have been,' he said.

'I've bolted the front door.'

'Is anything the matter?'

'I didn't feel like going out this evening.'

'Your friend not with you?'

'He went some time ago.'

290

She turned along the landing.

'Do you want me to come to your room?' he asked.

'What for?'

'To say good night.'

'No, thank you, Bryan,' and, as she turned back along the landing, his door was closed with a bang.

He visited Mr Corrigan each evening; sometimes Mrs Corrigan came with him or, if she had visited Mr Corrigan during the day, he went alone. For several days he got no better, the dark eyes inanimate, the cheeks sallow, the voice slurred; then, after a week, he began to recover: he sat up in bed and took an interest in what Bryan had to tell him. He got out of bed; he sat in a chair; he talked of coming home. His emaciated figure, shrouded in a check dressing-gown, showed signs of impatience. 'You shall come home,' Mrs Corrigan told him on one of her visits, 'as soon as you're well.'

'I am well,' the emaciated face announced.

'As soon as the hospital gives permission.'

'I'll discharge myself,' Mr Corrigan said. 'I can't wait any longer.'

Even while Bryan was sitting with Mr Corrigan, and taking note of his returning health, as well as the residual signs of his illness, he was observing Mrs Corrigan's arm, the shape of her mouth, her nose, the colour of her make-up, the way she withdrew her hand from her glove: the suffusion on her cheek when, glancing up, she saw his look. At other moments, when they were in the street, and he glimpsed her reflection in the window of a shop, he thought that something in her life had now been broken. 'She has no centre to her life, other than the clothes she wears, the perfume she puts on, the looks that follow her,' he reflected, 'wherever she goes.'

'What are you thinking?' she asked on one occasion as they waited outside the hospital for the bus to Chevet.

'I'm wondering how long we'll be together.'

'You're always telling me for ever.' She laughed: the sound echoed in the street. Drawing him to her, she said, 'There's enough to keep us going for quite some time.' A moment later, she added, 'And all the while you're getting older.'

'So are you,' he said.

'I know,' she said, 'but a time will soon be reached when, in a street like this, we might easily be mistaken for a man and wife.'

He didn't refer to it again. 'Perhaps it's her nervousness that makes her like this,' he thought. 'Or a deeper disturbance altogether, one I've scarcely glimpsed before.'

'Do you want to take a taxi?' she asked.

'We'll wait for the bus,' he said, not wishing to be indebted to her for more than his mood could stand.

Other people came up and stood beside them; neither of them spoke. 'Our relationship is odd, maybe even mad,' he thought, and yet, in glancing up at her face, he saw no sign of apprehension.

When the bus arrived, its interior crowded, they sat on separate seats; only as they approached Chevet did he take a place beside her. 'I don't think there's any problem,' she said.

'What about?' he asked her.

'The future. It seems easier than the past. Much. Even,' she took his hand, 'more normal.'

She had left a light on in the house and, once inside, having taken off her coat, she walked through the hall as if she expected Mr Corrigan to emerge from the sitting-room to greet them: it was long after Bryan had gone to bed that he heard her come upstairs, call good night and, he assumed, still in her abstract mood, close her bedroom door without waiting for an answer.

'I'm sending Fay on holiday,' Mr Corrigan said one morning before Bryan left for school. He had recently come home from hospital and the routine of their life at Chevet had resumed along the lines which had prevailed before his illness. 'I shan't go away myself. There's too much to do. I thought,' he concluded, 'you ought to go with her.'

'My parents will be expecting me to stay at home,' he said.

'I'll talk to them,' Mr Corrigan said. 'I've spoken to them before. I'm sure they'll understand.' He added, 'How do you think she's been since I came back?'

'Much the same as before you went away,' Bryan said.

'The change will do her good. You're so much happier on your own than when there's someone else around.'

'I don't think so,' Bryan said.

'Oh, I know so.' Mr Corrigan laughed. 'She depends far more on you than she does on me.'

Later, that evening, when he got home from school and found Mrs Corrigan in the sitting-room, playing the piano, and told her about the holiday, she said, not glancing up, 'It was my decision, Bryan, to go away, not his.'

'You never told me,' Bryan said.

'I was waiting to see his reaction. He might have objected.' She added, 'I also have to wait for him to see your parents. We don't want to provoke them by taking you away when they're expecting you to spend the summer with them. I hope they'll agree. I thought, to put a gloss on it, we ought to take Margaret.'

'I'd prefer not to,' Bryan said.

'It'll look very odd, the two of us together.'

'I don't see why.'

'Perhaps you've a friend from school,' she said.

'I prefer to take Margaret,' Bryan said.

'Don't you like it at Peterson's?' she asked.

'I do,' he said. 'It's the one thing that excuses my seeing you.'

'That's true,' she said, returning to her playing, the tune changing to something brisker. 'So that's all decided,' she concluded. 'We'll go away together.'

By the end of the first week of the summer holidays Bryan, Margaret and Mrs Corrigan found themselves, each in a separate room, in a secluded hotel on the shores of a lake across which, beyond a line of wooded hills, were visible the peaks of several mountains.

A curious change had come over Mrs Corrigan: rather than appearing more relaxed she became withdrawn, and spent a great deal of her time alone in her room, seldom answering the door when either Bryan or Margaret knocked and sitting – Bryan observed from the lawn below – at her window, gazing across the lake towards the mountains on the other side. Occasionally, when she did come down, she would sit in much the same mood at a table on the terrace, looking out to the jetty, alongside which several boats were moored, or, idly, without any sign of interest, she would examine the figures sitting beside her on the terrace or at the tables on the lawn below.

'Aunt looks more like a schoolmistress than a courtesan,' Margaret said, watching Mrs Corrigan in her chair from across the terrace. 'She gives the impression, away on holiday, of being at home, and when at home,' she concluded, 'of being away on holiday.'

'There you are, Bryan,' Mrs Corrigan said when, on this occasion, after watching Margaret swim off from the jetty, he walked over to where she was sitting. 'Not swimming?'

'What would you like to do?' he asked.

'I'll sit here,' she said. 'You run off, if you like, with Margaret.'

'I'd prefer to stay with you,' he said.

'Margaret's more company.' She shielded her eyes, gazing out to where Margaret's shouts came up from the lake: amidst several bobbing heads a column of water shot into the air. 'I've never seen her look so happy. It's what she's needed all these years. To get away from Freddie. The farm's not a place for a girl like her.'

'What is?'

'It's too masculine for one thing. It's what drove Mary into her grave.'

A figure approached Bryan across the lawn and, laughing, flung out her hand and called, 'Are you coming in? It's nice?'

He shook his head: the figure ran off and plunged back in.

Sitting on the terrace beside Mrs Corrigan's chair he was conscious less of her abstracted mood than of something about her that was definitely 'odd': she didn't smile nor was she provoked when he made an allusion to Margaret's looks. 'She could,' Mrs Corrigan said, 'if she wished, be as pretty as her mother, before that farm, and my brother, ruined her looks.'

'I didn't think Mrs Spencer's looks were ruined,' Bryan said.

Mrs Corrigan glanced down. 'When she was young she was the prettiest woman I'd ever met. I was jealous of Freddie for having married her. She put me in the shade. I can tell you that.'

'Mr Proctor says the same about you,' he said.

'Does he?' She glanced back to the lake. 'Prettiness to him is any woman who wears a skirt.'

She crossed her legs.

'Is anything the matter?'

'Haven't you something you can do? Why don't you swim,' she added, 'or hire a boat?'

'I'd prefer to sit with you.'

'I don't like you sitting with me.'

'Why not?'

'You're here to relax.'

'Why don't we go inside and talk?' he asked.

'I've no intention of going inside,' she said.

'Why not?'

'The more time we spend apart,' she said, 'the better.'

'I don't understand,' he said. 'Not long ago you were saying we would never be apart.'

'It's become a disease.' Mrs Corrigan lowered her voice. 'We can't go on as we are at present.' She was gazing off across the lake: in a faint striation on the opposite shore stood the buildings of a village. 'If I were asked to acknowledge it I would have to kill myself.'

Bryan got up.

He wandered down to the jetty: the shouts of someone clinging to the supports beneath the jetty were interspersed with the shouts of someone holding to the mooring rope by one of the boats.

When he glanced back Mrs Corrigan had gone: her chair was being taken by a woman escorted by a man– a figure who, in plus-fours and a check jacket, and with a neckerchief in his open collar, was drawing up a chair to sit beside her.

He glanced up to her room and caught a glimpse, not of her, but of a maid passing to and fro across the window; finally, after one last look round, she moved in the direction of the door and disappeared.

He was inclined to go inside and find her but Margaret, hanging to the side of the boat below, called, 'Aren't you coming in? What's happened to Aunt Fay?'

'She went off,' he said.

'Why didn't you ask her to come in? It'll do you good. You're both a couple of grumpies.'

'I don't feel grumpy,' Bryan said.

'You look it.'

295

'I'll get my costume, in that case,' Bryan said, and was already walking back along the jetty when he saw Mrs Corrigan walking away from the hotel, across the lawn, towards a clump of trees at the opposite end.

'Hurry up!'

The voice came from the water and, having paused, he turned back to the terrace and started to his room.

He was already changed when the thought occured, 'She's dead!', the image so vividly evoked of her lying amongst the trees which enclosed the back of the hotel that he moved to the window and gazed down at the lawn, craning out to see if she might have reappeared: the same figure, foreshortened from this perspective, occupied her chair, with the foreshortened figure of the man beside her.

His towel in his hand he ran down to the jetty to find that Margaret was, in fact, some distance out, surrounded by several youths each of whom, effortlessly, she appeared capable of out-swimming, her breathless laughter coming back as, beside him, on the jetty, a man called, 'No swimming from the boats,' waving him towards the bank where a portion had been roped off for bathers.

Waiting for Margaret to acknowledge his arrival, he stepped in, gasped, felt the water lap between his legs, shivered, his arms held to him until, closing his eyes, he plunged forward and swam for several strokes, frenziedly, beneath the surface, coming up breathless, thinking, 'If only she could see me now it would wipe away our conversation and she'd forget everything she told me.' He glanced along the lawn, in the direction of the jetty.

'Bryan!'

He choked, swallowed, struggled, pushed up, pushed out and, surging upwards, reached the surface, retched, half-choked, felt his head pushed down again and, swimming, set off back, beneath the water, in the direction of the bank.

He caught his breath, clutched his chest and, still coughing, crawled up on the grass.

'You're not mad at me?'

He shook his head.

'I saw you come in.'

'You were miles out.'

'Part of the plan.' She laughed. 'You never saw me coming.'

He coughed again.

'You're a jolly good sport. I never thought you'd do it.' Glancing along the lawn, she added, 'Where's Aunt?'

'She went off to the woods.'

'In one of her moods.'

'What moods?' Bryan said.

'Doesn't like people having fun.'

'That's not like her at all,' he said. 'She could easily come in and swim.'

She turned to the bank, stamping at the water. 'Ten years ago she would, but not any longer. Race you to the boats.'

She disappeared beneath the surface.

When he came back up, after diving in, she was swimming on her back beside him.

'Go with it,' she called. 'You're fighting the water.'

A youth, having climbed into one of the moored boats, dived off.

His head came up beside them.

'Your brother?'

'My cousin,' Margaret said, and laughed.

Bryan swam round the edge of the nearest boat and caught hold of the rope at the bow.

'Are you all right?' she asked.

He nodded, swimming around the boat, releasing the rope and clutching the gunwale.

Margaret, having climbed up on one of the boats, dived off.

Bryan watched the disappearing legs, the brisk elevation of the head and shoulders and was conscious of a sudden warmth radiating now across his chest.

He recalled the softness of Margaret's body and when, a moment later, she came towards him, he began to smile, the smile expanding until, as she reached the boat, she called, 'Do I look funny?'

'No,' he said and added, for no reason he could account for, 'I feel very light.'

'What did I tell you?' She grabbed the gunwale of the boat herself. 'Not ticklish?'

'No,' he said.

Her arm was placed around his waist. 'Not even there?'

With his free arm he drew her to him.

The spray splashed in his ear; it filtered into his nose: in a moment, instead of coughing, he began to laugh.

'Are you all right?'

'Perfectly.'

'You're an awful ass. Race you to the bank.'

She swam on her back.

Bryan slowly followed.

Across his hips and against his chest he could still feel, rhythmically, the movement of her body: her arm curved, her wrist came down and, moments later, as she climbed up on the bank, he thought, 'She's like Mrs Corrigan must have been when she was a girl.'

'You don't swim badly, Bryan.' She picked up a towel and dried her hair.

'I don't swim fast.'

'Speed isn't important.'

'You swim quickly.'

'I like it.' She bowed her head, flung back her hair, and added, 'You don't strike me as a physical person. You never have.' She dried her legs, gasped, said, 'That feels better,' and lay back in the grass.

He spread his towel beside her.

'How many girls have you kissed?' she asked.

'Not many.'

'There aren't any at all at Peterson's.'

'There aren't any boys at St Margaret's.'

'We get Peterson's boys over,' she said.

'We get St Margaret's girls.'

'Not many.'

'One or two.'

'No one would be seen dead outside Peterson's,' she added. She pulled herself up.

'There were girls at Stainforth before I met you,' Bryan said.

'Were there?'

She leant on her side, picking at the grass between them and dropped several strands on Bryan's chest.

298

'Ticklish?'

'Not much.'

'I bet.'

With something of a laugh she knelt across his chest, ran her hands across his ribs, then, flushed, turned back to the lake and, laughing, ran down to the water and quickly plunged in.

He watched her swim out to the boats, glanced down at her rumpled towel, rolled over on his stomach and – listening to the voices from the lake – he dozed.

Cold water trickled on his back.

'Spoil-sport, Bryan,' she said, and laughed. 'Not coming in. We're thinking of swimming across tomorrow.'

'The lake?'

The nearest headland, on the opposite shore, was shrouded in mist.

'It's not far.'

'It looks it.'

'Three-quarters of a mile. Though they think, with a current, it's nearer two.'

'Are you telling Mrs Corrigan?'

'I can swim two miles without a rest. In any case,' she gestured off to the crowd of youths, 'one of their fathers has a boat and says he'll sail as pilot.'

She picked up her towel.

'I think I'll get changed. Race you to the door.'

She disappeared across the terrace.

He went up to his room, dressed, laid his towel on the window-ledge, and gazed down at the terrace.

'Bryan?'

She was standing in the door.

Her hair, still wet, had been drawn in a single swathe to the back of her neck: she wore a light-blue dress, belted at the waist. Her legs were bare.

She came to the window, avoiding his towel.

'Forget about her.'

'I wondered where she'd got to.'

'She'll be all right.' Her shoulder brushed against his. 'She'll have picked up a man.'

299

'Where?'

'In the woods.'

'I doubt if she's in the mood,' he said.

'She's always in the mood.'

'Are you glad you came away?' he asked.

'From what?'

'Feltham.'

She hunched her shoulders and glanced at the prostrate bodies on the lawn below. 'Are you?'

'I'm glad I came away with you.'

'Me, too. Though I don't know why.'

'When was the last time you had a holiday?'

'The year before my mother died.' She paused. 'And you?'

'I haven't been away for years.'

'I suppose you couldn't afford it.'

'No.'

'Shall we go down to the kiosk?'

'If you like.'

'Beat you downstairs.'

'I'll walk,' he said. 'I'm not used to swimming as far as that.'

'Come in the boat tomorrow.'

'I'd prefer to wait over here,' he said.

'Don't want to see me drown.'

'That's right.'

She laughed, waited for him to close the door, then added, 'You're not knocking?' as he went to Mrs Corrigan's door and, dissuaded by the tone of her voice, stooped to it, listened, then, lightly, his body shielding the action, tried the handle.

The door was locked.

'The way you run after her.'

'I don't.'

'Leave her alone.'

She took his hand and, side by side, they ran down to the terrace.

He was conscious of a figure moving across the dining-room whose gestures alone attracted his attention: her shoulders were bare; her face shone. Not until she was at the table did she glance at Margaret, nod at Bryan and, as her chair was held for her by the

300

waiter, inquire, 'Had a good day?' laying her handbag on the cloth beside her.

'Not bad,' Margaret said, glancing to the window and, beyond the window, to the evening light across the lake. 'Had one yourself?'

'Quiet,' Mrs Corrigan said.

'I swam,' Margaret said. 'Bryan drew.'

'What did you draw?'

'Nothing much,' he said.

'Drawing isn't your line,' she said. 'More, modelling, I should think, which is very messy. He hasn't, fortunately, brought any clay.'

Her features glowed; her hair shone: the dress she wore, a pale-blue, enhanced her colour.

The food was brought; as other groups finished they came across, offered invitations to Mrs Corrigan, and passed on to the lounge across the foyer.

It was to the terrace, however, that Mrs Corrigan led them when the meal was finished.

They sat at a table, Mrs Corrigan between them.

'I'll go up early this evening,' she said. 'Sitting out all day has tired me.'

'Why don't you have a swim, Aunt?' Margaret said. 'We could find somewhere around the lake if you're feeling shy.'

'I shouldn't feel shy,' Mrs Corrigan said. 'But,' she added, 'I don't anticipate swimming.'

'Or sun-bathing.'

Mrs Corrigan stood up. 'Let's see how I feel in the morning.' She kissed Margaret good night, kissed Bryan, and disappeared inside the foyer.

'All that preparation and she doesn't do anything with it,' Margaret said.

'What preparation?' Bryan moved up to the chair beside her.

'It must have taken hours, her hair. Even her dress. Just to sit down to a meal,' she added.

'Perhaps it's for our benefit,' Bryan said.

'She's far more selfish than that,' Margaret said.

'I wonder,' he said.

'You always see her as someone without motives,' Margaret said. 'At least, without the sort of motives I know she has.' Her arms swept down as she smoothed her dress. 'Shall we go for a walk?'

He took her hand; he glanced to Mrs Corrigan's window as they reached the jetty: the curtains had been drawn.

'She must have been in her room,' Margaret said, 'before we came down to dinner.'

'Perhaps she was busy.'

'In one of her moods.'

'What moods?'

'She has lots. Particularly,' Margaret said, 'when I'm around.'

They gazed down at the reflected lights in the water; the waves lapped against the moored boats: the sound reverberated beneath the jetty.

'We rub each other up the wrong way,' she added. 'It's a chemical reaction. Just as, with you, she feels compatible. With me, it's oil and water.'

'You're both women,' Bryan said.

'Temperament, mainly,' Margaret said. 'Aunt is an artist. Only, she creates herself instead of pictures.'

'Why do you dislike her?' he said.

'I don't dislike her. But there's a lot I ought to criticize. And a lot,' she concluded, 'that needs explaining.'

Other figures drifted past, paused to glance out across the lake, turned, and drifted back towards the terrace.

'Do you want to walk far?' she asked.

'I'm feeling tired.'

'Me, too. I'm beginning to ache,' she said. 'I mightn't swim across tomorrow.'

'I thought you'd arranged it,' Bryan said.

'I can easily dis-arrange it,' she said. 'They do anything I ask them as a matter of fact.'

'You talk like Mrs Corrigan,' he said.

'I suppose there is a part of her in me,' she said. 'Which is another reason, no doubt, why we rub each other up.' And when, finally, they stepped inside the foyer, she added, 'Are you going up?'

'I think I shall,' he said.

'I might stay down.' An arm was raised in her direction. 'See

302

you,' she added and, having released his hand, she started to the lounge: he saw her sink down in a waiting chair and two figures, who had stood for her, sat down beside her.

He knocked on Mrs Corrigan's door.

She stood there, blinking, not glancing down but, beyond him, to the landing.

The room was in darkness behind.

'Are you all right?'

'I was resting,' she said.

'Haven't you gone to bed?'

'I sleep very badly at present, Bryan.'

Clothes, worn earlier that day, were lying on a chair.

'Why don't you open the curtains?'

'What for?'

'You can look at the lake.'

'I'm not very keen on the lake,' she said.

'I thought you were.'

'Not much.'

He could see the impression of the straps on her shoulders from the dress she had worn that morning, and the flush of colour on her upper arm.

'Are you going to bed?'

'I shall be.'

'Do you want me to stay?'

'No, thanks.'

'Why have you cut yourself off?' he asked.

'You've Margaret to talk to,' she said.

'I'd like to talk to you,' he said.

'I'm tired.'

'Shall I kiss you good night?'

'If you like.'

She averted her cheek.

'I'll sit with you, if you like,' he said.

'Go and find Margaret if you want to chatter,' she said and, adding, 'Good night,' she closed the door.

It was Margaret who, some time later, tapped on his door and, having waited for an answer, and received none, tapped on Mrs Corrigan's, called, 'Good night,' and, having received no reply there

303

either, called, 'Good night,' again, and closed her door with a bang.

She was standing by the window, and had only come in perhaps moments before for she turned and called, 'It's you,' and he saw that, previous to his entry, she must have been crying.

'Is anything wrong?'

'Nothing,' she said.

He closed the door and, as she came back from the window, she asked, 'Have you had your lunch?'

'I've just come up,' he said.

'Is Margaret about?'

'She's over the lake.'

'Who with?'

'People with a boat.' He gestured to the window.

'What do you mean by over the lake?'

'They have a yacht.'

'Weren't you invited?'

'No.'

'She never mentioned it to me.'

'Why don't we go for a walk?' he asked.

'No, thanks.'

'Do you want me to go?'

'I'd like it.'

'I'll see you later,' he said and added, from the door, 'Knock on the wall if you want me.'

As he lay on his bed he imagined her sitting there, and thought, 'She is seeing how far she can go and when she sees I won't be moved she'll respond by coming closer.' Then, to his surprise, he heard her knock and when he went to her room he found her standing by the bed, and as if in the interval she hadn't stirred, she said, 'It's you I should be blaming. All I did was give you a chance you never had.'

'It's not like that at all,' he said.

'Why is it me who always fails?'

'Do you want me to go?' he said and, when she didn't answer, he added, 'Back to Stainforth?'

'No, thank you.'

304

'Why not?'

'I'd have to go with you. I mean to enjoy myself. Margaret deserves a holiday, too.'

'When we get back home I'll give up Peterson's.'

'You'd like that.'

'I'd prefer to stay with you.'

'And prolong the torment.'

He closed the door; even when he'd returned to his room and lain down on the bed he couldn't restrain himself from shaking. When, finally, he thought he could stand, he got into his costume and ran downstairs and, in a rage with himself as much as he was with her, ran across the lawn and into the lake.

Perhaps it was the coldness that brought him to his senses; perhaps it was the thought, also, that this was a test, not only of his feelings but of his courage: perhaps it was a combination of both these things which compelled him, swallowing water, to fight to the surface.

A hand clasped his shoulder; it grasped his chest: 'Cough it up. Spit it out,' came a bland instruction. His arms were pumped; his back was slapped.

The sky gave way to the ceiling of the foyer.

He heard Mrs Corrigan inquire, 'Who is it?'

A moment later he was lying on her bed.

'He'll be all right,' a voice suggested.

'He'll be all right,' came the voice again.

He was turned on his side.

A towel had been placed beneath his head.

'It was an accident,' he said.

'I watched you. Without that man,' she said, 'you would have drowned.'

'No,' he said. 'I didn't intend to. I could easily have swum back. I'll go out now and prove it.'

'No,' she said.

She was pressing him down.

'Will you forget what I told you?' she added. 'I can't imagine what made me do it.'

His head was raised; the towel was replaced.

A hand brushed back his hair.

The light, when he woke, was fading in the window; across the room, her head bowed, the figure of Mrs Corrigan was sleeping in a chair.

'What's all this about drowning?' Margaret asked.

'I swam out too far,' Bryan said.

He was waiting for breakfast, sitting on the terrace, gazing out across the lake.

'When I told her where I'd been she bit my head off.'

'Did you make it to the other side?' he asked.

'Easily.'

'What about the others?'

'One kept up. The others dropped out.'

She sat in the chair beside him.

'Did they give you a prize?'

'They gave me lunch. And dinner last night. You look pretty well,' she added.

'Not really.'

'Better than ever.' She sat forward, her arms wrapped round her knees.

'I feel all right.'

'She said you were lifted out.'

'I could have managed.'

'She says you might have drowned.'

He could see Mrs Corrigan through the dinning-room window; she was speaking to the waiter who, having held her chair, stooped forward and, in response to something she had said, glanced out to the terrace.

'Slept well?' she said when they went in to her.

'I have,' Margaret said. 'Dinner was super, Aunt. You ought to have come.'

And later, when they sat out on the lawn, a motor-boat had appeared from beyond an adjacent headland and, turning in circles, cut a wake in front of the jetty.

'The Pettingers,' Margaret said. 'They're coming this morning to pick me up.'

'What for?' Mrs Corrigan asked.

306

'I was invited,' Margaret said.

'Where are they taking you?' Mrs Corrigan asked.

'I've no idea.'

'Not swimming?'

'I shouldn't think so.' She stretched her arms. 'I'm stiffer today than I've ever been.' She glanced to the lake. 'I could have swum back if they hadn't stopped me.'

'I'm glad they did.'

'I'll stay behind if you want me to.'

'You go,' Mrs Corrigan said. 'If that's what you promised.'

And later, when the motor-boat came in, she ran down to the jetty; an arm was waved: the boat moved off.

A crescent of foam rocked the tethered rowing-boats and, in successive waves, lapped against the bank.

'You feeling all right?'

'I am.'

'Better than yesterday?' he asked.

'Much, thank you.'

The bay was enclosed at the water's edge by rocks and, on the grassy slope above, by trees: out on the lake the motor-boat, its bow raised, a line of white spume thrown up on either side, was turning in circles.

'I wanted to drown.' He paused. 'But I couldn't.'

'I don't want to talk about it, Bryan.'

'If anything happened to you I'd feel the same.'

'Would you?' After a while, she added, 'If anything happened to you I'd be the only one to blame.'

'I wouldn't do anything to harm you,' he said. 'Everything I do is because of you.'

'It's time,' Mrs Corrigan said, 'you were thinking of something else.'

'There's nothing else I care about.'

'I'm sure there is.'

'Nothing.'

'If you want to stand a chance there has to be.'

'A chance of what?'

'Of living a life with other people.'

307

'I'm not complaining,' Bryan said. 'But there's no reason now,' he concluded, 'we should ever be apart.'

The sound of the motor-boat grew fainter.

'You'll grow away from me,' she said and, looking up from where she was sitting in the direction of the distant boat, she added, 'If not with Margaret, then with friends from school.'

'I don't have any friends from school.'

'Because I've taken up too much of your life which, normally, you would have spent with other people.'

'I was like that before I met you,' he said. 'I'm like that now. I'm proud of what we are.'

'I don't see why.'

'I'd never disown it.'

'You'd be in no position to,' she said.

'I would be,' he said. 'And more so,' he concluded, 'the older I get.'

'I see further ahead than you,' Mrs Corrigan said.

'You only imagine it,' Bryan said. 'All we know for certain is what exists between us now,' and, glancing at her as she sat beside him, her arm pushed back, her legs thrust out, he thought, 'Outside of our feelings for one another we don't exist: everything is there merely to make sure that we look like everyone else.'

'Why don't we have a swim?' he asked.

'I haven't brought a costume.'

'There's no one about.'

'Only a dozen people in passing boats.'

'They're too busy with other things,' he said. 'Once we were in,' he added, 'no one would know.'

She swam out several strokes and turned on her back.

She waited, treading water.

'Can you feel the bottom?' she asked.

'It's deep,' he said.

'Swim together.'

He could feel her abdomen beneath him.

'Anything the matter?'

'No,' he said.

'What you wanted?'

308

'Yes,' he said.

'You look much prettier in the water.'

'So do you.'

'How much?'

'Lots.'

She drew him to her.

He felt the pressure of her arm around his waist.

Lapped by the waves, the shore invisible beyond her head, it was as if they were elements of the lake itself, their figures loosely joined, their legs entwined.

'Fay,' he said, and saw her smile.

'Are you all right?' she asked.

TWENTY-TWO

All evening and into the night the bombs had fallen; glass had broken at the front of the house and come into the bedrooms and into the hall: cracks showed across the panes that were still intact.

From the door of the shelter Bryan gazed out to the windows of the summer-house, their dull, dust-streaked panes, by a peculiar conjunction of adjacent surfaces, reflecting, from the rear windows of the house, the cone-shaped beams of the searchlights.

'They won't bomb us,' he said. 'What have we got to bomb at Chevet?' when, from overhead, came a sound of rushing air: the sound grew louder. He closed the shelter door: the sound intensified. It expanded to a shriek.

The ground shook. The shelter rattled.

A peculiar silence was followed by a trembling in his hands and feet.

'It didn't go off.'

Mrs Corrigan was old; never had she looked older than at that moment, her face illuminated by the glow from the lamp, her nose and mouth more sharply pronounced, the horizontal creases around her eyes echoed in profusion across her neck where they showed between the collar of her housecoat and the tugged down corners of the blanket draped across her back. She wore no make-up and her hair, concealed beneath a headscarf, lay in loose curls across her brow, dishevelled, pushed back, a loose strand hanging towards one eye and which – waiting for an outcome to the falling of the bomb – she pushed beneath the headscarf, the other hand clenched tightly around the corner of the blanket.

'I'm frightened.'

'No need to be,' he said.

'It must have landed close.'

'It fell in the garden,' Bryan said.

'Why hasn't it gone off?'

'It might be delayed.'

'We ought to get out.'

'And go where?' he said as a whistling sound, more distant, erupted overhead and suddenly, from further down the slope, towards the river, came a loud explosion, followed by a second, then a third; somewhere, close at hand, another pane of glass was shattered.

'It's a nightmare. I can't believe it's happening.'

Almost in that instant they were flung to the ground.

A tree fell in the garden.

Through the texture of the blanket he could feel her tremble, and feel, too, the guttural sob as she endeavoured to hide her terror, her head bowed, her shoulders stooped.

'One went off,' he said. 'Shall I look outside?'

'I shouldn't.'

Having lifted her, he held her to him, felt the slightness of her figure, the strange delicacy of her figure drawn against him until, releasing her, he opened the door.

The house still stood.

'It was further away than it sounds,' he said.

Her face, lit by the lamp, was turned towards the door. She extended her hand: a dull percussion of explosions echoed from the town; a splatter of shrapnel fell across the shelter.

He closed the metal door.

'All the windows are broken, Bryan.'

'Most of them.'

'It's terrible.' She waited. 'I feel so ill. I thought I was feeling better.'

Her legs were thin; her figure had lost its shape: a stoop was evident in her shoulders, her head thrust down. 'Is the war,' he thought, 'in the hands of those who planned my life? Is this something I have to endure, and something, too, which I may not even survive? And if I do,' he reflected, 'is that, too, a part of the plan? Something, as yet, I can't imagine?'

In holding her hand he was conscious of how cold she was: 'Like holding a ghost.'

311

'It's strange to be sitting here,' she added, 'the two of us together.'

Her pale eyes, almost colourless in the light from the oil-lit lamp, gazed out at him from beneath the edge of her headscarf with its strange, incongruous pattern of flowers. 'Even here, amidst all this destruction, she thinks of things that might attract me, and a long time,' Bryan reflected, 'since the time when she might have attracted another man.'

The roar of an aeroplane made her flinch: it passed above the house.

'The most important thing for me,' he said, 'is you.'

'It won't always be.'

'It is.'

'And here we are.' She flinched. 'On the edge of destruction and talking of love!'

The town had been bombed four times that week; in previous weeks neighbouring towns had also been attacked: the first night that the familiar drone of oscillating engines had been accompanied by the roar of a loud explosion Bryan, who had been lying in bed, the daylight still showing beneath his curtains, had been flung on to the floor, spread-eagled, and had heard Mrs Corrigan calling, and, moments later, more strangely, had come the rush of air preceding yet another blast in which the floor of his bedroom shook, the walls vibrated, and glass shattered in his window.

Then, on three successive nights, more bombs had fallen and, each morning, on his way to school, he had seen the streets of broken houses, and had had to walk along certain thoroughfares and roads where the bus itself could no longer travel, and had made his way to Stainforth, noting there the broken windows but relieved that the estate as a whole was only slightly damaged.

'After this, nothing will be the same again,' she said. 'If it's not destroyed it'll all be changed.'

'We won't be destroyed,' he said.

'In a way,' she said, 'we already are.'

The clamour towards the town died down; the drone of aircraft faded: the wail of a siren, shrill, sustained, followed by another, was taken up by a third, then a fourth, echoing from the village, drawn out – so long and sustained that, before it faded, he imagined in the

312

streets beside the river, where the mills and the manufactures stood, the survivors of the air-raid raising their heads.

'They've gone.'

He helped her up, opened the metal-barred door of the shelter, and gazed out at the darkened house, at the trees enclosing the garden and made out, finally, directly overhead, a star and the shape, fused by vapour, of a crescent moon.

'It's over.'

The freshness of the air, for a moment, overcame them both; she picked up the lamp and turned it off.

'Are you all right?'

He was stooping in the door; the thinness of the arm beneath the blanket, the delicacy of the wrist, the lightness of the hand, the slightness of her waist: he might have lifted her up, carried her across the garden and into the house.

'Is it safe?'

He could see the dampness of the grass glistening by his feet and, behind them, at the end of the lawn, the glassless windows of the summer-house.

'Has the house been hit?'

He was craning his head to the tiles: smoke trailed off from one of the chimneys. 'The sitting-room fire's been burning all the time,' he said, and was suddenly aware of the brightness in the sky which enabled him to see the details of the garden, as well as of the house itself.

'It looks all right, apart from the glass.'

'It'll take ages to replace.'

'We'll see about it in the morning.'

'That last explosion was in the village.'

'A stray.'

'Does it matter what it is?' she said.

Glass crumbled in the kitchen: more glass crumbled in the hall. He could hear her calling, 'Don't put on the light,' and the squeak of the oil-lamp as he realized, absurdly, she'd brought it with her.

'I'll make the tea,' he said. 'You sit down and I'll sweep this up.'

'Oh, I'll help,' she said, the light, from the re-lit oil-lamp, illuminating her features in such a way that her eyes appeared dark

313

hollows and her nose extended; then, as the light was turned to the floor, she added, 'I've never seen such a mess. We'll never set it right.'

'We'll sleep down here. There's too much glass upstairs,' he said.

Having made the tea they sat in the kitchen, the curtains pinned down at the edges, the blanket still draped around her shoulders, for he could see now that she had begun to tremble, minutely, her hand shaking at one time so severely that she put down her cup and sat with her hand in both of his, their fingers clenched together.

Finally, to distract her, he secured the other curtains, put on the lights, and began to sweep the floor. The telephone rang: he heard her answer, 'We're both all right. We're clearing up the mess,' and when she came back she said, 'Mrs Meredith's all right. The village isn't damaged!'

They fell asleep in the sitting-room and when, much later, Mrs Meredith arrived, they recommenced the clearing-up, a man appearing later in the day to begin the task of replacing the glass and, once the glass itself was in, Mrs Corrigan and Mrs Meredith began, meticulously, to tape each pane while Bryan went off to the town from where, in the afternoon, he called, reporting the damage, and describing the scenes of destruction in the streets around.

TWENTY-THREE

His father was standing at the gate, about to depart, the lane darkening, his dynamo switched on so that, as he had wheeled the bike across the yard, Bryan had seen the spluttering of the lamp, its light flickering down across the ruts, and had wondered if it were his father at all. The fact was, he invariably came to Feltham in the evenings, when he knew, in winter, his father would have gone.

'Can you manage on your own up there?' his father asked.

'There's Mrs Meredith as well,' he said.

His father nodded, looking across the lane to the lighted forecourt of the Three Bells public house. The murmur of the stream came from the direction of the hump-backed bridge.

It was seven years since Bryan had gone to live at Chevet. Two years after the war had started Mr Corrigan had died: the shop had been sold and, rather than distress Mrs Corrigan by his leaving, his parents had agreed to his staying on.

'We saw thy work in the paper. "Exhibited in town". I never thought you would make it.'

'Why not?'

'Nay, a sculptor.' Having prepared to mount the bike, drawing down the pedal, his father still stood there, looking off across the road.

'Do you want a drink?' Bryan asked.

His father ducked his head.

'I'll buy you one.'

'All right,' his father said. 'You're on.'

He wheeled his bike across the yard, the tyres rasping on the pebbles, his feet crunching, his back straightening suddenly as he leant his bike by the wall.

315

But for one other figure, the bar was deserted.

Bryan took their drinks to a corner table.

'Been in here before?' his father asked.

'Once or twice.'

'Who with?'

'Margaret.'

'She's grown into a handsome woman.'

'Do you think so?'

'She knows her own mind. More than her father does at present.'

'How do you get on with him?'

'All right.' Unsure how much he ought to relish the drink, he raised the glass slowly and sipped from the edge. 'He ne'er recovered from the death of his wife. Margaret took over after that, and never looked back. She fills the space two women might have had. That's why she's blossomed.'

His father's hands were black, the palms and the backs of them covered by mittens, the fingers bare, the dirt ingrained.

'Let me get you another.'

'Nay, one's enough, one better be enough, if I'm going back to your mother.' His father laughed, yet made no further objection when Bryan got up and crossed to the bar.

And yet, in a curious way, he despised his father: in glancing back, and seeing his figure shrouded in his overcoat – an army greatcoat dyed brown – and his cap and mittens, with their peculiar perversity in baring his fingers to the cold, he wished he'd had more pride.

'Don't you think that you've been used?' Bryan asked, returning to the table.

'In what way?'

'Making wealth for other people of which you've scarcely had a share yourself. Or, at least,' he added, 'a share which has only been sufficient to keep you going.'

'I haven't had much choice,' his father said. 'I wa' lucky to get a job. There weren't many going when I started here.'

'Yet you ought to own a third, perhaps a half of this farm, for the work you've done.'

His father drank slowly from his second glass. 'Your mother won't be pleased with this,' he said. 'Me supping here. The rows

316

we've had about it in the past. But even that has changed. The war changed that. We see things differently. You might even say we've come together.' After a moment, he added, 'Because we had nought to start with, I count myself a rich man, Bryan.'

'Why's that?'

'Thy's thinking of material wealth.' He glanced up at him from beneath his cap. 'It's a knot I never unravelled: how you split up the world's wealth in such a way that you don't do away with each man's effort.'

'I might come home to live,' he said.

'What about Mrs Corrigan?'

'It's what we planned. I shan't stay long. After that I'll go to London.'

'And Margaret?'

'It's time I left. I've made mistakes in the past I never recognized till now.'

'I wa' ne'er much keen on your going.' His father lowered his head. 'To Chevet.'

'It was what I wanted,' Bryan said.

'It wa' more your mother's thing than mine.'

'If I'd stayed at home I'd never have been what I am,' Bryan said.

'Is it that much different?' his father asked.

'It has been.' He glanced at his father's face again, the reddened cheeks, the stubbled chin, a smear of earth where he'd brushed his hand across it: 'I'd like to come home,' he said.

'It was here,' his father gestured to the door and, beyond the door, to the darkened farm outside, 'I brought you on your bike.' He lifted the glass, then, without drinking, lowered it again. 'I always thought we ducked out,' he added.

'From what?'

'From raising you in the way we should. That we all ducked out. We should have known better.'

'If we did,' Bryan said, 'it's over now. We can make,' he added, 'a fresh beginning.'

'With something missing,' his father said.

'We can still go on without it,' Bryan said. 'Even if,' he added, 'we know it was there in the first place.'

He glanced at his father's face again, with its day's growth of beard, with its frosted cheeks, and recognized in its expression a devotion he had never seen before, something intractable, that couldn't be moved, was constant and which, in its having been created, he knew was there for good.

TWENTY-FOUR

Tables had been set out in the field at the back of the houses; bunting had been hung from wooden poles: pieces of coloured cloth and Union Jacks had been strewn along the fences. At the far end of the field, where it abutted on to the back gardens of the houses flanking Spinney Moor Crescent, two poles supported a banner which read 'LONG LIVE OUR QUEEN'. A picture of Queen Elizabeth, in colour, was secured to a placard at the foot of each of the poles.

A gramophone was playing and several couples had begun to dance, the groups of children, still sitting at the tables, pushing back the chairs and benches.

Bryan had just come in from the field with Margaret; she wore a pale-blue dress, belted at the waist and, on coming into the house, had taken off her wide-brimmed hat, sitting at the table in the living-room in much the same fashion as he had first seen her sitting there, years before, on her first visit to the house.

And yet, as he brought in a tray with a pot of fresh tea and cups and saucers, he was reminded more distinctly of someone else – a figure so elusive that only when Margaret reached out to the teapot, and righted one of the cups, and insisted on pouring the tea herself, did he finally recognize, seated there, a youthful Mrs Corrigan – younger even than that first moment when he'd glimpsed her, seated at the kitchen table, at Feltham, in her blue-spotted dress and her wide-brimmed hat; and as her look came up, and he saw her smile, and he recognized, too, the Spencer eyes – set in a broader and more expansive face – she asked, 'What are you gazing at? Anything wrong?'

'Nothing,' he said, glancing to the field where the dancing couples gyrated in the sun – his parents, he noticed, presently

319

amongst them – and thought, 'It's strange how everything that is full of life has come back here. Like a heart from which the blood is pumped, expanding beyond this room, beyond these houses, beyond Spinney Top, out to the world, like that time,' he reflected, 'when I used to imagine a spirit at Christmas passing overhead, focusing its journey on every house and moving with the speed of light through a world that expanded to infinity in every direction.'

She followed his gaze herself, and specifically, Bryan thought, to where his brother had come into view dancing with his wife; almost aimlessly, having poured the tea, she said, 'I read about your work. "A prodigal talent. Bought by several private collections."' She smiled. 'So that's what you meant by someone special.' And, half anxiously, she asked, 'What happens next?'

'I mean to go on,' he said, and wondered if he might tell her of his life-long dream that he was the successor to a line of monarchs, stretching back into the mists of time, and realized, in that moment, 'But this is my kingdom, the kingdom of the heart; this is my rule: we are all a part of it,' and he began, carelessly at first, to arrange the pieces on the tray before him, arranging, rearranging, and perhaps something in his movements persuaded Margaret to look across.

'Yes,' she said. 'I see it '